Book of Lost Spells

Authors: Faisal Abdullah, Scott Alvarado, Jose De La Puente Alvarez, Antony Ball, Erica Balsley, Robert Baxter, David Best, Rick Bibeault, Jeff Binder, Terje Erwing Bjelkholm, Christopher Bjork, N. E. Bloom, Mario Boulanger, Ed Bourelle, Bret Boyd, Joseph Boyd, David Brohman, Deirdre Brooks, Michelle Brooks-Nimmo, Glenn David Brown, Christopher Bundy, Chris Campbell, Bernard Cana, Joseph Carriker, Jr., Stephen Cheney, Casey W. Chrisofferson, Aaron Clancy, Casey C. Clark, Bill Collins, Jim Collura, Wendy Connick, David S. Corcoran, Charles Corley, Chad Coulter, Colin W. Cross, Mihael D'Andrea, Aaron Day, David Ayala De Garay, Tom deMayo, David Dolph, Peter Donis, Sean Duncan, Steven Ehrbar, Adam Eichelberger, Roosevelt T. Eldridge, Robert N. Emerson, Dale Earnest, John D. Faugno, Guillerjo Sanchez Fernandez, James Fischer, Brett Friley, Tom Frisby, Jason Fultz, James Garr, Brendan Gasparin, Brian Giammalva, Michael Gill, Travis N. Gillespie, Kelly Golden, Patrick Goulah, Skeeter Green, Scott Greene, Allan Grohe, Eric Guindon, Bruce Gulke, C. J. Hammer, Jeff Harkness, Eric Harry, Lance Hawwermale, Travis Hawwermale, Jess Heinig, Christopher Henry, Matt Holman, Robert Holmberg, James Holt, Nathan Hook, Clifford Horowitz, Richard Hughes, Ryan C. Houle, Conrad Hubbard, Stefan Huddleston, C. Erich Hudson, Robert Hunter, Andrew Hurwitz, Ben Iglaur, Gabe Ivan, Evan Jamieson, Eric Jansing, J. S. Johnson, Spike Y. Jones, Chad Justice, Lysle Kapp, Ryan Karr, Shawn Kehoe, Christopher Kennedy, Michael Koal, Alan I. Kravit, Al Krombach, George Krubski, John Kubisz, Benjamin Lam, Jean Michel Lavarenne, Patrick Lawinger, Michael P. Lazure, Clyde Lekel, Lizard, Rhiannon Louve, James Maliszewski, David Mannes, Rob Mason, Matt McGee, Mike Mearls, Doug Meerschaert, Krister Michl, Adam Silva Miramon, James Mishler, Ben Monk, Clinton Clark Napper, Geoffrey T. Nelson, Scott Nimmo, Matt Noble, Robert Olla, Pier Giorgio Pacifici, Michael Paddock, Lee Palmer, Dean Paolilo, William Patterson, W. Jason Peck, E. A. Penna, Steve Peterson, Clark Peterson, Kimberly Pino-DiGennaro, Anthony Pitman, Anthony Pryor, Greg Ragland, Lawson Reilly, Stuart Renton, Darrell Ridley, Jeffrey A. Robbins, T. Patrick Rooney, Aaron Rosenberg, Chris Ryan, Gary Schafer, Michael Schell, Gary Schotter, Elias Scorsone, J. T. Scott, Jason Scott, Daniel Shaefer, James Sharkey, Jr., Bryan R. Shipp, Christopher Shiverdecker, Andrew Shockney, Dean Shomshak, Catrion Singfield, Ethan Skemp, Richard Smith II, William D. Smith Jr., Andrew Snow, Julian Soullard, John Henry Stam, Michael Strauss, Christina Stiles, James Sverapa IV, Jeff Tabrum, Eric Tam, Laban Tatro, Jeff Taylor, Paul Thompson, Lawrence Thurman, William H. Timmins, John D. Tolin, Sean Treacy, Jason Treon, Kieran Turley, Ian Turner, Matt Tweedt, Bradford Walker, Joe Walmsley, Greg Weatherford, Bill Webb, George Trace Webster, David A. Wendt, Jeff Weskamp, Erik Lees White, Stewart Wieck, James Wilbur, Brian Williams, Clifford Wolter, R.L. Wood, Wayne Woodman, Jason B. Wyrick, Karlo Yeager, Fred Yelk, Jeffrey Yurkiw, Bernardo Perez Zamorano

Developer: Steven Winter

Editors: Steven Winter, Merric Blackman

Layout, Typesetting: Charles A. Wright

Cover Art: Feleipe Gaon

Interior Art: Felipe Gaon, Brian LeBlanc, Llyn Hunter, Tom Biondillo, D. Malachai Penney, Eric Lofgren, Jeremy McHugh, Mike Chaney

NECROMANCER GAMES

5th Edition Rules,
1st Edition Feel

I0611110

Table of Contents

Spells in Alphabetical Order

Foreword

Welcome to the *Book of Lost Spells*! Within its pages, you'll find a large number of spells originally designed for previous versions of the game, newly updated to the latest edition. The necromancers have been very busy, delivering a number of musty old tomes to my tower. I spent many happy hours examining the contents and choosing the best spells to present to you. The result is the tome you are now reading.

Not every spell managed to make its way across. There are some spells that were deemed to be too similar to other spells, and others that used mechanics that are no longer in the current edition. A number of spells managed to sneak their name across, but their effects are quite different to how they were originally presented. The new edition may evoke older editions, but its biggest changes may be in how magic works, especially enhancement spells.

Steve and I wanted to draw your attention to the spells that care about alignment. The significance of alignment has been depreciated in the most current rules, but we thought it would be a good idea to bring a few across. After all, they're part of the feel of the earlier editions. We'd be careful of the *know alignment* spell, though. There are good reasons that spell disappeared from the lists of common spells. We wanted it for the sake of completeness, but it's a spell that can utterly change how the game plays.

This is true of many spells, of course. There should be a label on this book. "Use with care!" Perhaps the best way of using these spells is to slowly drop them into a campaign, with rumours of arcane secrets and mysterious tomes. In the dungeon of an elder lich – a scroll with three previously unknown spells! Treasure!

I'm indebted to the work of Steve Winter in creating this tome. Apart from his advice and editorial skills, both incredibly significant, he shaped the format we used to present the spells. We've given you a little extra detail in the header of each spell, which we hope you'll find useful.

Finally, this tome wouldn't exist without the faith and passion of Bill Webb. Thank you very much, Bill!

Merric Blackman
merricb.com
11 February 2015

On Reading Spell Entries

Spell descriptions in *The Book of Lost Spells* follow some standard conventions and some nonstandard ones. Knowing what those are before you start reading will help you understand these new spells.

Each entry begins with the spell's **name**, **level**, **school** or type, and the character **classes** that can cast it.

This is followed by standard notations for **components**: V for verbal, S for somatic, and M for material. Material components are specified where they apply.

Casting time is 1 action in most cases. These entries are self-explanatory.

Duration describes the length of time that the spell's magic is active. The spell's effects can linger much longer, obviously. Exceptions and unusual cases are spelled out in the main text. Most "permanent" spells can still be dispelled or ended with other magic.

Range describes how far from the caster the spell's target or origin point can be. Range is always assumed to be a limiting factor when casting a spell, even if text doesn't explicitly state "within range" when describing how a spell is targeted. For example, many spell descriptions instruct the caster to "select a target you can see," without stipulating that the target must be within the spell's range. Assume the range restriction is always in force unless text explicitly states that it's not.

Range only restricts the spell's target point, not its effect. An area of effect can extend beyond the spell's range. For example, *acid storm* has a range of 120 feet, and it affects a cylindrical area with a radius of 20 feet around the target point. If the spell is targeted at the full extent of its range, the area of effect will reach another 20 feet farther; it could attack a creature 140 feet away from the spellcaster. That's fine by the rules, unless the spell description specifically says the whole effect needs to be kept within range.

Area of Effect describes the spell's most obvious effect. Many spells have secondary or lingering effects that extend beyond the initial area described in the summary.

Saving Throw gives only the first or most obvious saving throw against the spell and its effect. Like areas of effect, many spells call for continuing or secondary saving throws that aren't mentioned in the summary. In many cases, saving throws are triggered when a creature "starts its turn in or enters the area of affect." The default rule in these cases is that a creature never needs to make more than one saving throw per turn against a particular spell, even if it starts its turn in the area, leaves it, and re-enters. Exceptions are noted explicitly in the few cases where they occur.

In short, always read spell descriptions thoroughly and carefully! Magic is tricky.

Finally, the GM is the ultimate arbiter of whether any particular spell can be used in his or her campaign. Some of these Lost Spells have dramatic effects, and they aren't all thematically suitable in every setting. In particular, be sure to check with your GM before adding alignment-detecting spells to your spell book. The ability to detect alignment, especially Good and Evil, is significantly (and intentionally) restricted in Fifth Edition. Giving heroes the ability to unerringly identify Evil creatures has far-reaching implications in the game world and on adventures; your GM might want to keep a tight lid on that particular can of worms. Such spells are included for those who prefer an older style of play where the ability to detect alignment was relatively common. We leave the decision of whether it's right for your game up to you.

Spell Lists

The lists in this section are organized by class and level. For wizard spells grouped by school, see the appendix.

Bard

Cantrips (Level 0)
Decorate Object
Detect Charm
Detune
Dissonance
Encrypt
Pepper's Purpose
Shield Open Flame

Level 1
Bewitch
Copy
Decrypt
Enhance Oration
Flash of Light
Forked Tongue
Quick Change
Serpent's Gaze
Slow Draw
Sonic Boom
Twitch
Unchained Melody
<3>Level 2
Bead of Blazing
Damage Morale
Detect Illusion
Harmony of Heroes
Helpless Grief
Menace
Phantom Accompaniment
Shadow Embrace
Taunt
Undetectable Charm

Level 3
Air of Nobility
Babel's Curse
Bad Luck
Barbaric Yawp
Blade Song
Cacophony
Curse of Horror
Dancer's Grace
Detect Land
Dread Scream
Firm Ally
Musical Mural
Player Instrument
Resonant Imbalance
Sound Worm
Spiteful Images
Twisted Magic
Unfasten
Wailing Dirge

Level 4
Association

Bait
Bead of Blasting
Bladelust
Crystal Wail
Distance Distortion
Harmonic DIscord
Maligned Performance
Paean of Greater Glory
Paper Tigers
Portrait
Stupefy
Voice of Confession

Level 5
Cone of Silence
Dance of Seduction
Discordant Chorus
Euphoric Ecstasy
Fugue
Harmony of the Gods
Interrogation
Mantle of Dread
Reverence
Shattering Cry
Song of Vengeance
Violent Scream
Voice of Memories
Wail of Fate

Level 6
Confounding Battlefield
Illusory Illusion
Instant Fluency
Nymph's Aura
Song Barrier
Words of Thunder

Level 7
Agitate Crowd
Charismatic Shield
Pocket Paradise
Revelation Field

Level 8
Greater Curse
Harmonic Dissolution
Imbue Passion
Xenophobic Rage

Level 9
Curse of the Ancient Mariner

Cleric

Cantrips (Level 0)
Decorate Object
Detect Charm

Level 1
Battle Wisdom
Bubble Net
Cloud Burst
Detect Disease
Detect Life
Empathic Resonance
Enhance Oration
Heraldic Mastiff
Heraldic Owl
Heraldic Ox
Hives
Mercurial Smite
Necrotic Feast
Putrefy Food and Drink

Level 2
Air Forge
Augment Skeleton
Battle Guidance
Battle Insight
Blessed Harvest
Blessed Watchman
Blessing of the Dawn
Blood Geyser
Bolster Mental Fortitude
Boost Potency
Bug Bites
Chanting
Charnel Stench
Damage Morale
Detect Curse
Energetic Burst
Faerie Ward
Find Corpse
Fortify Armor
Fresh Seal
Glowing Bones
Heraldic Fox
Heraldic Horse
Know Alignment
Luck of the Saints
Menace
Protection from Paralysis
Slur
Speed Undead
Willful Transformation
Wisdom of the Divine
Wound Reading
Wyvern Guard

Level 3
Air Bridge
Air of Nobility
Aspect Tattoo
Babel's Curse
Bad Luck
Blinding Ash
Bone Armor
Cause the Bends

Choose Fate
Corpse Armor
Curse of Horror
Curse of Light
Delay Death
Detect Land
Divine Mantle
Expunge Shadow
Fire Gills
Firm Ally
Godly Patronage
Health Transfer
Heraldic Lion
Liar's Remorse
Lifebread
Mind Link
Protection from Pressure
Restore the Undead
Retribution
Speak with Objects
Squeaking Floor Alarm
Summon Undead
Walk in the Moonlight
Weeping Wounds
Whirlwind of Gore
Whisper Wind
Wine Fount
Wise Defense

Level 4
Air Sphere
Association
Assume True Form
Aura of Tsathogga
Balance of the Mind
Barbaric Rage
Bastion
Comrades in Arms
Demon Flesh
Divine Communion
Exorcise
Force Corporeality
Heraldic Leopard
Heraldic Tortoise
Infuse Shadow
Iron Bones
Iron Core
Light Control
Lock Form
Negative Energy Aura
Null the Soothing Touch
Profane Link
Righteous Cloak
Snakes into Staves
Stonefast
Twig Torture
Umbral Touch

Level 5
Billow the Sails
Blessing of the Forge

Bone Blight
Cloak of Serpents
Clot
Corrupt Water
Dark Empowerment
Deathly Gaze
Earthen Snare
Ethereal Shield
Forced March
Heraldic Bear
Interrogation
Intimate Knowledge
Mystic Negation
Necrotic Touch
Reverence
Sacred Champion
Skull Bomb
Slime Bucket
Spellcaster's Refusal
Tracker's Gaze
Transfer of Vigor
Unholy Glare
Vile Vintage
Wail of Fate
Watery Blood

Level 6

Angel's Cloak
Arcane Obstruction
Black Exhalation
Call the Heart
Ebon Water
Elemental Cloak
Extract Life
Giant's Potency
Healing Draught
Hound of Hell
Instant Fluency
Invigorating Touch
Lost Wanderer
One with the Earth
Torrent

Level 7

Bound Hearts
Charismatic Shield
Chill of Evil
Create Crypt Thing
Disassemble
Divine Intervention
Grim Harvest
Heraldic Boar
Immunity to Energy
Mark of Exile
Purple Haze
Revelation Field
Sacred Aegis
Sanguine Creatures

Level 8

Blazing Blood
Call Divine Warrior
Death Bringer
Divine Assimilation
Elemental Infusion
Godsblood
Greater Curse

Halt Aging
Heraldic Hydra
Impart Strength
Solar Flare
Soul Strike
Strength of the Wyrm
Xenophobic Rage
Zone of Metamagic Minimization

Level 9

Annihilate Soul
Curse of the Ancient Mariner
Disable
Divine Inspiration
Heraldic Phoenix
Heraldic Wyrm
Hide the Soul
Phoenix Cloak
Wither Limb

Druid

Cantrips (Level 0)

Alter Normal Fires
Daze Animal
Drench
Headwind
Pepper's Purpose
Shield Open Flame

Level 1

Affect Normal Fog
Alter Scent
Bee Sting
Binding Sap
Bubble Net
Buoyancy
Call of the Wild Companion
Camouflage
Chlorophyll
Claws of the Beast
Cloud Burst
Detect Disease
Divining Rod
Feather Step
Fists of Stone
Hound's Scent
Locate Fish
Locate Water
Otter's Grace
Pattern Grass
Protection from Oozes
Pummel
Putrefy Food and Drink
Quill Skin
Signal Flare
Tree Ladder
Wind Speak
Woodland Shriek

Level 2

Air Forge
Augment Flames
Blessed Harvest
Boost Potency

Branch Assault
Bug Bites
Catnip
Cave Walker
Chatterwild
Constant Heat
Dolphin Fins
Dust to Death
Earth Ear
Energetic Burst
Eyes of the Hawk
Fleet Feet
Forecast
Fresh Seal
Icy Hammer
Identify Tracks
Jungle Cry
Keen Ears
Leaf Fall
Leaf Tide
Melt
Molten Strike
Nature's Aura
Net
Open Trail
Pollen Cloud
Quell the Wild
Regenerate Plant
Rooted in Place
Sandbody
Scent Mask
Silver Spear
Stench of Death
Sticky Tongue
Thorn Snare
Tremorsense
Wolf's Hearing
Wolf's Howl
Wound Reading

Level 3

Air Breathing
Air Bridge
Animal Mask
Aspect Tattoo
Bestow Speech
Charged Touch
Detect Land
Discern Lycanthrope
Earthen Concealment
Essence of the Wild
Exile from Nature
Far Strike
Fire Gills
Halt Plant
Hornet Wall
Locust Leap
Moonbeam
Nature's Repast
Nature's Strength
Spyworm
Steam Bolt
Undulating Earth
Volley of Thorns
Walk in the Moonlight
Wall of Water
Weather Calming

Level 4

Absorption
Air Sphere
Assume True Form
Bramble Armor
Desert Refuge
Earthburst
Enliven Wood
Fluid Form
Forest Home
Forgebane
Green Slime
Iceform
Infinite Knowledge
Quicksand
Snakes into Staves
Stonefast
Transform Boulder to Pebble
Transform Pebble to Boulder
Vines of Binding

Level 5

Billow the Sails
Blades of Bone
Cloak of Serpents
Corrupt Water
Death Spores
Divine Burden
Earth Shift
Earthen Snare
Enrich Soil
Gutsprout
Improve Senses
Inner Storm
Kiss of the Nereid
Mystic Negation
Prey's Scent
Transfer of Vigor
Vengeful Environs
Vile Vintage
Watery Blood

Level 6

Acorn Grove
Blades of Jade
Blood of the Hydra
Change Dust to Water
Change Water to Dust
Chrysalis
Claws of Digging
Elemental Cloak
Elemental Scimitar
Ice Sled
Invigorating Touch
Landslide
Lightning Wheel
Lost Wanderer
Nature's Support
One with the Earth
Plant Form
Serpent Hands
Solar Fury
Torrent

Level 7

Acid Swamp
Assault of Stone

Create Iceberg
Deep Freeze
Divine Disconnection
Electrical Storm
Establish Foundation
Grim Harvest
Immunity to Energy

Level 8
Chariot of Fire
Darken Forest
Deny Succor
Elemental Infusion
Tranquil Grove

Level 9
Creation's Fury
Ravaging Fire
Rimeshatter

Ranger

Level 1
Alter Scent
Bee Sting
Bewildering Tracks
Binding Sap
Buoyancy
Call of the Wild Companion
Camouflage
Detect Disease
Divining Rod
Empower Companion
Feather Step
Locate Fish
Locate Water
Otter's Grace
Pattern Grass
Signal Flare
Tree Ladder
Wind Speak

Level 2
Biting Blade
Boost Potency
Bug Bites
Catnip
Charged Missile
Constant Heat
Dust to Death
Earth Ear
Eyes of the Hawk
Fleet Feet
Forecast
Hunter's Insight
Identify Tracks
Jungle Cry
Keen Ears
Leaf Fall
Leaf Tide
Nature's Aura
Open Trail
Quell the Wild
Scent Mask
Shifter's Bane
Swirling Leaves

Tremorsense
Wolf's Hearing
Wolf's Howl
Wound Reading

Level 3
Air Breathing
Animal Mask
Axe of Destruction
Bestow Speech
Detect Land
Dire Rage
Discern Lycanthrope
Earthen Concealment
Nature's Strength
Smart Arrow
Unstoppable Tracker

Level 4
Assume True Form
Desert Refuge
Enliven Wood
Forgebane
Track Magic

Level 5
Vengeful Environs

Paladin

Level 1
Battle Wisdom
Cloth of Honorable Melee
Divine Beacon
Heraldic Mastiff
Heraldic Owl
Heraldic Ox
Holy Infusion
Mercurial Smite
Unfettered Steed

Level 2
Battle Guidance
Battle Insight
Blade of Light
Chanting
Energetic Burst
Fortify Armor
Heraldic Fox
Heraldic Horse
Luck of the Saints
Sanctified Reverie of Arms
Vigil of Enlightenment
Willful Transformation
Wisdom of the Divine

Level 3
Favor Mount
Health Transfer
Heraldic Lion
Mighty Steed
Retribution
Weapon of Retribution
Wings of Heaven
Wise Defense

Level 4
Circle of Divine Censure
Comrades in Arms
Divine Charge
Hand of Judgment
Heraldic Leopard
Heraldic Tortoise
Iron Core
Iron Judgment
Paean of the Holy
Peacebinding
Righteous Cloak
Silver Shield

Level 5
Divine Beacon's Answer
Divine Sovereignty
Heraldic Bear
Holy Blazon
Sacred Champion
Zone of Ablation

Sorcerer

Cantrips (Level 0)
Alter Normal Fires
Burden

Level 1
Acid Wind
Bubble Net
Caustic Spittle
Debilitate
Dragon's Gauntlet
Earthen Blast
Fire Burst
Flaming Bolts
Flash of Light
Frostfire
Gossamer Webbing
Ice Bolts
Push
With the Wind

Level 2
Bead of Blazing
Bead of Frost
Dragon Scales
Ethereal Strike
Flame of Chaos
Flameswell
Force Wave
Frost Snap
Ignite
Molten Strike
Net
Silver Spear
Smothering Cloud
Spirit Blast

Level 3
Air Breathing
Arcane Spear
Barbaric Yawp

Battle Double
Breath of the Dragon
Chaos Bolt
Electromagnetic Storm
Far Strike
Frost Shards
Hard Water Blast
Heat Flesh
Ooze Bolt
Sand Blast
Shadow Bolt
Steam Bolt

Level 4
Abiding Webs
Air Sphere
Bead of Blasting
Bubble Goop
Desail
Earthburst
Enduring Missiles
Fiery Blast
Flame Spiral
Flames of Purification
Rainbow Spear
Scalding Sea
Slimeball
Solar Spear
Steam Cloud

Level 5
Arcane Shield
Devouring Darkness
Earthen Snare
Ethereal Blast
Euphoric Ecstasy
Rainbow Staff
Shattering Cry
Violent Scream
Wail of Fate
Weaken Fiendish Will

Level 6
Acid Blast
Chilling Gaze
Cold Fog
Curse of Infirmity
Death's Imposition
Fangstorm
Fiery Constrictor
Life Shot
Lightning Storm
Lightning Wheel
Words of Thunder

Level 7
Acid Storm
Crawling Chaos
Deep Freeze
Ebon Lightning
Electrical Storm
Forceful Crush
Liquid Fire
Magma Eruption
Scorching Air
Searing Flash

Level 8
Ebonflame
Ice Geyser

Level 9
Arcane Censure
Conflagration
Scintillating Doom
Storm of Vitriol
Tendrils of Night

Warlock

Cantrips (Level 0)
Alter Normal Fires
Assassin's Mark
Detect Charm

Level 1
Assassin's Coin
Farsighted
Fiery Grasp
Fire Burst
Flame Water
Flash of Light
Frostfire
Gossamer Webbing
Grave-Touched Weapon
Hives
Know the Mark
Nearsighted
Pilfer Sleep
Serpent's Gaze
Shroud the Shadow

Level 2
Blindfold
Blood Bath
Burn the Sight
Charnel Stench
Damage Morale
Death Rattle
Dream Speaker
Faerie Ward
False Gold
Frame
Ghostly Throttle
Glowing Bones
Hesitate
Insomnia
Inverted Compass
Menace
Pain of Giving
Precision of Arms
Slur

Level 3
Babel's Curse
Bad Luck
Battle Double
Blackout
Blinding Ash

Bone Trap
Delay Death
Hemophilia
Infuse Weapon
Life Leech Weapon
Link Perception
See the Ephemeral
Spell Kill
Tenacious Blade

Level 4
Aura of Tsathogga
Bait
Corpulent Bloat
Demon Flesh
Flames of Darkness
Flames of Purification
Force Corporeality
Fumble
Gallows Tree
Infirmity
Purifying Bath
Shadow Form
Twig Torture
Warrior's Touch

Level 5
Arcane Retribution
Arcane Shield
Blades of Bone
Bloody Tentacles
Bone Blight
Clot
Corrupt Water
Dark Curtain
Dark Empowerment
Divine Burden
Donor
Euphoric Ecstasy
Foggy Flying Carpet
Fugue
Grim Resilience
Heat Bone
Mantle of Dread
Mystic Negation
Spirit Doll
Transfer of Vigor

Level 6
Advance the Years
Bead of Iron
Blight Fog
Breach Defenses
Chilling Gaze
Crew with the Dead
Curse of Infirmity
Death Gaze
Ebon Water
Extract Life
Giant's Potency
Hound of Hell
Illusory Illusion
Inflict Lycanthropy
Lost Wanderer
Negative Energy Mantle
Spiritbreaker

Level 7
Cone of Decay
Divine Disconnection
Interdiction
Obliterate Soul

Level 8
Deny Succor
Destined Doom
Devour Essence
Ebonflame
Fuse Joints
Imbue Passion

Level 9
Arcane Censure
Eternal Sleep
Hide the Soul
Quicken Assassin

Wizard

Cantrips (Level 0)
Alter Normal Fires
Assassin's Mark
Befuddle
Burden
Decorate Object
Detect Charm
Encrypt
Ferment
Itemize
Pepper's Purpose
Shield Open Flame

Level 1
Acid Wind
Assassin's Coin
Bewitch
Bubble Net
Caustic Spittle
Commune with Shade
Copy
Dead Man's Hands
Debilitate
Decrypt
Dragon's Gauntlet
Earthen Blast
Enhance Oration
Erase
Farsighted
Fiery Cloth
Fiery Grasp
Fire Burst
Flame Water
Flaming Bolts
Flash of Light
Frostfire
Gossamer Webbing
Grave-Touched Weapon
Hives
Ice Bolts
Impressive Blow
Know the Mark

Lasting Breath
Malicious Intent
Morph Shadow
Mucilage
Muddy Appearance
Nearsighted
Necrotic Feast
Pilfer Sleep
Push
Quick Change
Rock Bolt
Serpent's Gaze
Shroud the Shadow
Signal Flare
Slow Draw
Twitch
Web Orb
With the Wind

Level 2
Air Forge
Augment Flames
Augment Skeleton
Bead of Blazing
Bead of Frost
Biting Blade
Blindfold
Blood Bath
Blood Geyser
Blunt the Edge
Boarding Plank
Bolster Mental Fortitude
Brittle
Burn the Sight
Buttress
Character Flaw
Charged Missile
Combat Mind
Damage Morale
Death March
Death Rattle
Delude
Detect Curse
Detect Illusion
Dragon Scales
Dream Speaker
Ethereal Blade
Ethereal Strike
Faerie Ward
False Gold
Fiery Shield
Flame of Chaos
Flameswell
Force Wave
Frame
Frost Snap
Gaze Mirroring
Ghostly Howl
Ghostly Throttle
Glide
Glowing Bones
Hesitate
Ignite
Insomnia
Inverted Compass
Ironshot
Melt
Menace

Molten Strike
Net
Pain of Giving
Precision of Arms
Protection from Paralysis
Safeguarded Slumber
Scent Mask
Shadow Sight
Silver Spear
Slur
Smothering Cloud
Soul Shield
Spirit Blast
Spirit Cartographer
Undead Alteration
Undertow
Undetectable Charm

Level 3

Aerial Pilot
Air Breathing
Air Bridge
Anchor
Arcane Spear
Babel's Curse
Bad Luck
Barbaric Yawp
Battle Double
Binding Chains
Blackout
Blade Song
Blinding Ash
Blinding Flare
Bone Trap
Breath of the Dragon
Cacophony
Cause the Bends
Chaos Bolt
Charged Touch
Delay Death
Detect Land
Electromagnetic Storm
Explosive Cloud
Far Strike
Finger Missile
Frost Shards
Glass House
Hard Water Blast
Heat Flesh
Hemophilia
Infuse Weapon
Life Leech Weapon
Link Perception
Lustful Gaze
Ooze Bolt
Protection from Pressure
Reshape Metal
Restore the Undead
Sand Blast
See the Ephemeral
Shadow Bolt
Silver Bones
Speak with Objects
Spell Kill
Spiteful Images
Steam Bolt
Summon Undead
Tenacious Blade

Twisted Magic
Umbral Images
Umbral Strike
Undulating Earth
Unfasten
Wall of Water
Water Double
Whisper Wind
Yellow Smoke

Level 4

Abiding Webs
Aetheric Shield
Air Sphere
Association
Aura of Tsathogga
Bait
Bastion
Bead of Blasting
Bead of Luck
Bladelust
Bloodburn
Bubble Goop
Charge
Circle of Scrying
Corpulent Bloat
Creeping Eye
Deflect Ram
Desail
Dig
Distance Distortion
Earthburst
Endless Abyss
Enduring Missiles
Fiery Blast
Fire Fascination
Flame Spiral
Flames of Darkness
Flames of Purification
Fluid Form
Force Corporeality
Fumble
Gallows Tree
Hard Water Weapon
Iceform
Infirmity
Infuse Shadow
Instant Exit
Iron Bones
Iron Rope
Lock Form
Maligned Performance
Mark of Ownership
Megalomania
Mind Carve
Multiple Shot
Negative Energy Aura
Piercing Vision
Portrait
Profane Link
Projectile Link
Purifying Bath
Rainbow Spear
Remember Seas
Scalding Sea
Searing Projectiles
Shadow Form
Shadowbind

Slimeball
Solar Spear
Spectral Archers
Steam Cloud
Steel Butterflies
Stonefast
Stupefy
Transform Boulder to Pebble
Transform Pebble to Boulder
Twig Torture
Umbral Touch
Vermin Swarm
Wall of Blood
Warrior's Touch
Zombify Self

Level 5

Absorb Object
Arcane Retribution
Arcane Shield
Blades of Bone
Blood Blade
Blood Purge
Bloody Tentacles
Clot
Cone of Silence
Corrupt Water
Dance of Seduction
Dark Curtain
Dark Empowerment
Devouring Darkness
Divine Burden
Donor
Earthen Snare
Ethereal Blast
Ethereal Shield
Euphoric Ecstasy
Foggy Flying Carpet
Forced March
Fugue
Grim Resilience
Heat Bone
Jolt
Lower Spell Resistance
Mantle of Dread
Mark of Fire
Mark of Ice
Mark of Ooze
Memento
Mystic Negation
Necrotic Touch
Nullifying Cloak
Rainbow Staff
Resist Channeling
Shattering Cry
Skull Bomb
Soul Shatter
Spell Legs
Spellcaster's Refusal
Spirit Doll
Tattoo Object
Transfer of Vigor
Transform Zombie
Umbral Weapon
Unyielding Durability
Vile Vintage
Violent Scream
Wail of Fate

Weaken Fiendish Will

Level 6

Acid Blast
Adamantine Bones
Bead of Iron
Black Exhalation
Blade Bond
Breach Defenses
Change Dust to Water
Change Water to Dust
Chilling Gaze
Claws of Digging
Cold Fog
Confounding Battlefield
Crew with the Dead
Curse of Infirmity
Death Gaze
Death's Imposition
Dust of Death
Ebon Water
Extract Life
Fangstorm
Farvision
Fiery Constrictor
Giant's Potency
Glass Window
Hound of Hell
Ice Sled
Illusory Illusion
Inflict Lycanthropy
Instant Fluency
Judicious Concealment
Life Shot
Lightning Storm
Lightning Wheel
Lost Wanderer
Merge into Art
Negative Energy Mantle
Ogre's Visage
Serpent Hands
Shade Swarm
Spell Inhibitor
Spilling of Blood
Spiritbreaker
Transmute Gold to Steel
Transparent Steel
Umbral Transformation
Words of Thunder

Level 7

Acid Storm
Acid Swamp
Burning Rain
Chain Enervation
Chronal Displacement
Cone of Decay
Containment Orbs
Crawling Chaos
Create Crypt Thing
Create Iceberg
Dancing Daggers
Deep Freeze
Divine Disconnection
Ebon Lightning
Electrical Storm
Establish Foundation
Forceful Crush

BOOK OF LOST SPELLS

Hovership
Icebreaker
Immunity to Energy
Interdiction
Liquid Fire
Magma Eruption
Mangling Foot
Obliterate Soul
Raise Island
Revelation Field
Scorching Air
Searing Flash
Shield of Crackling Fire
Sleep of Power

Volley Spell

Level 8
Dark Geyser
Death Bringer
Deny Succor
Destined Doom
Ebonflame
Elemental Infusion
Fuse Joints
Glass into Iron
Greater Curse
Halt Aging
Ice Geyser

Imbue Passion
Impart Strength
Life Leech
Outside of Time
Raise Shipwreck
Shadowstaff
Soul Strike
Spirit Disk
Strength of the Wyrm
Touch of Madness
Umbral Storm
Xenophobic Rage
Zephyr of Death
Zone of Metamagic Minimization

Level 9
Arcane Censure
Conflagration
Crag Warrior
Curtain of Fire
Eternal Sleep
Hide the Soul
Quicken Assassin
Rimeshatter
Scintillating Doom
Storm of Vitriol
Tendrils of Night
Wrack the Mind

Spells in Alphabetical Order

Abiding Webs

4th-level conjuration
Sorcerer, Wizard
Components: V, S, M (spider and a bit of webbing frozen in amber)
Casting Time: 1 action
Duration: Permanent
Range: 100 ft.
Area of Effect: Cube, 20 ft. square
Saving Throw: Dex / avoids

You create a 20-foot cube of sticky webs at a point you can see. *Abiding webs* works identically to *web*, except as noted otherwise.

These webs are crawling with tiny, harmless spiders. Damage to the web is repaired by the spiders that live in it, at the rate of one 5-foot cube per round (125 cubic feet; the entire volume of the webs can be sixteen times this size). This repair occurs on initiative count 20. If the webs are completely destroyed, the spell ends. The spiders themselves are immortal and need neither air nor food to survive; the magic of the spell produces more spiders as needed.

Absorb Object

5th-level transmutation
Wizard
Components: V, S, M (seven drops of the host's blood, a bit of gauze, and 100 gp in ritual items that are consumed during casting)
Casting Time: 1 hour
Duration: Permanent
Range: Touch
Area of Effect: 1 object weighing up to 1 lb.
Saving Throw: None

You cause a small object of up to a pound in weight to sink harmlessly into the flesh of the target. Magical rings, amulets, or other items melded in this way still give their benefits to the wearer as if they were being worn. A slight warping of the flesh and a magical aura are the only clues to the item's existence. Items carried in this way are considered attuned to the recipient and count toward the limit of how many items can be attuned. If the creature is already at the limit, the spell fails to take effect.

If *absorb object* is dispelled or otherwise ends early, the object tears itself free of its recipient, doing 2d8 piercing damage in the process. The original spell-caster can end the spell as an action, causing the item to be expelled harmlessly.

Absorption

4th-level transmutation
Druid
Components: V, S, M (a pinch of sand)
Casting Time: 1 action
Duration: Instantaneous
Range: 30 ft.
Area of Effect: 1 creature
Saving Throw: Wis / negates effect

You cause liquids carried by a creature to dry up. All nonmagical liquid (water, alcohol, lamp oil) evaporates instantly unless the target creature makes a successful Wisdom saving throw. In addition, three potions carried by the target will also be affected by this spell. If the target carries more than three potions, the three that dry up are selected randomly.

Absorption has no direct effect on living (or unliving) creatures or plants, only on liquids they carry.

Acid Blast

6th-level evocation
Sorcerer, Wizard
Components: V, S
Casting Time: 1 action
Duration: Instantaneous
Range: Self
Area of Effect: Cone, 30 ft. long
Saving Throw: Dex / half damage

A blast of caustic acid erupts from your fingers. Every creature in the cone takes 6d8 acid damage, or half damage with a successful Dexterity saving throw. Creatures that fail their saving throw also take an additional 2d8 acid damage at the end of their next turn.

Enhancement: For each spell slot used higher than 6th level, the subsequent damage increases by 1d8.

Acid Storm

7th-level evocation
Sorcerer, Wizard
Components: V, S, M (a small vial of acid)
Casting Time: 1 action
Duration: Concentration, up to 1 minute
Range: 120 ft.
Area of Effect: Cylinder, 20-ft. radius, 30 ft. high
Saving Throw: None

You create a caustic downpour of acid in a cylindrical area with a 20-foot radius, 30 feet high, extending downward from a point you can see. For the duration, each creature that starts its turn in the area or enters the area takes 5d8 acid damage. Even after leaving the area, a creature is still coated with the acid and continues taking 2d8 acid damage at the end of each of its turns. A creature can use an action to rinse off the acid if it has water, vinegar, or another suitable substance available. All ongoing damage ends when the spell ends.

The acid can also damage objects in the affected area, but the extent of this damage must be determined by the GM.

Acid Swamp

7th-level transmutation
Druid, Wizard
Components: V, S, M (a small vial of acid)
Casting Time: 1 action
Duration: Concentration, up to 1 minute
Range: 120 ft.
Area of Effect: Up to 100 ft. by 100 ft. by 20 ft. of water
Saving Throw: Con / half damage

You transform a normal body of water into a pool of thick, bubbling acid. The spell affects an area up to 100 ft. by 100 feet by 20 feet deep. The acid is black and opaque and reeks of sulfur. Anyone splashed by the acid takes 2d6 acid damage. A creature that starts its turn in the acid or that enters the acid takes 10d6 acid damage, or half damage with a successful Constitution saving throw.

Acid Wind

1st-level evocation
Sorcerer, Wizard
Components: V, S, M (a dried lemon peel)
Casting Time: 1 action

Duration: Instantaneous
Range: Self
Area of Effect: 15-ft. cube
Saving Throw: Con / half damage, no blindness

You call forth a breeze full of stinging acid droplets from your outstretched hand. Each creature in a 15-foot cube originating from you must make a Constitution saving throw. On a failed save, a creature takes 2d6 acid damage and is blinded until the end of your next turn. On a successful save, the creature takes half as much damage and isn't blinded.

Enhancement: For each spell slot used higher than 1st level, the damage increases by 1d6.

Acorn Grove

6th-level conjuration
Druid
Components: V, S, M (acorns)
Casting Time: 1 action
Duration: 24 hours
Range: Touch
Area of Effect: 6 acorns
Saving Throw: None

As part of casting this spell, you throw up to six acorns, which take root and rapidly grow into adult trees where they land. The acorns can be thrown up to 60 feet. They can all be thrown in the same direction, or in different directions. They must land in fertile ground (not on bare rock or a wooden floor, for example) for the spell to be effective, and they must have enough space to grow. You have a special bond with this grove; it grants you tactical advantage on saving throws you make within 30 feet of one of the trees. This benefit ends if all of the trees are destroyed.

The trees shrink back into acorns when the spell ends.

Adamantine Bones

6th-level necromancy
Wizard
Components: V, S, M (1 pound of adamantine, which is consumed in the casting)
Casting Time: 1 action
Duration: Permanent
Range: Touch
Area of Effect: 1 skeleton
Saving Throw: None

One skeleton that you touch gains immunity to bludgeoning, slashing, and piercing damage from nonmagical weapons that are not made of adamantine, and resistance to bludgeoning, slashing, and piercing damage from magical weapons that are not made of adamantine.

Enhancement: For each spell slot used higher than 6th level, you can affect one additional skeleton.

Advance the Years

6th-level necromancy
Warlock
Components: V, S, M (a lock of an elderly person's hair)
Casting Time: 1 action
Duration: Permanent
Range: Touch
Area of Effect: 1 creature
Saving Throw: Con / negates effect

You touch a creature, and that creature becomes cursed with age unless is makes a successful Constitution saving throw. The creature becomes wizened and enfeebled and has disadvantage on Strength, Dexterity, and Constitution-based ability checks, attack rolls, skill rolls, and saving throws. It does half damage with weapon attacks.

This effect can be ended by magic that removes curses.

Aerial Pilot

3rd-level conjuration
Wizard
Components: V, S, M (a piece of string and a bit of wood)
Casting Time: 1 action
Duration: 12 hours
Range: 60 ft.
Area of Effect: 1 summoned creature
Saving Throw: None

You summon an invisible creature capable of steering and navigating any vessel competently. It follows simple instructions you give it regarding the bearing and speed of the vessel. Treat the creature as if it had a +6 bonus to relevant ability checks when performing its duties.

The creature has AC 10, 1 hit point, Strength 10, and it can't attack. If it drops to 0 hit points, the spell ends.

Aetheric Shield

4th-level abjuration
Wizard
Components: V, S, M (a glass lens)
Casting Time: 1 action
Duration: Concentration, up to 1 minute
Range: 30 ft.
Area of Effect: 1 lens, 10-ft. diameter
Saving Throw: None

You conjure an aetheric lens, 10 feet wide, within 30 feet of you. The lens protects those behind it from magic; any spell of 4th level or lower that requires a clear path through the lens is stopped entirely. The lens doesn't interfere with spells you cast, and it doesn't block area effects. For example, a *fireball* couldn't be aimed directly through the lens, but if it was set off immediately in front of the lens, the blast would still affect people on the other side of the lens and within the *fireball's* radius. You can spend a bonus action to move the lens to any point within 30 feet of you.

Enhancement: If *aetheric shield* is cast using a spell slot higher than 4th level, the lens protects against spells of equal or lower level than the spell slot you used.

Affect Normal Fog

1st-level transmutation
Druid
Components: V, S, M (a tiny candle and a small horn)
Casting Time: 1 action
Duration: Concentration, up to 1 hour
Range: 120 ft.
Area of Effect: 1,000 cubic ft.
Saving Throw: None

You can manipulate a normal fog bank of up to 1,000 cubic feet you can see within range. The fog can be gathered into a thick mass of opaque fog, creating a heavily obscured area, or dispersed to create an area of patchy fog that lightly obscures its area. Magically-created fog can't be affected by this spell.

Agitate Crowd

7th-level enchantment
Bard
Components: V, S
Casting Time: 10 minutes
Duration: 8 hours
Range: Self
Area of Effect: Sphere, 60-ft. radius
Saving Throw: Wis / negates effect

This spell enables you to sway a large group of people toward accomplishing a specific goal. You must speak emphatically on the subject for 10 minutes, playing on the crowd's emotions and reason, to inflame their fervor for or against a cause or person. You must be clear about the specific goal you want to achieve. For example, shouting that "The Academy of Wizards is evil and corrupt!" might make people dislike the academy, but it won't spur them to action because it doesn't tell them what to do. Adding "Follow me, and we'll burn it to the ground!" will send a crowd of torch-bearing arsonists to the academy tower.

The spell affects all sentient creatures that are able to hear and understand you within 60 feet.

When you finish casting the spell, all potential targets of the spell who fail a Wisdom saving throw are compelled to follow your instructions for the duration of the spell, as long as those orders are in keeping with the goal stated in the speech and you personally lead them. If these conditions aren't met, the spell ends and the crowd becomes hostile toward you. The spell also ends when the goal has been achieved.

Air Breathing

3rd-level transmutation (ritual)
Druid, Ranger, Sorcerer, Wizard
Components: V, S, M (a sliver of copper)
Casting Time: 1 action
Duration: 24 hours
Range: 30 ft.
Area of Effect: 1 to 10 creatures
Saving Throw: None

You grant up to ten willing creatures you can see the ability to breathe air until the spell ends. These creatures retain the ability to breathe in their normal element.

Air Bridge

3rd-level transmutation (ritual)
Cleric, Druid, Wizard
Components: V, S, M (a tiny model bridge)
Casting Time: 1 action
Duration: 10 minutes
Range: 120 ft.
Area of Effect: 1 bridge, 60 ft. long, 10 ft. wide
Saving Throw: None

You create an invisible bridge up to 60 feet long and 10 feet wide that connects two points of your choosing. Both ends of the bridge must be within the spell's range, and both must be solid objects that can support the weight of whatever physical objects cross the bridge. The bridge itself has no weight. Anyone can cross this bridge while it exists, provided they know where it is.

Enhancement: When you cast *air bridge* using a slot of 5th level or higher, the bridge is substantial only to those you nominate; to all others, it does not exist. This is also true if you cast the spell as a ritual and are capable of casting 5th level spells.

Air Forge

2nd-level transmutation (ritual)
Cleric, Druid, Wizard
Components: V, S
Casting Time: 1 action
Duration: 8 hours
Range: 30 ft.
Area of Effect: 2 cubic ft. of air
Saving Throw: None

You heat a patch of air to the great temperatures of a forge. You can hold up metal to that area and soften it just as a real forge would and then work the metal appropriately. Only items placed in the heated area by the caster are affected; the heat doesn't affect anything else, and it

Air Bridge

can't be felt by living creatures at all. This spell, along with a portable anvil, greatly lessens the difficulty for a craftsman repairing equipment in the field.

Enhancement: If *air forge* is cast using a spell slot higher than 2nd level, it heats a number of cubic feet of air equal to the spell slot used.

Air of Nobility

3rd-level enchantment
Bard, Cleric
Components: V, S, M (A ring)
Casting Time: 1 action
Duration: Concentration, up to 1 hour
Range: Touch
Area of Effect: 1 creature
Saving Throw: None

A willing creature gains an aura of nobility, which gives it tactical advantage on Charisma ability checks made to influence others.

Air Sphere

4th-level conjuration
Cleric, Druid, Sorcerer, Wizard
Components: V, S
Casting Time: 1 action
Duration: 12 hours
Range: Self
Area of Effect: Sphere, 5-ft. radius
Saving Throw: None

The spell creates a 5-foot-radius sphere of pure, fresh air that forms around you and moves with you. The spell keeps out hazardous gases and water, but solid objects can pass into the sphere. The air remains pure and clean for the duration of the spell.

Alter Normal Fires

Transmutation cantrip
Druid, Sorcerer, Warlock, Wizard
Components: V, S
Casting Time: 1 action
Duration: Concentration, up to 10 minutes.
Range: 30 ft.
Area of Effect: 1 fire
Saving Throw: None

You cause an existing fire of Medium or smaller size to reduce in size and light to that of a match, or increase in brightness – but not size – to that of a *light* spell. Reducing a fire also reduces its consumption of fuel by half, with the effect of doubling its remaining duration, while increasing a fire doubles its fuel consumption. This spell doesn't change the heat output of the fire.

Alter Scent

1st-level transmutation
Druid, Ranger
Components: V, S
Casting Time: 1 action
Duration: Concentration, up to 1 hour
Range: 30 ft.
Area of Effect: 1 creature
Saving Throw: None

This spell changes the target's scent to any other of the caster's choice. Creatures attempting to track the target by scent have tactical disadvantage on ability checks to follow the target.

Anchor

3rd-level evocation (ritual)
Wizard
Components: V, S, M (a small bit of iron and a string)
Casting Time: 1 action
Duration: 12 hours
Range: Touch
Area of Effect: 1 anchor
Saving Throw: None

You create an anchor and chain of pure force that attach to a ship and maintain its position against current and strong wind. Creatures aboard the ship can raise the anchor by using an action to touch the chain and command it, and they can lower the anchor the same way. The anchor disappears when the spell ends.

Angel's Cloak

6th-level abjuration
Cleric
Components: V, S, M (a feather)
Casting Time: 1 action
Duration: Concentration, up to 10 minutes
Range: Touch
Area of Effect: 1 creature
Saving Throw: None

One willing creature you touch is blessed with the protective qualities of angels. For the duration of the spell, the target creature gains resistance to radiant damage and to nonmagical bludgeoning, piercing, and slashing damage. It also has tactical advantage on saving throws against spells and other magical effects.

Animal Mask

3rd-level illusion
Druid, Ranger
Components: V, S, M (a tuft of fur)
Casting Time: 1 action
Duration: 1 hour
Range: Touch
Area of Effect: Self plus 1, 2, or 3 other creatures
Saving Throw: None

This spell allows you and up to three more willing creatures to take on the appearance of any one species of beast of CR 1 or less, but only to members of that species. All creatures of that species perceive affected creatures not only as their own kind but also as members of their own pack, herd, flock, or group. The spell does not guarantee safety; affected creatures might still be challenged as rivals for mates or dominance, but such challenges are no more severe than they would be for a genuine rival beast.

Annihilate Soul

9th-level necromancy
Cleric
Components: V, S, M (a glass figurine worth 1,000 gp, which is consumed by the spell)
Casting Time: 1 action
Duration: Instantaneous (see text)
Range: 30 ft.
Area of Effect: 1 living creature
Saving Throw: Con / half damage

This spell unleashes magic that rips the soul from a living creature you can see. The target takes 8d6 + 50 necrotic damage, or half damage if it makes a successful Constitution saving throw.

If the creature is reduced to 0 hit points after failing the saving throw against this spell, it dies and its soul shatters into 2d6 spirit shards that take up residence in random life forms in a 10-mile radius. The spirit shards prefer intelligent creatures over unintelligent ones. The creatures that become hosts to these shards are unaware of their presence, but they can start having strange dreams and displaying odd habits picked up from the soul shard. Each shard-bearer also gains proficiency in one random skill possessed by the original creature; if they already are proficient in the skill, they become expert in the skill, and if already expert, they gain tactical advantage on all uses of that skill.

The original creature can't be resurrected unless all bearers of shards are gathered into the same area before the resurrection magic is used; shard-bearers lose all benefits gained from the spirit shards at that time.

If a shard-bearer dies, the spirit shard transfers to another creature within 10 miles.

Arcane Censure

9th-level abjuration
Sorcerer, Warlock, Wizard
Components: V, S, M (a diamond worth 1,000 gp)
Casting Time: 1 action
Duration: Concentration, up to 10 minutes
Range: 60 ft.
Area of Effect: 1 creature
Saving Throw: None

You point at a creature and disrupt the ether around it. For the duration of *arcane censure*, the creature can't cast spells or use innate spellcasting. As an action, it can make an ability check using its spellcasting ability against your spell saving throw DC. A successful save ends the *arcane censure's* effect.

Arcane Obstruction

6th-level abjuration
Cleric
Components: V, S
Casting Time: 1 action
Duration: Concentration, up to 10 minutes
Range: Self
Area of Effect: Sphere, 50-ft. radius
Saving Throw: None

You create an aura in a 50-foot radius around yourself that is antithetical to arcane magic. Arcane spellcasters in the sphere require additional time to cast their spells: spells that take a bonus action to cast now require 1 action; 1 action increases to 1 round; and other spells have their casting times doubled. The sphere of effect moves with you.

Arcane Retribution

5th-level evocation
Warlock, Wizard
Components: V, S, M (a pinch of ash from a cremated spell-caster)
Casting Time: 1 action
Duration: Concentration, up to 10 minutes
Range: 120 ft.
Area of Effect: Sphere, 30-ft. radius
Saving Throw: Con / half damage

You create a 30-foot-radius sphere of unstable magic centered on a point you can see. For the duration of the spell, any creature casting an arcane spell within the area of the sphere takes 6d6 fire damage, or half damage with a successful Constitution saving throw, as their casting ignites the magic of your spell.

Arcane Shield

5th-level abjuration
Sorcerer, Warlock, Wizard
Components: V, S
Casting Time: 1 action

Duration: 1 minute
Range: Self
Area of Effect: Self
Saving Throw: None

You summon power to protect yourself against outside magic. You get tactical advantage on saving throws against magic that specifically targets you. *Arcane shield* provides no protection against area-effect spells.

Arcane Spear

3rd-level evocation
Sorcerer, Wizard
Components: V, S, M (a miniature wooden spear)
Casting Time: 1 action
Duration: Instantaneous
Range: 60 ft.
Area of Effect: 1 creature
Saving Throw: None

You hurl a spear made of magical force at one creature within range. Make a ranged spell attack against the target. If it hits, the spear does 3d10 force damage. If the target is a spellcaster, the hit also wipes out one of its available, lowest-level spell slots as if the spell had been expended.

Enhancement: For each spell slot used higher than 3rd level, damage increases by 1d10. When you cast *arcane spear* using a spell slot of 6th level or higher, a hit also wipes out two of the target's spell slots instead of one.

Aspect Tattoo

3rd-level abjuration (ritual)
Cleric, Druid
Components: V, S, M (special ink worth 200 gp)
Casting Time: 10 minutes
Duration: Permanent until discharged
Range: Touch
Area of Effect: 1 creature
Saving Throw: None

You scribe a tattoo on a willing creature's skin that holds a portion of an animal's energy and ability. A creature can only hold one aspect tattoo at a time; scribing another eliminates the previous one. The animal being represented must be present when the aspect tattoo is created.

The recipient of the tattoo can activate the tattoo's effect as a bonus action. Once the tattoo is scribed, it remains until the effect is activated.

The known tattoos are as follows:
• Badger: The recipient goes into a battle frenzy, gaining tactical advantage on melee attacks for 1 minute.
• Bear: The recipient's Strength score increases to 19 for 10 minutes.
• Cheetah: The recipient's speed increases to 60 feet for 1 minute, and opportunity attacks against the recipient have tactical disadvantage.
• Panther: The recipient gains tactical advantage on Stealth checks for 10 minutes.

Other animal tattoos could be discovered that grant different powers.

Assassin's Coin

1st-level conjuration (ritual)
Warlock, Wizard
Components: V, S, M (a coin)
Casting Time: 1 action
Duration: Permanent until discharged
Range: Touch
Area of Effect: 1 coin
Saving Throw: None

A coin that you received in payment becomes imbued with a magical charm. Once the spell is cast, you must return the coin to the person or being who gave it to you. As an action, they can throw the coin into the air while speaking your name (or whatever name you gave them). The coin then vanishes and reappears in your pocket, along with a mental image of whoever spoke your name. No message can be transferred along with the coin.

Assassin's Mark

Transmutation cantrip
Warlock, Wizard
Components: V, S
Casting Time: 1 bonus action
Duration: Permanent
Range: 30 ft.
Area of Effect: 1 creature
Saving Throw: None

When cast upon a creature killed by you within one minute of its death, *assassin's mark* reshapes the fatal wound in a way that unmistakably identifies you as the killer. You select the form this mark will take when you learn the spell, and you can't change it later except through exceptional magic such as a *wish* spell. No two creatures can share the same *assassin's mark*.

Assault of Stone

7th-level conjuration
Druid
Components: V, S, M (a hatndful of pebbles)
Casting Time: 1 action
Duration: Instantaneous; stones remain for 1 minute
Range: 400 ft.
Area of Effect: Up to 1,200 sq. ft.
Saving Throw: Dex / half damage

When you cast this spell, rocks, boulders, and other large stones are summoned from the Elemental Plane of Earth and rain down on the area of effect, which can be up to 1,200 square feet (twelve 10-by-10-foot squares). The area can be laid out as you wish, but it must be contiguous, at least 10 feet across at every point, entirely within the spell's range, and entirely within your line of sight.

Each creature in the area must make a Dexterity saving throw. If the saving throw fails, the creature takes 8d8 bludgeoning damage, falls prone, and is restrained beneath boulders until they escape or the stones disappear. A successful save means the creature takes half damage and isn't knocked prone or restrained. A restrained creature can escape from under the boulders by using an action and making a successful Strength (Athletics) check against your spell saving throw DC.

The stones remain on the ground for 1 minute after they fall, making the area difficult terrain and providing plenty of places to find cover.

Association

4th-level enchantment
Bard, Cleric, Wizard
Components: V, S, M (a sketch of the target)
Casting Time: 1 hour
Duration: 1 day
Range: 120 ft.
Area of Effect: All creatures within range
Saving Throw: Wis / negates effect

You select an animal (for example, a lion) or image (such as a shining sword) or ideal (such as honor) and associate it with a specific individual. Each creature within the spell's range must make a Wisdom saving throw. Each creature that fails the saving throw associates the person with the animal, image, or ideal for as long as the spell lasts. A positive association increases the starting attitude of those around the affected target by one step; hostile becomes indifferent, indifferent becomes friendly. Likewise, a negative association decreases the starting attitude by one.

This can be a subtle way to influence a group: By planting an association

Assault of Stone

that links a lord to wickedness or to a serpent, the caster can undermine morale in that lord's dominion for days. Friendly advisers become indifferent, for example, and unfriendly rivals become hostile.

Enhancement: For each spell slot used higher than 4th level, the *association* lasts for an additional day.

Assume True Form

4th-level transmutation
Cleric, Druid, Ranger
Components: V, S, M (a sprig of wolfsbane)
Casting Time: 1 action
Duration: 1 minute
Range: Self
Area of Effect: Sphere, 20-ft. radius
Saving Throw: Con / negates effect

You create an aura around yourself that forces all shapeshifted creatures to resort to their normal forms. The spell affects lycanthropes, therianthropes, doppelgangers, mimics, and creatures under the effect of *polymorph* magic. A shapechanged creature that begins its turn within the aura is forced to resume its natural form unless it makes a successful Constitution saving throw. If the saving throw fails, it reverts to its normal form immediately, and it can't alter its form voluntarily again until it leaves the spell's area of effect.

Augment Flames

2nd-level transmutation
Druid, Wizard
Components: V, S, M (an ordinary fire)
Casting Time: 1 action
Duration: Instantaneous
Range: 400 ft.
Area of Effect: Cone, 30 ft. long
Saving Throw: Dex / half damage

You cause one normal fire to flare out in a 30-foot cone in the direction of your choice. Each creature in the cone takes 4d6 fire damage, or half damage with a successful Dexterity saving throw.

Enhancement: When you cast *augment flames* using a spell slot of 3rd level or higher, the damage increases by 1d6 for each slot level above 2nd.

Augment Skeleton

2nd-level transmutation
Cleric, Wizard
Components: V, S, M (a small piece of metal)
Casting Time: 1 action
Duration: 1 hour
Range: Touch
Area of Effect: 1 skeleton
Saving Throw: None

Your magic imbues an undead skeleton with unnatural hardness; its base AC becomes 16 + its Dexterity modifier.

Enhancement: When you cast *augment skeleton* using a spell slot of 3rd level or higher, you can affect two additional skeletons for each slot level above 2nd.

Aura of Tsathogga

4th-level conjuration
Cleric, Warlock, Wizard
Components: V, S, M (a small piece of a bombardier beetle)
Casting Time: 1 action
Duration: Concentration, up to 1 hour
Range: Self
Area of Effect: Self

Saving Throw: None

A swirling mist of corrosive green vapor engulfs your body for the duration of this spell. Any creature that strikes you with a melee attack takes 4d6 acid damage, and you gain resistance to acid damage.

As an action, you can make a melee spell attack against one creature within your reach; a hit does 10d6 acid damage and ends this spell.

Axe of Destruction

3rd-level transmutation
Ranger
Components: V, S, M (an axe)
Casting Time: 1 action
Duration: Concentration, up to 1 minute
Range: Touch
Area of Effect: 1 axe
Saving Throw: None

One axe becomes magically effective against objects. For the duration of the spell, the axe is considered to be made of adamantine and does an additional 2d6 damage against inanimate objects and constructs.

Babel's Curse

3rd-level enchantment
Bard, Cleric, Warlock, Wizard
Components: V
Casting Time: 1 action
Duration: Concentration, up to 1 minute.
Range: 100 ft.
Area of Effect: 1 creature
Saving Throw: Wis / negates effect

One creature you can see must make a Wisdom saving throw. If the saving throw fails, the creature is cursed and becomes incapable of producing intelligible speech for the duration of the spell. The creature is also unable to cast spells with a verbal component. At the end of each of the creature's turns, it can repeat the saving throw. A successful save ends the spell. A spell that removes a curse can also end *Babel's curse*.

Enhancement: If you cast *Babel's curse* with a 5th-level or higher spell slot, the creature is also unable to understand spoken language for the duration of the spell. If you use an 8th-level or higher spell slot, the duration becomes permanent and the creature can't make saving throws to end the effect.

Bad Luck

3rd-level enchantment
Bard, Cleric, Warlock, Wizard
Components: V, S
Casting Time: 1 action
Duration: Concentration, up to 1 minute
Range: 60 ft.
Area of Effect: 1 creature
Saving Throw: Wis / negates effect

Bad luck curses one creature to become incredibly unlucky. The affected creature has tactical disadvantage on saving throws for the duration of the spell unless it makes a successful Wisdom saving throw when *bad luck* is first cast. The spell also ends if the creature rolls a natural 20 on a saving throw, or by magic that removes a curse.

Bait

4th-level enchantment
Bard, Warlock, Wizard
Components: V, S, M (a shiny piece of glass)
Casting Time: 1 action
Duration: 1 minute

16

Range: 60 ft.
Area of Effect: 1 creature and 1 object
Saving Throw: Wis / negates effect

When you cast *bait*, choose a creature and an object. Both must be within 60 feet of you. If the creature fails a Wisdom saving throw, it experiences an overwhelming desire to possess the object. On its turn, the affected creature must move directly toward the object, ignoring all danger. Upon reaching the object, it does everything within its power to remain within 5 feet of the object and to prevent anyone else from possessing it, even if that means taking it away from its current owner. The affected creature can repeat the saving throw at the end of each of its turns; a successful save ends the effect.

Balance of the Mind

4th-level enchantment
Cleric
Components: V, S, M (a blindfold and a set of scales)
Casting Time: 10 minutes
Duration: 8 hours
Range: Touch
Area of Effect: 1 creature
Saving Throw: None

By calling on the gods of Law, you temporarily alter a willing creature's alignment to Lawful Neutral and remove all emotional attachments or biases the creature might have. While under the effect of this spell, the creature gains tactical advantage on saving throws against enchantment spells. All decisions the creature makes while under the spell's influence must follow the spirit and letter of the law, and the subject is incapable of showing favoritism. A creature under the effect of *balance of the mind* can judge the actions of even his most hated enemy fairly and impartially.

Barbaric Rage

4th-level enchantment
Cleric
Components: V, S
Casting Time: 1 action
Duration: Concentration, up to 1 minute
Range: 30 ft.
Area of Effect: 1 creature
Saving Throw: None

One willing creature you can see rages like a barbarian. The creature has tactical advantage on Strength checks and Strength saving throws, gains a +2 bonus to damage dealt with Strength-based melee weapons, and has resistance to bludgeoning, piercing, and slashing damage. The creature is unable to cast spells or concentrate on spells when raging.

The spell ends if the creature ends its turn without either attacking a hostile creature or being attacked since its previous turn.

Barbaric Yawp

3rd-level evocation
Bard, Sorcerer, Wizard
Components: V, S
Casting Time: 1 action
Duration: Instantaneous
Range: Self
Area of Effect: Cone, 30 ft. long
Saving Throw: Con / negates effect

You release a hoarse cry that reverberates in a 30-foot cone in front of you. Each creature in the cone must make a Constitution saving throw. If the saving throw fails, the creature drops everything it is holding, is

Battle Double

incapacitated until the end of its next turn, and is frightened. A frightened creature can make a Wisdom saving throw at the end of each of its turns; a successful save ends the fright.

Bastion

4th-level abjuration
Cleric, Wizard
Components: V, S, M (a diamond worth at least 1,000 gp, which is consumed in the casting)
Casting Time: 1 hour
Duration: Permanent
Range: Touch
Area of Effect: 1 structure up to 100 sq. ft.
Saving Throw: None

When you touch a structure, a soft glow spreads from your hands and flows across the walls until it envelops the entire structure. The glow is absorbed into the building, leaving behind a faint, permanent sparkle to the stone, wood, brick, or clay. The structure's current and maximum hit points are doubled.

Battle Double

3rd-level illusion
Sorcerer, Warlock, Wizard
Components: V, S
Casting Time: 1 action
Duration: Concentration, up to 1 minute
Range: Self
Area of Effect: 1 double
Saving Throw: None

You create a shadowy double of yourself that superimposes itself on you. As a bonus action, you can move the double up to 20 feet away from you; you can then use it as the source of any weapon attack you make or spell you cast, as if you were standing in the double's spot. At the end of your turn, the double returns to your space.

The battle double can't be damaged or even attacked. It has no real, physical presence except in the moment when it attacks.

Battle Guidance

2nd-level divination
Cleric, Paladin
Components: V
Casting Time: 1 bonus action
Duration: Concentration, up to 3 rounds
Range: 30 ft.
Area of Effect: 1 creature
Saving Throw: None

You pray for insight into the defenses of one creature you can see. You have tactical advantage on your next two attack rolls against the target before the spell ends.

Battle Insight

2nd-level divination
Cleric, Paladin
Components: V, S, M (a small looking glass)
Casting Time: 10 minutes
Duration: Concentration, up to 8 hours
Range: Self
Area of Effect: Self
Saving Throw: None

You become supernaturally alert to danger. While the spell is in effect, you can add 1d6 to your initiative rolls.

Battle Wisdom

1st-level divination
Cleric, Paladin
Components: V, S
Casting Time: 1 action
Duration: Concentration, up to 1 minute
Range: 50 ft.
Area of Effect: 1, 2, or 3 creatures
Saving Throw: None

You fill up to three creatures of your choice within range with battle insight and the ability to perform tasks better. Each creature can add 1d4 to its attack rolls and Wisdom checks.

Enhancement: For each spell slot used higher than 1st level, you can affect one additional creature.

Bead of Blasting

4th-level evocation
Bard, Sorcerer, Wizard
Components: V, S, M (a bone bead)
Casting Time: 1 action
Duration: Instantaneous
Range: 60 ft.
Area of Effect: Sphere, 15-ft. radius
Saving Throw: Con / half damage

A small bead of concentrated sound travels from your hand to a point within range that you select, where it explodes in a 15-foot-radius sphere. Each creature in the radius takes 5d8 thunder damage and is deafened for 1 minute, or takes half damage and is not deafened with a successful Constitution saving throw.

Enhancement: For each spell slot used higher than 4th level, *bead of blasting* does an additional 1d8 damage.

Bead of Blazing

2nd-level evocation
Bard, Sorcerer, Wizard
Components: V, S, M (a handful of small glass beads)
Casting Time: 1 action
Duration: Instantaneous
Range: 120 ft.
Area of Effect: 1, 2, or 3 creatures
Saving Throw: Dex / half damage

You propel 5d6 small beads at up to three creatures you can see. The beads can be divided between the targets as desired. Each target takes 1 bludgeoning damage per bead, or half damage with a successful Dexterity saving throw.

Enhancement: For each spell slot used higher than 2nd level, you propel an additional 1d6 beads and can target one additional creature.

Bead of Frost

2nd-level evocation
Sorcerer, Wizard
Components: V, S, M (a glass bead)
Casting Time: 1 action
Duration: Instantaneous
Range: 60 ft.
Area of Effect: 1 creature or object
Saving Throw: None

You create a small bead of elemental frost that you then hurl at a target within range. If you make a successful ranged spell attack roll, the target takes 5d6 cold damage and is unable to move until the beginning of your next turn.

Enhancement: When you cast *bead of frost* using a spell slot of 3rd level or higher, you deal an additional 1d6 damage for each slot level above 2nd.

Bead of Iron

6th-level abjuration
Warlock, Wizard
Components: V, S, M (an iron bead strung on an oxen-hide thong)
Casting Time: 1 action
Duration: Concentration, up to 1 hour
Range: Self
Area of Effect: Self
Saving Throw: None

You imbue a small iron bead with a protective aura. For the duration of the spell, while you wear the bead, you have resistance to bludgeoning, piercing, and slashing damage from nonadamantine weapons, and your AC increases by 2. Keep track of how much damage is prevented by this spell's resistance; the spell ends once it has prevented 100 points of damage.

Bead of Luck

4th-level abjuration
Wizard
Components: V, S, M (a bone bead with the rune of luck carved on it)
Casting Time: 1 action
Duration: 1 hour
Range: Self
Area of Effect: Self
Saving Throw: None

You imbue a small bone bead with an aura of luck. While you wear the bead, you can reroll any attack roll, ability check, or saving throw you make that results in a natural 1. You must keep the second result, even if it's another 1.

Bee Sting

1st-level conjuration
Druid, Ranger
Components: V, S, M (a bumblebee's stinger)
Casting Time: 1 action
Duration: Instantaneous
Range: 60 ft.
Area of Effect: 1 creature
Saving Throw: Con / half damage, no poisoning

You conjure a small bee that stings one creature within range. The stung creature must make a Constitution saving throw against poison. If the saving throw fails, the creature takes 2d8 poison damage and becomes poisoned until the end of your next turn. If the save succeeds, the creature takes half damage and is not poisoned.

Enhancement: When you cast *bee sting* using a spell slot of 2nd level or higher, you do an additional 1d8 damage for each slot level above 1st.

Befuddle

Enchantment cantrip
Wizard
Components: V, S
Casting Time: 1 action
Duration: 1 round
Range: 30 ft.
Area of Effect: 1 creature
Saving Throw: Wis / negates effect

One creature you can see must make a Wisdom saving throw. If the saving throw fails, the creature becomes confused and loses its train of thought.

Note that this spell does no real damage, doesn't affect the target's Intelligence, and doesn't negate the target's next action; it simply erases the target's current thought. The thought probably will reoccur to the creature naturally at some time in the future. For example, if a lady sees someone running from her husband's room with a dagger, this spell compels her to forget that image. But if the person with the dagger is still visible a second later, she'll wonder about it all over again. Similarly, an opponent in combat can forget what strike he was planning but still realizes he's in combat and attack on his next action. The spell's effect ends at the start of the target's next action, so you must be quick to make certain that something forgotten isn't instantly remembered.

Bestow Speech

3rd-level transmutation
Druid, Ranger
Components: V, S, M (a small lexicon)
Casting Time: 1 action
Duration: Concentration, up to 1 hour
Range: Touch
Area of Effect: 1 beast
Saving Throw: None

One beast gains the ability to speak and understand a single language you know. The spell does not increase the beast's intelligence, nor does it make the beast friendly toward you if it wasn't before.

Bewildering Tracks

1st-level transmutation
Ranger
Components: V, S
Casting Time: 1 action
Duration: 1 hour
Range: Touch
Area of Effect: 1 creature
Saving Throw: None

By casting this spell on a creature, you cause the tracks they leave for the duration of this spell to assume the form of one natural animal or humanoid that is within one size category of the creature, of your choosing.

Bewitch

1st-level illusion
Bard, Wizard
Components: V, S
Casting Time: 1 action
Duration: Concentration, up to 1 hour
Range: Self
Area of Effect: Self
Saving Throw: None

You become more likable, attractive, and easier to talk to. For the duration of the spell, you can add 1d4 to your Charisma (Deception) and Charisma (Diplomacy) checks.

Billow the Sails

5th-level transmutation
Cleric, Druid
Components: V, S, M (scrap of sailcloth)
Casting Time: 10 minutes
Duration: Concentration, up to 8 hours
Range: 100 ft.
Area of Effect: 1 ship
Saving Throw: None

You gain control of the wind in a limited area, and can cause it to fill the sails of a ship, even on a calm day. The wind blows in the direction you desire, without weakening or shifting, for the duration of the spell.

The area around the ship is unaffected by this spell; only its sails feel the wind. You must remain in range of the sails throughout the duration of the spell or the effect ends.

Binding Chains

3rd-level conjuration
Wizard
Components: V, S, M (a hooked chain from a torture chamber)
Casting Time: 1 action
Duration: Concentration, up to 1 minute
Range: 120 ft.
Area of Effect: 1 creature
Saving Throw: Dex / negates effect

You conjure four hooked chains that burst out of the ground at a spot you can see. The chains lash at one creature within 10 feet of their location in an attempt to hook into its flesh, clothing, or gear. Each chain has AC 18, 10 hit points, resistance to bludgeoning, piercing and slashing damage from non-adamantine weapons, and immunity to fire, necrotic, poison, psychic, and radiant damage. A chain disappears if it is reduced to 0 hit points.

The creature being attacked by the chains must make a Dexterity saving throw. If the saving throw fails, all four chains attach themselves to the creature and restrain it. At the beginning of each of the creature's turns, it takes 1d6 piercing damage per chain attached to it. As an action, a creature can make a Strength check against your spell save DC to break free from the chains; the DC increases by 1 for each chain attached to the victim. If the victim escapes, the spell ends.

If the targeted creature avoids the chains, every other creature within reach of the chains must make a successful Dexterity saving throw or be hooked and restrained by one chain, with effects as described above.

Binding Sap

1st-level transmutation
Druid, Ranger
Components: V, S, M (a lichen)
Casting Time: 1 action
Duration: Concentration, up to 10 minutes
Range: Self
Area of Effect: Self
Saving Throw: None

You cause parts of your skin to exude a sticky sap that allows you to cling to wooden surfaces. You can change which parts exude the sap at will. This allows you to climb or perch on wooden surfaces with no chance of falling. Climbing still costs double normal movement.

Biting Blade

2nd-level transmutation
Ranger, Wizard
Components: V, S, M (a whetstone)
Casting Time: 1 action
Duration: Concentration, up to 1 minute
Range: 60 ft.
Area of Effect: 1 slashing weapon
Saving Throw: None

One weapon you can see that deals slashing damage becomes incredibly sharp. For the duration of the spell, its damage dice become one category larger: d4 becomes d6, d6 becomes d8, and so on; d12 becomes 2d8.

Black Exhalation

6th-level necromancy
Cleric, Wizard
Components: V, S, M (a fungi)
Casting Time: 1 action
Duration: Instantaneous
Range: Self
Area of Effect: Cone, 30 ft. long
Saving Throw: Con / half damage

You exhale a 30-foot cone of deadly spores. Each creature in the cone must make a Constitution saving throw against poison. If the saving throw fails, the creature takes 6d6 poison damage and loses 1d3 points of Intelligence. With a successful save, the creature takes half damage and loses no Intelligence.

A creature that loses Intelligence because of *black exhalation* must repeat the saving throw at the end of each of its turns. If the saving throw fails, it loses an additional point of Intelligence; if the save succeeds, the spell effect ends. Intelligence loss is permanent until restored by magic.

Blackout

3rd-level abjuration
Warlock, Wizard
Components: V, S, M (a smoky quartz crystal)
Casting Time: 1 action
Duration: 10 minutes
Range: 30 ft.
Area of Effect: Sphere, 20-ft. radius
Saving Throw: None

You gesture at a point within range. A sphere of shifting shadows with a 20-foot radius emanates from that point, visible only to those with darkvision. Creatures with darkvision can't see into or through this area. Creatures without darkvision are not affected.

Blade Bond

6th-level transmutation
Wizard
Components: V, S, M (a shard of a blade and a ball of tar)
Casting Time: 1 action
Duration: Concentration, up to 1 minute
Range: Self
Area of Effect: Self
Saving Throw: Dex / negates effect

You become capable of absorbing metal weapons that strike you. When you are struck by a metallic melee weapon, its wielder must make a Dexterity saving throw or the weapon is absorbed into your flesh and you take no damage from the attack. If the weapon is magical, its enhancement bonus is added to the creature's saving throw.

An absorbed weapon is stuck in your flesh and can't be removed. You can have up to five weapons absorbed at one time. Once this limit is reached, you take damage normally from subsequent attacks.

As a bonus action, you can expel all absorbed weapons. The weapons also are expelled when the spell ends. Expelled weapons fall to the ground around you.

Blade of Light

2nd-level conjuration
Paladin
Components: V, S
Casting Time: 1 bonus action
Duration: 1 minute
Range: Self
Area of Effect: Self
Saving Throw: None

You conjure a blade of light in your hand. Treat this blade as a *longsword +1, +2 vs. evil creatures*. The blade emits bright light in a 20-foot radius.

Enhancement: When you cast *blade of light* using a spell slot of 4th level or higher, the enhancement increases to +2, +3 vs evil creatures. At 6th level, the enhancement increases to +3, +4 vs evil creatures.

Blade Song

3rd-level evocation
Bard, Wizard
Components: V, S, M (a toy horn)
Casting Time: 1 bonus action
Duration: Concentration, up to 1 minute.
Range: Self
Area of Effect: 1 melee weapon
Saving Throw: None

You imbue your weapon with the essence of concentrated sound. When it strikes a creature, it does an additional 2d6 thunder damage. The spell ends if you relinquish or lose your grip on the weapon.

Bladelust

4th-level transmutation
Bard, Wizard
Components: V, S
Casting Time: 1 action
Duration: Concentration, up to 1 minute
Range: Self
Area of Effect: 1 bladed weapon you're holding
Saving Throw: Wis / partial

You cause a slashing or piercing weapon you are holding to achieve a form of limited sentience that hungers for blood. For every 4 points (rounded up) of damage you inflict with the weapon on a living creature, your next attack with that weapon has a bonus of +1 to hit and to damage.

Non-Evil creatures damaged by your weapon also suffer a -2 penalty to hit you with their next attack, unless they make a successful Wisdom saving throw.

Blades of Bone

5th-level necromancy
Druid, Warlock, Wizard
Components: V, S, M (a needle made from bone)
Casting Time: 1 action
Duration: 10 minutes
Range: Touch
Area of Effect: 1 creature
Saving Throw: None

One willing creature you touch sprouts long, sharp spurs of bone all over its body. The creature does 2d6 piercing damage to its target when it successfully initiates a grapple. It does another 2d6 damage at the start of its turn to any creature it has grappled.

Blades of Jade

6th-level transmutation
Druid
Components: V, S
Casting Time: 1 action
Duration: Concentration, up to 1 hour
Range: 120 ft.
Area of Effect: Sphere, 30-ft. radius
Saving Throw: Dex partial

You cause all leaves, petals, and blades of grass within 30 feet of a point you can see to become unnaturally hard and sharp. Each creature that starts its turn in or enters the affected area has its speed reduced by 10 feet until the end of its turn unless it makes a successful Dexterity saving throw. In addition, any creature that moves in the affected area suffers 1d6 slashing damage for every 5 feet moved.

21

If *blades of jade* is cast in an area with especially thick underbrush (as determined by the GM), the spell becomes more dangerous: damage increases to 2d6 per 5 feet in lightly obscuring foliage, and to 4d6 per 5 feet in heavily obscuring foliage.

Blazing Blood

8th-level transmutation
Cleric
Components: V, S, M (holy symbol)
Casting Time: 1 action
Duration: Instantaneous
Range: 60 ft.
Area of Effect: 1, 2, or 3 creatures
Saving Throw: Con / half damage

You attempt to transform the blood of up to three creatures you can see into a blazing fluid. Each creature takes 10d8 fire damage, or half damage with a successful Constitution saving throw. If the creature has imbibed alcohol within the last hour, the damage increases to 10d10 fire damage.

Creatures without blood are immune to this spell.

Blessed Harvest

2nd-level transmutation
Cleric, Druid
Components: V, S
Casting Time: 1 hour
Duration: 1 year
Range: Touch
Area of Effect: 1 acre
Saving Throw: None

You bless a field of up to 1 acre, granting it unusual fertility. Crops grown on the field provide a harvest that is one-third more than the field would have produced normally; or up to 33 percent more animals can be grazed on it.

Blessed Watchman

2nd-level enchantment
Cleric
Components: V, S
Casting Time: 1 action
Duration: 8 hours
Range: Touch
Area of Effect: 1 creature
Saving Throw: None

Your touch grants a creature a +2 bonus on Wisdom (Perception) checks and tactical advantage on saving throws against charm effects for the duration of the spell. In addition, the creature can't be surprised.

Blessing of the Dawn

2nd-level abjuration
Cleric
Components: V, S
Casting Time: 1 action
Duration: 10 minutes
Range: Self
Area of Effect: Sphere, 50-ft. radius
Saving Throw: None

You create an aura that emanates from you in a 50-foot-radius sphere and moves with you. This aura negates magical darkness within its area. In addition, creatures inside the aura add 1d4 to their Wisdom (Medicine) checks.

Blessing of the Forge

5th-level transmutation
Cleric
Components: V, S
Casting Time: 1 action
Duration: Concentration, up to 1 minute
Range: Self
Area of Effect: Self
Saving Throw: No

You call upon the god of craftsmen and seek his blessing. All attack rolls against you with forged or crafted items have tactical disadvantage, and you gain resistance to damage done by such items.

Blight Fog

6th-level necromancy
Warlock
Components: V, S
Casting Time: 1 action
Duration: Concentration, up to 1 minute
Range: 120 ft.
Area of Effect: Sphere, 20-ft. radius
Saving Throw: Con / half damage

You create a thick, gray, 40-foot cloud of deadly mist at a point you can see. The mist is deadly to plants; normal plants wither immediately upon being touched by the fog. Each plant-based creature that begins its turn in the cloud or enters the cloud takes 5d6 + 20 necrotic damage, or half damage with a successful Constitution saving throw.

The magic is specifically designed to affect plants; it has no effect on other creatures.

The cloud moves away from the caster at 10 feet per round. It is dispersed by moderate wind (10 mph or greater). The area of the mist is heavily obscured.

Blindfold

2nd-level transmutation
Warlock, Wizard
Components: V, S, M (Spirit doll)
Casting Time: 1 action
Duration: 1 day
Range: 400 ft.
Area of Effect: 1 creature
Saving Throw: Con / impaired sight rather than blinded

By covering the eyes of a previously constructed *spirit doll*, you force the creature linked to that doll to make a Constitution saving throw. If the saving throw fails, the creature is blinded for the duration of the spell. If the save succeeds, the creature's sight is impaired so that it has a -2 penalty on Wisdom (Perception) checks for the spell's duration. Either effect can be removed by any magic that cures blindness, such as *lesser restoration*.

Blinding Ash

3rd-level conjuration
Cleric, Warlock, Wizard
Components: V, S
Casting Time: 1 action
Duration: Concentration, up to 1 minute
Range: 60 ft.
Area of Effect: Sphere, 30-ft. radius
Saving Throw: None

You create a cloud of thick ash in a 30-foot radius sphere around a point you can see. The cloud spreads around corners, and its area is heavily obscured. Fire spells do not burn off the mist, but water- and cold-based spells do dispel the magic. Each creature in the cloud takes 2d6 fire damage at the beginning of its turn. The cloud lasts for the duration of the spell or until a wind of moderate or greater speed (10 miles per hour) disperses it.

Blinding Flare

3rd-level evocation
Wizard
Components: V, S, M (a bit of tinder)
Casting Time: 1 action
Duration: Concentration, up to 1 minute
Range: 20 ft.
Area of Effect: 1 arrow
Saving Throw: Con / negates effect

You enchant an arrow or bolt you can see. The projectile erupts in a burst of light when it strikes a solid object or at the height of its arc (your choice). Anyone within 30 feet of this eruption who can see it must make a Constitution saving throw or be blinded. A blinded creature can repeat the saving throw at the end of each of its turns; a successful save ends the blindness.

Blood Bath

2nd-level necromancy
Warlock, Wizard
Components: V, S, M (a drop of blood)
Casting Time: 1 action
Duration: Instantaneous
Range: 120 ft.
Area of Effect: 1 creature
Saving Throw: Con / half damage

One creature that you can see must make a Constitution saving throw. If the saving throw fails, the creature suffers 3d8 necrotic damage and is blinded for 1 round as blood spurts from its eyes, ears, mouth, and nose. If the saving throw succeeds, it takes half damage and is not blinded.

Blood Blade

5th-level transmutation
Wizard
Components: V, S, M (a whetstone)
Casting Time: 1 action
Duration: Concentration, up to 1 minute
Range: Touch
Area of Effect: 1 weapon
Saving Throw: None

You transform the edge of one slashing weapon you touch, making it unnaturally sharp. Any creature struck by the weapon begins bleeding, suffering 3d6 damage at the beginning of each of its turn until the wound is stanched, either with magical healing or by spending an action and making a successful DC 10 Wisdom (Medicine) check. The Medicine check can be performed by the bleeding creature or by an adjacent ally. Creatures without blood are not affected by the blade. When the spell ends, the blade returns to its natural sharpness, but bleeding caused by the blade doesn't end automatically.

Blood Geyser

2nd-level transmutation
Cleric, Wizard
Components: V, S
Casting Time: 1 action
Duration: Instantaneous
Range: 60 ft.
Area of Effect: Cylinder, 10-ft. radius, 20 ft. high

Saving Throw: Dex / half damage

You select a point on the ground that you can see. A geyser of blood filled with the caustic anger of the defeated erupts from that point and rains down in a 20-foot high, 10-foot radius cylinder. Each creature in the area takes 4d6 acid damage, or half damage with a successful Dexterity saving throw.

Blood of the Hydra

6th-level conjuration
Druid
Components: V, S, M (a drop of venom)
Casting Time: 1 action
Duration: Concentration, up to 1 minute
Range: Touch
Area of Effect: 1 weapon
Saving Throw: Con / negates effect

The edge of a piercing or slashing weapon that you touch becomes poisoned. For the duration of the spell, each time the weapon hits a creature, that creature must make a successful Constitution saving throw against poison or take 3d8 poison damage and become poisoned. A poisoned creature can repeat the saving throw at the end of each of its turns; on a successful save, it is no longer poisoned.

Blood Purge

5th-level necromancy
Wizard
Components: V, S, M (a glass tube filled with blood)
Casting Time: 1 action
Duration: Instantaneous
Range: 30 ft.
Area of Effect: 1 creature
Saving Throw: Con / negates effect

You choose a creature you can see and try to make it violently disgorge blood from its body. The creature must make a Constitution saving throw. If the saving throw fails, it loses 2d4 points of Constitution. A creature reduced to 0 Constitution dies immediately. Creatures without blood are immune to this effect.

Bloodburn

4th-level necromancy
Wizard
Components: V, S, M (a pinch of sulfur)
Casting Time: 1 action
Duration: Concentration, up to 1 minute
Range: 120 ft.
Area of Effect: 1 creature
Saving Throw: Con / negates effect

Select one creature within range that has been wounded in the last minute and hasn't yet received any healing. If the creature fails a Constitution saving throw, the blood flowing from its wounds bursts into fire, inflicting 5d8 fire damage to the creature at the start of each of its turns and preventing it from receiving any healing while the spell is in effect. The creature can repeat the saving throw at the end of each its turns; the spell ends when it has made two successful saves, which need not be consecutive.

Bloody Tentacles

5th-level necromancy
Warlock, Wizard
Components: V, S, M (a handful of dirt from a strangled man's grave)
Casting Time: 1 action

Bloodburn

Eric Lofgren

Duration: 8 hours
Range: Self
Area of Effect: Sphere, 30-ft. radius
Saving Throw: See text

When you cast this spell, tentacles of blood erupt from the bodies of all dead or dying creatures within 30 feet of you. A dying creature must make a Constitution saving throw; a successful save negates the effect for that creature, but a failure results in the creature dying immediately as its blood erupts from inside it.

Each tentacle has AC 15, 10 hit points, reach 5 ft., and your saving throw modifiers. At the beginning of your turn, each tentacle attacks one creature within 10 feet of it using your spell attack bonus. You choose the targets if you can see the tentacles; otherwise they attack the closest creature, friend or foe. A successful hit does 1d8 + 4 bludgeoning damage and the target creature is grappled. A tentacle doesn't attack any other target while it's grappling a creature.

A grappled creature can't breathe, and is suffocating. A creature can escape from a tentacle by using an action and making a successful Strength (Athletics) check against your spell save DC. Tentacles disappear when they are reduced to 0 hit points.

If no enemies are in reach, the tentacles retreat inside their hosts and remain dormant until a creature approaches. The tentacles never attack you.

Blunt the Edge

2nd-level transmutation
Wizard
Components: V, S, M (a blunt razor)
Casting Time: 1 action
Duration: Concentration, up to 1 minute

Range: 10 ft.
Area of Effect: 1 weapon
Saving Throw: Wis / negates effect

You cause one weapon within range that does piercing or slashing damage to become blunt. If the weapon's wielder fails a Wisdom saving throw, then for the duration of the spell, the weapon does only half damage and can't score critical hits.

Boarding Plank

2nd-level conjuration
Wizard
Components: V, S
Casting Time: 1 action
Duration: 1 hour
Range: Touch
Area of Effect: 4 ft. wide by 25 ft. long
Saving Throw: None

You create a shimmering plank of force, 4 feet wide and up to 25 feet long, originating from a point that you touch. It doesn't need to be supported physically at either end. The board keeps itself level at all times and can support up to 3,000 lbs. If the weight limit is exceeded, the spell ends immediately.

Bolster Mental Fortitude

2nd-level abjuration
Cleric, Wizard
Components: V, S
Casting Time: 1 action

Duration: Concentration, up to 10 minutes
Range: Touch
Area of Effect: 1 creature
Saving Throw: None

A willing creature you touch gains tactical advantage on Intelligence, Wisdom, and Charisma saving throws for the duration of this spell.

Bone Armor

3rd-level conjuration
Cleric
Components: V, S, M (holy symbol)
Casting Time: 1 action
Duration: Concentration, up to 10 minutes
Range: Touch
Area of Effect: 1 creature
Saving Throw: None

You strengthen the bones of a willing creature you touch. The creature gains resistance against bludgeoning damage for the duration of the spell.

Bone Blight

5th-level necromancy
Cleric, Warlock
Components: V, S, M (a bit of powdered bone)
Casting Time: 1 action
Duration: Permanent
Range: 60 ft.
Area of Effect: 1 creature
Saving Throw: Con / negates effect

You inflict a powerful curse on a creature you can see, unless that creature makes a successful Constitution saving throw.

Creatures cursed with *bone blight* have dangerously brittle bones. They gain vulnerability to bludgeoning and slashing damage, and if they take 20 or more damage from any attack, they must make a successful Constitution saving throw or suffer a broken bone. A broken bone reduces movement to half speed and imposes disadvantage on Dexterity checks. The penalties for a broken bone are removed when the character receives magical healing or finishes a long rest with all of their hit points and hit dice restored.

At the end of each long rest, a character suffering *bone blight* must make a Constitution saving throw. The curse ends after two successful saves, which need not be consecutive. The curse can also be ended by magic that removes curses.

Bone Trap

3rd-level necromancy
Warlock, Wizard
Components: V, S, M (a pinch of dust taken from a defeated wight or vampire)
Casting Time: 1 action
Duration: Permanent until discharged.
Range: Touch
Area of Effect: 1 bone
Saving Throw: Con / half damage

You enchant an arm or leg bone taken from a skeleton or corpse of a Medium or smaller creature. When any creature touches that bone, it explodes in a blast of red and violet energy. Every creature within 10 feet of the bone takes 4d10 necrotic damage, or half damage with a successful Constitution saving throw.

Boost Potency

2nd-level transmutation
Cleric, Druid, Ranger
Components: V, S
Casting Time: 1 action
Duration: Concentration, up to 10 minutes
Range: Touch
Area of Effect: 1 creature or plant
Saving Throw: None

You cause the natural poison of one willing creature or plant to increase in potency; the DC of its saving throw increases by 2 for the duration of the spell.

Bound Hearts

7th-level enchantment
Cleric
Components: V, S, M (holy symbol)
Casting Time: 1 hour
Duration: 1 year
Range: Touch
Area of Effect: 2 creatures
Saving Throw: None

You cause two willing creatures to become linked with a psychic bond. Each becomes perpetually aware of the other's location accurately enough to find the other even when blindfolded. They are aware of each other's physical and emotional condition at all times. This knowledge doesn't give any information about the subject's surroundings — one of the spell's recipients could know that the other is 10 miles away in a castle and distraught, for example, but wouldn't know that the other person is chained to a wall and awaiting trial for witchcraft.

A person can be under the effect of only one *bound hearts* spell at a time, and it's not possible for more than two people to be simultaneously linked by this spell.

Enhancement: If *bound hearts* is cast using a 9th-level slot, the duration becomes permanent.

Bramble Armor

4th-level conjuration
Druid
Components: V, S, M (a thorny vine)
Casting Time: 1 action
Duration: 1 hour
Range: Touch
Area of Effect: 1 creature
Saving Throw: None

A multitude of thorny vines burst from your fingers and enwrap a willing, nonarmored creature you touch to form a suit of fibrous armor around the target. This armor is treated as medium armor with a base AC of 15 + Dexterity modifier (max 2). Normal penalties apply if the armored creature doesn't have proficiency with medium armor. Any foe that strikes a creature encased in *bramble armor* with a melee attack takes 1d4 piercing damage.

Branch Assault

2nd-level transmutation
Druid
Components: V, S
Casting Time: 1 action
Duration: Concentration, up to 1 minute
Range: 120 ft.
Area of Effect: 1 tree
Saving Throw: None

You imbue one tree you can see with the ability to strike creatures with its branches. The tree remains immobile otherwise. When you cast the spell, and as an action on your turn, you direct the tree to attack one target that it can reach. Make a melee spell attack against the target; a successful hit does 2d10 + 5 bludgeoning damage.

Breach Defenses

6th-level transmutation
Warlock, Wizard
Components: V, S
Casting Time: 1 action
Duration: Concentration, up to 1 minute
Range: 60 ft.
Area of Effect: 1 creature
Saving Throw: Con / negates effect

You attempt to nullify the resistances of one creature you can see. The creature loses all of its resistance to bludgeoning, piercing, and slashing damage for the duration of the spell unless it makes a successful Constitution saving throw. The spell doesn't affect the creature's immunities.

Breath of the Dragon

3rd-level evocation
Sorcerer, Wizard
Components: V, M (a small statuette of a dragon god)
Casting Time: 1 bonus action
Duration: 1 minute
Range: Self
Area of Effect: See text
Saving Throw: Dex / half damage

This spell grants you the ability to spew a breath attack similar to a dragon's breath weapon. You gain a pool of 10d6 that you can use as damage dice in your attacks.

As an action, you can breathe a 60-foot cone of fire or cold, or a 60-foot-long, 5-foot-wide line of acid or lightning. Each creature in the affected area takes damage, or half damage with a successful Dexterity saving throw.

When you use the breath weapon, you can expend up to five dice from the damage pool at one time; the breath weapon does that much acid, fire, cold, or lightning damage, as appropriate. You must decide how many dice to use before targets make their saving throws.

The spell ends when no dice are left in the damage pool.

Enhancement: For each spell slot used higher than 3rd level, add 2d6 to the damage pool and 1d6 to the maximum dice you can expend in a single attack.

Brittle

2nd-level transmutation
Wizard
Components: V, S, M (a drop of acid)
Casting Time: 1 action
Duration: Concentration, up to 1 minute
Range: 30 ft.
Area of Effect: 1 object
Saving Throw: Con / negates effect

One object you can see becomes brittle and vulnerable to bludgeoning damage. If the object is held by a creature or is magically animated, a successful Constitution saving throw negates the effect.

Bubble Goop

4th-level conjuration
Sorcerer, Wizard
Components: V, S, M (tree sap)
Casting Time: 1 action
Duration: Until scraped off
Range: 120 ft.
Area of Effect: 1 creature
Saving Throw: Dex / negates effect

You breathe out a bubble that floats quickly toward one creature within range. If the creature fails a Dexterity saving throw, the bubble bursts over it and covers it with goo. Creatures covered with goo suffer a -2 penalty to attack rolls and Dexterity checks, and their speed is reduced by 10 feet. In addition, creatures covered in *bubble boop* can't cast spells with somatic components.

The *bubble goop* remains until an affected creature or an adjacent ally uses an action to scrape it off and the affected creature makes a successful Dexterity check.

Enhancement: For each spell slot used higher than 4th level, you can create one additional bubble. Each bubble can be targeted against a different creature.

Bubble Net

1st-level conjuration
Cleric, Druid, Sorcerer, Wizard
Components: S, M (palm-sized net)
Casting Time: 1 action
Duration: Concentration, up to 1 minute
Range: 120 ft.
Area of Effect: 1 creature
Saving Throw: Dex / negates effect

You cause an underwater creature you can see within range to be wrapped in a magical net of air bubbles that rises to the water's surface. The creature must make a Dexterity saving throw. If the saving throw fails, the creature is restrained by the net and it rises 120 feet toward the surface at the end of each of its turns. Once the net reaches the surface, it remains there and keeps the creature restrained. As an action, a restrained creature can make a Strength or Dexterity check against your spell save DC to escape from the net. If the save succeeds, the net disappears and the spell ends.

Bug Bites

2nd-level conjuration
Cleric, Druid, Ranger
Components: V, S, M (honey)
Casting Time: 1 action
Duration: 24 hours
Range: Touch
Area of Effect: 1 sleeping creature
Saving Throw: None

You cause one sleeping creature to become covered in itchy insect bites. The target has a -2 penalty to attack rolls and ability checks for the next 24 hours, after which the bites disappear. There is no saving throw, but the caster might awaken the creature before the spell can take effect if the caster is not appropriately stealthy. This spell has no effect if cast on a creature that is not asleep.

Buoyancy

1st-level transmutation
Druid, Ranger
Components: V, S, M (a small white ring)
Casting Time: 1 action
Duration: 1 hour
Range: Touch
Area of Effect: 1 creature
Saving Throw: None

One willing creature you touch becomes naturally buoyant and rises to the surface of any liquid it is immersed in, regardless of weight, at the rate of 10 feet per round.

Burden

Transmutation cantrip
Sorcerer, Wizard
Components: V, S, M (a small stone)
Casting Time: 1 action

Duration: Concentration, up to 10 minutes
Range: 60 ft.
Area of Effect: 1 object weighing up to 1 lb.
Saving Throw: None

You double the weight of one inanimate object you can see. At 5th level, you can affect an object weighing up to 5 lbs. and quadruple its weight. At 10th level, you can affect an object weighing up to 20 lbs. and increase its weight by a factor of six.

Burn the Sight

2nd-level transmutation
Warlock, Wizard
Components: V, S, M (spirit doll)
Casting Time: 10 minutes
Duration: 8 hours
Range: 30 ft.
Area of Effect: 1 creature
Saving Throw: None

If this spell is cast on a *spirit doll* and the doll is placed within 6 inches of a light source (a lit candle or lantern, for example, or an object with a *light* spell cast on it), then the creature associated with that *spirit doll* has darkvision (60 feet) for the duration of this spell.

Burning Rain

7th-level transmutation
Wizard
Components: V, S, M (a small vial of acid)
Casting Time: 1 action
Duration: Concentration, up to 1 minute
Range: 300 ft.
Area of Effect: Cylinder, 100-ft. radius, 50 ft. high
Saving Throw: None

Burning rain transforms natural rain into droplets of liquid fire. It affects a cylindrical area 100 feet in radius and 50 feet high. A creature that starts its turn in the affected area or enters the area takes 4d6 fire damage. The spell has no effect unless rain is already falling.

Burning rain also damages objects in the area and ignites unattended, flammable objects, but the extent of this damage must be determined by the GM.

Buttress

2nd-level transmutation
Wizard
Components: V, S
Casting Time: 1 action
Duration: Concentration, up to 10 minutes
Range: 60 ft.
Area of Effect: 1 object
Saving Throw: None

You cause one item weighing up to 10 lbs. to become stronger and less likely to break. It gains resistance against bludgeoning, piercing, and slashing damage and gains temporary hit points equal to its current hit points. The temporary hit points disappear when the spell ends.

Cacophony

3rd-level evocation
Bard, Wizard
Components: V, S
Casting Time: 1 action
Duration: Instantaneous
Range: 60 ft.

Area of Effect: Sphere, 20-ft. radius
Saving Throw: Con / negates effect

You create a great burst of sound emanating from a point you can see. All creatures within 20 feet of that point are deafened for 10 minutes unless they make successful Constitution saving throws. Brittle objects and creatures made of crystal also take 6d6 thunder damage, or half damage with a successful saving throw.

Call Divine Warrior

8th-level conjuration
Cleric
Components: V, S, M (holy relic)
Casting Time: 10 minutes
Duration: 24 hours
Range: 60 ft.
Area of Effect: 1 champion
Saving Throw: None

You summon the spirit of a powerful, once-living champion of your deity and give it physical form. The spirit champion arrives within range, looking as it did in the prime of its life. The spell must be cast at a site hallowed to the caster's deity.

The spirit champion possesses all abilities and items that it possessed during life. In addition, the spirit champion is able to cast *command* or *suggestion* as an action on any worshipper of the caster's deity. Its exact statistics are determined by the GM; we suggest using the planetar's stat block as a starting point, but the specifics are entirely up to the GM. It won't give or loan items to other characters.

The spirit champion is not under the control of the caster. It acts in the best interest of its deity as it sees it. Often, a spirit champion will take command of the situation. Followers of the deity are always well-disposed toward taking commands from a *divine warrior*.

The champion and all its items disappear when it is slain or when the spell ends.

Call of the Wild Companion

1st-level evocation
Druid, Ranger
Components: S, M (mistletoe)
Casting Time: 1 action
Duration: Instantaneous
Range: 10 miles
Area of Effect: 1 animal companion
Saving Throw: None

You transmit a silent, one-word message to your animal companion, if it is within 10 miles. The spell does not require line-of-sight. If the message is "come," the animal also learns your location. Only an animal companion or an animal bonded to the caster through *animal friendship* or similar magic can be the target of this spell.

Call the Heart

6th-level necromancy
Cleric
Components: V, S
Casting Time: 1 action
Duration: Instantaneous
Range: 60 ft.
Area of Effect: 1 creature
Saving Throw: Con / half damage

One living creature that you point at takes 6d10 + 20 necrotic damage, or half damage with a successful Constitution saving throw. If the creature is reduced to 0 hit points by this attack, it must make another Constitution saving throw immediately. If this saving throw fails, the creature's heart is ripped out of its chest and flies to your hand; the creature dies instantly.

Camouflage

1st-level transmutation
Druid, Ranger
Components: V, S
Casting Time: 1 action
Duration: Concentration, up to 10 minutes
Range: Touch
Area of Effect: 1 creature
Saving Throw: None

You grant a creature the ability to change colors to match its surroundings. The creature can make Dexterity (Stealth) checks to hide if it has cover or is lightly obscured.

Catnip

2nd-level enchantment
Druid, Ranger
Components: V, S, M (berries)
Casting Time: 1 action
Duration: 10 minutes
Range: Touch
Area of Effect: 1 handful of berries
Saving Throw: Con / negates poisoning; special

You infuse a handful of berries with the power to lure and intoxicate animals. Choose a type of beast when you cast the spell. Beasts of that type within 60 feet of the berries are drawn to them unerringly. The first beast to reach the berries devours them in one round and becomes poisoned unless it makes a successful Constitution saving throw. The poisoning lasts until the end of the beast's next long rest. Beasts with an Intelligence of 6 or higher can resist the lure of the berries with a successful Wisdom saving throw.

Cause the Bends

3rd-level necromancy
Cleric, Wizard
Components: V, S
Casting Time: 1 action
Duration: Concentration, up to 1 minute
Range: Touch
Area of Effect: 1 creature
Saving Throw: Con / negates effect

One creature you touch is afflicted with pain from high-pressure gas bubbles forced into its bloodstream. The creature must make a Constitution saving throw. On a successful save, the spell has no effect. If the saving throw fails, then the creature takes 2d6 necrotic damage at the end of each of its turns and it must subtract 1d4 from its attack rolls and ability checks for the duration of the spell. The creature can repeat the saving throw at the end of each of its turns (after taking damage from the spell); a successful save ends the spell.

Caustic Spittle

1st-level evocation
Sorcerer, Wizard
Components: V, S, M (a small vial of wine)
Casting Time: 1 bonus action
Duration: Concentration, up to 1 minute
Range: Self
Area of Effect: Self
Saving Throw: None

You produce a small, viscous glob of acid and hold it in your belly. As an action, you can spit the acid at one creature within 20 feet. Make a ranged spell attack roll. On a hit, the target takes 3d6 acid damage plus 1d6 for each round since you cast the spell. Thus, the spell does 3d6 damage on the round you cast it, 4d6 on the round after, etc. If the spell ends before you make the attack, you must make a Constitution saving throw or take the damage yourself. The spell ends after the attack is made.

Cave Walker

2nd-level transmutation
Druid
Components: V, S
Casting Time: 1 action
Duration: Concentration, up to 1 hour
Range: Self
Area of Effect: Self
Saving Throw: None

You adapt yourself for survival in an underground environment. While underground, you gain darkvision (60 feet) and have tactical advantage on Strength (Athletics) and Dexterity (Acrobatics) checks used to traverse natural (unworked) stone. You also gain light sensitivity; you have tactical disadvantage on attack rolls and ability checks if you are in sunlight or if you are attacking a creature in sunlight.

Chain Enervation

7th-level evocation
Wizard
Components: V, S, M (finger bone of a wight)
Casting Time: 1 action
Duration: Instantaneous
Range: 200 ft.
Area of Effect: 1 or more creatures
Saving Throw: Con partial

You fire a bolt of negative energy at one creature you can see. Make a ranged spell attack against the target. On a hit, the bolt does 12d6 necrotic damage and the creature must make a successful Constitution saving throw or gain two levels of exhaustion. The bolt then leaps to another target within 50 feet of the previous target that hasn't already been targeted by the spell; you choose which target to attack, if more than one is available. The effect continues attacking creatures one after another in a chain until it misses or there are no more creatures eligible to be hit.

Change Dust to Water

6th-level transmutation
Druid, Wizard
Components: V, S, M (a seashell)
Casting Time: 1 action
Duration: Permanent
Range: 120 ft.
Area of Effect: Up to 10,000 cubic ft. of dust
Saving Throw: None

You transmute an area of dust or dirt into fresh, potable water. You can affect up to 10,000 cubic feet (10 cubes, each 10 feet on a side), but the effect can't extend more than 10 feet into the ground. The spell doesn't work on rock or stone and has no effect on creatures.

Change Water to Dust

6th-level transmutation
Druid, Wizard
Components: V, S, M (a pinch of dust)
Casting Time: 1 action
Duration: Permanent
Range: 120 ft.
Area of Effect: Up to 10,000 cubic ft. of water
Saving Throw: None

You transmute normal water into fine dust. Up to 10,000 cubic feet (10 cubes, each 10 feet on a side) can be affected, but the effect can go no deeper than the top 10 feet of a pool of water. A creature in the affected water is trapped in the dust unless it makes a successful Dexterity saving throw, in which case it escapes to the nearest clear, safe space.

This spell has no effect on most creatures. If cast directly on a water creature, however, such as a water elemental, the creature must make a Constitution saving throw. If the saving throw fails, the creature is killed instantly; on a successful save, it takes 5d6 fire damage instead.

Chanting

2nd-level conjuration
Cleric, Paladin
Components: V, S
Casting Time: 1 action
Duration: Concentration, up to 1 minute
Range: Self
Area of Effect: Sphere, 30-ft. radius
Saving Throw: None

You begin a chant of devotion to your deity. The chant creates an aura in a 30-foot-radius sphere around you, that moves with you. The aura brings luck to your allies and disfavor to your enemies. Each ally in the aura adds 1d4 to its attack rolls and saving throws. Enemies must subtract 1d4 from their attack rolls and saving throws while they are inside the aura.

You must maintain the chant for the duration of the spell; the spell ends if you lose concentration or if you are silenced or unable to speak. You can't cast spells with a verbal component while chanting.

Chaos Bolt

3rd-level evocation
Sorcerer, Wizard
Components: V, S
Casting Time: 1 action
Duration: Instantaneous
Range: 30 ft.
Area of Effect: 1 creature
Saving Throw: None

You release a bolt of pure chaos. Make a ranged spell attack against one creature you can see. If it hits, the target takes 4d10 force damage and is confused on its next turn.

A confused creature can't take reactions and must roll 1d10 at the start of its turn to determine what it does that turn.

d10	Behavior
1	Creature is incapacitated and moves as far as it can in a random direction.
2-6	Creature is incapacitated and can't move.
7-8	Creature can't move, but it makes a melee attack against the nearest creature within reach. If no target is within reach, it does nothing.
9-10	The creature can move and act normally.

Character Flaw

2nd-level enchantment
Wizard
Components: S
Casting Time: 1 action
Duration: Concentration, up to 10 minutes
Range: Touch
Area of Effect: 1 creature
Saving Throw: Wis / negates effect

One creature that you touch becomes unpleasant and gaffe-prone, provided it fails a Wisdom saving throw. Until the spell ends, the target creature has tactical disadvantage on Charisma checks when interacting with other creatures.

Charge

4th-level abjuration
Wizard
Components: V, S, M
Casting Time: 10 minutes
Duration: Permanent until discharged
Range: Touch
Area of Effect: 1 object
Saving Throw: Dex / negates effect

You infuse one object with a magical trap. Anyone other than you who touches the object takes 10d6 lightning damage, or half damage with a successful Dexterity saving throw. You can create a command word when the spell is cast that will allow other creatures to handle the item safely.

The presence of a *charge* on an object can be detected with a successful Intelligence (Investigation) check; the DC equals your spell saving throw.

Charged Missile

2nd-level evocation
Ranger, Wizard
Components: V, S
Casting Time: 1 bonus action
Duration: Concentration, up to 1 minute
Range: Touch
Area of Effect: 1 projectile
Saving Throw: None

One arrow, bolt, or sling bullet you touch becomes infused with electrical energy. A successful attack with the affected ammunition does its normal damage plus 5d6 lightning damage. The spell ends after the projectile is used, whether it hits or misses.

Enhancement: For each spell slot used higher than 2nd level, the missile does an additional 1d6 damage.

Charged Touch

3rd-level transmutation
Druid, Wizard
Components: S
Casting Time: 1 action
Duration: 1 minute or until discharged
Range: Self
Area of Effect: Self
Saving Throw: Con / half damage

Your body becomes the reservoir of an electric charge. The next time you are struck by a melee attack during the spell's duration, the attacker takes 8d6 lightning damage, or half damage with a successful Constitution saving throw.

Chariot of Fire

8th-level conjuration
Druid
Components: V, S, M (small wheel)
Casting Time: 10 minutes
Duration: 3 hours
Range: 60 ft.
Area of Effect: 1 chariot
Saving Throw: None

You bring forth a large chariot made of flames and two fiery horses to draw it in an unoccupied space within range. The chariot and horses have

Chariot of Fire

a land speed of 70 feet and a fly speed of 140 feet. The chariot can carry up to eight Medium or Small creatures; you must touch them as you cast the spell for them to ride the chariot safely.

Other creatures that begin their turn within 10 feet of the chariot or who approach within 10 feet during their turn take 2d6 fire damage.

While aboard the chariot, a creature has resistance to fire damage (but only selected creatures can get aboard).

The chariot and horses follow your verbal commands.

The chariot and horses can be damaged. Treat the entire assemblage as have AC 18 and 100 hit points. It uses your saving throws, and is immune to fire damage and to bludgeoning, slashing, and piercing damage from nonmagical weapons. The spell ends if the chariot is reduced to 0 hit points.

The chariot and horses disappear immediately when the spell ends, which can leave passengers falling to the ground.

Charismatic Shield

7th-level enchantment
Bard, Cleric
Components: V, S, M (a flower)
Casting Time: 1 action
Duration: Concentration, up to 10 minutes
Range: Self
Area of Effect: Self
Saving Throw: Wis / negates effect

For the duration of this spell, you add your Charisma modifier to your AC. In addition, each creature within 50 feet of you that targets you with an attack or a harmful spell must make a Wisdom saving throw. If the saving throw fails, the creature must target another creature or lose the action, and it can't target you again for the duration of the spell. If you attack or cast a harmful spell against that creature, the spell's effect against that creature is broken, and it can target you normally.

Charnel Stench

2nd-level necromancy
Cleric, Warlock
Components: V, S, M (rotting organs)
Casting Time: 1 action
Duration: Concentration, up to 1 minute
Range: Self
Area of Effect: Sphere, 10-ft. radius
Saving Throw: Con / negates effect

You exude a sickening, carrion stench. Every living creature that begins its turn within 10 feet of you or that enters the area of effect must make a Constitution saving throw. If the saving throw fails, the creature is poisoned for as long as it stays in the area of effect and for an additional 1d4 rounds after it leaves the area. A creature that makes a successful save is immune to the effect of this casting of *charnel stench*.

Chatterwild

2nd-level divination
Druid
Components: V, S, M (feathers from a parrot)
Casting Time: 1 action
Duration: Concentration, up to 1 hour
Range: Touch
Area of Effect: 1 to 6 creatures
Saving Throw: None normally; special

You can touch up to six willing creatures when you cast this spell. For the duration of the spell, the affected creatures can communicate with each other using the languages of fauna native to the area. Everyone who is not under the effect of a *chatterwild* spell hears their words as the barking of coyotes, the chattering of squirrels, or the clacking, hooting, or shrieking of birds. If a listener has a reason to question what they're hearing–for example, if the spell is used inside a normally quiet temple–the GM can allow a Wisdom saving throw to negate the effect.

Chill of Evil

7th-level enchantment
Cleric
Components: V, M (the preserved heart of a good creature)
Casting Time: 1 action
Duration: 1 week
Range: Touch
Area of Effect: 1 creature
Saving Throw: Wis / negates effect

The creature you touch when you cast this spell is filled with the deep chill of evil. The targeted creature must make a Wisdom saving throw. If the saving throw fails, the creature's compassion is stripped away and it becomes cruel and paranoid for the duration of the spell.

This is a subtle effect calling for adjudication by the GM. The affected creature doesn't go berserk or turn into a serial murderer. Most often, this spell causes the affected creature's normal acts to become twisted perversions of their original intent. For example, a noble knight afflicted by the *chill of evil* might decide that defeating his opponent honorably on the field of battle isn't enough "justice" for the harm that opponent caused. Instead, that foe must be "purified" through pain, so the knight imprisons him and tortures him to death over the week of the spell's duration. An artist could turn to portraying only evil or grisly subjects in his paintings, and a merchant might suddenly start hawking poisons on the street. Essentially, the affected creature acts as if its alignment is aggressively Neutral Evil; it greedily seeks its own interests with no regard for how others are hurt. If the creature was Evil to begin with, this might not be much of a change.

People who know the target well can make a Wisdom (Insight) check to determine why the person is acting so uncharacteristically.

Chill of evil is most often used by evil clerics against paladins and good clerics. Their victims are likely to fall from grace for the duration of the spell at least, and their reputations might be ruined for far longer. The target of the spell recalls everything after it ends. Since the person doesn't necessarily know they were enchanted, a Good character is likely to feel tremendous remorse over his or her actions.

Chilling Gaze

6th-level transmutation
Sorcerer, Warlock, Wizard
Components: V, S, M (a glass cube)
Casting Time: 1 action
Duration: Concentration, up to 1 minute
Range: Self
Area of Effect: Self
Saving Throw: Con / negates effect

Your eyes become cold and frosty. For the duration of this spell, whenever a creature starts its turn within 30 feet of you, you can force it to make a Constitution saving throw. The creature must be able to see your eyes, and you must be able to see it. If the saving throw fails, the creature takes 2d10 cold damage and becomes paralyzed by supernatural chills. The paralysis lasts 2d4 days; this decreases to 1 day if the victim is warmed in a dwelling, bundled in furs, etc. The paralysis can also be ended by magic capable of removing paralysis.

Creatures that are resistant to or immune to cold damage are not paralyzed by this spell.

Chlorophyll

1st-level transmutation
Druid
Components: V, S, M (a green leaf)
Casting Time: 1 action
Duration: 24 hours
Range: Self
Area of Effect: Self
Saving Throw: None

Your skin takes on a green hue that allows you to draw energy from the sun. While you are affected by this spell, you do not need to eat and can survive indefinitely, provided you get four hours of sunlight per 24-hour period. You still require normal amounts of water and air. If you spend a short rest in direct sunlight, you regain an additional hit point per hit die expended during that short rest.

Choose Fate

3rd-level divination
Cleric
Components: V, S, M (two grains of salt and a rose petal)
Casting Time: 1 action
Duration: 1 minute
Range: Touch
Area of Effect: 1 creature
Saving Throw: None

You grant a willing creature a brief glimpse into the future and the ability to rearrange its fate. The creature 1d20 twice and notes the rolls. The creature must use those two results for its next two d20 rolls during the spell's duration, but it can choose the order in which the results are used.

Enhancement: For each spell slot used higher than 3rd level, you can affect one additional creature.

Chronal Displacement

7th-level transmutation
Wizard
Components: V, S, M (intricate and accurate planetary model)
Casting Time: 1 hour
Duration: 1 year
Range: Touch
Area of Effect: 1 creature
Saving Throw: None

A willing creature you touch becomes disconnected from time and doesn't age for the duration of the spell.

The spell's magic is erratic. Each day, there is a 5% chance that time slows for the creature for 24 hours, causing the creature to act as if under the influence of a *slow* spell for the entire day. In addition, the creature has disadvantage on any saving throw against any magic involving time or aging during that 24-hour period.

Chrysalis

6th-level transmutation
Druid
Components: V, S, M (a cocoon)
Casting Time: 10 minutes
Duration: 1 hour
Range: Touch
Area of Effect: 1 creature
Saving Throw: None

A willing creature you touch becomes wrapped in a silky cocoon. While in the cocoon, the subject doesn't need to eat or drink. At the end of the hour, it emerges from the cocoon as if it had just completed a long rest. While within the cocoon, however, the creature is helpless and can do nothing. If awakened before the end of the spell's duration, the subject can break free from the cocoon as an action, but this does provoke opportunity attacks from adjacent enemies. The creature has tactical disadvantage on Wisdom (Perception) checks while cocooned.

The chrysalis has 1 hit point and AC 10. If it is destroyed, the spell ends and the creature is stunned until the end of its next turn.

Circle of Divine Censure

4th-level abjuration
Paladin
Components: V, S, M (holy symbol)
Casting Time: 1 action
Duration: Concentration, up to 1 minute
Range: Self
Area of Effect: Sphere, 30-ft. radius
Saving Throw: Cha / partial

You radiate a holy aura in a 30-foot radius that is anathema to undead and fiends. Any undead or fiend that enters the aura or begins its turn in the aura takes 2d6 radiant damage and must make a Charisma saving throw; if the saving throw fails, the creature must move out of the aura as soon it can.

Circle of Scrying

4th-level divination
Wizard
Components: V, S
Casting Time: 1 minute
Duration: Concentration, up to 8 hours
Range: Self
Area of Effect: 1 magic circle
Saving Throw: None

You empower a magic circle that links to sigils of seeing you previously created. You can select a number of sigils up to your Intelligence modifier (minimum of 1). The distance between the *circle of scrying* and the sigils of seeing is not a factor, and the sigils can even be on other planes of existence.

When you stand inside your *circle of scrying*, you can view the area around any of the linked sigils as if you were actually standing at the location of the sigil. You can switch between different sigils as an action.

The casting time for the spell depends on whether the circle is being drawn anew or a previously placed, permanent circle is being empowered. Drawing a new circle takes one day. Empowering a previously placed, permanent circle takes 1 minute.

Drawing a new circle requires material components costing 250 gold pieces. The circle is typically a flat design of a geometric shape with a 5-foot radius.

A sigil of seeing is created spending one minute drawing the sigil on a flat surface. Each sigil requires special ink that costs 100 gold pieces per sigil. The sigil disappears within moments of being drawn, but it reappears when you are scrying through it. A sigil is typically no more an inch in diameter. While a sigil is in use, it can be noticed by anyone who examines the spot where it's drawn and makes a successful DC 10 Wisdom (Perception) or Intelligence (Investigation) check. While the sigil isn't in use, finding it requires a deliberate search of the correct area and a successful Intelligence (Investigation) check against your spell saving throw DC.

Cirrem's Bewilderment

1st-level illusion
Bard, Warlock
Components: S
Casting Time: 1 bonus action
Duration: 1 turn
Range: Self
Area of Effect: Self
Saving Throw: None

You become invisible until the end of the current turn.

Claws of Digging

6th-level transmutation
Druid, Wizard
Components: V, S, M (a claw)
Casting Time: 1 action
Duration: Concentration, up to 1 hour
Range: Touch
Area of Effect: 1 creature
Saving Throw: None

You transform one willing creature's hands into thick, wide claws that enable it to burrow through earth and stone. The creature can burrow through earth at a rate equal to its land speed, and through rock or stone at one-quarter of that rate.

A creature that burrows through stone leaves a tunnel behind it. If it burrows through soft earth, the tunnel fills in behind it (with earth excavated from ahead of the creature) unless the creature slows down to half speed.

In addition, the creature's unarmed attacks do 2d6 slashing damage. The claws are considered adamantine.

Claws of the Beast

1st-level transmutation
Druid
Components: V, S, M (a claw)
Casting Time: 1 action
Duration: 1 minute
Range: Self
Area of Effect: Self
Saving Throw: None

Your hands transform into wicked claws, so that your unarmed strikes do 2d6 slashing damage. You are proficient with your unarmed strikes.

Cloak of Serpents

5th-level abjuration
Cleric, Druid
Components: V, S, DF
Casting Time: 1 bonus action
Duration: Concentration, up to 1 minute
Range: Self
Area of Effect: Self
Saving Throw: See text

A writhing, twisting, hissing mass of snakes surrounds you and protects you. For the duration of the spell, your Armor Class increases by 2 and you can use an action to attack an adjacent creature with the snakes. Make a melee spell attack against one adjacent creature. If it hits, the creature takes 6d6 poison damage and is poisoned. The poisoned creature must make a Constitution saving throw against poison at the end of each of its turns; a successful save ends the poisoning.

Clot

5th-level necromancy
Cleric, Warlock, Wizard
Components: V, S, M (a strip of cloth)
Casting Time: 1 action
Duration: Instantaneous
Range: Touch
Area of Effect: 1 creature
Saving Throw: Con / half damage

You touch a creature and cause its blood to solidify within its body. The creature must make a Constitution saving throw. If the saving throw fails, the creature takes 8d6 necrotic damage and loses 2 points of Constitution. With a successful saving throw, the creature takes half damage and loses no Constitution.

Cloth of Honorable Melee

1st-level abjuration
Paladin
Components: V, S, M (a cloth emblazoned with holy symbol)
Casting Time: 1 bonus action

Duration: 1 minute
Range: Touch
Area of Effect: 1 strip of cloth
Saving Throw: None

You invest your god's power into a strip of cloth that animates beside you and interposes itself against ranged attacks. You gain a +2 bonus to AC against ranged attacks for the duration of the spell.

Cloud Burst

1st-level transmutation
Cleric, Druid
Components: V, S, M (a pinch of silver dust)
Casting Time: 1 action
Duration: 1 minute
Range: 50 ft.
Area of Effect: Cylinder, 60-ft. radius, 20 ft. high
Saving Throw: None

You collect existing water vapor from the atmosphere and release it as light rain, sleet, or snow in a cylindrical area that's 60 feet in radius and 20 feet high, within 50 feet of you. The precipitation lasts for the duration of the spell. If the temperature in the surrounding area is 90° F (32° C) or higher, the duration doubles, except in desert areas. In an area where the temperature is between 31° and 33° F (-1° to 1° C), the precipitation takes the form of sleet. At temperatures of 30° F (-2° C) or less, the precipitation takes the form of snow.

If *cloud burst* is cast on a Large or larger fire source (such as a *wall of fire*) or if magical heat or fire (such as a *fireball* or *flame strike*) is cast in the area of *cloud burst*, a cloud of warm fog (treat as a *fog cloud* spell) billows through the area of effect for 3 rounds. If a cold-based spell or effect is used on an area soaked by *cloud burst* (such as a *cone of cold* cast on rain-soaked ground), normal ice is formed. Such ice remains for the duration of this spell if the temperature is below 32° F; otherwise the ice melts normally when the temperature rises above freezing.

Cold Fog

6th-level conjuration
Sorcerer, Wizard
Components: V, S, M (a pinch of powdered crystal or glass)
Casting Time: 1 action
Duration: Concentration, up to 1 minute
Range: 120 ft.
Area of Effect: Sphere, 20-ft. radius
Saving Throw: None

You create a cloud of icy fog in a 20-foot-radius sphere centered on a point you can see. The sphere extends around corners, and its area is heavily obscured. The fog is semi-solid, and its area is considered difficult terrain.

Each creature that starts its turn in the fog, or enters it, takes 4d6 cold damage and its speed is reduced by 10 feet until the end of its turn.

The fog lasts for the duration of the spell or until it's dispersed by a wind of moderate or greater speed (at least 10 mph).

Combat Mind

2nd-level divination
Wizard
Components: V, S, M (a copper piece)
Casting Time: 1 action
Duration: Concentration, up to 10 minutes
Range: Self
Area of Effect: Self
Saving Throw: None

You gain a limited form of telepathy that enables you to anticipate the moves of your opponents in combat. This grants you a +2 armor class bonus against melee attacks and a +3 armor class bonus against ranged attacks. The spell doesn't work against attackers that have no minds (automatons, mindless undead) or whose thoughts are shielded.

Commune with Shade

1st-level necromancy
Wizard
Components: V, S, M (a wineskin full of fresh blood)
Casting Time: 1 action
Duration: See text
Range: Personal
Area of Effect: 1-mile radius
Saving Throw: None

You attempt to contact the spirit of a specific dead entity by name. The spell contacts the spirit and lets it know that you want to meet; it doesn't compel the spirit to appear before you. This spell is most useful in the Underworld or another realm where finding one shade among countless hosts of the dead can be nigh impossible. The spell conveys your call to the shade you desire, along with your location and a sense of urgency. The shade is under no obligation to respond, but most do simply to break the eternal tedium of death. If the shade chooses to answer your call in the Underworld, it arrives within ten minutes. If you are somewhere else, the shade arrives within 24 hours.

If cast within the Underworld, the spell's range is unlimited. If cast from the material world or any other plane, the site of the spirit's death must be on the same plane and within the spell's range of the caster. Note that the range refers to the site of the creature's death, not its current location.

This spell can also be used to contact an intelligent undead creature within range; for example, it could contact the spirit of a drowned sailor if cast within a mile of the site of the drowning.

Note that this spell does not alter the subject's personality or willingness to help you. Once the target spirit arrives, you must persuade it to help through negotiation, payment, or coercion of some sort. Family members, loved ones, friends, and slain companions are more inclined to help than are strangers or someone who was killed by the caster. Another spell, such as *speak with dead*, might be needed to compel answers from an uncooperative or unresponsive shade.

Comrades in Arms

4th-level transmutation
Cleric, Paladin
Components: V, S
Casting Time: 1 action
Duration: 1 minute
Range: 30 ft.
Area of Effect: 1 to 4 creatures
Saving Throw: None

You create a bond between up to four willing creatures you can see. All must be within 30 feet of you. For the duration of the spell, a creature may, as a bonus action, transfer any number of its hit points to another creature affected by the spell. Any hit points that would raise a creature over its maximum number of hit points are gained as temporary hit points. Temporary hit points gained through this spell vanish when the spell ends, but other hit point changes are permanent.

Cone of Decay

7th-level necromancy
Warlock, Wizard
Components: V, S, M (a carrion beetle)
Casting Time: 1 action
Duration: Instantaneous
Range: Self
Area of Effect: Cone, 60 ft. long
Saving Throw: Con / negates effect

You create a 60-foot-long cone originating from your hand. All unattended, nonliving, organic matter within the cone crumbles to dust.

Each creature in the cone must make a Constitution saving throw. If the saving throw fails, all the creature's nonmagical, organic gear (food, drink, cloth, leather, etc.) is destroyed.

Undead creatures additionally lose 4 points of Constitution, or 2 points if they made a successful Constitution saving throw.

Cone of Silence

5th-level abjuration
Bard, Wizard
Components: V, S, M (a tuning fork)
Casting Time: 1 action
Duration: Concentration, up to 10 minutes
Range: Self
Area of Effect: Sphere, 20-ft. radius
Saving Throw: None

You create an aura of silence in a 20-foot-radius sphere around yourself that moves with you. Within the aura, only you can make noise; all other noises are silenced. In addition, no creature inside the affected area can take thunder damage or be affected by sound-related spells unless the spell was cast by you.

Conflagration

9th-level evocation
Sorcerer, Wizard
Components: V, S, M (a small wax doll)
Casting Time: 1 action
Duration: Concentration, up to 1 minute
Range: 50 ft.
Area of Effect: 1 creature
Saving Throw: Dex / half damage

You point at a creature within range and mentally command it to burst into flame. The creature must make a Dexterity saving throw. If the saving throw fails, it takes 6d10 + 20 fire damage and begins burning; on a successful save, it takes half damage and suffers no other effect.

A burning creature takes 2d10 fire damage at the end of each of its turns. The fire can't be extinguished by natural means; it burns for the duration of the spell.

Confounding Battlefield

6th-level illusion
Bard, Wizard
Components: V, S, M (a cracked prism)
Casting Time: 1 action
Duration: Concentration, up to 1 minute
Range: Self
Area of Effect: Sphere, 60-ft. radius
Saving Throw: Int / negates effect

Every intelligent creature within 60 feet of yourself (including you) takes on the appearance of one other creature in the area. The creature that everyone and everything resembles should be selected randomly. Every creature in the area of effect becomes an exact copy of the original, from the items it carries to the sound of its voice.

A creature that sees the spell's effect can make an Intelligence saving throw. If the saving throw fails, the creature can't distinguish which creature is which by sight or sound. On a successful save, the creature still sees the illusion but can tell which creature is which from subtle clues such as posture or manner of movement.

As an action, a creature can make an Intelligence (Investigation) check against your spell saving throw DC; if it succeeds, they can correctly identify each creature affected by the illusion, the same as if they'd made a successful saving throw.

Constant Heat

2nd-level transmutation
Druid, Ranger
Components: V, S
Casting Time: 1 action
Duration: 8 hours
Range: Touch
Area of Effect: 1 rock
Saving Throw: None

You enchant a rock so that it warms with some of the heat from its creation. The rock glows red-hot and radiates enough heat to warm a normal-sized room or a small cave to 70 degrees. The rock must weigh at least 10 pounds. Anyone who touches the rock directly takes 1d6 fire damage.

Containment Orbs

7th-level abjuration
Wizard
Components: V, S
Casting Time: 1 action
Duration: Concentration, up to 10 minutes
Range: Self
Area of Effect: Self
Saving Throw: Dex / half damage

You are surrounded by three small orbs of multicolored force that can absorb certain spells. When you cast *containment orbs*, you choose a school of magic for each orb (e.g., abjuration, evocation, transmutation). Any spells of the appropriate type that would affect you are absorbed by the corresponding orb and have no further effect.

Each orb can absorb only one spell. Once an orb has absorbed a spell, you can use an action to cause it to explode. All creatures within 20 feet of you take 2d6 damage per level of the spell the orb absorbed, or half damage with a successful Dexterity saving throw. The DC for the saving throw is set by you, not by the spell's original caster.

As an action, you can instead choose an orb to discharge the absorbed spell with no effect.

An orb is destroyed after it has discharged a spell or exploded. All orbs disappear with no further effect when the spell ends.

Copy

1st-level transmutation (ritual)
Bard, Wizard
Components: V, S, M (a drop of black ink)
Casting Time: 1 action
Duration: Instantaneous
Range: Touch
Area of Effect: 10 pages of writing
Saving Throw: None

This spell creates a perfect duplicate of any written or drawn document that you touch onto blank pages you supply. You can copy up to 10 pages of text with one casting of this spell. Magical writing, including spellbook pages, can't be copied with this spell.

Corpse Armor

3rd-level necromancy
Cleric
Components: V, S
Casting Time: 1 action
Duration: 12 hours
Range: Self
Area of Effect: 1 corpse
Saving Throw: None

Corpse Armor

You create magical armor from the remains of a dead humanoid that is the same size as you or larger. You touch the corpse, which then bends and twists itself around you to form a gruesome suit of armor from bones and dead flesh. Treat the armor as *half-plate +1* (AC 16). You take normal penalties for wearing *corpse armor* if you aren't proficient with medium armor.

You also gain 25 temporary hit points. The spell ends when these temporary hit points are all gone (you've taken 25 points of damage). At that point, the remnants of the corpse disintegrate into dust.

Corpulent Bloat

4th-level transmutation
Warlock, Wizard
Components: V, S, M (handful of raw animal fat)
Casting Time: 1 action
Duration: Permanent
Range: 30 ft.
Area of Effect: 1 creature
Saving Throw: Con / negates effect

You curse one creature you can see. The creature must make a Constitution saving throw against the curse. If the saving throw fails, the target creature bloats into a horrific mockery of itself. Nonmagical belts, buckles, armor, clothes, shoes, and other garments are all destroyed by rapidly expanding rolls of flesh. The now-obese victim quadruples in weight and girth, loses 4 points of Strength and 6 points of Dexterity, and its speed is reduced by 10 feet. Each month, it loses an additional point of Constitution. Ability scores can't be reduced below 1 by this spell.

The creature returns to its previous size instantly if the curse is lifted by magic.

Corrupt Water

5th-level transmutation
Cleric, Druid, Warlock, Wizard
Components: V, S, M
Casting Time: 1 action
Duration: Concentration, up to 1 minute
Range: 60 ft.
Area of Effect: Up to 10,000 cubic ft. of water
Saving Throw: Con / negates effect

You change an area of water you can see into a poisonous, toxic substance. The spell affects a maximum of 10,000 cubic feet of water (picture ten cubes, each 10 feet on a side). Each creature that begins its turn in the water or that enters the water takes 5d6 poison damage and becomes poisoned for as long as it stays in the *corrupt water*; a successful Constitution saving throw negates the effect on that creature. If the affected area is part of a larger body of water, new water entering the area becomes poisonous while water leaving the area is no longer affected.

Crag Warrior

9th-level conjuration
Wizard
Components: V, S, M (a handful of crushed gemstones worth 1,000 gp)
Casting Time: 1 bonus action
Duration: Concentration, up to 1 minute
Range: 60 ft.
Area of Effect: 100 lbs. of rocks

Saving Throw: None

You transform nearby rocks and stones into an animated stone figure that fights for you. The objects don't need to be in humanoid form beforehand; they are magically shaped by the spell as if a master sculptor had carved them into a great statue.

The resulting *crag warrior* has stats identical to a stone golem, except it doesn't have that creature's Slow ability. The crag warrior doesn't act unless you spend an action commanding it, in which case it moves and takes actions on your turn according to your wishes.

When the crag warrior is reduced to 0 hit points, the spell ends and the rocks return to their natural forms.

Crawling Chaos

7th-level conjuration
Sorcerer, Wizard
Components: V, S, M (an iridescent gem worth 500 gp)
Casting Time: 1 round
Duration: Concentration, up to 1 minute
Range: 120 ft.
Area of Effect: 1 creature
Saving Throw: None

You create a field of malign, chaotic energy adjacent to you and choose a creature you can see to be its target. The field is a 5-foot cube that appears adjacent to you. At the end of each of your turns, the cube moves 30 feet toward its target along the shortest path. The field can fly and can pass through creatures and solid objects. Creatures that occupy the same space as the cube at any time must make a Charisma saving throw. On a failure, roll 1d10 on the table below to discover its effect on their behavior.

You can change the field's target to another creature you can see as a bonus action; the field then pursues that target.

d10	Behavior
1	Creature is incapacitated until the start of your next turn. If it moves, it must move as far as it can in a random direction.
2-6	The creature is stunned until the start of your next turn.
7-8	The creature immediately makes a melee attack against the nearest creature within its reach.
9-10	The creature is unaffected.

Create Crypt Thing

7th-level necromancy
Cleric, Wizard
Components: V, S, M (a clay pot filled with grave dirt and a black pearl worth at least 100 gp)
Casting Time: 1 action
Duration: Permanent
Range: 30 ft.
Area of Effect: 1 corpse
Saving Throw: None

You animate one medium or large corpse you can see into a crypt thing (see *Fifth Edition Foes* from Frog God Games). The newly-created crypt thing guards the area where it was created.

Create Iceberg

7th-level transmutation
Druid, Wizard
Components: V, S, M (a translucent gemstone worth at least 100 gp)
Casting Time: 1 action

Duration: Permanent
Range: 200 ft.
Area of Effect: Up to 8,000 cu. ft. of water
Saving Throw: None

You freeze seawater to create a chunk of ice with a volume of up to 8,000 cubic feet. Sufficient seawater must be present to support the iceberg, or the spell fails. A simple way to envision 8,000 cubic feet is a cube with 20-foot sides, or a cone 20 feet high and 40 feet in diameter at the base.

Unless the iceberg is in arctic conditions, it melts at a rate determined by the GM, but usually 5 cubic feet per hour in temperate conditions.

Creation's Fury

9th-level transmutation
Druid
Components: V, S
Casting Time: 10 minutes
Duration: Instantaneous
Range: Sight
Area of Effect: 1-mile radius of land
Saving Throw: Dex / half damage

You unleash cataclysmic forces of nature over a vast area. The area affected is an entire geographic region within sight of the caster, such as a valley, the caverns beneath a mountain, or a lake from shore to shore. If the geographical area is especially large (a great plain, an ocean, etc.), then even this spell can't affect it entirely. Assume a maximum 1-mile-radius area of effect centered on a point chosen by the caster. To properly channel the massive energy this spell requires, the caster must be within the area of effect, if only at its periphery.

The entire chosen region becomes a nightmare of natural disasters. Scalding geysers erupt. Caverns collapse. Crevasses split wide open. All structures and living creatures in the area of effect sustain 5d6 points of bludgeoning damage, or half damage with a successful Dexterity saving throw. You are knocked prone and stunned for 2d6 rounds immediately after casting *creation's fury*, and you can't cast any spells except cantrips for 30 days afterward.

The exact effect of the destruction wrought by this spell must be determined by the GM.

Creeping Eye

4th-level conjuration
Wizard
Components: V, S
Casting Time: 1 hour
Duration: Permanent
Range: Self
Area of Effect: 1 eye
Saving Throw: None

One of your eyes extrudes from its socket until it pops loose, when it is replaced by another eye that grew behind the original. The eye that popped out of your head becomes a mobile, eyelike object that can animate its ganglia of trailing nerves to crawl 5 feet per minute, as long as you concentrate on its movement. You can see whatever the eye can see.

An *identify* spell cast on the eye reveals your name. The eye has AC 10 and 1 hit point. It disappears when reduced to 0 hit points, and its destruction stuns you for 1d4 rounds and blinds you for 1d6 minutes.

Crew with the Dead

6th-level necromancy
Warlock, Wizard
Components: V, S
Casting Time: 10 minutes
Duration: 24 hours
Range: Self

Crystal Wail

Area of Effect: All dead humanoids within 60 ft. of you
Saving Throw: None

You animate all dead humanoid creatures you can see within 60 feet of yourself to act as a crew for a ship or boat. Treat the animated corpses as zombies or skeletons, as appropriate. They have a +8 bonus on skill checks related to crewing the ship, but they are incapable of doing anything else. They must be constantly commanded (by your mental commands) or they do nothing. If your concentration is broken, they halt their activity immediately and you must spend an action to regain control over them.

The undead crew does not fight, even if commanded to do so. If instructed to do anything but operate a boat, they simply stand in place, doing nothing.

Crystal Wail

4th-level evocation
Bard
Components: V
Casting Time: 1 action
Duration: Instantaneous
Range: Self
Area of Effect: Sphere, 40-ft. radius
Saving Throw: Con / half damage

You give a piercing scream that vibrates in a 40-foot radius sphere centered on you. Unattended crystal or glass items in the affected area take 7d6 thunder damage. Each creature in the area takes 7d6 thunder damage and is deafened, or takes half damage and is not deafened with a successful Constitution saving throw.

A deafened creature can repeat the saving throw at the end of each of its turns; a successful save restores its hearing.

Enhancement: For each spell slot used higher than 4th level, the spell does 1d6 extra damage.

Curse of Horror

3rd-level enchantment
Bard, Cleric
Components: V, S
Casting Time: 1 action
Duration: Permanent
Range: 60 ft.
Area of Effect: 1 creature
Saving Throw: Wis / negates effect

You choose a creature you can see and name an object. The creature instantly develops a powerful phobia of that object unless it makes a successful Wisdom saving throw against curses. If the creature can see the object it fears at the start of its turn, it must make a successful Wisdom saving throw or become frightened until the start of its next turn.

The curse can be ended only by magic that lifts a curse.

Curse of Infirmity

6th-level necromancy
Sorcerer, Warlock, Wizard
Components: V, S, M (a pinch of ground bone)
Casting Time: 1 action
Duration: Permanent or 1 minute
Range: 60 ft.
Area of Effect: 1 creature
Saving Throw: Con / negates effect

You curse a creature you can see. The creature loses 4 points of Strength and Dexterity (to a minimum of 1) and must make a Constitution saving throw. If the saving throw fails, the curse is permanent until it's lifted by magic. A successful save means the curse lasts only one minute, unless it's ended magically before then.

Curse of Light

3rd-level transmutation
Cleric
Components: V, S
Casting Time: 1 action
Duration: 10 minutes
Range: 60 ft.
Area of Effect: 1 creature
Saving Throw: Con / negates effect

You curse one creature you can see. That creature becomes highly sensitive to light unless it makes a successful Constitution saving throw. The cursed creature has tactical disadvantage on attack rolls and on Wisdom (Perception) checks that rely on sight when it, you, or whatever it is trying to perceive or attack is in bright light.

Curse of the Ancient Mariner

9th-level transmutation
Bard, Cleric
Components: V, S, M (a dead albatross)
Casting Time: 1 hour
Duration: Permanent
Range: Touch
Area of Effect: 1 creature
Saving Throw: None

This ancient and powerful rite causes disastrous luck to befall the captain of a sea vessel. The captain can never again safely sail the seas or be part of the crew on a seagoing ship.

The target of this curse has the material component hung around his neck, marking him as cursed. Placing the component around the target's neck requires a successful melee attack. Even if it is removed immediately, the curse takes effect. From this point on, the target can never safely set foot on a ship again.

The effects of the curse can be manifold; a colossal sea monster might attack the ship the cursed creature is on, or terrible weather could becalm it, smash it, or the ship could spring leaks, or its food and water supplies could rot, etc. The GM is encouraged to be creative about plaguing the ship; many unfortunate things can happen before the ship is destroyed or sunk to make the crew's lives miserable and make them hate the cursed mariner. Eventually, however, the curse always destroys a ship that the target sails on.

This curse can be removed only with a *wish* spell or comparable magic.

Curtain of Fire

9th-level conjuration
Wizard
Components: V, S, M (a fire opal worth 1,000 gp)
Casting Time: 1 action
Duration: Concentration, up to 10 minutes
Range: 200 ft.
Area of Effect: 1 wall, up to 400 ft. long, 20 ft. high, 1 inch thick
Saving Throw: Con / half damage

You bring into existence a curtain of flickering purple and pink flames that burns the life out of everything it touches. The curtain is 1 inch thick, up to 20 feet high, and up to 400 feet long. It is roughly straight; it can't be curved or folded. You must be able to see the entire curtain when the spell is cast.

The curtain moves in a direction of your choice at a rate of 5 feet per round, consuming all organic matter in its path. Once a direction is chosen, the curtain moves that direction for the spell's duration. If the spell is maintained for its full duration, the *curtain of fire* will advance 500 feet and leave a scorched area 500 feet long by 400 feet wide.

The flames generate no heat, but all organic material coming into contact with the curtain is treated as if struck by a *disintegrate* spell. Buildings and items made from stone or metal are unharmed, but the magical fire can pass through up to 2 feet of stone or 2 inches of any metal and continue advancing. The magical fire burns life out of the soil as well, extending its horrid power to a depth of 5 feet beneath the surface of the earth.

Areas struck by a *curtain of fire* are easy to identify, as they are nothing but burned-out scars of black dust and sand unable to support any life.

Damage Morale

2nd-level enchantment
Bard, Cleric, Warlock, Wizard
Components: V, S
Casting Time: 1 action
Duration: Concentration, up to 10 minutes
Range: 30 ft.
Area of Effect: 1 creature
Saving Throw: Wis / negates effect

You select one creature you can see. The creature must make a Wisdom saving throw. If it fails, the creature has tactical disadvantage on morale checks and on saving throws against fear, and a -2 penalty on attack rolls, for the duration of the spell.

Dance of Seduction

5th-level evocation
Bard, Wizard
Components: V, S
Casting Time: 1 action
Duration: 12 hours
Range: 30 ft.
Area of Effect: All humanoids within range
Saving Throw: Wis / negates effect

By dancing and moving seductively, you attempt to charm humanoids within range. Each creature that can see you must make a Wisdom saving throw, with tactical advantage if you or your companions are fighting it. If the saving throw fails, it is charmed by you until the spell ends or until you or your companions do anything harmful to it. Charmed creatures regard you as a friendly acquaintance. When the spell ends, affected creatures do not realize they were charmed by you.

Dancer's Grace

3rd-level evocation
Bard
Components: V, S
Casting Time: 1 action
Duration: 10 minutes
Range: Touch
Area of Effect: 1 creature
Saving Throw: None

You grant one creature 15 temporary hit points for the duration of the spell. While any those hit points remain, the creature does not take any penalties for exhaustion, although levels of exhaustion remain and affect the creature when the spell ends.

Enhancement: If you use a 4th-level or higher slot to cast *dancer's grace*, you grant an additional 5 temporary hit points for each slot level above 3rd.

Dancing Daggers

7th-level conjuration
Wizard
Components: V, S, M (a dagger)
Casting Time: 1 action
Duration: Concentration, up to 1 minute
Range: 150 ft.
Area of Effect: 1 creature
Saving Throw: Dex / half damage

You conjure a cloud of daggers into existence and select one creature you can see for them to attack. The targeted creature takes 6d4 + 30 piercing damage at the start of each of its turns, or half damage with a successful Dexterity saving throw. The daggers follow the creature as it moves. If the creature teleports or moves to another plane, the daggers stay where they are and don't follow. They attack only the creature they're targeted against; others can walk through them without harm.

As an action, you can redirect the daggers to attack another creature you can see within 100 feet of their current position.

The daggers disappear when the spell ends.

Dark Curtain

5th-level evocation
Warlock, Wizard
Components: S
Casting Time: 1 action
Duration: Concentration, up to 1 minute
Range: 200 ft.
Area of Effect: Varies
Saving Throw: Dex or Con / half damage

You create a dark curtain that must stand on a solid surface within range. You can form it into a hemispherical dome or a sphere with a radius of up to 10 feet, or you can shape a flat surface made of up to ten 10-foot-square panels. Each panel must be contiguous with another panel. In all forms, the curtain is 1 inch thick and lasts for the duration of the spell.

Each creature in the area of the curtain when it appears is pushed to one side of the curtain and takes 4d6 necrotic damage, or half damage with a successful Dexterity saving throw.

The dark curtain blocks all vision through it. Any creature trying to pass through the curtain takes 4d6 necrotic damage and must make a Constitution saving throw. If the saving throw fails, the creature fails to pass through the curtain and becomes frightened of it until the end of its next turn.

Dark Empowerment

5th-level conjuration
Cleric, Warlock, Wizard
Components: V, S, M (a small idol of a fiendish creature)
Casting Time: 1 action
Duration: 1 minute
Range: Self
Area of Effect: Self
Saving Throw: Cha special

You summon a fiend to inhabit your body and grant you its strength. For the duration of the spell, your Strength score becomes 21, you gain 40 temporary hit points, and you gain a +2 bonus to AC. You also grow wicked claws on your hands, so your unarmed attacks do 2d8 slashing damage; the claws are magical, so you get a +1 bonus to hit and to damage with them.

At the start of each of your turns, you must make a DC 10 Charisma saving throw. If the saving throw fails, the fiend takes control of your actions for the remaining duration of the spell. It has full access to your abilities. Most demons will wreak as much havoc as possible during this time, attacking your allies if possible.

Dark Geyser

8th-level necromancy
Wizard
Components: V, S
Casting Time: 1 action
Duration: 2 rounds
Range: 400 ft.
Area of Effect: Cylinder, 5-ft. radius, 30 ft. high
Saving Throw: Con / half damage

You select a point on the ground that you can see. A small gate to another plane of existence opens there, expelling pure negative energy in a 5-foot radius, 30-foot high cylinder of magical darkness. At the beginning of your next turn, the cylinder grows to a 30-foot radius and 60 feet high. At the beginning of your turn after that, it vanishes from existence.

Any living creature that's in the area when the spell is cast, moves through it, or ends its turn in it, takes 8d8 necrotic damage, or half damage with a successful Constitution saving throw. Undead creatures are immune to this effect; in fact, they heal 8d8 hit points if they end their turn in the area of effect.

Darken Forest

8th-level transmutation
Druid
Components: V, S
Casting Time: 1 action
Duration: Concentration, up to 1 minute
Range: 40 ft.
Area of Effect: 1, 2, or 3 trees
Saving Throw: Wis / negates effect

You animate up to three trees you can see within 40 feet. The trees are treated as awakened trees (per the *awaken* spell). The trees won't attack you, but they are not under your control and they do attack all other living creatures in the area without distinction.

The dark and angry power animating these trees also creates an aura of panic. Every creature that starts its turn within 40 feet of one of these trees becomes frightened unless it makes a successful Wisdom saving throw. A frightened creature must take the Dash action and move out of the area by the safest path. If it starts its turn more than 40 feet from a darkly *awakened* tree, a frightened creature can repeat the saving throw; a successful save ends the fright and leaves the creature immune to the fright effect from this batch of trees for 24 hours.

Daze Animal

Enchantment cantrip
Druid
Components: V, S
Casting Time: 1 action
Duration: 1 round
Range: 60 ft.
Area of Effect: 1 creature
Saving Throw: Cha / negates effect

Choose a Medium-size or smaller beast you can see. The beast makes a Charisma saving throw. If it fails, it can't take actions or reactions until the start of your next turn.

Dead Man's Hands

1st-level transmutation
Wizard
Components: V, S
Casting Time: 1 bonus action
Duration: 1 minute
Range: Self
Area of Effect: Caster's hands
Saving Throw: None

You transform your hands into filthy, dirt-caked claws so that while the spell lasts, you are proficient with unarmed strikes and your unarmed strikes do 1d6 slashing damage. If you do 5 or more damage with an unarmed strike, your opponent must make a Constitution saving throw. If it fails, the target creature is poisoned until the end of your next turn.

Death Bringer

8th-level necromancy
Cleric, Wizard
Components: V, S, M (a bone dagger made from an animated skeleton)
Casting Time: 1 action
Duration: Instantaneous
Range: Self
Area of Effect: Sphere, 1-mi. radius
Saving Throw: Con / negates effect

Using an ancient evil spell, you stab yourself in the chest and magically spread the pain over a wide area, potentially bringing death to sleeping creatures as far as a mile away. You take 5d8 piercing damage (which can't be reduced) and are stunned for 5 rounds. Sleeping creatures with fewer than 25 hit points within 1 mile of you die instantly unless they make successful Constitution saving throws. Survivors, as well as creatures with more than 25 hit points, awaken suddenly from a nightmare that included the figure of Death looming over them and trying to slay them.

Death Gaze

6th-level necromancy
Warlock, Wizard
Components: V, S, M (two bone marbles)
Casting Time: 1 action
Duration: Concentration, up to 1 minute
Range: Self
Area of Effect: Self
Saving Throw: Con / negates effect

Your pupils reshape to resemble skulls. When a creature starts its turn within 30 feet of you, you can force it to make a Constitution saving throw if it can see your eyes and you can see it. If the saving throw fails, the creature takes 6d8 necrotic damage and is incapacitated until the start of its next turn.

A creature that isn't surprised can avoid the saving throw by averting its gaze at the start of its turn. It takes the normal penalty for attacking an unseen target if it attacks you before the start of its next turn.

If you meet your own gaze through a reflection, you must also make the saving throw.

Death March

2nd-level evocation
Wizard
Components: V, S
Casting Time: 1 action
Duration: Concentration, up to 1 minute
Range: 60 ft.
Area of Effect: 1 drummer
Saving Throw: Dex / half damage

You create the image of an undead drummer in a tattered military uniform in an unoccupied space you can see. The drummer is completely incorporeal and unable to interact with anything around it. As a bonus action on your turn, you can cause it to move 25 feet in any direction. This may take it outside the initial range of the spell. The skeletal drummer taps out a death cadence on its drum as it moves.

Either at the end of the spell's duration or anytime at your command, the drummer explodes in a fiery burst. Every creature within 10 feet of the drummer takes 4d6 fire damage, or half damage with a successful Dexterity saving throw.

Death Rattle

2nd-level necromancy
Warlock, Wizard
Components: V, S

Casting Time: 1 action
Duration: 1 minute
Range: 60 ft.
Area of Effect: 1 creature
Saving Throw: Con / negates effect

You exhale a foul-smelling gust toward a creature you can see. The creature must make a Constitution saving throw. If the saving throw fails, the target gains one level of exhaustion that lasts for the duration of the spell. The affected creature can repeat the saving throw at the end of each of its turns; a successful save ends the spell.

Death Spores

5th-level conjuration
Druid
Components: V, S, M (a toadstool)
Casting Time: 1 action
Duration: Instantaneous
Range: Self
Area of Effect: Cone, 30 ft.
Saving Throw: Con / half damage

You exhale a 30-foot cone of infectious spores. Each creature in the cone must make a Constitution saving throw against disease. If the saving throw fails, the creature takes 6d6 poison damage and becomes poisoned and infected, or it takes half damage and suffers no other effect with a successful save.

Purple-black fungus oozes from the eyes and nose of infected creatures. Any creature touching the infected creature must make a Constitution saving throw or be affected the same as by the initial effect; a successful save means the creature is unaffected.

Only magic that cures diseases can end the effect. If the caster must touch the patient to cast the spell, then the caster is also exposed to the fungus and must make a Constitution saving throw against it.

Death's Imposition

6th-level enchantment
Sorcerer, Wizard
Components: V, S
Casting Time: 1 action
Duration: Concentration, up to 1 minute
Range: 120 ft.
Area of Effect: 1 creature
Saving Throw: Cha / negates effect

The magic you weave around one living creature makes it believe it has died. It falls unconscious unless it makes a successful Charisma saving throw.

At the end of each of its turns, the creature can repeat the saving throw. If the saving throw succeeds, it wakes up and the spell ends. Otherwise, it takes 4d8 necrotic damage, remains unconscious, and the spell continues. If an adjacent creature spends an action trying to awaken the affected creature, it gets tactical advantage on its next saving throw.

If the creature remains unconscious but alive for ten rounds (1 minute, the spell's full duration), it must make a Constitution saving throw at the end of its turn instead of a Charisma saving throw. If the Constitution saving throw fails, the creature dies.

The creature instantly awakes when the spell ends. Creatures immune to charming are not affected by *death's imposition*.

Deathly Gaze

5th-level transmutation
Cleric
Components: V, S, M (two jade eyeballs worth 100 gp)
Casting Time: 1 action
Duration: Concentration, up to 1 minute
Range: 60 ft.
Area of Effect: Undead creatures that can see you

Saving Throw: Con / negates effect

You gain a gaze attack that only affects undead. Every undead creature that starts its turn within 30 feet of you must either avert its gaze or make a Constitution saving throw; if the saving throw fails, the creature takes 5d8 radiant damage. To be affected, the undead creature must be able to see your eyes, and you must be able to see it. A creature that averts its gaze suffers the usual penalties for attacking an unseen target, if it attacks you. Once a creature averts its gaze, it remains averted until the start of its next turn. A creature can't avert its gaze while it's surprised.

Enhancement: For each spell slot used higher than 5th level, the damage from *deathly gaze* increases by 1d8.

Debilitate

1st-level necromancy
Sorcerer, Wizard
Components: V, S, M (a needle)
Casting Time: 1 action
Duration: Concentration, up to 1 minute
Range: 60 ft.
Area of Effect: 1 creature
Saving Throw: Con / negates effect

Choose one creature within range you can see. If the creature fails a Constitution saving throw, it feels a shooting pain in its limbs. For the duration of the spell, when it uses a thrown or ranged weapon except for a crossbow or similar mechanical weapon, the range of that weapon is reduced by half and it has tactical disadvantage on its attack. The target creature also suffers a 10-foot reduction in its speed. At the end of its turn, the creature can make another Constitution saving throw; the spell ends if the save succeeds.

Decorate Object

Transmutation cantrip
Bard, Cleric, Wizard
Components: S
Casting Time: 1 action
Duration: Permanent
Range: Touch
Area of Effect: 1 object
Saving Throw: None

You add details to one crafted object you touch, or alter its existing details. The changes are purely cosmetic and do not alter its properties in any way.

Decrypt

1st-level transmutation (ritual)
Bard, Wizard
Components: V, S
Casting Time: 1 action
Duration: Concentration, up to 1 hour
Range: Self
Area of Effect: Self
Saving Throw: None

You gain insight into an encrypted message you are holding when you cast this spell. This spell gives you tactical advantage on ability checks you make to decipher the document. It doesn't grant understanding of languages you don't know; *comprehend languages* or similar magic might also be necessary to make the message legible.

Deep Freeze

7th-level transmutation
Druid, Sorcerer, Wizard
Components: V, S, M (a sliver of glass)
Casting Time: 1 action

Duration: Concentration, up to 1 minute
Range: Touch
Area of Effect: 1 creature
Saving Throw: Con / partial

You touch a creature and attempt to freeze its body. The creature must make a Constitution saving throw. If the saving throw fails, the creature is restrained for the duration as its body becomes covered in ice, and it takes 3d8 cold damage at the start of each of its turns. On a successful save, it takes 5d8 cold damage immediately but suffers no other effect.

A creature restrained by the spell repeats the saving throw at the end of each of its turns. If the saving throw fails, the creature completely freezes and becomes ice; treat it as petrified. If the creature makes three successful saving throws (which don't need to be consecutive), the spell ends and it is no longer restrained. Note that the creature continues making Constitution saving throws even while petrified, unless the condition becomes permanent (see below).

If the caster maintains concentration for the full minute, a creature turned to ice is permanently frozen in that form; it stops making Constitution saving throws to end the effect. It remains frozen, however, only if the ambient temperature is below freezing. The creature can be returned to normal by being gradually thawed.

Deflect Ram

4th-level abjuration
Wizard
Components: V, S
Casting Time: 1 action
Duration: Concentration, up to 1 hour
Range: Touch
Area of Effect: 1 ship
Saving Throw: None

You protect the ship you are on from ramming attacks. Your ship gains resistance to bludgeoning damage for the duration of the spell.

Delay Death

3rd-level necromancy
Cleric, Warlock, Wizard
Components: V, S, M (a piece of stone from a tombstone)
Casting Time: 1 Action
Duration: 1 minute
Range: 60 ft.
Area of Effect: 1 creature
Saving Throw: None

You give one willing creature you can see the ability to keep fighting despite near-lethal wounds. When the creature drops to 0 hit points without being instantly killed, it does not become unconscious but can keep acting normally. The creature still makes death saving throws and dies if it fails three times or if it takes enough damage to cause instant death. The creature does not automatically fail death saving throws when it takes damage. *Delay death* has no effect on a creature already at 0 hit points when the spell is cast.

Delude

2nd-level abjuration
Wizard
Components: V, S
Casting Time: 1 action
Duration: 1 hour
Range: 30 ft.
Area of Effect: Self
Saving Throw: None

You change your alignment aura to be that of one creature you can see within range. Spells that detect your alignment thus give a false reading. The alignment aura of the creature you have copied doesn't change.

Demon Flesh

4th-level abjuration
Cleric, Warlock
Components: V, S, M (a bit of flesh from a demon)
Casting Time: 1 action
Duration: Concentration, up to 10 minutes
Range: Touch
Area of Effect: 1 creature
Saving Throw: None

You touch a willing creature and give its skin the defensive properties of demon flesh. The creature gains resistance to cold and fire damage and to damage from nonsilvered, nonmagical bludgeoning, piercing, and slashing weapons.

Enhancement: When you cast *demon flesh* using an 8th-level or higher spell slot, the creature gains immunity to cold and fire damage instead of resistance.

Deny Succor

8th-level necromancy
Druid, Warlock, Wizard
Components: V, S
Casting Time: 1 action
Duration: Permanent
Range: 120 ft.
Area of Effect: 1 creature
Saving Throw: Wis / negates effect

You curse a creature you can see within range. That creature must make a Wisdom saving throw with tactical disadvantage. If it fails the saving throw, it is unable to regain hit points by any means until the curse is lifted by magic. *Remove curse* and similar magic is effective against this curse only if cast using a spell slot of 6th level or higher.

Desail

4th-level transmutation
Sorcerer, Wizard
Components: V, S, M (a tiny candle)
Casting Time: 1 action
Duration: Concentration, up to 1 hour
Range: 200 ft.
Area of Effect: 1 ship
Saving Throw: None

The mainsail of one ship you can see becomes insubstantial for the duration of this spell. The loss of a mainsail reduces the ship's speed by a percentage equal to the sail's percentage of the ship's total sails. On many smaller ships, this will be 50% or more. On larger ships, it always reduces the ship's speed by at least 25%.

Desert Refuge

4th-level abjuration
Druid, Ranger
Components: V, S, M (a piece of tarpaulin)
Casting Time: 1 action
Duration: 24 hours
Range: Touch
Area of Effect: 1 creature
Saving Throw: None

A willing creature you touch becomes surrounded by an aura that maintains a constant temperature of 70 degrees Fahrenheit and protects the creature from the blazing heat of day and the freezing cold of night. It also shields the creature from the effects of exposure to sun and wind but not from objects propelled by the wind, such as sand blown by a sandstorm.

Destined Doom

8th-level necromancy
Warlock, Wizard
Components: V, S
Casting Time: 1 action
Duration: Permanent
Range: 30 ft.
Area of Effect: 1 creature
Saving Throw: None

You curse one creature you can see within range to be vulnerable to a specific doom. You can select a specific person, a type of weapon or creature, or a location. When the person, weapon, or creature attacks the target, or the target is in the location, they suffer a -4 penalty to their AC and take an additional 5 damage from each attack.

Destined doom lasts until broken by magic that can remove a curse.

Detect Charm

Divination cantrip
Bard, Cleric, Warlock, Wizard
Components: V, S
Casting Time: 1 action
Duration: Instantaneous
Range: 30 ft.
Area of Effect: 1 creature
Saving Throw: None

You recognize automatically whether one creature you can see within range is currently charmed.

Detect Curse

2nd-level divination (ritual)
Cleric, Wizard
Components: V, S
Casting Time: 1 action
Duration: Instantaneous
Range: Self
Area of Effect: 1 creature, object, or small area within 30 ft. of you
Saving Throw: None

You determine whether a creature, object, or area you can see within 30 feet of you is affected by a curse. With a successful DC 20 Intelligence or Wisdom check, you can also determine the exact type of curse and its effects.

The spell doesn't function when used on an artifact.

Detect Disease

1st-level divination (ritual)
Cleric, Druid, Ranger
Components: V, S
Casting Time: 1 action
Duration: Instantaneous
Range: 30 ft.
Area of Effect: 1 creature, object, or 30-ft.-by-30-ft. area
Saving Throw: None

You automatically determine whether a creature, object, or area within range that you can see is diseased. If you make a successful DC 20 Wisdom (Medicine) check, you also determine the exact type of disease and its effects.

Detect Illusion

2nd-level divination
Bard, Wizard
Components: V, S
Casting Time: 1 action
Duration: Concentration, up to 1 minute
Range: Self
Area of Effect: Self
Saving Throw: None

You are able to identify illusions within 60 feet of you. In the first round, you become aware of the presence or absence of illusions. In the second round, you determine the number of illusions. In the third round, you learn the location of each illusion.

For the duration of this spell, you have tactical advantage on saving throws against illusions.

Detect Land

3rd-level divination
Bard, Cleric, Druid, Ranger, Wizard
Components: V, S
Casting Time: 1 action
Duration: Concentration, up to 10 minutes
Range: 10 miles
Area of Effect: Self
Saving Throw: None

You become aware of the location of any and all islands and continents within the spell's range. You only learn their location, not their size nor composition.

Enhancement: For each spell slot used higher than 3rd level, the range increases by 10 miles per level.

Detect Life

1st-level divination (ritual)
Cleric
Components: V, S
Casting Time: 1 action
Duration: Instantaneous
Range: 30 ft.
Area of Effect: 1 creature
Saving Throw: None

You determine whether a creature within range that you can see is living or dead. The true status of a creature in a coma, suspended animation, or even masked with a *feign death* spell can be determined with this spell. Undead and animated constructs such as golems register as neither alive nor dead.

Detune

Transmutation cantrip
Bard
Components: V, S, M (a broken tuning fork)
Casting Time: 1 action
Duration: Instantaneous
Range: 50 ft.
Area of Effect: 1 instrument
Saving Throw: Wis / negates effect

One instrument you can see becomes detuned. Anyone using the instrument in a performance has tactical disadvantage on their ability checks to play it. If the instrument is held by a creature, that creature makes a Wisdom saving throw when the cantrip is cast; a successful save negates the effect.

Devour Essence

8th-level necromancy
Warlock
Components: V, S
Casting Time: 1 action
Duration: Instantaneous

Range: Touch
Area of Effect: 1 corpse
Saving Throw: None

You consume the essence of a creature that died within the past day. By doing so, you gain some of the general knowledge of that creature. This gives you a +5 bonus and tactical advantage on Charisma (Deception) checks when pretending to be that person. Until you are slain, the creature can't be brought back to life by any means, as you have prevented the creature's soul or spirit from going to its reward.

Devouring Darkness

5th-level conjuration
Sorcerer, Wizard
Components: V, S
Casting Time: 1 action
Duration: 1 minute
Range: 150 ft.
Area of Effect: Sphere, 20-ft. radius
Saving Throw: Con / half damage

A cloud of darkness erupts from a point that you can see. The cloud fills a 20-foot-radius sphere around the target point. Everything inside the affected area is heavily obscured. Each creature in the cloud when it appears takes 8d6 necrotic damage, or half damage with a successful Constitution saving throw.

Creatures slain by *devouring darkness* rise 1d4 rounds later as shadows.

Dig

4th-level transmutation
Wizard
Components: V, S, M (a tooth)
Casting Time: 1 action

Duration: Concentration, up to 1 minute
Range: 50 ft.
Area of Effect: Cube, 10 ft. square
Saving Throw: None

For the duration of this spell, you can excavate 1,000 cubic feet (a cube 10 feet square) of earth, sand, or mud each round. You can expand an existing hole or start a new one. You can't dig through solid stone or mortared stone walls.

The earth removed from the hole is scattered evenly around the hole. If you dig deeper than 20 feet, the hole has a 15% chance of collapsing (roll of 1-3 on 1d20). The chance the hole collapses increases by 5% for every 5 feet you dig beyond 20 feet unless it is braced or supported.

You can also use this spell to tunnel through earth. If the tunnel is longer than 10 feet, it has a 30% chance of collapsing (1-6 on 1d20), +5% for every 5 feet beyond 30 feet, unless the tunnel is braced or supported.

Most creatures can easily react quickly enough to step aside automatically if you try digging beneath them.

Dire Rage

3rd-level transmutation
Ranger
Components: V, S, M (a tooth)
Casting Time: 1 action
Duration: Concentration, up to 1 minute
Range: Touch
Area of Effect: 1 animal companion
Saving Throw: None

Your animal companion takes on an unnaturally ferocious appearance and its muscles throb with adrenaline. Until the spell ends, its melee attacks do an additional 2d6 damage and it has tactical advantage on attack rolls, but all creatures attacking it also have tactical advantage on their attacks. When the spell ends, the creature gains one level of exhaustion.

Disable

9th-level necromancy
Cleric
Components: V, S
Casting Time: 1 action
Duration: Permanent
Range: Touch
Area of Effect: 1 creature
Saving Throw: Con / negates effect

A creature you touch must make a Constitution saving throw. If the saving throw fails, it is cursed and all of its ability scores are reduced to 3. The curse and the ability reduction can be ended by *remove curse* or comparable magic.

Disassemble

7th-level transmutation
Cleric
Components: S
Casting Time: 1 action
Duration: Instantaneous
Range: Touch
Area of Effect: 1 object, up to 100 lbs. in weight
Saving Throw: Wis / negates effect

One constructed object you touch falls to pieces, separating into its component parts. For instance, a sword separates into a blade, handle, guard, and pommel, while a chariot collapses into nails, wood, and metal. If the item is in the possession of a creature, the creature can make a Wisdom saving throw. On a successful save, the item is unaffected.

Discern Lycanthrope

3rd-level divination
Druid, Ranger
Components: V, S, M (a piece of wolfsbane)
Casting Time: 1 action
Duration: Instantaneous
Range: 30 ft.
Area of Effect: 1 creature
Saving Throw: Wis / negates effect

Choose a creature you can see within range. If that creature fails a Wisdom saving throw, you determine whether or not the creature is a lycanthrope. You can determine what kind of lycanthrope the creature is with a successful DC 20 Intelligence (Nature) check.

Discordant Chorus

5th-level evocation
Bard
Components: V, S
Casting Time: 1 action
Duration: Concentration, up to 1 minute
Range: 120 ft.
Area of Effect: Sphere, 30-ft. radius
Saving Throw: Con / negates effect

You create powerful strains of music that emanate from a point you can see to fill a 60-foot sphere. The music is so loud inside that area that only shouting can be heard over it. No spells with a verbal component can be cast in the area. All creatures have tactical disadvantage on Wisdom saving throws and Wisdom ability checks while in the affected area.

Dissonance

Transmutation cantrip

Bard
Components: V, S
Casting Time: 1 action
Duration: 1 minute
Range: 60 ft.
Area of Effect: 1 creature
Saving Throw: Wis / negates effect

One creature you can see takes a -2 penalty on the next ability check it makes as part of a performance unless it makes a successful Wisdom saving throw.

Distance Distortion

4th-level illusion
Bard, Wizard
Components: V, S, M (a lump of soft clay)
Casting Time: 1 action
Duration: 12 hours
Range: 120 ft.
Area of Effect: Up to 8,000 cu. ft.
Saving Throw: None

Select an area of up to 8,000 cubic feet. (An easy way to picture this is eight 10-foot cubes.) The selected area must be contiguous and can't be less than 10 feet across at any point. The entire area must be within the spell's range. Inside that area, distance is distorted to be twice or half what it actually is (your choice). The change must be the same in the entire area.

For example, if distance is doubled in a 30-foot section of corridor, creatures moving, attacking, or looking along it would treat it as if it were 60 feet long. A 20-foot-deep pit could become effectively 40 feet deep. Conversely, if distance is halved, a 60-foot corridor would be treated as only 30 feet long. Weapon and spell ranges are affected by the change, as is falling damage. There is no apparent change in the size of creatures or objects in the affected space, but the space itself appears longer or shorter. That is, a 60-foot corridor that's *distorted* to be 120 feet long does look 120 feet long from both ends, and someone in the middle of it sees the end as being 60 feet away.

Divine Assimilation

8th-level transmutation
Cleric
Components: V, S, M (holy symbol)
Casting Time: 1 action
Duration: Concentration, up to 10 minutes
Range: Self
Area of Effect: Self
Saving Throw: None

You take on some of the attributes of your deity. The exact attributes depend on your deity's alignment:

Lawful Good: You gain +2 AC, 30 temporary hit points, and resistance to bludgeoning, piercing, and slashing damage. Chaotic Evil creatures must make a successful Wisdom saving throw when they first see you or become frightened for the duration of the spell.

Neutral Good: As a bonus action, three times during the duration of this spell, you can provide 5d6 points of healing to all allies within 30 feet of you. Creatures attempting to attack you or include you in the area of an offensive spell must make a Charisma saving throw; if the saving throw fails, they can take no action that turn. Neutral Evil creatures must make a successful Wisdom saving throw when they first see you or become frightened for the duration of the spell.

Chaotic Good: You get tactical advantage on ranged attacks, and ranged attacks against you have tactical disadvantage. Lawful Evil creatures must make a successful Wisdom saving throw when they first see you or become frightened for the duration of the spell.

Lawful Neutral: You gain +4 AC and are immune to charm, fright, and exhaustion. Chaotic Neutral creatures must make a successful Wisdom saving throw when they first see you or become frightened for the duration of the spell.

Chaotic Neutral: You add 1d4 to your saving throws, ability checks, skill checks, and attack rolls, as you become infused with unpredictable luck. You can detect Law at will, and Lawful Neutral creatures must make a successful Wisdom saving throw when they first see you or become frightened for the duration of the spell.

Lawful Evil: You gain a 2d6 bonus on melee damage rolls, and your weapon is considered magical. Chaotic Good creatures must make a successful Wisdom saving throw when they first see you or become frightened for the duration of the spell.

Neutral Evil: While the spell lasts, you can use an action to make a melee spell attack against a creature you can reach. If the attack hits, the creature takes 5d8 necrotic damage and must make a successful Constitution saving throw or become paralyzed. A paralyzed creature can repeat the saving throw at the end of each of its turns; a successful save ends the paralysis. Neutral Good creatures must make a successful Wisdom saving throw when they first see you or become frightened for the duration of the spell.

Chaotic Evil: You are surrounded by hot flames as the spell *fire shield.* As an action, you can cause the flames to flare briefly around you; each creature within 20 feet of you takes 6d8 fire damage, or half damage with a successful Dexterity saving throw. Lawful Good creatures must make a successful Wisdom saving throw when they first see you or become frightened for the duration of the spell.

True Neutral: You can choose the effects of one other alignment when you first cast this spell; you must always then use that choice.

Divine Beacon

1st-level abjuration
Paladin
Components: V, S, M (Holy symbol)
Casting Time: 1 action
Duration: 24 hours
Range: Self
Area of Effect: Self
Saving Throw: None

When you suffer one of the following conditions, this spell causes a great beacon of light, visible only to paladins, to appear in the sky overhead. The circumstance that befell you determines the color of the beacon.

Color	Condition
Red	Falling unconscious during combat
Orange	Falling unconscious outside of combat
Yellow	Critical hunger or thirst that causes you to suffer penalties
Blue	Voluntarily triggering the beacon as an action
White	Your death

The beacon can be seen by paladins from up to 50 miles away even in daylight, provided it's not obscured by fog or rain, or blocked by obstacles such as mountains or towering trees. If the fallen paladin is underground, the beacon appears in the subterranean chamber where the paladin fell and also in the sky above. Paladins of 10th level or higher have a 10% chance per level above 9 to see the beacon despite all obstacles.

Divine Beacon's Answer

5th-level conjuration
Paladin
Components: V, S, M (Holy symbol)
Casting Time: 1 action
Duration: Instantaneous
Range: Self

Area of Effect: Self
Saving Throw: None

You can cast this spell only if you can see a *divine beacon* (q.v.). When you cast *divine beacon's answer*, you are transported, along with all items you are carrying, to the location of the paladin in distress. No other living creatures can be transported by this spell.

Divine Burden

5th-level transmutation
Druid, Warlock, Wizard
Components: V, S
Casting Time: 1 action
Duration: Concentration, up to 10 minutes
Range: 120 ft.
Area of Effect: Sphere, 30-ft. radius
Saving Throw: Con / negates effect

This spell places a spiritual burden on creatures that can cast divine spells. Every such creature within 30 feet of you must make a Constitution saving throw. If the saving throw fails, the creature moves at half speed, has tactical disadvantage on attack rolls, and has tactical disadvantage on Strength and Dexterity ability and skill checks. It also gains one level of exhaustion if it uses the Dash action.

Divine Charge

4th-level transmutation
Paladin
Components: V, S
Casting Time: 1 bonus action
Duration: 1 round
Range: Self
Area of Effect: Self
Saving Throw: None

Until the end of the round, your movement speed is doubled and, as long as you move only in a straight line, you can make a normal melee attack against each creature you move adjacent to. If your attack hits, the creature is knocked prone in addition to other effects. You do not provoke opportunity attacks while moving in this fashion.

Divine Communion

4th-level divination
Cleric
Components: V, S, M (100 gp worth of incense, which is consumed by the spell)
Casting Time: 1 action
Duration: Concentration, up to 10 minutes
Range: Self
Area of Effect: Self
Saving Throw: None

You become a channel for your god, allowing your deity to converse with others through your body. You are unaware of all that occurs or is said during this conversation. The spell doesn't compel the attention of your deity, who can choose to ignore its effects.

Enhancement: When you cast *divine communion* using a 6th-level or higher spell slot, you can instead touch a willing creature and allow it to commune with its god.

Divine Disconnection

7th-level abjuration
Druid, Warlock, Wizard
Components: V, S, M (holy symbol)
Casting Time: 1 action
Duration: 1 minute

Range: 150 ft.
Area of Effect: 1 creature
Saving Throw: Wis / negates effect

You sever the connection between one creature you can see and its deity. If the creature fails a Wisdom saving throw, it can't cast divine spells or channel divinity for the duration of the spell. At the end of each of its turns, the creature can repeat the saving throw with tactical disadvantage; a successful save ends the spell's effect.

Divine Inspiration

9th-level transmutation
Cleric
Components: V, S, M (holy symbol)
Casting Time: 1 action
Duration: Concentration, up to 1 minute
Range: Self
Area of Effect: Sphere, 100-ft. radius
Saving Throw: None

All creatures within 100 feet of you who worship your god get tactical advantage on attack rolls, ability checks, skill checks, and saving throws while the *divine inspiration* spell is in effect.

Divine Intervention

7th-level abjuration
Cleric
Components: V, S, M (holy symbol)
Casting Time: 1 action
Duration: Concentration, up to 10 minutes
Range: 60 ft.
Area of Effect: 1 creature
Saving Throw: Wis / negates effect

One creature you can see within range is protected from the magic of other gods. If the creature is unwilling, it can make a Wisdom saving throw to negate the effect. If the creature is affected, it has tactical advantage on saving throws against divine spells granted by deities other than your own. Divine spells that are beneficial (and thus require no saving throw) have a 50% chance of failing when cast on the creature, if they originate from a different deity than yours.

Divine Mantle

3rd-level abjuration
Cleric
Components: V, S, M (holy symbol)
Casting Time: 1 action
Duration: Concentration, up to 1 minute
Range: Touch
Area of Effect: 1 creature
Saving Throw: see below

One creature you touch becomes warded against attack. While *divine mantle* is in effect, any creature that intends to aim an attack or a harmful spell at the warded creature must make a Wisdom saving throw before resolving the attack. If the saving throw fails, the attacker changes its mind at the last moment and either redirects the attack against a different target or doesn't attack at all (its choice). The warded creature can be included in area effects without first making a saving throw.

Divine Sovereignty

5th-level enchantment
Paladin
Components: V, S, M (holy symbol)
Casting Time: 1 action
Duration: Concentration, up to 24 hours
Range: Self
Area of Effect: Self
Saving Throw: None

Your god imbues you with divine presence; all creatures of 4 Hit Dice or fewer view you as being their legitimate ruler and treat you with the reverence due a king. Alignment matters; Lawful creatures are more likely to obey your commands than are Chaotic creatures. Paladins have been known to use this spell to nullify the commands of rulers they believe are wielding power illegitimately.

Divining Rod

1st-level divination (ritual)
Druid, Ranger
Components: M (a forked stick)
Casting Time: 1 action
Duration: Concentration, up to 8 hours
Range: Self
Area of Effect: 1 mile
Saving Throw: None

You call upon the natural spirits of a region to guide you to water, natural shelter, or food, assuming that such exists within a radius of 1 mile. The rod points in the direction of the object you seek but does not indicate danger along the way.

Dolphin Fins

2nd-level transmutation
Druid
Components: V, S, M (wooden figurine of a dolphin)
Casting Time: 1 action
Duration: Concentration, up to 10 minutes
Range: Touch
Area of Effect: 1 creature
Saving Throw: None

One willing creature you touch gains webbed feet and hands, and is able to see normally while under water. The creature also gains tactical advantage on ability checks related to swimming and moving under water.

Enhancement: For each spell slot used higher than 2nd level, you can affect one additional creature with this spell.

Donor

5th-level necromancy
Warlock, Wizard
Components: V, S, M
Casting Time: 1 action
Duration: Instantaneous
Range: Touch
Area of Effect: 2 creatures
Saving Throw: Con / negates effect

By touching two creatures simultaneously, you can transfer any number of hit points between them. Neither creature can have its hit points raised above its maximum (no temporary hit points) or lowered below 1. An unwilling creature can make a Constitution saving throw; a successful save negates the spell.

Dragon Scales

2nd-level transmutation
Sorcerer, Wizard
Components: V, S
Casting Time: 1 action
Duration: 10 minutes
Range: Self

Area of Effect: Self
Saving Throw: None

Your skin hardens and turns the shade and texture of a dragon's hide. Your base AC is 15 + your Dexterity modifier (maximum +2) for the duration of this spell.

Dragon's Gauntlet

1st-level conjuration
Sorcerer, Wizard
Components: V, S
Casting Time: 1 action
Duration: Concentration, up to 1 minute
Range: Self
Area of Effect: 1 hand
Saving Throw: None

Your hand transforms into a dragon's claw. For the duration of the spell, you can use your action to make a melee spell attack against a creature within reach; a hit does 2d6 slashing damage. When you hit, you can spend a sorcery point to do 1d6 additional acid, cold, fire, lightning, or poison damage.

Dread Scream

3rd-level enchantment
Bard
Components: V, S
Casting Time: 1 action
Duration: Concentration, up to 1 minute
Range: Self
Area of Effect: Cone, 40 ft. long
Saving Throw: Wis partial

You create sound vibrations in a 40-foot cone that produce deep feelings of dread in target creatures. Each creature in the cone must make a Wisdom saving throw. If the saving throw fails, the creature becomes frightened of you for the duration of the spell. On a successful save, the creature isn't frightened but does suffer a -2 penalty on saving throws against fright for the duration of the spell. Affected creatures can repeat the saving throw at the ends of their turns; a successful save ends the effect on that creature.

Although this spell is based on sound, it is vibrations that cause the fear effect. Deaf or deafened creatures are not immune, but they do get tactical advantage on their Wisdom saving throws.

Dream Speaker

2nd-level enchantment
Warlock, Wizard
Components: V, S
Casting Time: 1 action
Duration: Concentration, up to 10 minutes
Range: Touch
Area of Effect: 1 creature
Saving Throw: Cha / negates effect

You touch one sleeping creature, which must make a Charisma saving throw. If the saving throw fails, you are able to whisper questions into its ear and have it answer in its native language. If an answer would divulge information the creature wants especially to keep secret, it can make another Charisma saving throw to avoid answering and end the spell.

Drench

Conjuration cantrip
Druid
Components: V, S
Casting Time: 1 action
Duration: Instantaneous
Range: 60 ft.
Area of Effect: Cylinder, 5-ft. radius, 10 ft. high
Saving Throw: None

You trigger a sudden, short, freezing-cold downpour just big enough to drench a single creature, or several creatures if they're standing close together. This downpour also quenches candles or a small fire.

Dread Scream

48

Dust of Death

6th-level transmutation
Wizard
Components: V, S
Casting Time: 1 action
Duration: 1 hour
Range: Touch
Area of Effect: 1 oz. of sand
Saving Throw: Con / half damage

For the duration of the spell, you transform one ounce of normal sand into deadly poison (enough to affect just one creature). The poison is a fine powder that can be sprinkled on food or stirred into a drink. When mixed this way, it is difficult to detect; a successful Wisdom (Perception) check against your spell saving throw DC is needed to notice the poison before enough has been ingested to cause harm. Only the creature that is eating or drinking the poison can attempt this check, and only if they are suspicious of the food or drink. If the victim doesn't suspect the food is contaminated, no check is allowed.

A creature that consumes the poison must make a Constitution saving throw against poison at the end of each of its turns. The creature takes 6d6 poison damage if the saving throw fails, or half damage on a successful save. A creature that makes two successful saving throws is no longer affected by the poison; it still takes half damage from the second successful save, but then the poison is neutralized. The successful saves don't need to be consecutive.

Dust to Death

2nd-level transmutation
Druid, Ranger
Components: V, S
Casting Time: 1 action
Duration: Instantaneous
Range: Touch
Area of Effect: 1 corpse
Saving Throw: None

You instantly transmute one corpse into dust. It can't be magically animated or turned into an undead creature. The spell has no effect on undead or living creatures.

Earth Ear

2nd-level divination (ritual)
Druid, Ranger
Components: S
Casting Time: 1 action
Duration: Concentration, up to 1 minute
Range: Self
Area of Effect: Sphere, 100-ft. radius
Saving Throw: None

By placing one ear to the ground, you determine the location and size of all creatures moving beneath or on the ground within 100 feet of you.

Earth Shift

5th-level transmutation
Druid
Components: V, S
Casting Time: 1 action
Duration: Instantaneous
Range: Self
Area of Effect: Self
Saving Throw: None

You select a point within 300 feet that you have either traveled across or can see. You then instantly sink into the ground beneath you and a few moments later, rise up from the target point. Both the starting and ending points must be natural ground, not a constructed floor or water, but what lies between them doesn't matter.

Earthburst

4th-level transmutation
Druid, Sorcerer, Wizard
Components: V, S, M (piece of volcanic rock)
Casting Time: 1 action
Duration: Instantaneous
Range: 150 ft.
Area of Effect: Cylinder, 30-ft. radius, 30 ft. high
Saving Throw: Dex / half damage

You touch the ground and send a furrow of displaced earth 5 feet wide toward a point you can see. Upon reaching the target point, the earth erupts in a cylinder 30 feet in radius and 30 feet high. Creatures that were standing on top of the furrow as it passed underfoot are knocked prone unless they make successful Dexterity saving throws. Creatures in the area of the eruption take 7d6 bludgeoning damage and are knocked prone, or take half damage and are not knocked prone with a successful Dexterity saving throw.

Enhancement: For each spell slot used higher than 4th level, the spell does an additional 1d6 damage.

Earthen Blast

1st-level evocation
Sorcerer, Wizard
Components: V, S
Casting Time: 1 action
Duration: Instantaneous
Range: Self
Area of Effect: Cone, 15 ft. long
Saving Throw: Dex / half damage, no immobilization

Stone and earth erupt from your fingers in a 15-foot cone. Each creature in the area of effect takes 2d6 bludgeoning damage and can't move until the end of its next turn, or takes half damage and is not immobilized if it makes a successful Dexterity saving throw.

Enhancement: For each spell slot used higher than 1st level, the damage increases by 1d6.

Earthen Concealment

3rd-level transmutation
Druid, Ranger
Components: V, S, M (piece of soft clay)
Casting Time: 1 action
Duration: 1 minute
Range: 30 ft.
Area of Effect: Wall, 20 ft. long, 20 ft. tall, 6 in. thick
Saving Throw: None

The ground reshapes itself to form a wall that is 6 inches thick, 20 feet wide, and 2 feet high. You must be able to see the entire area of affect, and it all must be within the spell's range. The wall can curve however you choose. It has AC 15 and 50 hit points. The wall provides cover the same as any earthen wall. The ground returns to its natural shape when the spell ends or when the wall is reduced to 0 hit points.

Earthen Snare

5th-level conjuration
Cleric, Druid, Sorcerer, Wizard
Components: V, S
Casting Time: 1 action
Duration: Concentration, up to 1 minute

Range: 50 ft.
Area of Effect: 1 creature
Saving Throw: Dex / negates effect

You select one creature you can see within range. The creature must make a Dexterity saving throw. If the saving throw fails, the creature disappears as it is sucked into a small, spherical, extraplanar trap just large enough to hold the creature while allowing it to turn around.

The trap is surrounded by earthen walls that are not impervious to attacks; they have AC 14, 100 hit points, and are immune to all but bludgeoning, piercing, slashing, force, and thunder damage. When the spell ends or the creature destroys the walls, the trapped creature takes 4d6 force damage and returns to the space it originally occupied or the nearest unoccupied space, where it falls prone.

Ebon Lightning

7th-level evocation
Sorcerer, Wizard
Components: V, S, M (a piece of blackened amber)
Casting Time: 1 action
Duration: Instantaneous
Range: Self
Area of Effect: Line, 150 ft. long, 5 ft. wide
Saving Throw: Dex / half damage

Ebon lightning streaks from your fingers as you cast this spell. Each creature in the line must make a Dexterity saving throw. If the saving throw fails, the creature takes 8d8 lightning damage and loses (expends) its highest-level spell slot for no effect. On a successful save, the creature takes half damage and doesn't lose a spell slot. Creatures with innate spellcasting lose one use of their highest-level spell instead.

Enhancement: For each spell slot used higher than 7th level, the damage increases by 1d8.

Ebon Water

6th-level necromancy
Cleric, Warlock, Wizard
Components: V, S, M (bone dust from an undead creature)
Casting Time: 1 action
Duration: Concentration, up to 1 minute
Range: 150 ft.
Area of Effect: 1,000 cubic ft. of water
Saving Throw: Con / half damage

You instill necrotic energy into up to 1,000 cubic feet (a cube 10 feet on a side) of water you can see. Each creature that enters the water or ends its turn in the water (not both in a single turn) takes 8d6 necrotic damage, or half damage with a successful Constitution saving throw.

A creature that drinks the water takes 8d6 necrotic damage and its maximum hit points are reduced by the same number, or it takes half damage and its maximum hit points aren't reduced with a successful Constitution saving throw.

At the beginning of your turn, you can use a bonus action to move the necrotic energy up to 10 feet in any direction, as long as it remains in the body of water.

Ebonflame

8th-level evocation
Sorcerer, Warlock, Wizard
Components: S
Casting Time: 1 action
Duration: 1 minute
Range: 150 ft.
Area of Effect: 1 creature
Saving Throw: Con / negates effect for one round

You select one creature you can see; the creature is engulfed in an aura of black flames. At the beginning of each of its turns, the creature must make a Constitution saving throw. If the saving throw fails, the creature takes 3d10 necrotic damage and is frightened; on its turn, it must move as far away from the caster as it can. The spell and the fright effect end only when the spell's duration expires.

Ebonflame can't be cast on a target that's underwater. The flames follow the affected creature when it moves, but it it is magically transported out of the flames, such as by *teleportation*, the spell ends.

Electrical Storm

7th-level evocation
Druid, Sorcerer, Wizard
Components: V, S, M (a bit of fur and an amber rod)
Casting Time: 1 action
Duration: Instantaneous
Range: Self
Area of Effect: Sphere, 100-ft. radius
Saving Throw: Dex / half damage

The surrounding air within 100 feet of you erupts in a violent electrical storm. Each creature in the affected area other than you takes 12d6 lightning damage, or half damage with a successful Dexterity saving throw.

The electrical storm sets fire to combustibles and damages objects in the area. It can melt metals with a low melting point such as lead, gold, copper, silver, or bronze. The extent of this damage must be determined by the GM. If the damage caused to an interposing barrier shatters or breaks through it, the burst can continue beyond the barrier to the limit of the spell's range. Otherwise, it stops at the barrier, the same as any other spell effect.

Electromagnetic Storm

3rd-level evocation
Sorcerer, Wizard
Components: V, S, M (iron filings)
Casting Time: 1 action
Duration: Concentration, up to 1 minute
Range: 120 ft.
Area of Effect: Cylinder, 20-ft. radius, 20 ft. high
Saving Throw: Dex / negates effect

You cause an intense electromagnetic storm to break out in a cylindrical zone with a 20-foot radius and 20 feet high, at a point you can see. The spell has three effects.

First, each creature that starts its turn in the area of effect takes 1d10 lightning damage unless it makes a successful Dexterity saving throw.

Second, any attempt to use magnetism within the area of effect (to navigate, for example) is spoiled by the storm's intense magnetic field unless the opposed magnetic field is generated by a spell of level 4 or higher.

Third, any electrical current (magical or otherwise) that passes within 60 feet of the *electromagnetic storm* is drawn into the storm, causing everyone in the storm's area to take whatever damage the electricity would normally do. For example, assume a wizard casts *lightning bolt* within 60 feet of an *electromagnetic storm*. The bolt is drawn into the storm and it terminates there, causing its normal damage to everyone inside the *electromagnetic storm*.

Elemental Cloak

6th-level transmutation
Cleric, Druid
Components: V, S
Casting Time: 1 action
Duration: 24 hours
Range: Touch
Area of Effect: 1 creature
Saving Throw: None

You infuse a willing creature with properties of creatures of either ice or fire. The creature is affected as described below, depending on which

Eletromagnetic Storm

element it's infused with. These resistances and vulnerabilities completely replace any existing resistance or vulnerability to fire and cold damage that the creature had when *elemental cloak* was cast on it.

- *Fire:* Resistance to fire damage, vulnerability to cold damage.
- *Ice:* Resistance to cold damage, vulnerability to fire damage.

Elemental Infusion

8th-level transmutation
Cleric, Druid, Wizard
Components: V, S
Casting Time: 1 action
Duration: Concentration, up to 1 minute
Range: Touch
Area of Effect: 1 creature
Saving Throw: None

You infuse one willing creature with elemental energy. The creature gains 50 temporary hit points; remaining points disappear when the spell ends. For the duration of the spell, the creature is immune to poison damage and the poisoned condition, gains darkvision (60 feet), and has resistance to bludgeoning, piercing, and slashing damage from nonmagical weapons. The creature also gains immunity to one of the following (your choice): acid, cold, electricity, or fire damage. The affected creature's eyes faintly glow with the color of the chosen element.

Elemental Scimitar

6th-level conjuration
Druid
Components: V, S
Casting Time: 1 action
Duration: 1 minute
Range: Self
Area of Effect: Self
Saving Throw: None

You conjure an elemental scimitar into your hand. You choose which element it is affiliated with when you cast the spell. The scimitar acts as a *+1 scimitar* and has the additional abilities listed below.

Scimitar of Air: A creature struck by the scimitar must make a successful Strength saving throw or be pushed up to 30 feet in the direction of your choice and knocked prone. The scimitar's attacks score critical hits on a natural roll of 19 or 20.

Scimitar of Earth: A creature struck by the scimitar must make a successful Constitution saving or become restrained. It repeats the saving throw at the end of its next turn; a successful save ends the effect, but a failure results in the creature becoming petrified. A petrified creature repeats the saving throw at the end of each of its turns; a successful save ends the petrification.

Scimitar of Fire: A creature struck by the scimitar catches on fire. It takes 5d6 fire damage at the beginning of each of its turns until either it or an adjacent ally uses an action to extinguish the flames.

Scimitar of Water: As an action, you can slash the air with the scimitar to create a spray of acid in a 15-foot cone. Each creature in the cone takes 6d6 acid damage, or half damage with a successful Dexterity saving throw.

Empathic Resonance

1st-level enchantment
Cleric
Components: V, S, M (holy symbol)
Casting Time: 1 action
Duration: 1 hour
Range: Touch
Area of Effect: 1 creature

Saving Throw: Wis / negates effect

One creature you touch becomes aware of the suffering it causes. Whenever the creature injures another creature, it must make a Wisdom saving throw. If the saving throw fails, then it must subtract 1d4 from every attack roll it makes for the next five rounds. Roll the d4 anew for every attack.

Empower Companion

1st-level enchantment
Ranger
Components: V, S
Casting Time: 1 action
Duration: Concentration, up to 1 minute
Range: Touch
Area of Effect: 1 animal companion
Saving Throw: None

You touch your animal companion and give it tactical advantage on all ability checks it makes for the duration of this spell.

Encrypt

Transmutation cantrip
Bard, Wizard
Components: V, S
Casting Time: 1 action
Duration: Permanent
Range: Touch
Area of Effect: 1 scroll
Saving Throw: None

You alter the writing on a scroll or piece of paper, making it unintelligible. A creature that spends a minute or more trying to decipher the text can make an Intelligence check against your spell saving throw DC; success indicates they decipher the text.

Endless Abyss

4th-level conjuration
Wizard
Components: V, S
Casting Time: 1 action
Duration: 8 hours
Range: 60 ft.
Area of Effect: Hole, 10 ft. square
Saving Throw: None

You open a 10-foot square hole in the floor within range. The hole can't appear under an occupied space. The hole is an extra-dimensional space with no bottom. Any creature falling into the pit never hits the bottom. To observers outside the hole, a creature or object that fell in appears to be just 20 feet below the level of the ground or floor, and falling endlessly without ever getting farther away. A creature who looks up after falling into the hole sees the lip of the hole receding farther and farther behind.

Flying creatures can get out of the pit without difficulty. A 20-foot rope will reach anyone who fell in, but the falling creature must make a successful Dexterity saving throw to catch the rope; if the saving throw fails, they perceive the rope as being too short to reach them.

When the spell ends, the hole closes. Every creature inside it at that moment is trapped and will plunge forever unless another *endless abyss* spell is cast on the same location; this reopens the pit and makes it possible to rescue trapped creatures. Other magical rescues might be possible, at the discretion of the GM.

Enduring Missiles

4th-level evocation
Sorcerer, Wizard
Components: V, S, M (a handful of glass marbles)

Casting Time: 1 action
Duration: Concentration, up to 1 minute
Range: 120 ft.
Area of Effect: 1, 2, or 3 targets
Saving Throw: None

You create three missiles that unerringly strike creatures you can see, doing 1d6 + 1 force damage each. You can choose to have the missiles strike the same creature or split them between different creatures. After the missiles strike their targets, they return to your side and hover. As a bonus action on each of your subsequent turns, you can launch the missiles again. The missiles disappear when the spell ends.

A missile that strikes a *shield* spell is dispelled and doesn't return.

Enhancement: For each spell slot used higher than 4th level, you gain one additional missile.

Energetic Burst

2nd-level conjuration
Cleric, Druid, Paladin
Components: V
Casting Time: 1 action
Duration: Concentration, up to 1 minute
Range: Self
Area of Effect: Self
Saving Throw: None

You gain 10 temporary hit points. For the duration of the spell, you can add 1d4 to your saving throws. Unused temporary hit points are lost when the spell ends.

Enhance Oration

1st-level illusion (ritual)
Bard, Cleric, Wizard
Components: V, S, M (a small cone of paper)
Casting Time: 1 action
Duration: Concentration, up to 1 minute
Range: Touch
Area of Effect: 1 creature
Saving Throw: None

You enhance the voice of one willing creature you touch, allowing that creature to be heard clearly by all creatures that can hear within 300 feet of it, regardless of background noise.

Enliven Wood

4th-level transmutation
Druid, Ranger
Components: V, S
Casting Time: 1 action
Duration: Concentration, up to 1 minute
Range: Touch
Area of Effect: 3 plants or wooden objects
Saving Throw: None

Up to three plants or wooden objects gain the ability to regenerate. At the beginning of each of their turns, they regain 10 hit points. An *enlivened* plant or object doesn't regenerate if it took fire or acid damage since its previous turn.

Enrich Soil

5th-level transmutation
Druid
Components: V, S
Casting Time: 1 action
Duration: Instantaneous
Range: 200 ft.

Eternal Sleep

Area of Effect: 1 acre of land
Saving Throw: None

You restore the soil of up to one acre of land so that it can support plant life native to the area. This spell is typically used when magic or a natural disaster has spoiled the land and made it unable to support life.

Erase

1st-level transmutation
Wizard
Components: V, S
Casting Time: 1 action
Duration: Instantaneous
Range: Touch
Area of Effect: 1 scroll, 2 pages, 9 in. x 12 in.
Saving Throw: None

You automatically remove mundane writing from up to two sheets of paper or parchment, from a single scroll, or from a surface no larger than 9 inches by 12 inches. This spell can remove magical writing (including a *glyph of warding*) if the caster makes a successful Intelligence (Arcana) check against the original caster's spell save DC. The caster of *erase* must be aware of the writing for the spell to be effective; it has no effect if cast blindly or experimentally.

Essence of the Wild

3rd-level transmutation
Druid
Components: V, S, M (a claw)
Casting Time: 1 action
Duration: Concentration, up to 10 minutes

Range: Self
Area of Effect: Self
Saving Throw: None

You gain one ability chosen from the list below until the spell ends.

• Echolocation: While you can hear, you have blindsight 60 feet.

• Keen Hearing: You have tactical advantage on Wisdom (Perception) checks that rely on hearing.

• Keen Sight: You have tactical advantage on Wisdom (Perception) checks that rely on sight.

• Keen Smell: You have tactical advantage on Wisdom (Perception) checks that rely on smell.

• Pack Tactics: You have tactical advantage on attack rolls against creatures that are within 5 feet of at least one of your non-incapacitated allies.

• Pounce: If you move at least 20 feet straight toward a creature immediately before hitting it with a melee attack, the creature must make a Strength saving throw or be knocked prone. If the creature is knocked prone, you can use a bonus action to make a melee attack against it.

• Relentless: If you take damage that would reduce you to 0 hit points, you drop to 1 hit point instead. The spell then ends.

Establish Foundation

7th-level transmutation (ritual)
Druid, Wizard
Components: V, S, M (a granite pebble)
Casting Time: 1 hour
Duration: Permanent
Range: Self
Area of Effect: See text
Saving Throw: None

You cause stone to rise up from the ground beneath you, in either a circle with a 60-foot diameter or a square with 60-foot sides, centered on you. The stone is solid and stable and perfect for use as a building foundation. The foundation is 20 feet thick, and you can choose to have it flush with the ground or as much as half of it above ground level.

Enhancement: When you cast *establish foundation* with a 9th-level spell slot, you can raise dirt as well as stone in a 60-foot radius around you; this will effectively fill in marshes or lakes.

Eternal Sleep

9th-level transmutation
Warlock, Wizard
Components: V, S, M (a small cone of paper)
Casting Time: 1 action
Duration: Permanent
Range: Touch
Area of Effect: 1 creature
Saving Throw: Wis / negates effect

One creature you touch must make a successful Wisdom saving throw or fall into an enchanted slumber that lasts until dispelled or until a condition selected by you at the time of casting is fulfilled. The creature doesn't age or decay while slumbering.

Eternal sleep is notoriously difficult to dispel. Attempts to do so are made with tactical disadvantage on the spellcasting ability check.

Ethereal Blade

2nd-level evocation
Wizard
Components: V, S
Casting Time: 1 bonus action
Duration: Concentration, up to 1 minute
Range: Self
Area of Effect: 1 blade
Saving Throw: None

You create a blade of ethereal energy in your hand, similar in dimensions to a longsword, which lasts for the duration of the spell. As an action, you can make a melee spell attack with the blade against one creature within your reach. On a hit, the blade does 2d6 radiant damage plus 1d6 cold damage.

If you let go of the blade, it disappears, but while the spell is in effect, you can create it again with a bonus action.

Enhancement: When you cast *ethereal blade* using a spell slot of 4th level or higher, the damage increases by 1d6 radiant damage for every two levels above 2nd.

Ethereal Blast

5th-level necromancy
Sorcerer, Wizard
Components: V, S
Casting Time: 1 action
Duration: Instantaneous
Range: Self
Area of Effect: Cone, 30 ft. long
Saving Throw: Con / half damage

You create a disruption in the ether that erupts in a 30-foot cone from your outstretched hand. Each creature in the cone takes 6d6 radiant damage and 3d6 cold damage, or half damage with a successful Constitution saving throw.

Enhancement: For each spell slot used higher than 5th level, the spell does an additional 1d6 damage. You choose whether the extra dice do radiant damage, cold damage, or a mix of both.

Ethereal Shield

5th-level necromancy
Cleric, Wizard
Components: V, S, M (fingernail of a wight)
Casting Time: 1 action
Duration: 1 minute
Range: Self
Area of Effect: Self
Saving Throw: None

Wisps of dark flame surround you. You gain resistance to necrotic damage and your maximum hit points can't be reduced for the spell's duration. If a creature within 5 feet of you strikes you with a melee attack while you're protected by *ethereal shield*, the attacker takes 3d10 radiant damage.

Ethereal Strike

2nd-level evocation
Sorcerer, Wizard
Components: V, S
Casting Time: 1 action
Duration: Instantaneous
Range: 100 ft.
Area of Effect: 1 creature
Saving Throw: Dex / half damage

One incorporeal creature you can see takes 2d10 force damage, or half damage with a successful Dexterity saving throw. If the creature fails its saving throw, it loses any resistance it had to bludgeoning, slashing, or piercing damage for 1 minute.

Euphoric Ecstasy

5th-level enchantment
Bard, Sorcerer, Warlock, Wizard
Components: V, S
Casting Time: 1 action
Duration: Concentration, up to 1 minute
Range: Touch
Area of Effect: 1 creature
Saving Throw: Wis / negates effect

A creature that you touch must make a successful Wisdom saving throw or be overwhelmed by feelings of bliss and euphoria. The creature has tactical disadvantage on attack rolls, ability checks, and skill checks, and it must make a Wisdom saving throw at the beginning of each of its turns. If the saving throw fails, the creature loses 1 point of Wisdom and is incapacitated until the start of its next turn. The spell ends when the creature makes two successful saves, which don't need to be consecutive.

Exile from Nature

3rd-level transmutation
Druid
Components: V, S
Casting Time: 1 action
Duration: Permanent
Range: Touch
Area of Effect: 1 creature
Saving Throw: Cha / negates effect

One creature you touch must make a Charisma saving throw against curses or become cursed so that the natural world considers them anathema. The creature has tactical disadvantage on Charisma ability and skill checks when interacting with any creature that has a close tie to nature. In addition, while in an area away from civilization, its chance to encounter hostile creatures is doubled and it has tactical disadvantage on ability checks involving any sort of interaction with nature, not just those related to Charisma.

Exorcise

4th-level abjuration
Cleric
Components: V, S
Casting Time: 10 minutes
Duration: Instantaneous
Range: 10 ft.
Area of Effect: 1 creature or object
Saving Throw: Cha negates effect

You call upon your deity in an elaborate ceremony to end the possession of a creature or object by any force, whether creature or magic.

The source of the possession must make a Charisma saving throw. It has tactical disadvantage on the save if holy water is sprinkled on the target during the casting of the spell. If the saving throw fails, the possession ends; the responsible creature (if any) is ejected from the body and appears in the nearest unoccupied space.

Exorcise can also be cast on a lich's phylactery, a mummy lord's heart, or a vampire's coffin, in which case the soul immediately tries to possess the nearest material body. The two souls switch places unless the current inhabitant of the body makes a successful Charisma saving throw; the DC equals the monster's CR.

Explosive Cloud

3rd-level conjuration
Wizard
Components: V, S
Casting Time: 1 action
Duration: Concentration, up to 1 minute
Range: 120 ft.
Area of Effect: Sphere, 20-ft. radius
Saving Throw: Dex / half damage

You summon a cloud of invisible, explosive gas that spreads out into a 20-foot-radius sphere around a point you can see. If fire is brought into contact with the cloud, the gas ignites and does 6d6 fire damage to creatures inside the cloud, or half damage to creatures that make a successful Dexterity saving throw. The cloud of gas can be noticed only with a successful Wisdom (Perception) check against your spell DC.

Expunge Shadow

3rd-level abjuration
Cleric
Components: V, S, M (holy symbol)
Casting Time: 10 minutes
Duration: Instantaneous
Range: 120 ft.
Area of Effect: 1 creature
Saving Throw: Cha / damage instead of banishment

You force one creature that originates from the plane of Shadow to return to that plane unless it makes a successful Charisma saving throw. If the saving throw succeeds, the target creature still takes 3d6 force damage.

Extract Life

6th-level necromancy
Cleric, Warlock, Wizard
Components: V, S, M (an onyx vial filled with the caster's blood)
Casting Time: 10 minutes
Duration: Instantaneous
Range: Touch
Area of Effect: Self
Saving Throw: None

You must sacrifice one helpless creature of your race as you cast this spell. Their life force is transferred to you, and you gain immunity to aging and its effects for 1 month per hit die of the creature sacrificed.

Eyes of the Hawk

2nd-level transmutation
Druid, Ranger
Components: V, S
Casting Time: 1 action
Duration: 10 minutes
Range: Touch
Area of Effect: 1 creature
Saving Throw: None

A willing creature you touch gains tactical advantage on Wisdom (Perception) checks that rely on sight for the duration of the spell.

Enhancement: If you cast *eyes of the hawk* with a 5th-level or higher slot, the creature also gains immunity to blindness, and any blindness effect on it ends.

Faerie Ward

2nd-level abjuration
Cleric, Warlock, Wizard
Components: V, S, M (powdered iron)
Casting Time: 1 action
Duration: 1 minute
Range: Touch
Area of Effect: Sphere, 10-ft. radius
Saving Throw: Con / half damage

You create an aura in a 10-foot radius sphere that emanates from a creature or object you touch. Every fey creature in the area when the spell is cast or at the start of its turn takes 3d8 force damage, or half damage with a successful Constitution saving throw.

Enhancement: For each spell slot used higher than 2nd level, *faerie ward* does an additional 1d8 damage.

False Gold

2nd-level transmutation
Warlock, Wizard
Components: V, S, M (a piece of pyrite)
Casting Time: 1 action
Duration: 24 hours
Range: Touch
Area of Effect: 3 cubic ft.
Saving Throw: None

You convert up to 3 cubic feet of copper or brass items (about 6,000 cp) into gold. A creature who sees the false gold for the first time can make an Intelligence saving throw to detect the falsehood. The gold is peculiarly vulnerable to iron; the spell ends if iron touches the gold.

It's worth noting that word spreads quickly among the merchants in a community if this spell is used to purchase goods or pay debts, and commercial guilds take a very dim view of those who stoop to such tricks.

Enhancement: By using a valuable gem, which is expended in the casting of the spell, the gold can be made less vulnerable to iron. A citrine (50 gp) lowers the chance to 30% that iron will dispel the transmutation. A piece of amber (100 gp) makes the chance 25%. Topaz (500 gp) drops it to 10%, and a yellow sapphire (1,000 gp) to 1%.

Fangstorm

6th-level evocation
Sorcerer, Wizard
Components: V, S
Casting Time: 1 action
Duration: Instantaneous
Range: 250 ft.
Area of Effect: Sphere, 20-ft. radius

Saving Throw: Dex / half damage

Choose a point you can see within range. The air within 20 feet of that point fills with glowing fangs of force that slash at all creatures in the affected area. Each creature in the affected area must make a Dexterity saving throw. If the saving throw fails, the creature takes 10d6 slashing damage and begins bleeding, which causes an additional 5 points of damage at the start of each of the creature's turns; on a successful save, it takes half damage and doesn't bleed. Bleeding continues until the creature regains hit points or is attended to with a successful Wisdom (Medicine) check against your spell save DC, made by the bleeding creature or by an adjacent ally.

Incorporeal creatures can't benefit from damage resistance against the damage from this spell, but they never bleed.

Enhancement: For each spell slot used higher than 6th level, the slashing damage increases by 1d6 and the bleeding increases by 1 point.

Far Strike

3rd-level evocation
Druid, Sorcerer, Wizard
Components: V, S
Casting Time: 1 action
Duration: Instantaneous
Range: Sight
Area of Effect: 1 creature
Saving Throw: None

You throw a bolt of fire at one creature you can see. Make a ranged spell attack against the target. If it hits, the bolt does 5d10 fire damage.

Enhancement: For each spell slot used higher than 3rd level, the spell does an additional 1d10 damage.

Farsighted

1st-level transmutation
Warlock, Wizard
Components: V, S, M (a cloudy gem)
Casting Time: 1 action
Duration: Concentration, up to 1 minute
Range: Touch
Area of Effect: 1 creature
Saving Throw: Con / negates effect

You attempt to blur the near vision of one creature. If the creature fails a Constitution saving throw, it suffers tactical disadvantage on attack rolls against creatures within 30 feet of it. The target creature can repeat the saving throw at the end of each of its turns; a successful save ends the spell.

Farvision

6th-level transmutation
Wizard
Components: V, S
Casting Time: 1 action
Duration: 8 hours
Range: Touch
Area of Effect: 12 sq. in. of transparent object
Saving Throw: None

You transform any object made from transparent material into spectacles or into a handheld item similar to a magnifying glass. For example, *farvision* could be cast on a window pane, a clear crystal goblet, or a glass mirror. While a creature looks through the transformed item, it has darkvision (90 feet).

Favor Mount

3rd-level transmutation
Paladin
Components: V, S, M (holy symbol)
Casting Time: 1 action

Duration: Concentration, up to 10 minutes
Range: Touch
Area of Effect: 1 mount
Saving Throw: None

You infuse your mount with divine vigor. While you are riding it, it gains tactical advantage on attack rolls and saving throws and increases its land speed by 30 feet.

Feather Step

1st-level transmutation
Druid, Ranger
Components: S
Casting Time: 1 action
Duration: 1 minute
Range: 150 ft.
Area of Effect: 1 creature
Saving Throw: None

One creature you touch becomes able to step lightly across snow, leaves, earth, and loose sand without sinking in or having its movement affected. In addition, the creature can add 1d4 to its Dexterity (Stealth) checks.

Ferment

Transmutation cantrip
Wizard
Components: V, S, M (a grape)
Casting Time: 1 action
Duration: Instantaneous
Range: Touch
Area of Effect: Up to 1 pint of liquid
Saving Throw: None

The liquid in one container becomes alcoholic, but it looks, tastes, and smells exactly as it did before.

Fiery Blast

4th-level evocation
Sorcerer, Wizard
Components: V, S, M (a pinch of sulfur and a bit of candle wax)
Casting Time: 1 action
Duration: Instantaneous
Range: Self
Area of Effect: Cone, 60 ft. long
Saving Throw: Dex / half damage

A fan of flames bursts in a 60-foot cone from your outstretched hand. Each creature in the cone takes 5d8 fire damage, or half as much with a successful Dexterity saving throw.

The spell sets fire to unattended flammable materials.

Enhancement: For each spell slot used higher than 4th level, *fiery blast* does an additional 1d8 damage.

Fiery Cloth

1st-level transmutation
Wizard
Components: V, S, M (flint and tinder)
Casting Time: 1 action
Duration: 12 hours before igniting; concentration, up to 1 minute
Range: Touch
Area of Effect: 1 piece of cloth
Saving Throw: None

You imbue up to 1 square yard of cloth with the essence of fire. Its appearance doesn't change, but as an action, you can cause it to burst into flame. You must have line of sight to the cloth to ignite it. It burns for up to 1 minute and does 1d6 fire damage at the start of each of the caster's turns to a creature that is in contact with more than half of the cloth. The spell ends if the flame is put out.

Fiery Constrictor

6th-level transmutation
Sorcerer, Wizard
Components: V, S
Casting Time: 1 action
Duration: Concentration, up to 1 minute
Range: 60 ft.
Area of Effect: 1 fire
Saving Throw: Dex / negates effect

You cause a great tendril, 20 feet long, to lash out from an existing source of fire you can see. The tendril tries to wrap around a creature within its reach (20 feet) that you can also see. The creature must make a Dexterity saving throw. If it fails, it takes 6d6 fire damage and is restrained until the spell ends. At the end of each of its turns, it can repeat the saving throw; it escapes if the save succeeds, but it takes another 6d6 fire damage if the saving throw fails.

At the beginning of your turn, if the tendril is not restraining a creature, it can attack a creature within reach that you can see, the same as the initial attack.

Enhancement: For each spell slot used higher than 6th level, the tendril's attacks do an additional 1d6 fire damage.

Fiery Grasp

1st-level evocation
Warlock, Wizard
Components: V, S
Casting Time: 1 action
Duration: Concentration, up to 1 minute
Range: Self
Area of Effect: 2 hands
Saving Throw: None

Your hands burst into flames. Until the spell ends, you can use an action to make a melee spell attack against a creature you can reach. A hit does 2d6 fire damage.

Enhancement: The damage dealt by this spell increases to 3d6 if you use a 3rd level slot, 4d6 if you use a 6th level slot, or 6d6 if you use an 8th level or higher slot.

Fiery Shield

2nd-level evocation
Wizard
Components: V, S, M (a gold coin)
Casting Time: 1 action
Duration: 1 hour
Range: Self
Area of Effect: Self
Saving Throw: None

You cause a great shield of flame and force to come into existence on your arm. The shield acts in all ways as a regular large shield, and you must be proficient with shields to get the full AC benefit from it. Regardless of proficiency, any creature within 5 feet of you that hits you with a melee attack takes 2d6 fire damage.

Find Corpse

2nd-level divination
Cleric
Components: V, S, M (a parchment with the name of the

Fiery Constrictor

57

deceased written on it and a small candle)
Casting Time: 1 action
Duration: Concentration, up to 10 minutes
Range: Self
Area of Effect: Self
Saving Throw: None

For the duration of this spell, you can determine the location of the corpse of a named individual, provided it is within 1 mile of you. The spell provides no information if the corpse is too far away or if the corpse has been disintegrated or destroyed.

Finger Missile

3rd-level necromancy
Wizard
Components: V, S, M (a gem worth at least 100 gp, which is consumed in the casting)
Casting Time: 1 action
Duration: Permanent
Range: Touch
Area of Effect: 1 skeleton
Saving Throw: None

You touch a skeleton and imbue it with the ability to launch its finger bones as missiles. As an action, the skeleton can make a ranged weapon attack against one creature within 30 feet; a hit does 1d6 piercing damage. The skeleton's attack bonus equals its Dexterity modifier + 2. If the skeleton makes more than five *finger missile* attacks, it can no longer make claw attacks.

Enhancement: For each spell slot used higher than 3rd level, the spell affects one additional skeleton.

Fire Burst

1st-level transmutation
Sorcerer, Warlock, Wizard
Components: V, S
Casting Time: 1 action
Duration: Instantaneous
Range: 60 ft.
Area of Effect: 1 fire
Saving Throw: Dex / half damage

One existing fire source bursts into a large conflagration for a moment. Each creature within 10 feet of the source takes 3d6 fire damage, or half as much with a successful Dexterity saving throw.

Enhancement: For each spell slot used higher than 1st level, the spell does an additional 1d6 fire damage.

Fire Fascination

4th-level illusion
Wizard
Components: V, S, M (a small piece of multicolored silk)
Casting Time: 1 action
Duration: 1 minute
Range: 50 ft.
Area of Effect: 1 fire up to 10 ft. in diameter
Saving Throw: Wis / negates effect

You cause an existing fire (10-foot diameter or smaller) to become covered in a multi-hued veil of dancing flames. Touching the multicolored flames does 1d6 points of fire damage. Creatures within 30 feet of the fire who can see it must make Wisdom saving throws at the beginning of each of their turns. A creature that fails the saving throw stands transfixed and can do nothing except watch the fire until the beginning of its next turn.

While a creature is transfixed, it has tactical disadvantage on saving throws against enchantment spells.

Any physical attack or attack that triggers a saving throw against a fire-fascinated creature automatically breaks the effect on that creature. Likewise, interposing a solid barrier between a fascinated creature and the veil of flames breaks the effect.

Fire Gills

3rd-level transmutation
Cleric, Druid
Components: V, S
Casting Time: 1 action
Duration: 1 hour
Range: Touch
Area of Effect: 1 creature
Saving Throw: None

One willing creature you touch grows reddish gills that allow it to breathe safely in areas of high heat, smoke, and lava. The spell doesn't grant any resistance or immunity to fire damage, nor do the gills enable the creature to breathe underwater.

Enhancement: For each spell slot used higher than 3rd level, you can affect one additional willing creature.

Firm Ally

3rd-level abjuration
Bard, Cleric
Components: V, S
Casting Time: 1 action
Duration: 1 hour
Range: Touch
Area of Effect: 1 creature
Saving Throw: None

One willing creature you touch gets tactical advantage on saving throws against charm effects.

Fists of Stone

1st-level transmutation
Druid
Components: V, S, M (a pebble)
Casting Time: 1 action
Duration: 1 minute
Range: Self
Area of Effect: 2 hands
Saving Throw: None

Your hands become as hard as stone. For the duration of the spell, you are proficient with unarmed strikes and your unarmed strikes do 1d12 bludgeoning damage.

Flame of Chaos

2nd-level evocation
Sorcerer, Wizard
Components: V, S
Casting Time: 1 action
Duration: Concentration, up to 1 minute
Range: 150 ft.
Area of Effect: 1 ball of fire, approx. 3 ft. in diameter
Saving Throw: None

You create a ball of fire in an unoccupied space you can see. Immediately when the ball appears, and at the beginning of each of your turns, you must make a DC 15 Charisma check. If the check is successful, the ball attacks the creature of your choice anywhere within 150 feet of you and in your line of vision. Otherwise, it attacks a randomly-selected creature within 30 feet of its position after moving to an unoccupied space adjacent to that creature. The fire ball's attack is resolved with a melee spell attack against the target's AC; if it hits, the ball does 4d6 fire damage.

Enhancement: For each spell slot used higher than 2nd level, the spell does an additional 1d6 fire damage.

Flame Spiral

4th-level invocation
Sorcerer, Wizard
Components: V, S
Casting Time: 1 action
Duration: Instantaneous
Range: Self
Area of Effect: Sphere, 30-ft. radius
Saving Throw: Dexterity half

Flames spiral out from you to fill a 30-foot-radius sphere. Each creature apart from you in the area must make a Dexterity saving throw. If the saving throw fails, the creature takes 6d6 fire damage and is incapacitated until the end of your next turn. If the save succeeds, the creature takes half damage and is not incapacitated. Creatures with resistance or immunity to fire are never incapacitated by a *flame spiral*.

Enhancement: For each spell slot used higher than 4th level, the spell does an additional 1d6 damage.

Flame Water

1st-level transmutation
Warlock, Wizard
Components: V, S
Casting Time: 1 action
Duration: Permanent
Range: Touch
Area of Effect: 1 pint of water
Saving Throw: None

You transmute up to 1 pint of water in a container into a flammable liquid akin to alcohol. It ignites if it is exposed to fire. If a container of burning flame water is thrown against a creature or shattered against the ground, all creatures within 5 feet of it take 2d6 fire damage, or half damage with a successful Dexterity saving throw. The liquid burns out in 1 round.

Flames of Darkness

4th-level transmutation
Warlock, Wizard
Components: V, S
Casting Time: 1 action
Duration: Concentration, up to 4 hours
Range: Touch
Area of Effect: 1 object
Saving Throw: None

An object that you touch bursts into dark red flames. The flames are harmless and give out minimal heat. For the duration of the spell, creatures within 20 feet of the flames have darkvision (60 feet).

Flames of Purification

4th-level evocation
Sorcerer, Warlock, Wizard
Components: V, S, M (a piece of sulfur)
Casting Time: 1 action
Duration: Concentration, up to 1 minute
Range: Touch
Area of Effect: 1 creature
Saving Throw: Dex / half damage

One creature you touch bursts into flame. At the beginning of each of its turns, the creature takes 4d6 fire damage, or half damage with a successful Dexterity saving throw. The fire is extinguished after two successful saving throws, which do not need to be consecutive. The flames also do damage to equipment the creature is wearing if it burns for more than two rounds.

Creatures standing adjacent to the burning creature may also take damage; each takes 2d6 fire damage at the beginning of its turn unless is makes a successful Dexterity saving throw.

Flameswell

2nd-level evocation
Sorcerer, Wizard
Components: V, S
Casting Time: 1 action
Duration: Instantaneous
Range: 30 ft.
Area of Effect: Cylinder, 10-ft. radius, 40 feet high
Saving Throw: Dex / half damage

An existing fire swirls upward in a 10-foot-radius, 40-foot-high cylinder. Each creature in the area takes 4d6 fire damage, or half damage with a successful Dexterity saving throw. The original fire is extinguished by this spell.

Flaming Bolts

1st-level evocation
Sorcerer, Wizard
Components: V, S
Casting Time: 1 action
Duration: Instantaneous
Range: 120 ft.
Area of Effect: 1, 2, or 3 creatures
Saving Throw: None

You create three bolts of fire that you direct at one or more creatures you can see within range. Each bolt hits automatically and does 1d6 fire damage. The bolts all strike simultaneously.

Enhancement: For each spell slot used higher than 1st level, you create one additional bolt.

Flash of Light

1st-level evocation
Bard, Sorcerer, Warlock, Wizard
Components: V, S
Casting Time: 1 action
Duration: 1 round
Range: 20 ft.
Area of Effect: Sphere, 10-ft. radius
Saving Throw: Con / negates effect

A bright light flashes from a point you can see within range. All creatures in a 10-foot radius sphere centered on that point are blinded until the end of your next turn unless they make a successful Constitution saving throw.

Fleet Feet

2nd-level transmutation
Druid, Ranger
Components: V, S
Casting Time: 1 action
Duration: Concentration, up to 10 minutes
Range: Self
Area of Effect: Self
Saving Throw: None

Your speed increases by 20 feet for the duration of this spell.

Fluid Form

4th-level transmutation

Flameswell

Druid, Wizard
Components: V
Casting Time: 1 action
Duration: Concentration, up to 10 minutes
Range: Self
Area of Effect: Self
Saving Throw: None

You transform yourself and all items you are carrying into thick liquid. The amount of liquid has the same mass and volume as your normal body, but it is amorphous, allowing you to can squeeze through gaps that are at least an inch wide. In this form, you are immune to poison, paralysis, and stun. Your speed becomes 20 feet. You can flow up gently slanted surfaces, but can't climb stairs.

You can't speak, attack, or cast spells in fluid form. You gain resistance to bludgeoning, slashing, and piercing damage done by nonmagical weapons.

You can end this spell as an action. If the spell ends when you are in a container that's too tight for your full form, the container shatters if it can; if it can't, then you remain in fluid form until you are released from the container.

Foggy Flying Carpet

5th-level conjuration
Warlock, Wizard
Components: V, S
Casting Time: 1 action
Duration: Concentration, up to 1 hour
Range: Self
Area of Effect: 1 carpet of cloud
Saving Throw: None

You conjure a supernaturally thick fog beneath your feet that lifts you into the air. You can create a carpet that ranges from 5 feet square up to 20 feet square. You choose the size at the time of casting. Whatever its size, the carpet can carry up to 1,000 lbs.

The *foggy flying carpet* flies at a speed of 40 feet and is steered by the mental direction of the caster. The fog, though magical, can be dissipated by gale-force wind (greater than 50 mph). If dissipated or dispelled, any characters or items on board plummet to earth unless they have some means of preventing a fall.

Force Corporeality

4th-level transmutation
Cleric, Warlock, Wizard
Components: V, S, M (a pinch of powdered lead)
Casting Time: 1 action
Duration: Concentration, up to 1 minute
Range: 30 ft.
Area of Effect: 1 creature
Saving Throw: Con / negates effect

You attempt to wrap one incorporeal creature you can see within a physical shell. The creature makes a Constitution saving throw. If the saving throw fails, the creature becomes corporeal. While under the effect of this spell, it can't make use of incorporeal movement and it loses all resistance and vulnerability to weapon damage and to being grappled, paralyzed, petrified, prone, and restrained. It also can't enter the Ethereal Plane.

The creature can repeat the saving throw at the end of each of its turns. The spell ends when the creature makes its second successful save. The two successes don't need to be consecutive.

Force Wave

2nd-level evocation
Sorcerer, Wizard
Components: V, S

60

Casting Time: 1 Action
Duration: Instantaneous
Range: Self
Area of Effect: Sphere, 15-ft. radius
Saving Throw: Con / half damage

A sphere of force expands from you to a radius of 15 feet. Each creature in the area must make a Constitution saving throw. If the saving throw fails, the creature takes 3d8 force damage and is pushed 10 feet away from you. On a successful save, the creature takes half damage and is not pushed.

Enhancement: For each spell slot used higher than 2nd level, the damage increases by 1d8.

Forced March

5th-level transmutation
Cleric, Wizard
Components: V, S
Casting Time: 1 action
Duration: 24 hours
Range: Touch
Area of Effect: Up to 6 creatures
Saving Throw: None

Your touch instills a reservoir of energy in up to six willing creatures. For the duration of the spell, the creatures automatically succeed at Constitution checks required during forced march movement, as described in the Movement rules.

Forceful Crush

7th-level evocation
Sorcerer, Wizard
Components: V, S
Casting Time: 1 action
Duration: Instantaneous
Range: 400 ft.
Area of Effect: 1 creature
Saving Throw: Dex / half damage

One creature you can see must make a Dexterity saving throw to evade a hammer and anvil of pure force that are trying to crush it. If the saving throw fails, the creature takes 10d10 force damage and is incapacitated. On a successful save, the creature takes half damage and is not otherwise affected.

An incapacitated creature can repeat the saving throw at the end of each of its turns; a successful save ends the incapacitation.

Forecast

2nd-level divination (ritual)
Druid, Ranger
Components: V, S
Casting Time: 1 action
Duration: Instantaneous
Range: Self
Area of Effect: Self
Saving Throw: None

You predict the weather conditions for the area within 30 miles of your current location for the next three days with 90% accuracy.

Forest Home

4th-level transmutation (ritual)
Druid
Components: V, S
Casting Time: 1 minute
Duration: 12 hours

Range: Touch
Area of Effect: 1 shelter
Saving Throw: None

You create an earthen shelter under the roots of a tree. A door appears at the base of the tree, or in the ground if the tree is not wide enough for a door. When opened, the door reveals steps that lead down into a 15-foot-square room. You can select up to nine individuals who can open the door and enter the underground space. You also designate the shelter's ambient temperature.

The shelter keeps occupants safe from storms, forest fires, and other natural hazards. The door is visible to anyone passing nearby with only a DC 10 Wisdom (Perception) check. It can be forced open with a Strength (Athletics) check, or it can be destroyed like any normal, 2-inch-thick wooden door.

Characters or creatures inside the shelter when the spell ends are expelled violently as the earth closes around them, and they take 3d6 points of bludgeoning damage in the process.

Forgebane

4th-level transmutation
Druid, Ranger
Components: V, S, M (a sprig of mistletoe)
Casting Time: 1 bonus action
Duration: Concentration, up to 1 minute
Range: Touch
Area of Effect: 1 weapon
Saving Throw: None

One nonmetallic weapon you touch when casting this spell becomes excellent for defeating metal armor. While the spell is in effect, the weapon's wielder has tactical advantage when using it to attack creatures clad in metal armor.

Forked Tongue

1st-level enchantment
Bard
Components: V, S, M (a bit of wool)
Casting Time: 1 action
Duration: Concentration, up to 1 minute
Range: Self
Area of Effect: Self
Saving Throw: None

For the duration, you have tactical advantage on Charisma (Deception) checks.

Fortify Armor

2nd-level transmutation
Cleric, Paladin
Components: V, S, M (an iron nail)
Casting Time: 1 bonus action
Duration: 10 minutes
Range: Touch
Area of Effect: 1 suit of armor
Saving Throw: None

One suit of nonmagical armor becomes stronger, so its inherent AC increases by 5 for the duration of the spell. Unfortunately, the armor crumbles to dust when the spell ends.

Frame

2nd-level abjuration
Warlock, Wizard
Components: V, S, M (a pair of loaded dice)
Casting Time: 1 action

Duration: Concentration, up to 1 minute
Range: 30 ft.
Area of Effect: 1 creature
Saving Throw: Wisdom / negates effect

One creature you can see must make a Wisdom saving throw. If it fails, your luck becomes entangled with that of the target. For the duration of the spell, whenever you make an ability check, saving throw, or attack roll that you dislike, make a note of your original result, then roll again and use the second result. The next time the targeted creature would make an ability check, saving throw, or attack roll, it automatically uses your original result instead. Only one roll can be held in reserve at a time; you can't make another reroll until your last one has been reassigned.

Fresh Seal

2nd-level transmutation
Cleric, Druid
Components: V, S
Casting Time: 1 action
Duration: 1 week
Range: 10 ft.
Area of Effect: Sphere, 5-ft. radius
Saving Throw: None

Nonmagical food and drink within 5 feet of you becomes fresh and safe to eat. If it was poisoned, the poison is neutralized. In addition, the food can't spoil or become poisoned while the spell lasts.

Enhancement: For each spell slot used higher than 2nd level, the spell lasts an additional week.

Frost Shards

3rd-level evocation
Sorcerer, Wizard
Components: V, S
Casting Time: 1 action
Duration: Concentration, up to 1 minute
Range: Self
Area of Effect: 3 shards
Saving Throw: None

You create three shards of ice that float around you.

While at least two shards survive, you have cover against attacks that are aimed at you. The shards don't hinder your attacks.

When you cast the spell, or as an action on a subsequent turn, you can direct a shard to attack a creature you can see within 30 feet. Make a ranged spell attack roll. If it hits, the creature takes 2d10 piercing plus 1d10 cold damage. The shard is destroyed whether it hits or misses.

Enhancement: For each spell slot used higher than 3rd level, the spell creates one additional shard.

Frost Snap

2nd-level evocation
Sorcerer, Wizard
Components: V, S, M (silver dust)
Casting Time: 1 action
Duration: Instantaneous
Range: 30 ft.
Area of Effect: 1 creature
Saving Throw: Con / half damage, no incapacitation

One creature you can see must make a Constitution saving throw. If the saving throw fails, it takes 2d10 cold damage and is incapacitated until the end of its next turn. On a successful save, it takes half damage and is not incapacitated.

Enhancement: If you use a 4th-level or higher slot to cast *frost snap*, it does an additional 1d10 cold damage for every two levels above 2nd.

Frostfire

1st-level evocation
Sorcerer, Warlock, Wizard
Components: V, S
Casting Time: 1 action
Duration: Instantaneous
Range: Self
Area of Effect: Cone, 15 ft. long
Saving Throw: Con / half damage, no speed reduction

A wave of cold fire spreads out from your fingertips. Each creature in a 15-foot cone takes 2d6 cold damage and has its speed reduced by 10 feet until the end of its next turn; a successful Constitution saving throw reduces damage to half and negates the speed penalty.

Enhancement: For each spell slot used higher than 1st level, the spell does 1d6 additional cold damage. At 5th level or above, the speed reduction is 20 feet. At 9th level, the speed reduction is 30 feet.

Fugue

5th-level enchantment
Bard, Warlock, Wizard
Components: V, S, M (a vial of wine)
Casting Time: 1 action
Duration: Concentration, up to 8 hours
Range: Touch
Area of Effect: 1 creature
Saving Throw: Wis / negates effect

Your touch causes a creature to forget its identity and history. The creature can make a Wisdom saving throw; a successful save negates the spell.

An affected creature retains all of abilities and spells, but it can't remember any details about its life, its mission, or its companions. If *fugue* is used in combat, the target creature can't remember why it is fighting and has tactical disadvantage on attack rolls until the combat ends.

Fumble

4th-level enchantment
Warlock, Wizard
Components: V, S, M (a broken finger bone)
Casting Time: 1 action
Duration: Concentration, up to 1 minute
Range: 30 ft.
Area of Effect: 1 creature
Saving Throw: Wis / negates effect

One creature you can see becomes cursed with clumsiness if it fails a Wisdom saving throw. While cursed, the creature must make a Dexterity saving throw whenever it moves 20 feet or farther during its turn. If the saving throw fails, the creature falls prone at the end of the movement. It also must make a Dexterity saving throw at the end of each of its turns in which it attacked with a hand-held weapon. If the saving throw fails, it drops the weapon.

The spell ends if the creature rolls a natural 20 on any of the saving throws required by the spell.

Fuse Joints

8th-level transmutation
Warlock, Wizard
Components: V, S
Casting Time: 1 action
Duration: Permanent
Range: 60 ft.
Area of Effect: 1 creature
Saving Throw: Con / negates effect

One creature you can see within range must make a successful Constitution saving throw or its joints fuse into near-immobility. The creature's Dexterity is reduced to 1, it is incapacitated, and it can't move. The spell doesn't affect creatures without bones. Its effect can be removed only by *heal* or *wish*.

Gallows Tree

4th-level conjuration (ritual)
Warlock, Wizard
Components: V, S
Casting Time: 1 action
Duration: 1 week
Range: Touch
Area of Effect: 1 creature
Saving Throw: Wis / negates effect

One creature you can see must make a Wisdom saving throw. If it fails, it becomes mystically linked to a structure or tree of your choosing on the same plane. If the creature dies during the duration of the spell, its body is instantly teleported to the structure or tree and bound to it by stout ropes.

Gaze Mirroring

2nd-level conjuration
Wizard
Components: V, S
Casting Time: 1 action
Duration: 1 minute
Range: Self
Area of Effect: Self
Saving Throw: None

This spell creates a shimmering veil, akin to a mirror, in the air in front of your face. The veil makes you immune to gaze attacks for the duration of the spell. Gaze attacks directed against you are reflected by the mirror back at their originator. The veil moves with you, and you can see normally through it.

Ghostly Howl

2nd-level necromancy
Wizard
Components: V, S
Casting Time: 1 action
Duration: Instantaneous
Range: 50 ft.
Area of Effect: Sphere, 20-ft. radius
Saving Throw: Wis partial

You evoke the spirits of the dead in a 20-foot-radius sphere centered about a point you can see. These spirits emit an unearthly howl. Each creature in the sphere must make a Wisdom saving throw. If the saving throw fails, it has tactical disadvantage on ability checks and attack rolls until the end of your next turn. On a successful save, it has tactical disadvantage on its next attack roll before the end of your next turn. Undead and creatures that can't hear the ghosts are immune to this effect.

Ghostly Throttle

2nd-level evocation
Warlock, Wizard
Components: V, S, M (a pair of silk gloves)
Casting Time: 1 action
Duration: Concentration, up to 1 minute
Range: 50 ft.
Area of Effect: 1 creature

Gaze Mirroring

Saving Throw: Special

You create a pair of ghostly hands that try to throttle one creature you can see. The target creature must be Medium or smaller, and it must be a creature that breathes. At the beginning of each of its turns, the creature must make a Strength or Dexterity saving throw (its choice). If the saving throw fails, it can't breathe or speak until it makes the saving throw successfully or the spell ends. This can cause it to suffocate.

Enhancement: If you use a 5th-level or higher slot to cast *ghostly throttle*, it can affect a Large creature. An 8th-level or higher slot allows it to affect a Huge creature.

Giant's Potency

6th-level transmutation
Cleric, Warlock, Wizard
Components: V, S, M (a few hairs from a giant)
Casting Time: 1 action
Duration: Concentration, up to 10 minutes
Range: Touch
Area of Effect: 1 creature
Saving Throw: None

You imbue one willing creature with the strength of a giant. Until the spell ends, the creature's Strength increases to 21 and it gains 30 temporary hit points. Any remaining temporary hit points vanish when the spell ends.

Glass House

3rd-level conjuration
Wizard
Components: V, S, M (a one-inch cube of glass)
Casting Time: 1 action
Duration: Concentration, up to 10 minutes
Range: 50 ft.
Area of Effect: Cube of glass, 10 ft. square
Saving Throw: Dex / escape

You create a 10-foot-square hollow cube of glass in an area you can see. If a creature is in the area where the cube is created, it escapes with a successful Dexterity save and moves automatically to a space adjacent to the cube. Creatures that fail the saving throw are trapped inside the cube and cannot leave it except by teleportation or similar means. The cube has AC 12 and 100 hit points. It is immune to acid, necrotic, poison, and psychic damage, but is vulnerable to force and thunder damage. Creatures inside the cube when it is destroyed take 5d6 slashing damage from shards of glass.

Glass into Iron

8th-level transmutation
Wizard
Components: V, S, M (a piece of glass and a piece of steel)
Casting Time: 1 action
Duration: Permanent
Range: Touch
Area of Effect: 1 object weighing up to 200 lbs.
Saving Throw: None

One glass or crystal item you touch gains the strength and resiliency of steel, although it doesn't change its appearance. The spell doesn't affect objects weighing more than 200 pounds.

Glass Window

6th-level transmutation
Wizard
Components: V, S, M (a piece of crystal)
Casting Time: 1 action
Duration: Concentration, up to 1 minute
Range: Touch
Area of Effect: Wall section, 3-ft.-by-3-ft.
Saving Throw: None

A 3 foot by 3 foot section of wall becomes transparent as glass at your touch. The spell doesn't work on particularly thick walls; up to 4 inches of metal, up to 6 feet of stone, or up to 20 feet of wood is the maximum thickness it will function on.

You can choose one of two modes for the spell. In its standard mode, creatures on both sides of the wall can see through the window. In one-way mode, only creatures on your side of wall can see through the window; from the other side, the wall looks unchanged.

Glass window doesn't work on lead, gold or platinum.

Glide

2nd-level transmutation
Wizard
Components: V, M (a piece of cloth)
Casting Time: 1 reaction, which you take when you or a creature within 30 ft. of you falls
Duration: 1 minute
Range: 30 ft.
Area of Effect: 1 creature
Saving Throw: None

One willing creature gains the ability to glide when falling. For the duration of the spell, it falls only 30 feet per round and can move up to 30 feet horizontally as well.

Enhancement: For each spell slot used higher than 2nd level, you can affect one additional target.

Glowing Bones

2nd-level necromancy
Cleric, Warlock, Wizard
Components: V, S
Casting Time: 1 action
Duration: 10 minutes
Range: Self
Area of Effect: Sphere, 20-ft. radius
Saving Throw: Wis / negates effect

Every creature within 20 feet of you when the spell is cast must make a Wisdom saving throw; if the saving throw fails, the creature has tactical disadvantage on Dexterity (Stealth) checks until the spell ends. Failing the saving throw causes the creatures' bones to glow with such intensity that they can be seen through the creature's skin. You are not affected by the spell, and neither are creatures without internal skeletons.

Godly Patronage

3rd-level abjuration
Cleric
Components: V, S
Casting Time: 1 action
Duration: Concentration, up to 10 minutes
Range: Touch
Area of Effect: 1 creature
Saving Throw: None

You draw down a portion of your god's aura and drape it around one willing creature. For the duration of the spell, the creature gains +2 AC, has a +4 bonus on Charisma (Intimidate) checks, and a +2 bonus on saving throws. The aura is faintly visible and resembles your god's image.

Godsblood

8th-level transmutation
Cleric
Components: V, S, M (a vial of holy water, which is

consumed in the casting)
Casting Time: 10 minutes
Duration: 1 day
Range: Touch
Area of Effect: 1 vial
Saving Throw: None

You transform holy water in a single vial into *godsblood*, a representation of the blood of your deity. As an action, the *godsblood* can be used for one of the following purposes.

• As a *heal* spell, when consumed;

• As a *raise dead* spell, when anointed to the eyes and mouth of a dead creature;

• As a *purify food and water* spell, when sprinkled over the consumables;

• To transform one melee weapon into a *mace of disruption* for one minute, when sprinkled on the weapon.

Gossamer Webbing

1st-level conjuration
Sorcerer, Warlock, Wizard
Components: V, S, M (a bit of spiderweb)
Casting Time: 1 action
Duration: Concentration, up to 1 minute
Range: 60 ft.
Area of Effect: Cube, 20 ft. square
Saving Throw: None

You conjure a mass of flimsy webbing that expands into a 20-foot cube from a point you can see within range. The webs must be anchored to at least two solid surfaces. Creatures in the affected area pay twice the normal movement cost when moving and have a -1 penalty on attack their rolls. The webs immediately burn away if touched by flame, doing 1d6 fire damage to each creature in their area.

Grave-Touched Weapon

1st-level necromancy
Warlock, Wizard
Components: V, S
Casting Time: 1 action
Duration: Concentration, up to 1 minute
Range: Touch
Area of Effect: 1 weapon
Saving Throw: Con / negates effect

One weapon you touch is infused with necrotic energy. Each time it hits a creature, the creature must make a Constitution saving throw or lose 1 point of Strength. All lost Strength is restored automatically when the spell ends.

Greater Curse

8th-level necromancy
Bard, Cleric, Wizard
Components: V, S
Casting Time: 1 action
Duration: Permanent
Range: Touch
Area of Effect: 1 creature
Saving Throw: Wis / negates effect

Gossamer Webbing

You touch a creature; that creature must make a successful Wisdom saving throw or become cursed. The cursed creature has tactical disadvantage on attack rolls, ability checks, and saving throws.

A *remove curse* spell or comparable magic ends the curse.

Green Slime

4th-level transmutation
Druid
Components: V, S, M (green dye)
Casting Time: 1 action
Duration: Permanent
Range: 30 ft.
Area of Effect: 25 cubic ft. of water
Saving Throw: None

You cause 25 cubic feet (a volume 5 feet by 5 feet by 1 foot) of water to turn into green slime.

Grim Harvest

7th-level transmutation
Cleric, Druid
Components: V, S
Casting Time: 1 minute
Duration: Permanent
Range: 800 ft.
Area of Effect: 1 acre of land
Saving Throw: None

One acre of land you can see becomes blighted. The soil becomes incapable of supporting plant life, and all plants in the area immediately wither and die. Plant creatures take 6d10 necrotic damage, or half damage with a successful Constitution saving throw.

Grim Resilience

5th-level necromancy
Warlock, Wizard
Components: V, S, M (flesh from a zombie)
Casting Time: 1 action
Duration: Concentration, up to 1 minute
Range: Self
Area of Effect: Self
Saving Throw: None

You can't die from damage or from failed death saving throws while this spell is in effect, but the effort wracks you with pain. If you have 0 hit points while you're under the effect of *grim resilience*, you continue acting and fighting normally. You must make a death saving roll at the start of each of your turns, and for each failure, you suffer a cumulative -1 penalty to attack rolls, saving throws (including death saving throws), and ability checks. Successful death saves have no effect, but a natural 20 restores 1 hit point as usual, which means you don't need to keep making death saving throws.

If you have 0 hit points when this spell ends, you die instantly.

Gutsprout

5th-level transmutation
Druid
Components: V, S, M (a seed)
Casting Time: 1 action
Duration: Instantaneous
Range: 60 ft.
Area of Effect: 1 creature
Saving Throw: Con / negates effect

One creature you can see must make a Constitution saving throw. If the saving throw fails, sprouts and roots grow inside the creature's stomach, doing 8d10 piercing damage.

If the creature dies while under the effect of *gutsprout*, the roots force their way out of the creature's mouth and skin within a few rounds.

Halt Aging

8th-level evocation
Cleric, Wizard
Components: V, S, M (a diamond worth at least 5,000 gold pieces)
Casting Time: 1 action
Duration: Permanent
Range: Touch
Area of Effect: 1 creature
Saving Throw: None

One willing creature you touch stops aging for the next 1d10 years, extending its lifespan by a corresponding amount. Any effects that age the creature reduce the effect of this spell first before taking effect on the creature.

Halt Plant

3rd-level enchantment
Druid
Components: V, S
Casting Time: 1 action
Duration: Concentration, up to 1 minute
Range: 120 ft.
Area of Effect: 1 plant creature
Saving Throw: Wis / negates effect

One plant creature you can see becomes paralyzed for the duration of the spell unless it makes a successful Wisdom saving throw. An affected plant can repeat the saving throw at the end of each of its turns to end the spell.

Enhancement: For each spell slot used higher than 3rd level, you can affect one additional plant creature.

Hand of Judgment

4th-level transmutation
Paladin
Components: V, S
Casting Time: 1 bonus action
Duration: 1 minute
Range: Self
Area of Effect: Self
Saving Throw: None

When you cast this spell, you must select to implement either the right hand or the left hand of judgment effect.

Left Hand: Whenever you are struck by an opponent's melee attack, you can use your reaction to attack that opponent.

Right Hand: Whenever you spend your action dodging during combat, you accumulate one charge. When you make a successful attack during the spell's duration, you can expend one charge to turn the normal hit into a critical hit.

Hard Water Blast

3rd-level evocation
Sorcerer, Wizard
Components: V, S
Casting Time: 1 action
Duration: Instantaneous
Range: 150 ft.
Area of Effect: 1 creature
Saving Throw: None

You project a blast of water from your hand at one creature you can see. Make a ranged spell attack against that creature. If it hits, the creature takes 5d10 bludgeoning damage and is knocked prone.

Enhancement: For each spell slot used higher than 3rd level, the attack does an additional 1d10 damage.

Hard Water Weapon

4th-level transmutation
Wizard
Components: V, S
Casting Time: 1 action
Duration: 10 minutes
Range: Touch
Area of Effect: 1 weapon
Saving Throw: None

You transform normal water into a solid version of any simple weapon. It maintains its watery appearance.

Enhancement: For each spell slot used higher than 4th level, you can create one additional weapon.

Harmonic Discord

4th-level enchantment
Bard
Components: V, S
Casting Time: 1 action
Duration: Concentration, up to 1 minute
Range: Self

Area of Effect: Sphere, 60-ft. radius
Saving Throw: None

You create a discordant ringing sound that fills a 60-foot-radius sphere centered on you. When you move, the sphere moves with you. Any creature in the area, including you, must make a Constitution saving throw against your spell save DC when they try to cast a spell; if the saving throw fails, the spell also fails (it has no effect) and the spell slot is expended. A creature maintaining a spell that requires concentration must make this saving throw at the beginning of each of its turns or it loses concentration and the spell ends.

Creatures that can't hear are immune to this effect.

Harmonic Dissolution

8th-level evocation
Bard
Components: V, S
Casting Time: 1 action
Duration: Instantaneous
Range: 60 ft.
Area of Effect: Sphere, 10-ft. radius.
Saving Throw: Con / half damage

You create a 20-foot sphere of harmonic vibration at a point you can see within range. All creatures in the area of that sphere take 8d10 force damage, or half damage with a successful Constitution saving throw. If this damage reduces the creature to 0 hit points, it is disintegrated.

Unattended, nonmagical objects (or portions of them) that are inside the area are automatically disintegrated.

Hard Water Blast

Harmony of Heroes

2nd-level enchantment
Bard
Components: V, S
Casting Time: 1 action
Duration: Concentration, up to 1 minute
Range: 60 ft.
Area of Effect: 1 to 4 creatures
Saving Throw: None

Choose up to four willing creatures within range when you cast this spell. For the duration of the spell, whenever you give your Bardic Inspiration die to one of those creatures, every creature affected by this spell gains a copy of that die. The copied dice disappear when they're used or when the spell ends.

Harmony of the Gods

5th-level transmutation
Bard
Components: V, S, M (a holy symbol of the selected faith)
Casting Time: 1 action
Duration: Instantaneous
Range: 30 ft.
Area of Effect: All allied divine spellcasters
Saving Throw: None

All divine spellcasters belonging to a single faith you select, who are within 30 feet of you, regain one expended spell slot of 4th level or lower when you cast this spell.

Headwind

Evocation cantrip
Druid
Components: V, S
Casting Time: 1 action
Duration: Instantaneous
Range: 30 ft.
Area of Effect: 1 creature
Saving Throw: Str / negates effect

You send a burst of air against one creature you can see. The creature must make a Strength saving throw. If the saving throw fails, it is pushed 10 feet away from you and knocked prone.

Healing Draught

6th-level transmutation
Cleric
Components: V, S
Casting Time: 1 action
Duration: 1 minute
Range: Touch
Area of Effect: 1 bottle of wine
Saving Throw: None

You transform wine into a potent healing draught. Any creature that drinks the wine during the spell's duration regains 10d6 hit points; any diseases it has are cured, poison is neutralized, and lost ability points are restored. The spell transforms enough wine to affect three creatures.

Enhancement: For each spell slot used higher than 6th level, the wine heals an additional 2d6 hit points and one additional dose is created.

Health Transfer

3rd-level necromancy
Cleric, Paladin
Components: V, S
Casting Time: 1 action
Duration: Instantaneous
Range: Touch
Area of Effect: 1 creature
Saving Throw: None

You lay your hands on one willing creature and absorb their wounds onto yourself. For every 6 points of damage you heal (rounded up) on the affected creature, you take 1d6 necrotic damage. This damage can't be reduced by resistance, immunity, or any other means as you're absorbing it, but once you've taken the damage, it can be healed normally. A target creature can't heal more than 60 hit points from one casting of this spell.

Heat Bone

5th-level necromancy
Warlock, Wizard
Components: V, S
Casting Time: 1 action
Duration: Concentration, up to 1 minute
Range: Touch
Area of Effect: 1 creature
Saving Throw: Con / half damage

Your touch causes a creature's skeleton to become dangerously hot. For the duration of the spell, the creature must make a Constitution saving throw at the start of each of its turns. If the saving throw fails, the creature takes 4d10 fire damage, its speed is reduced to half, and it has tactical disadvantage on attack rolls until the start of its next turn. On a successful save, it takes half damage and suffers no additional effects.

The spell ends when the creature makes its second successful saving throw against the effect. The saves don't need to be consecutive.

Heat Flesh

3rd-level transmutation
Sorcerer, Wizard
Components: V, S
Casting Time: 1 action
Duration: Instantaneous
Range: 30 ft.
Area of Effect: 1 creature
Saving Throw: Con / half damage

You sear the flesh of one creature you can see. The target creature must make a Constitution saving throw. If the saving throw fails, it takes 4d10 fire damage and loses 1d4 points of Dexterity. If the saving throw succeeds, it takes half damage and loses no Dexterity.

Enhancement: For each spell slot used higher than 3rd level, *heat flesh* does an additional 1d10 fire damage.

Helpless Grief

2nd-level enchantment
Bard
Components: V, S, M (small onion)
Casting Time: 1 action
Duration: Concentration, up to 1 minute
Range: 30 ft.
Area of Effect: 1 creature
Saving Throw: Wis / negates effect

A living creature of your choice that you can see is overcome with grief unless it makes a successful Wisdom saving throw. A grief-stricken creature falls prone and can't stand up, and is incapacitated for the duration of the spell.

At the end of each of its turns, and each time it takes damage, the creature can repeat the saving throw. On a successful save, the spell ends.

Hemophilia

3rd-level necromancy
Warlock, Wizard
Components: V, S, M (a drop of venom from an adder or cobra)
Casting Time: 1 action
Duration: 1 minute
Range: 30 ft.
Area of Effect: 1 creature
Saving Throw: Con / negates effect

One living creature you can see must make a Constitution saving throw. If the saving throw fails, its blood loses the ability to clot, so that it takes an additional 1d6 damage from any attack that does piercing or slashing damage to it for the duration of the spell. An affected creature can repeat the saving throw at the end of each of its turns; a successful save ends the spell.

Creatures without blood are immune to this spell.

Heraldic Bear

5th-level abjuration
Cleric, Paladin
Components: V, S
Casting Time: 1 action
Duration: Concentration, up to 10 minutes
Range: Touch
Area of Effect: 1 shield
Saving Throw: None

A shield that you touch gains a shimmering aura in the shape of a bear that inspires whoever wields it. A creature wielding the shield gains a +2 bonus to AC and has tactical advantage on attack rolls, ability checks, and skill checks that use Strength. The creature also does 1d6 additional damage with melee weapon attacks.

Heraldic Boar

7th-level abjuration
Cleric
Components: V, S
Casting Time: 1 action
Duration: Concentration, up to 10 minutes
Range: Touch
Area of Effect: 1 shield
Saving Throw: None

A shield that you touch gains a shimmering aura in the shape of a boar that inspires whoever wields it. A creature wielding the shield has tactical advantage on attack rolls, ability checks, and skill checks based on Strength or Constitution. In addition, the creature does 1d6 additional damage with melee weapons. At the beginning of each of the creature's rounds, it gains 10 temporary hit points. The temporary hit points vanish if the shield is relinquished or when the spell ends.

When a creature wielding the shield drops to 0 hit points, it does not drop unconscious, but can keep acting normally. The creature must make death saving throws, however, and it dies if it fails three times. It can't be stabilized while it continues fighting and casting offensive spells at 0 hit points, either by a Wisdom (Medicine) skill check or by a third successful death saving throw. If it relinquishes the shield or the spell ends, the creature drops to 0 hit points and all normal rules for that situation take over.

Heraldic Fox

2nd-level transmutation
Cleric, Paladin
Components: V, S
Casting Time: 1 action
Duration: Concentration, up to 10 minutes
Range: Touch
Area of Effect: 1 shield
Saving Throw: None

A shield that you touch gains a shimmering aura in the shape of a fox that inspires whoever wields it. The creature wielding the shield gains a +1 bonus to AC and has tactical advantage on Dexterity saving throws. In addition, if the creature would take half damage because of a successful Dexterity saving throw, it takes no damage instead.

Heraldic Horse

2nd-level transmutation
Cleric, Paladin
Components: V, S
Casting Time: 1 action
Duration: 10 minutes
Range: Touch
Area of Effect: 1 shield
Saving Throw: None

A shield that you touch gains a shimmering aura in the shape of a horse that inspires whoever wields it. A creature wielding the shield gains a +5 bonus to initiative rolls and can't be surprised.

Heraldic Hydra

8th-level transmutation
Cleric
Components: V, S
Casting Time: 1 action
Duration: Concentration, up to 10 minutes
Range: Touch
Area of Effect: 1 shield
Saving Throw: None

A shield that you touch gains a shimmering aura in the shape of a hydra that inspires whoever wields it. A creature wielding the shield gains a +3 bonus to AC. Also, its weapon attacks against creatures at least one size category larger than itself do an additional 5d6 radiant damage.

Heraldic Leopard

4th-level transmutation
Cleric, Paladin
Components: V, S
Casting Time: 1 action
Duration: Concentration, up to 10 minutes
Range: Touch
Area of Effect: 1 shield
Saving Throw: None

A shield that you touch gains a shimmering aura in the shape of a leopard that inspires whoever wields it. A creature wielding the shield has tactical advantage on Constitution saving throws and ability checks. At the beginning of each of its turns, the creature gains 10 temporary hit points. Remaining temporary hit points gained from this spell are lost when the spell ends.

Heraldic Lion

3rd-level transmutation
Cleric, Paladin
Components: V, S

Casting Time: 1 action
Duration: Concentration, up to 10 minutes
Range: Touch
Area of Effect: 1 shield
Saving Throw: None

By touching a shield, you give it a shimmering aura in the shape of a lion that inspires whoever wields it. The shield's user adds 1d4 to its attack rolls and gets tactical advantage on saving throws against fright.

Heraldic Mastiff

1st-level transmutation
Cleric, Paladin
Components: V, S
Casting Time: 1 action
Duration: Concentration, up to 10 minutes
Range: Touch
Area of Effect: 1 shield
Saving Throw: None

A shield that you touch gains a shimmering aura in the shape of a mastiff that inspires whoever wields it. A creature that wields the shield can add 1d6 to its saving throws.

Heraldic Owl

1st-level transmutation
Cleric, Paladin
Components: V, S
Casting Time: 1 action
Duration: Concentration, up to 10 minutes
Range: Touch
Area of Effect: 1 shield
Saving Throw: None

A shield that you touch gains a shimmering aura in the shape of an owl that inspires whoever wields it. A creature that wields the shield can add 1d6 to its Wisdom (Insight) and Wisdom (Perception) checks.

Heraldic Ox

1st-level abjuration
Cleric, Paladin
Components: V, S
Casting Time: 1 action
Duration: Concentration, up to 10 minutes
Range: Touch
Area of Effect: 1 shield
Saving Throw: None

A shield that you touch gains a shimmering aura in the shape of an ox that inspires whoever wields it. A creature that wields the shield ignores the effects of exhaustion for the duration of the spell. The targeted creature can't gain exhaustion while the spell is in effect. Pre-existing exhaustion isn't removed by the spell; if the creature had levels of exhaustion when the spell was cast, the effects return when the spell ends.

Heraldic Phoenix

9th-level necromancy
Cleric
Components: V, S, M (a ruby worth at least 1,000 gold pieces)
Casting Time: 1 action
Duration: 10 minutes
Range: Touch
Area of Effect: 1 shield
Saving Throw: None

A shield that you touch gains a shimmering aura in the shape of a phoenix that inspires whoever wields it. When a creature wielding the shield dies, it returns to life with full hit points at the beginning of its next turn.

Heraldic Tortoise

4th-level transmutation
Cleric, Paladin
Components: V, S
Casting Time: 1 action
Duration: 10 minutes
Range: Touch
Area of Effect: 1 shield
Saving Throw: None

A shield that you touch gains a shimmering aura in the shape of a tortoise that inspires whoever wields it. A creature wielding the shield gains a +5 bonus to AC whenever it takes the Dodge action.

Heraldic Wyrm

9th-level transmutation
Cleric
Components: V, S
Casting Time: 1 action
Duration: Concentration, up to 10 minutes
Range: Touch
Area of Effect: 1 shield
Saving Throw: Wis / negates effect

A shield that you touch gains a shimmering aura in the shape of a wyrm that inspires whoever wields it. Whenever a creature wielding the shield strikes another creature with a melee attack, the target of the attack must make a successful Wisdom saving throw or become frightened for the spell's duration.

Hesitate

2nd-level enchantment
Warlock, Wizard
Components: V, S, M (a seed)
Casting Time: 1 action
Duration: Instantaneous
Range: 60 ft.
Area of Effect: Sphere, 20-ft. radius
Saving Throw: Wis / negates effect

All creatures in a 20-foot-radius sphere centered on a point you can see must make Wisdom saving throws. Each creature that fails the saving throw hesitates briefly, reducing its initiative score by 5. If this changes its place in the initiative order, the creature uses the new position for the rest of the combat.

Hide the Soul

9th-level abjuration
Cleric, Warlock, Wizard
Components: V, S, M (a black sapphire gem worth at least 5,000 gp)
Casting Time: 10 minutes
Duration: Permanent
Range: Touch
Area of Effect: 1 creature
Saving Throw: None

You extract the soul from one willing creature you touch and sequester it in the body of an animal for safe-keeping. The affected creature can act normally while its soul is sequestered.

The creature becomes immune to all effects that damage or affect the soul. It can't be affected by the *clone* spell or be *raised* unless the animal housing its soul is present. The creature's Wisdom and Charisma saving

throws succeed automatically.

The creature can regain its soul by drinking the blood of its animal host. If the animal is killed, the creature must make a successful DC 20 Constitution saving throw or die instantly; the soul returns unharmed if the saving throw succeeds.

A *true seeing* spell can reveal the location of the creature's soul.

Hives

1st-level necromancy
Cleric, Warlock, Wizard
Components: V, S, M (poison ivy leaves)
Casting Time: 1 action
Duration: Concentration, up to 1 minute
Range: 30 ft.
Area of Effect: 1 creature
Saving Throw: Con / negates effect

Choose a creature you can see within range. The creature makes a Constitution saving throw. On a failed save, it breaks into an itchy rash that gives it a -2 penalty to AC and attack rolls for the duration of the spell. At the end of each of its turns, the creature can make another Constitution saving throw; a successful save ends the spell.

Enhancement: For each spell slot used higher than 1st level, you can target one additional creature.

Holy Blazon

5th-level abjuration
Paladin
Components: V, S
Casting Time: 1 action
Duration: Concentration, up to 1 minute
Range: Touch
Area of Effect: Self
Saving Throw: None

Your god's symbol appears on your shield, tabard, or other clothing. For the duration of the spell, you have resistance to acid, cold, fire, lightning, and thunder damage, and you do an additional 2d6 damage with melee weapon attacks.

Holy Infusion

1st-level evocation
Paladin
Components: V
Casting Time: 1 bonus action
Duration: Concentration, up to 1 minute
Range: Self
Area of Effect: Self
Saving Throw: None

Your prayer infuses you with holy energy. Until the spell ends, your weapon attacks do an additional 1d6 radiant damage against undead creatures and fiends, and the weapon is treated as magical.

Hornet Wall

3rd-level conjuration
Druid
Components: V, S, M (a hornet's sting)
Casting Time: 1 action
Duration: Concentration, up to 1 minute
Range: 120 ft.
Area of Effect: 8 5 ft.-by-5 ft. squares, 10 ft. high wall
Saving Throw: Con / half damage

You conjure a "wall" of stinging hornets. The wall is 5 feet thick, 10 feet high, and up to 40 feet long. The wall must be contiguous and at least

Hornet Wall

5 feet thick along its entire length. A simple way to envision this is as eight sections, each covering a square of ground that's 5 feet by 5 feet, and 10 feet high. You select where the wall appears, but the entire length must be within your line of sight and within the spell's range from you.

A creature that starts its turn inside the *hornet wall* or that enters the wall during its turn must make a Constitution saving throw against poison. If the saving throw fails, the creature takes 6d6 poison damage and is incapacitated; if the saving throw succeeds, it takes half damage and no additional effect.

Hound of Hell

6th-level conjuration
Cleric, Warlock, Wizard
Components: V, S
Casting Time: 1 action
Duration: Concentration, up to 1 hour
Range: 60 ft.
Area of Effect: 1 hell hound
Saving Throw: None

You summon a hell hound, which appears in an unoccupied space you can see. The hound is friendly to you and your companions and follows your orders. Roll initiative for the hound; it takes its own turns in combat.

If your concentration is broken, the hound immediately becomes hostile to you and your companions. It's certain to turn against you and attack.

Enhancement: For each spell slot used higher than 6th level, one additional hell hound is summoned.

Hound's Scent

1st-level transmutation
Druid
Components: V, S
Casting Time: 1 action
Duration: Concentration, up to 1 hour
Range: Self
Area of Effect: Self
Saving Throw: None

You gain keen scent, which gives you tactical advantage on Wisdom (Perception) checks that rely on smell.

Hovership

7th-level transmutation
Wizard
Components: V, S, M (eagle feathers)
Casting Time: 10 minutes
Duration: 2 hours
Range: Touch
Area of Effect: 1 ship
Saving Throw: None

One ship you touch rises up until it hovers 5 feet above the water or ground. If it has sails, it can travel at its normal speed. Rowing won't work, but a vessel without sails could be propelled by poling.

When the spell ends, the ship sinks slowly and safely to rest on whatever surface is beneath it. If that isn't water, the ship is likely to keel over.

The ship can travel over almost any terrain, but extremely rugged ground presents problems because it has only 5 feet of ground clearance. It can't cross sheer chasms or other steep-sided escarpments. If it is propelled over a cliff more than 10 feet high, it plunges to the ground and crashes. The extent of the damage must be determined by the GM, but it's likely to be severe.

Hunter's Insight

2nd-level transmutation
Ranger
Components: V, S
Casting Time: 1 action
Duration: Concentration, up to 12 hours
Range: Self
Area of Effect: 1 creature
Saving Throw: None

By touching some of its fur or its tracks, you gain great insight into the behavior of a creature you wish to hunt. You gain tactical advantage on ability checks to find or track the animal, and whenever you make an attack roll against it, you can add 1d4 to your roll.

Ice Bolts

1st-level evocation
Sorcerer, Wizard
Components: V, S
Casting Time: 1 action
Duration: Instantaneous
Range: 120 ft.
Area of Effect: 1, 2, or 3 creatures
Saving Throw: None

You create three bolts of ice that you direct at one or more creatures within range and line of sight. Each bolt hits automatically and does 1d6 cold damage. The bolts all strike simultaneously.

Enhancement: For each spell slot used higher than 1st level, you create one additional bolt.

Ice Geyser

8th-level evocation
Sorcerer, Wizard
Components: V, S
Casting Time: 1 action
Duration: 2 rounds
Range: 150 ft.
Area of Effect: Cylinder, 10-ft. radius, 40 ft. high
Saving Throw: Dex / half damage, no speed reduction

Choose a point on the ground you can see. Ice and freezing water spray high into the sky from that point, filling a cylindrical area 40 feet high and with a 10-foot radius. Each creature in that area when you cast the spell takes 8d10 cold damage, or half damage with a successful Dexterity saving throw. A creature that fails the save also has its speed reduced by 20 feet. A slowed creature can repeat the saving throw at the end of each of its turns; a successful save ends the speed reduction.

At the beginning of your next turn, the geyser spouts again. This time, it affects a cylindrical area 20 feet high and 20 feet in radius. The affect on creatures in the area is the same as before. The spell ends after the second eruption.

Ice Sled

6th-level conjuration (ritual)
Druid, Wizard
Components: V, S, M (a ball of snow)

Casting Time: 1 minute
Duration: 12 hours
Range: 50 ft.
Area of Effect: 5 sleds
Saving Throw: None

You summon up to five sleds that can travel rapidly over snow and ice. Each sled can carry up to 500 lbs. of material, including passengers. The sleds are made of extremely sturdy ice and are connected to each other by 10-foot chains of ice.

As an action, you can cause the sleds to travel at a speed of 60 feet in the direction of your choice. The sleds can continue to move as long as one of their runners is on snow or ice. If a sled moves onto an area where there is no snow or ice, or if the spell ends, the sleds shatter and crumble into loose snow.

Icebreaker

7th-level transmutation
Wizard
Components: V, S, M (a miniature plow)
Casting Time: 1 action
Duration: Concentration, up to 8 hours
Range: 120 ft.
Area of Effect: Path, 600 ft. long, 35 ft. wide, 15 ft. deep
Saving Throw: None

This mighty spell assists ships moving through ice-locked seas. While the spell is in effect, you can point your finger at any sheet of solid ice and, as an action, cause the ice to shatter into small chunks that the ship's hull can easily push aside. The area affected is always a strip 35 feet wide, 15 feet deep, and 600 feet long, permitting all but the largest of vessels safe passage. This only affects ice that has formed over a body of water.

Iceform

4th-level transmutation
Druid, Wizard
Components: V, S, M (a translucent gem)
Casting Time: 1 action
Duration: Concentration, up to 1 minute
Range: Self
Area of Effect: Self
Saving Throw: None

Your body transforms into an icelike substance. Your possessions remain unchanged. You gain immunity to cold damage but vulnerability to fire damage. Your melee weapon attacks do an additional 2d6 cold damage when they hit, and you have tactical advantage on ability checks made to escape from a grapple.

Icy Hammer

2nd-level conjuration
Druid
Components: V, S, M (a miniature glass hammer)
Casting Time: 1 bonus action
Duration: Concentration, up to 1 minute
Range: Self
Area of Effect: 1 hammer
Saving Throw: None

You conjure a hammer made of ice into your hand. As an action, you can make a melee spell attack with the hammer against one creature within reach. You can also throw the hammer as an action at a target within 30 feet, using a ranged spell attack to determine whether it hits. On a hit, the hammer does 1d6 bludgeoning plus 2d6 cold damage. After an attack, or if you drop the hammer for any reason, it disappears, but while the spell lasts, you can conjure it again with a bonus action.

Icy Hammer

Identify Tracks

2nd-level divination
Druid, Ranger
Components: V, S
Casting Time: 1 action
Duration: Instantaneous
Range: 30 ft.
Area of Effect: 1 set of tracks
Saving Throw: None

You determine the size and type of creature that made tracks you can see. If the tracks were made within the last week, you also learn how old they are; if they are more than a week old, you learn only that.

Ignite

2nd-level evocation
Sorcerer, Wizard
Components: V, S
Casting Time: 1 action
Duration: Instantaneous
Range: 30 ft.
Area of Effect: 1 creature
Saving Throw: None

You send a thick orange-and-purple ray at one creature you can see. Make a ranged spell attack; if it hits, the creature takes 4d6 fire damage and catches fire. At the end of each of its turns, it takes 2d6 fire damage. A burning creature or an adjacent ally can spend an action to extinguish the fire.

Enhancement: For each spell slot used higher than 2nd level, the initial damage increases by 1d6. Damage at the end of a burning creature's turn is unchanged.

Illusory Illusion

6th-level illusion
Bard, Warlock, Wizard
Components: V, S
Casting Time: 1 action
Duration: Permanent
Range: 400 ft.
Area of Effect: 1 creature or object
Saving Throw: Int / negates effect

You create a devious illusion that makes real objects seem like illusions. One creature or object that you can see is affected by the spell. Creatures interacting with the object will assume it is an illusion and that any effects it causes, such as heat or damage, are likewise not real. The GM can track the real effects, if necessary. Creatures that carefully examine the target or that are damaged by it can make an Intelligence saving throw. On a successful save, they realize the object's real nature.

Like any illusion, this spell requires careful adjudication by the GM, especially if it is used against player characters.

Imbue Passion

8th-level enchantment
Bard, Warlock, Wizard
Components: V, S, M (two magnets)
Casting Time: 1 action
Duration: 12 hours
Range: 30 ft.
Area of Effect: 2 creatures
Saving Throw: Cha / negates effect

Select two creatures you can see; each must make a Charisma saving throw. If the saving throw fails, the creature is imbued with a powerful love or hate (your choice) for the other. This emotion overwhelms any previous feelings it held for the other. If only one creature fails the saving throw, it is still affected but the other isn't; the spell doesn't need both creatures to reciprocate the feeling. Both creatures must be affected by the same emotion.

The exact effect of this must be determined by the GM. In general, creatures in love will embrace and look for a quiet place where they can be alone, and creatures overcome by hate will fight each other viciously.

Immunity to Energy

7th-level abjuration
Cleric, Druid, Wizard
Components: V, S
Casting Time: 1 action
Duration: Concentration, up to 1 hour
Range: Touch
Area of Effect: 1 creature
Saving Throw: None

You grant a willing creature you touch immunity to one of the following damage types (your choice) for the duration of the spell: acid, cold, fire, lightning, or thunder.

Impart Strength

8th-level transmutation
Cleric, Wizard
Components: V, S, M (a pint of fresh blood, which is consumed by the spell)
Casting Time: 1 action
Duration: Concentration, up to 10 minutes
Range: Touch
Area of Effect: 1 creature
Saving Throw: None

You touch a willing creature and imbue it with the strength of another creature, whose blood is used when casting the spell. For example, the blood of an Ancient Green Dragon would grant the target creature a Strength score of 27 for the duration of the spell.

The blood from the sample creature must have been collected no more than 24 hours ago.

Impressive Blow

1st-level evocation
Wizard
Components: V, S
Casting Time: 1 bonus action
Duration: Concentration, up to 1 minute
Range: Touch
Area of Effect: 1 weapon
Saving Throw: None

This spell is cast on a weapon. The next time the weapon scores a hit, roll twice the normal number of dice for damage.

Improve Senses

5th-level transmutation
Druid
Components: V, S
Casting Time: 1 action
Duration: Concentration, up to 8 hours
Range: Touch
Area of Effect: 1 creature
Saving Throw: None

One willing creature you touch gains darkvision (120 feet) and has tactical advantage on Wisdom (Perception) checks that rely on hearing, sight, or smell.

Infinite Knowledge

4th-level divination
Druid
Components: V, S
Casting Time: 1 action
Duration: Concentration, up to 10 minutes
Range: Self
Area of Effect: Self
Saving Throw: None

For the duration of this spell, you gain blindsight (60 feet) and have tactical advantage on Wisdom (Perception) and Wisdom (Survival) checks.

Infirmity

4th-level necromancy
Warlock, Wizard
Components: V, S, M (ash from a cremated creature)
Casting Time: 1 action
Duration: Instantaneous
Range: 120 ft.
Area of Effect: Sphere, 20-ft. radius
Saving Throw: Con / negates effect

You create a charnel scent in a 20-foot radius radiating from a point you can see within range. Each creature in the affected area must make a Constitution saving throw. If the saving throw fails, the creature is enfeebled so that it does only half damage with Strength-based weapon attacks. At the end of each of its turns, it can repeat the saving throw; a successful save ends the effect on that creature.

Inflict Lycanthropy

6th-level transmutation
Warlock, Wizard
Components: V, S, M (fur from a lycanthrope)
Casting Time: 1 action
Duration: Permanent
Range: Touch
Area of Effect: 1 humanoid creature
Saving Throw: Con / negates effect

You attempt to change one humanoid into a lycanthrope. If the creature fails a Constitution saving throw, it becomes cursed with lycanthropy.

The type of lycanthropy you can inflict depends on the level of the spell slot used to cast the spell.

6th level: wererat, werewolf
7th level: wereboar, weretiger
8th level or higher: werebear

The effect of lycanthropy on player characters is discussed fully in the rulebooks. The lycanthropy can be ended by magic that lifts curses.

Infuse Shadow

4th-level necromancy
Cleric, Wizard
Components: V, S
Casting Time: 1 action
Duration: Permanent
Range: 60 ft.
Area of Effect: 1 shadow
Saving Throw: None

You infuse shadow-stuff into one living creature's shadow that you can see. The shadow then animates and is under your control. It uses the standard stat block for a shadow. As a bonus action on each of your turns, you can mentally command the shadow if it is within 120 feet of you. You decide where it will move and what its action will be. Alternatively, you can give it a general order such as "guard this area." If it has no orders to follow, it only defends itself against hostile creatures. Once given an order, the shadow continues following it until that order is complete. After 24 hours, the shadow is no longer under your control; it becomes a free-willed undead.

The original creature regains a shadow over the next 24 hours. It appears faintly after one hour, then gradually intensifies until it casts a normal shadow again.

Infuse Weapon

3rd-level necromancy
Warlock, Wizard
Components: V, S, M
Casting Time: 1 hour
Duration: 24 hours
Range: Touch
Area of Effect: 1 weapon
Saving Throw: None

You infuse part of your life force into your weapon. You lose 10 hit points and, for the duration of the spell, your maximum hit points are reduced by 10; if this can't occur, the spell fails.

The weapon gains one of the following benefits.
- +2 to attack rolls
- +2 to damage
- Scores critical hits on rolls of natural 19 or 20
- does magical damage

For each additional 5 hit points you sacrifice when you cast the spell, you can add one additional benefit to the weapon.

Inner Storm

5th-level evocation
Druid
Components: V, S, M (a thin piece of iron)
Casting Time: 1 action
Duration: 10 minutes
Range: Self
Area of Effect: Self
Saving Throw: Con / partial

Electrical sparks wreathe your body for the duration of the spell. Whenever a creature that's within 5 feet of you hits you with a melee attack, the creature takes 4d8 lightning damage. If the creature is wearing metal armor, it also is knocked prone unless it make a successful Constitution saving throw. You can end the spell early with an action.

Insomnia

2nd-level enchantment
Warlock, Wizard
Components: V, S
Casting Time: 1 action
Duration: 7 days
Range: Touch
Area of Effect: 1 creature
Saving Throw: Wis / negates effect

You attempt to curse one creature by robbing it of sleep. The creature makes a Wisdom saving throw. If the saving throw fails, it loses the ability to sleep or rest. It can't benefit from long rests, and it gains one level of exhaustion every 24 hours, to a maximum of five levels of exhaustion. The cursed creature can repeat the saving throw at the end of each long rest; the spell ends on a successful save. The spell can also be ended by magic that removes a curse.

Instant Exit

4th-level conjuration
Wizard
Components: V, S
Casting Time: 1 action
Duration: 1 round
Range: 30 ft.

Area of Effect: 1 portal
Saving Throw: None

You cause a doorlike portal to appear on a nearby wall you can see. Any creature that steps through the portal is instantly teleported to a random location within 1,000 feet of the door. You have no control over where the creatures are transported, but all creatures that step through will be transported to the same location. The door disappears at the end of your next turn.

There is a 5% chance the spell malfunctions and instead leads to the corresponding location on the Ethereal Plane. This is determined once, the first time a creature steps through the portal, and applies throughout the spell's duration.

Instant Fluency

6th-level divination
Bard, Cleric, Wizard
Components: V, S
Casting Time: 1 action
Duration: 1 week
Range: Touch
Area of Effect: 1 to 4 creatures
Saving Throw: None

You grant up to four willing creatures the ability to understand any language they read or hear. In addition, they gain the ability to speak that language, if they can speak normally.

Enhancement: For each spell slot used higher than 6th level, you can affect one additional creature.

Interdiction

7th-level enchantment
Warlock, Wizard
Components: V, S, M (diamond dust worth 500 gp, which is consumed)
Casting Time: 1 action
Duration: 1 minute
Range: 150 ft.
Area of Effect: 1 creature
Saving Throw: Cha / negates effect

Select one creature within range. That creature must make a Charisma saving throw. If the saving throw fails, it loses all ability to cast arcane spells for the duration of the *interdiction*. It can repeat the saving throw at the end of each of its turns; a successful save ends the effect.

Interrogation

5th-level enchantment
Bard, Cleric
Components: V, S
Casting Time: 1 action
Duration: 10 minutes
Range: Touch
Area of Effect: 1 creature
Saving Throw: Cha / negates effect

You compel one creature you touch to answer up to three questions truthfully. The creature must make a Charisma saving throw after each question is asked. If the saving throw fails, it must answer the question truthfully and must offer as much information as it can. If the save is successful, the creature can refuse to answer the question, but it can't lie. The creature must be able to understand your questions.

Intimate Knowledge

5th-level divination
Cleric
Components: V, S

Casting Time: 1 action
Duration: 10 minutes
Range: 120 ft.
Area of Effect: 1 creature
Saving Throw: None

You gain insight into how one creature you can see acts and thinks. For the duration, you have tactical advantage on attack rolls against that creature and it has tactical disadvantage on attack rolls against you.

You don't need to have a language in common with the target of the spell, but you gain no benefit if *intimate knowledge* is cast on a creature that doesn't think.

Inverted Compass

2nd-level enchantment
Warlock, Wizard
Components: V, S
Casting Time: 1 action
Duration: Concentration, up to 1 minute
Range: 30 ft.
Area of Effect: 1 creature
Saving Throw: Wis / negates effect

Choose one creature you can see. It must make a Wisdom saving throw. If the saving throw fails, then whenever the creature moves for the duration of the spell, it moves in a random direction. The player or GM controlling the creature decides how far it will move before the direction is determined.

Invigorating Touch

6th-level evocation
Cleric, Druid
Components: V, S
Casting Time: 1 action
Duration: Concentration, up to 1 minute
Range: Touch
Area of Effect: 1 creature
Saving Throw: None

You touch a willing creature and fill it with invigorating energy. For the duration of the *invigorating touch*, the creature gains 10 temporary hit points at the beginning of each of its turns, and it makes a Constitution saving throw; on a successful save, it loses one level of exhaustion. The creature also has tactical advantage on saves against poison and disease for the duration of the spell. Any remaining temporary hit points are lost at the end of the creature's next long rest.

Iron Bones

4th-level necromancy
Cleric, Wizard
Components: V, S, M (an iron nail)
Casting Time: 1 action
Duration: Permanent
Range: Touch

Iron Judgment

Area of Effect: 1 skeleton
Saving Throw: None

One undead skeleton you touch gains resistance to bludgeoning, piercing, and slashing damage from nonmagical weapons.

Enhancement: For each spell slot used higher than 4th level, you can affect one additional skeleton.

Iron Core

4th-level abjuration
Cleric, Paladin
Components: V, S
Casting Time: 1 action
Duration: 1 day
Range: Touch
Area of Effect: 1 creature
Saving Throw: None

One willing creature that you touch gains a pool of 5 fortune points. If the creature makes a saving throw and dislikes the result, it can spend a fortune point to reroll the save. The decision to reroll must be made immediately, before any effects of the failed saving throw are determined. The result from the reroll must be used. The spell ends when all the fortune points have been used or at the end of the creature's next long rest.

Iron Judgment

4th-level evocation
Paladin
Components: V, S
Casting Time: 1 action
Duration: Concentration, up to 1 minute
Range: Touch
Area of Effect: 1 creature
Saving Throw: Wis / negates effect

You call upon the power of your deity to expose evil for what it is. One creature that you touch, if it is evil, must make a Wisdom saving throw. If the saving fails, the creature becomes outlined in flickering, holy flames for the duration of the spell. The creature can't hide or teleport, and it takes 2d6 radiant damage at the start of each of its turns.

The spell has no effect if cast on a non-evil creature.

Iron Rope

4th-level transmutation
Wizard
Components: V, S, M (a pinch of iron)
Casting Time: 1 action
Duration: 1 day
Range: Touch
Area of Effect: 100 ft. of rope or 1,000 square ft. of rigging
Saving Throw: None

One rope up to 100 feet long gains the hardness of iron; it has resistance to bludgeoning, piercing, and slashing damage from weapons and resistance to fire damage. In addition, it gains a damage threshold of 5 (every attack against the rope has a damage penalty of -5).

The spell can also be cast on 1,000 square feet of ship's rigging.

Ironshot

2nd-level conjuration
Wizard
Components: V, S, M (three iron marbles)
Casting Time: 1 action
Duration: 1 minute
Range: 60 ft.

Jungle Cry

Area of Effect: 5 iron balls
Saving Throw: None

You conjure five 2-inch-diameter iron balls into the air next to you. On each of your turns, you can launch one iron ball at a creature within 60 feet and line of sight. Make a ranged spell attack against that creature. If it hits, a ball does 2d6 bludgeoning damage and the target is knocked prone. Unused iron balls move with you as you move. Balls disappear after they attack or when the spell ends.

Itemize

Divination cantrip
Wizard
Components: V, S
Casting Time: 1 action
Duration: Instantaneous
Range: 30 ft.
Area of Effect: 1 type of object
Saving Throw: None

You instantly learn the exact quantity of one type of item within 30 feet of you. It must be a type of item that you've handled in the past; you can't, for example, use *itemize* to find out how many *swords of sharpness* are nearby if you've never handled such a weapon. The object being itemized must also be reasonably specific. You can learn how many apples are nearby, for example, but not how much fruit.

Jolt

5th-level evocation
Wizard
Components: V, S
Casting Time: 1 action
Duration: Instantaneous
Range: 30 ft.
Area of Effect: 1 to 4 creatures
Saving Throw: None

You channel power into up to four willing creatures you can see. Each of those creatures can immediately make one weapon attack with a ready weapon; each can also move up to 10 feet before or after the attack.

Judicious Concealment

6th-level illusion
Wizard
Components: V, S
Casting Time: 1 action
Duration: Concentration, up to 10 minutes
Range: 30 ft.
Area of Effect: Any number of creatures
Saving Throw: None

Choose a number of willing creatures within range. While this spell is in effect, these creatures can hear each other normally but no other creatures can hear what they are saying; lip-reading is still possible. The spell ends for all affected creatures if any one of them makes an attack or casts a spell.

Enhancement: When you use an 8th-level or higher slot to cast *judicious concealment*, the creatures also become invisible to all other creatures.

Jungle Cry

2nd-level enchantment
Druid, Ranger
Components: V, S
Casting Time: 1 action
Duration: 1 hour

Range: 400 ft.
Area of Effect: Sphere, 400-ft. radius
Saving Throw: Wis / negates effect

You utter a loud, echoing cry. Every beast within 400 feet of you and able to hear the shout becomes hostile toward any humanoids it can see. Large or bigger beasts negate this effect with a successful Wisdom saving throw, but Medium and smaller beasts get no saving throw.

Keen Ears

2nd-level transmutation
Druid, Ranger
Components: V, S, M (a small metal cone)
Casting Time: 1 action
Duration: Concentration, up to 10 minutes
Range: Touch
Area of Effect: 1 creature
Saving Throw: None

One willing creature you touch gains superb hearing. It has tactical advantage on Wisdom (Perception) checks that rely on hearing.

Kiss of the Nereid

5th-level conjuration
Druid
Components: V, S, M (a few drops of water)
Casting Time: 1 action
Duration: Concentration, up to 1 minute
Range: 150 ft.
Area of Effect: 1 creature
Saving Throw: Con / negates effect

You conjure a nereid — a creature of living water that resembles a beautiful man or woman. The nereid attempts to kiss one creature you can see within range. The creature being kissed must make a Constitution saving throw. If the saving throw fails, the water of the nereid flows into its lungs and the creature begins suffocating. At the end of each of its turns, it can repeat the saving throw; a successful save allows it to cough up enough water to breathe normally again, and the spell ends.

Know Alignment

2nd-level divination
Cleric
Components: V, S
Casting Time: 1 action
Duration: Instantaneous
Range: 50 ft.
Area of Effect: 1 creature
Saving Throw: Wis / negates effect

You choose one creature you can see and attempt to discern its alignment. The creature makes a Wisdom saving throw. If the saving throw fails, you immediately learn its alignment.

Know the Mark

1st-level divination
Warlock, Wizard
Components: V, S, M (a spirit doll)
Casting Time: 10 minutes
Duration: Instantaneous
Range: Self
Area of Effect: Special
Saving Throw: None

Choose one creature for which you have previously constructed a *spirit doll*. You immediately become aware of its location, as long as

Kiss of the Nereid

it is on the same plane as you. You learn any conditions affecting the creature, as well as its general state of health–unharmed, wounded (has more than half its hit points), badly wounded (has 25 to 50 percent of its hit points), near death (less than 25 percent of its hit points), dying (0 hit points), or dead.

Landslide

6th-level conjuration
Druid
Components: V, S, M (a handful of snow)
Casting Time: 1 action
Duration: Concentration, up to 1 minute
Range: 400 ft.
Area of Effect: Tumbling wall of snow, 20 ft. high, 10 ft. thick, 120 ft. long
Saving Throw: Dex / half damage

Landslide can only be used in snowy, mountainous regions. You create a fast-moving wall of snow, 20 feet high, 10 feet thick, and 120 feet long. The entire wall must be within 400 feet of you. When you cast the spell and again at the beginning of each of your turns, the *landslide* moves 60 feet under your control; it must always move downhill, but it can move sideways at the same time.

Any creature engulfed by the wall must make a Dexterity saving throw. If the saving throw fails, the creature takes 12d6 cold damage and is knocked prone and buried by snow; a successful save results in half damage and no other effect. Buried creatures are considered prone and restrained until they escape, even if the spell has ended. A restrained creature can escape if it uses an action and makes a successful Strength (Athletics) check against your spell saving throw DC.

The wall disappears when it can no longer move downhill or when the spell ends, but a heavy dusting of snow will still cover the ground.

Lasting Breath

1st-level transmutation
Wizard
Components: S, M (a paper bag)
Casting Time: 1 action
Duration: See text
Range: 50 ft.
Area of Effect: 1 creature
Saving Throw: None

You or another creature you can see can hold its breath 1d4 + 1 rounds longer than usual. If the creature is already suffocating, it gets enough fresh air in its lungs to last 1d4 + 1 rounds.

Leaf Fall

2nd-level necromancy
Druid, Ranger
Components: V, S
Casting Time: 1 action
Duration: Instantaneous
Range: 50 ft.
Area of Effect: 1 tree or 100 sq. ft. of brush
Saving Throw: None

All the leaves or needles on a tree or an area of brush you can see instantly wither and fall to the ground, leaving bare branches and revealing any creatures that were hiding in the foliage.

Leaf Tide

2nd-level transmutation
Druid, Ranger
Components: V, S
Casting Time: 1 action
Duration: Instantaneous
Range: 50 ft.
Area of Effect: 1 creature
Saving Throw: Dex / negates effect

One pile of leaves within range rises in a wave and engulfs a creature you can see. The creature takes 5d6 bludgeoning damage, or half damage with a successful Dexterity saving throw.

Liar's Remorse

3rd-level necromancy
Cleric
Components: V, S
Casting Time: 1 action
Duration: 1 week
Range: Touch
Area of Effect: 1 creature
Saving Throw: Wis / negates effect

You curse one creature you touch. The creature must make a Wisdom saving throw. If the saving throw fails, it is cursed so that intentionally speaking a lie causes its tongue to swell grotesquely and protrude from its mouth, making it unable to speak. The tongue returns to normal size in 1d4 minutes.

The effect can be ended by magic that removes a curse.

Life Leech

8th-level necromancy
Wizard
Components: V, S
Casting Time: 1 action
Duration: Instantaneous
Range: Self
Area of Effect: Sphere, 30-ft. radius
Saving Throw: Con / half damage

You attempt to rip the life force from living creatures you can see. Every living creature within 30 feet of you that you can see takes 4d6 + 14 necrotic damage, or half damage with a successful Constitution saving throw.

You gain half of the total hit points lost by creatures affected by the spell as temporary hit points, which last until you take a long or short rest. You can't gain more temporary hit points than your hit point maximum (in other words, if you have 50 hit points at full health, you can't gain more than 50 temporary hit points from *life leech*).

If there are undead in the area affected by *life leech*, the spell malfunctions; it drains hit points from you along with other living creatures in the area, and the temporary hit points are gained by the undead creature with the most hit points in the area (determine randomly in case of a tie).

Life Leech Weapon

3rd-level necromancy
Warlock, Wizard
Components: V, S
Casting Time: 1 action
Duration: Concentration, up to 1 minute
Range: Self
Area of Effect: 1 weapon
Saving Throw: None

One melee weapon you hold is infused with necrotic energy. For the duration of the spell, that weapon's damage increases by an additional 1d6 necrotic damage. Every time it does necrotic damage, you gain an equal number of temporary hit points. Remaining temporary hit points disappear when the spell ends.

Life Shot

6th-level necromancy
Sorcerer, Wizard
Components: V, S
Casting Time: 1 action
Duration: Concentration, up to 1 minute
Range: Self
Area of Effect: Self
Saving Throw: None

You empower your ranged weapon attacks with your life force. Each time you make a ranged weapon attack, you can sacrifice up to 5 hit points before you make the attack roll. The weapon then does additional necrotic damage equal to twice the hit points you sacrificed, if the attack hits.

Lifebread

3rd-level evocation
Cleric
Components: V, S
Casting Time: 1 action
Duration: Permanent
Range: Touch
Area of Effect: 1 loaf
Saving Throw: None

One 2-lb. loaf of bread that you touch becomes infused with healing energy. One-fourth of the loaf is enough food to sustain a Small or Medium creature for one day, and that creature heals 1d8 hit points when the *lifebread* is consumed. One-half of the loaf will feed a Large creature and has the same healing effect. Eating more than one-fourth (or one-half) of the loaf in a 24-hour period has no additional effect.

Light Control

4th-level transmutation
Cleric
Components: V, S
Casting Time: 1 action
Duration: Concentration, up to 1 minute
Range: 50 ft.
Area of Effect: Sphere, 30-ft. radius
Saving Throw: None

You control the illumination in a 30-foot-radius sphere centered on a point you can see, choosing whether it's full darkness, dim light, or bright light. You can change the level of illumination by one level as a free action when you cast the spell and at the beginning of each of your turns.

Other forms of illumination initially function normally within the zone, but you can change their effectiveness on your subsequent turns.

Lightning Storm

6th-level evocation
Sorcerer, Wizard
Components: V, S
Casting Time: 1 action
Duration: Concentration, up to 3 rounds
Range: 150 ft.
Area of Effect: Cylinder, 20-ft. radius, 60 ft. tall
Saving Throw: Dex / half damage

You summon a lightning storm that fills a cylinder with a 20-foot radius and 60 feet tall, extending from a point you can see. Each creature in the affected area whey you cast the spell takes 8d6 lightning damage, or half damage with a successful Dexterity saving throw.

At the beginning of each of your turns, you can move the storm up to 20 feet. Each creature that the storm moves onto or that is in the affected area when it stops moving also takes 8d6 lightning damage, or half damage with a successful Dexterity saving throw. A creature never needs to make more than one saving throw against the *lightning storm* per turn.

The area of the storm is lightly obscured.

Lightning Wheel

6th-level evocation
Druid, Sorcerer, Wizard
Components: V, S
Casting Time: 1 action
Duration: Instantaneous
Range: 400 ft.
Area of Effect: 1 creature
Saving Throw: Dex / half damage

You throw a wheel of ferocious electrical energy at one creature you can see. The creature takes 3d10 + 10 lightning damage plus 3d10 + 10 thunder damage, or half damage with a successful Dexterity saving throw, as the wheel detonates with a shattering crack of thunder. Every creature within 20 feet of the target must make a successful Constitution saving throw or be deafened for 1 minute.

Link Perception

3rd-level divination
Warlock, Wizard
Components: V, S, M (spirit doll)
Casting Time: 10 minutes
Duration: Concentration, up to 10 minutes
Range: Self
Area of Effect: 1 spirit doll
Saving Throw: None

For the duration of the spell, you can see, hear, and smell everything that the creature linked to a specific *spirit doll* experiences, as long as you are both on the same plane of existence.

Liquid Fire

7th-level evocation
Sorcerer, Wizard
Components: V, S, M (a small amount of pitch mixed with sulfur)
Casting Time: 1 action
Duration: Instantaneous
Range: 400 ft.
Area of Effect: Sphere, 30-ft. radius
Saving Throw: Dex / half damage

82

A ball of liquid fire speeds from your outstretched hand to a point you can see, where it explodes. Every creature within 30 feet of the explosion takes 10d6 fire damage and catches fire, or takes half damage and doesn't catch fire if it makes a successful Dexterity saving throw. A creature that's on fire takes 5d6 fire damage at the end of each of its turns. The fire burns out naturally after three rounds, or a creature can spend an action extinguishing the fire on itself or an adjacent creature.

Locate Fish

1st-level divination (ritual)
Druid, Ranger
Components: V, S
Casting Time: 1 action
Duration: Concentration, up to 10 minutes
Range: Self
Area of Effect: Sphere, 100-ft. radius
Saving Throw: None

You learn the species, number, and depth of all fish within range, and you get tactical advantage on ability checks related to fishing.

Locate Water

1st-level divination (ritual)
Druid, Ranger
Components: S, M (a forked stick)
Casting Time: 1 action
Duration: Instantaneous
Range: Self
Area of Effect: Circle, 1-mile radius
Saving Throw: None

You learn the location of the nearest potable water on the surface within 1 mile, and the location of the nearest potable subterranean water within 100 feet.

Lock Form

4th-level abjuration
Cleric, Wizard
Components: V, S
Casting Time: 1 action
Duration: 1 hour
Range: Touch
Area of Effect: 1 creature
Saving Throw: None

You fix the target's true appearance and attributes so they can't be altered. For the duration of the spell, one willing creature gets tactical advantage on saving throws against transmutation spells. If a transmutation spell would not normally get a saving throw, or if the creature is a willing target, it still must make a saving throw, and the transmutation spell has no effect if the save succeeds.

Enhancement: For each spell slot used higher than 4th level, you can affect one additional creature.

Locust Leap

3rd-level transmutation
Druid
Components: V, S, M (a locust's leg)
Casting Time: 1 action
Duration: Concentration, up to 1 minute
Range: Self
Area of Effect: Self
Saving Throw: None

For the duration of the spell, you gain the ability to make incredible jumps. When you move, you can jump up to your speed in any direction, and always land safely on your feet.

Lost Wanderer

6th-level enchantment
Cleric, Druid, Warlock, Wizard
Components: V, S, M (a broken compass)
Casting Time: 1 action
Duration: 24 hours
Range: 50 ft.
Area of Effect: 1 creature
Saving Throw: Wis / negates effect

Select a creature you can see. The creature must make a Wisdom saving throw. If it fails, it is cursed with the inability to find its way for the duration of the spell. The creature can't read maps or remember the route to anywhere. The creature can be led to a destination by another creature, but otherwise, it selects its path randomly. The curse doesn't prevent the creature from making its way to destinations it can see.

The effect can be ended by magic that lifts a curse.

Lower Spell Resistance

5th-level transmutation
Wizard
Components: V, S
Casting Time: 1 action
Duration: Concentration, up to 1 minute
Range: 50 ft.
Area of Effect: 1 creature
Saving Throw: Con / negates effect

One creature you can see must make a Constitution saving throw. If the saving throw fails, the creature has tactical disadvantage on saving throws against magic for the duration of this spell.

Luck of the Saints

2nd-level enchantment
Cleric, Paladin
Components: V, S
Casting Time: 1 action
Duration: Concentration, up to 10 minutes
Range: Touch
Area of Effect: 1 creature
Saving Throw: None

You touch a willing creature and infuse it with luck. Before making an ability check, attack roll, or saving throw, the affected creature can declare it is using this ability, which lets it add 1d6 to the d20 result. The spell ends when the luck is used.

Lustful Gaze

3rd-level enchantment
Wizard
Components: V, S
Casting Time: 1 action
Duration: Concentration, up to 8 hours
Range: 30 ft.
Area of Effect: 1 creature
Saving Throw: Cha / negates effect

One creature you can see must make a Charisma saving throw as you gaze upon it. If the saving throw fails, the creature is captivated by you and can take no actions other than shuffling meekly behind you at half-speed for the spell's duration. If the creature is attacked by anyone, the spell immediately ends. The creature can make another saving throw at the end of each of its turns; a successful save ends the spell.

Magma Eruption

7th-level conjuration
Sorcerer, Wizard
Components: V, S, M (a bit of igneous rock)
Casting Time: 1 action
Duration: Concentration, up to 1 minute
Range: 150 ft.
Area of Effect: Cylinder, 40-ft. radius, 30 ft. high
Saving Throw: Dex / half damage

You cause the ground to explode and spew forth a geyser of molten rock that showers down in a 40-foot-radius, 30-foot-high cylinder. Creatures in the cylinder when the geyser erupts take 6d6 fire damage and 6d6 bludgeoning damage, or half damage with a successful Dexterity saving throw.

Rocks and ash continue falling for the duration of the spell; each creature in the area at the end of its turn takes 2d6 fire damage and 2d6 bludgeoning damage, or half damage with a successful Dexterity saving throw. The area is treated as difficult terrain.

They geyser ends at the end of the spell. The remaining lava melts away into the ground 1d3 rounds later, leaving behind scorched earth.

Malicious Intent

1st-level enchantment
Wizard
Components: V
Casting Time: 1 action
Duration: Concentration, up to 1 minute
Range: Self
Area of Effect: Sphere, 30-ft. radius
Saving Throw: Wis / negates effect

Each creature within 30 feet of you must make a Wisdom saving throw. On a failed save, the creature takes a -1 penalty on every saving throw it makes for the duration of this spell.

Enhancement: If you use a 4th-level or higher spell slot to cast *malicious intent*, the saving throw penalty increases to -2.

Maligned Performance

4th-level illusion
Bard, Wizard
Components: V, S, M (a broken mirror and an asp's tongue)

Casting Time: 1 action
Duration: Concentration, up to 1 minute
Range: 30 ft.
Area of Effect: 1 creature
Saving Throw: Wis / negates effect

You cause a creature's performance to go subtly wrong, whilst shielding it from awareness of the spell. The targeted creature must make a Wisdom saving throw. If the saving throw fails, it subtracts 1d6 from its Charisma (Performance) checks and Charisma checks using musical instruments, and it is unable to benefit from tactical advantage on those checks. It can't use any ability that would allow rerolls on these checks because it is unaware that the performance is going poorly.

The spell ends if the performer gets inescapable evidence of his or her bad performance, such as most of an audience getting up and leaving in disgust or being pelted with rotten tomatoes.

Mangling Foot

7th-level evocation
Wizard
Components: V, S
Casting Time: 1 action
Duration: Concentration, up to 1 minute
Range: 150 ft.
Area of Effect: 1 foot
Saving Throw: Str / half damage

You create an enormous, glowing, blue-white foot of magical force in an unoccupied space that you can see within range. The Medium-size foot hovers in the air, 3 to 4 feet above the ground. At the beginning of your turn, you can use a bonus action to move it up to 60 feet to an unoccupied space. The foot is immune to damage and all conditions.

As an action, you can direct the foot to stomp on a creature adjacent to it. Make a melee spell attack against that creature. If it hits, the foot does 10d8 force damage, knocks the target prone, and restrains it. A successful Strength saving throw halves the damage and prevents the target from being knocked prone or restrained. A restrained creature takes 4d8 force damage at the end of each of its turns. The restraint ends automatically if the foot moves or attacks again. Otherwise, a restrained creature can escape by using an action to make a successful Strength check against your spell saving throw DC.

Instead of stomping, you can also command the foot to kick; this also does 10d8 force damage, but instead of being knocked prone and restrained, the target is pushed up to 60 feet. A successful Strength saving throw by the target creature halves the damage and negates the push effect.

The foot is big enough to provide cover and to prevent movement through its space.

Mantle of Dread

5th-level enchantment
Bard, Warlock, Wizard
Components: V, S
Casting Time: 1 action
Duration: Concentration, up to 1 minute
Range: Self
Area of Effect: Sphere, 30-ft. radius
Saving Throw: Wis / negates effect

An aura that inflicts an overwhelming sense of despair radiates from you in a 30-foot-radius; the aura moves with you.

Each creature that's inside the aura when the spell is cast or that enters the aura must make a Wisdom saving throw. If the saving throw fails, the creature must subtract 1d6 from its attack rolls, saving throws, and ability checks that it makes inside the aura. In addition, a creature other than you inside the aura must also make a Charisma saving throw before attacking or casting a spell; If the saving throw fails, the creature hesitates instead and takes no action.

Mark of Exile

7th-level necromancy
Cleric
Components: V, S
Casting Time: 1 hour
Duration: Permanent
Range: Touch
Area of Effect: 1 creature
Saving Throw: None

You curse one living creature to never enter a location you name, upon pain of death. The location can't be larger than 1 square mile. If the creature approaches within 100 feet of the banned location, it becomes aware of the danger it is in. If the creature voluntarily enters the location, the creature immediately drops to 0 hit points, and it can't regain hit points while inside the area.

The *mark of exile* is an invisible sigil on the creature. It can be viewed with *detect magic* and similar magic.

The *mark of exile* can be removed with magic that lifts a curse, but only if the spell is cast with a 7th-level or higher spell slot.

Mark of Fire

5th-level transmutation
Wizard
Components: V, S
Casting Time: 1 action
Duration: Permanent
Range: 50 ft.
Area of Effect: 1 undead creature
Saving Throw: None

One undead creature you can see becomes imbued with the essence of fire. A flaming sigil appears above the creature's head, and the creature's eye sockets smoke and burn with orange flame. The creature gains resistance to fire damage and vulnerability to cold damage, and its melee attacks do an additional 2d6 fire damage when they hit.

Mark of Ice

5th-level transmutation
Wizard
Components: V, S
Casting Time: 1 action
Duration: Permanent
Range: 50 ft.
Area of Effect: 1 undead creature
Saving Throw: None

One undead creature you can see is imbued with the essence of ice. An icy sigil appears above the creature's head, and the creature's eye sockets glow with frigid blue energy. The creature gains resistance to cold damage and vulnerability to fire damage, and its melee attacks do an additional 2d6 cold damage when they hit.

Mark of Ooze

5th-level transmutation
Wizard
Components: V, S
Casting Time: 1 action
Duration: Permanent
Range: 50 ft.
Area of Effect: 1 undead creature
Saving Throw: None

One undead creature you can see is imbued with the essence of acid. A green sigil appears above the creature's head, and acid trickles from its eye sockets. The creature gains resistance to acid damage and vulnerability to lightning damage, and its melee attacks do an additional 2d6 acid damage when they hit.

Mark of Ownership

4th-level abjuration
Wizard
Components: V, S, M (a drop of the owner's blood)
Casting Time: 10 minutes
Duration: Permanent
Range: Touch
Area of Effect: 1 item
Saving Throw: None

You curse one item to only accept one creature you can see as its rightful owner. In the hands of any other creature, the item feels unnatural; that creature has tactical disadvantage on all ability checks and attack rolls when using the item.

Megalomania

4th-level enchantment
Wizard
Components: V, S
Casting Time: 1 action
Duration: Concentration, up to 1 minute
Range: 30 ft.
Area of Effect: 1 creature
Saving Throw: Wis / negates effect

You enchant one living creature you can see to believe it is more skilled than it really is. The creature must make a Wisdom saving throw. A successful save negates the spell, but if the saving throw fails, the creature's overconfidence causes it to act rashly and without forethought. For the duration of the spell, the creature can't move away from an opponent, and it provokes an opportunity attack from adjacent creatures whenever it takes an action. It also suffers a -2 penalty to damage rolls and Wisdom saving throws.

The creature can repeat the Wisdom saving throw at the end of each of its turns; the spell ends after two successful saves, which need not be consecutive.

Melt

2nd-level transmutation
Druid, Wizard
Components: V, S
Casting Time: 1 action
Duration: Instantaneous
Range: 50 ft.
Area of Effect: Sphere, 20-ft. radius
Saving Throw: Con / half damage

You melt all inanimate ice and snow within 20 feet of a point you can see. Creature made of ice or snow in the affected area take 4d6 fire damage, or half damage with a successful Constitution saving throw.

Memento

5th-level transmutation
Wizard
Components: V, S, M (a drop of your blood)
Casting Time: 1 hour
Duration: Permanent
Range: Touch
Area of Effect: 1 object weighing up to 10 lbs.
Saving Throw: None

Your touch binds an unattended item weighing no more than 10 lbs. to you. The object can't be lost, and it can't be separated from you by more than 10 feet. It floats and moves after you as if it were attached by an invisible string. The spell ends if you cast it on another item.

Menace

2nd-level illusion
Bard, Cleric, Warlock, Wizard
Components: V, S
Casting Time: 1 action
Duration: Concentration, up to 8 hours
Range: Self
Area of Effect: Self
Saving Throw: None

You create an illusion around yourself that makes you seem larger, fiercer, and more imposing. For the duration of the spell, add 1d6 to your Charisma (Intimidate) checks.

Mercurial Smite

1st-level evocation
Cleric, Paladin
Components: V, S
Casting Time: 1 bonus action
Duration: Concentration, up to 1 minute
Range: Touch
Area of Effect: 1 weapon
Saving Throw: None

Choose one alignment listed below when you cast this spell. Your weapon glows with energy corresponding to the alignment you chose. You can't choose an alignment that corresponds with your own.

Evil–White
Good–Dark red
Chaotic–Blue
Lawful–Multicolored

When you make your next attack roll, if your target is of the chosen alignment, you can add 1d6 to your attack roll. If the attack hits, it does an extra 1d6 radiant damage. The spell ends after one attack, regardless of whether it hits or misses.

Merge Into Art

6th-level transmutation
Wizard
Components: V, S
Casting Time: 1 action
Duration: Concentration, up to 1 hour
Range: Self
Area of Effect: Self
Saving Throw: None

You step into a painting, tapestry, or mosaic large enough to encompass your height. Your shape and form becomes woven into the tapestry or painted into the picture as if it were part of the original work, changing your coloration and form as necessary to match the style of the art.

You are aware of your surroundings as if watching through a window, but your field of view is restricted to a narrow band in front of the artwork. You can't speak or cast spells while merged into the art, but you can end the spell as an action. The spell also ends if the artwork becomes damaged. When the spell ends, you appear in an unoccupied space adjacent to the artwork.

Mighty Steed

3rd-level transmutation
Paladin
Components: V, S
Casting Time: 1 action

Merge Into Art

Duration: Concentration, up to 10 minutes
Range: Self
Area of Effect: 1 mount
Saving Throw: None

A mount you are riding is infused with divine power. For the duration of this spell, the mount gets tactical advantage on attack rolls and saving throws and its attacks do an additional 1d6 radiant damage. The spell is cast on you, so it affects whatever mount you are riding. Switching mounts transfers the bonus to the new animal.

Mind Carve

4th-level necromancy
Wizard
Components: V, S
Casting Time: 1 action
Duration: Instantaneous
Range: 50 ft.
Area of Effect: 1 creature
Saving Throw: Int / partial; Wis / partial

You point your finger at a creature you can see within range and a bolt of negative energy shoots at the target. The creature must make an Intelligence saving throw and a Wisdom saving throw. If it fails the Intelligence saving throw, it loses 1d6 points of Intelligence. If it fails the Wisdom saving throw, it loses 1d6 points of Wisdom. A creature's score can't be reduced to less than 1 in either ability.

Mind Link

3rd-level transmutation
Cleric
Components: V, S

Casting Time: 1 action
Duration: Concentration, up to 10 minutes
Range: Touch
Area of Effect: 2 creatures
Saving Throw: None

Your touch links the minds of two willing creatures so that they can communicate telepathically across any distance, as long as they are both on the same plane of existence.

Molten Strike

2nd-level evocation
Druid, Sorcerer, Wizard
Components: V, S, M (a volcanic stone)
Casting Time: 10 minutes
Duration: Instantaneous
Range: 50 ft.
Area of Effect: 1 creature
Saving Throw: None

You draw forth from a volcanic stone all the heat and energy that went into its making and blast it at one creature you can see. The stone must be within 5 feet of you. Make a ranged spell attack against the target creature. A hit does 2d6 bludgeoning damage plus 3d6 fire damage.

Enhancement: For each spell slot used higher than 2nd level, the attack does an additional 1d6 bludgeoning damage and 1d6 fire damage.

Moonbeam

3rd-level evocation
Druid
Components: V, S, M (a volcanic stone)
Casting Time: 1 action

Duration: 10 minutes
Range: 50 ft.
Area of Effect: Cylinder, 10-ft. radius, 60 ft. high
Saving Throw: Con / negates effect

You cause a shaft of moonlight to illuminate a 10-foot-radius, 60-foot high cylinder rising from a point you can see. The moonlight provides dim illumination inside the cylinder.

If a lycanthrope in human form is in the area of moonlight at the start of its turn, it must make a successful Constitution saving throw or be forced to spend its action transforming into its animal or hybrid form (its choice), and it can't revert to human form for the duration of the spell.

As an action, you can move the moonbeam up to 30 feet, but its center point must stay within the spell's range.

Morph Shadow

1st-level illusion
Wizard
Components: S, M (a piece of black cloth)
Casting Time: 1 action
Duration: 1 hour
Range: 120 ft.
Area of Effect: 1 shadow
Saving Throw: Con / half damage

You change the appearance of one normal shadow you can see within range into the form of your choice. If a shadow creature is the target, it takes 5d6 force damage, or half damage with a successful Constitution saving throw.

Mucilage

1st-level conjuration
Wizard
Components: V, S, M (a piece of pine sap)
Casting Time: 1 action
Duration: Concentration, up to 1 minute
Range: 50 ft.
Area of Effect: Square, 10 ft. x 10 ft.
Saving Throw: Str / negates effect

A 10-foot-by-10-foot surface you can see within range becomes covered with sticky sap. Any creature that begins its turn in the affected area or enters the area becomes stuck and can move no farther that turn unless it makes a successful Strength saving throw. A creature needs to make only one saving throw per turn, no matter how far it moves through the *mucilage*.

Muddy Appearance

1st-level illusion
Wizard
Components: V, S
Casting Time: 1 action
Duration: 1 minute
Range: 50 ft.
Area of Effect: 1 creature
Saving Throw: None

You cause the features of a creature you can see within range to blur slightly, obscuring the details of its appearance. Anyone relying on sight has tactical disadvantage on ability checks to recognize or remember the affected creature. The illusion is subtle, so observers are prone to think something is wrong with their eyesight (dust blew into their eyes, or their eyes are watering) rather than that the creature has been masked in any way.

Multiple Shot

4th-level divination
Wizard
Components: V, S

Casting Time: 1 bonus action
Duration: Concentration, up to 1 minute
Range: Self
Area of Effect: 1 creature
Saving Throw: None

You must cast this spell on the same turn that you hit a creature with a ranged attack. For the duration of the spell, you are mystically linked to the target and have tactical advantage on every ranged attack roll you make against the target.

Musical Mural

3rd-level illusion
Bard
Components: V, S
Casting Time: 1 action
Duration: Concentration, up to 10 minutes
Range: Self
Area of Effect: Sphere, 60-ft. radius
Saving Throw: Wis / negates effect

You play a song that creates an image in the mind of each creature that can hear you and is within 60 feet of you. The image is so vivid, creatures experience it as if they were there. The image can be frightening, beatific, or whatever else you choose. Creatures experiencing the *musical mural* have tactical disadvantage on Wisdom (Perception) checks as they lose track of their physical surroundings.

A creature that tries to resist the illusion can make a Wisdom saving throw when the spell is cast and at the beginning of each of its turns. A successful save ends the effect on that creature. A creature is also freed from the spell's effect if it is attacked.

Mystic Negation

5th-level abjuration
Cleric, Druid, Warlock, Wizard
Components: V, S
Casting Time: 1 action
Duration: Concentration, up to 1 minute
Range: 50 ft.
Area of Effect: Sphere, 30-ft. radius
Saving Throw: None

You create a dark, pulsing, 1-foot-diameter sphere of antimagic that hangs in the air at a point you can see within 50 feet of you. It automatically negates every spell (including your own) of 4th level or lower that's cast within 30 feet of the sphere. Spells of level 5 and higher are not affected. The sphere disappears after it counters three spells or when the spell's duration runs out.

At the beginning of your turn, you can move the sphere up to 60 feet as a bonus action.

Enhancement: For each spell slot used higher than 5th level, the maximum spell level the sphere can negate increases by one.

Nature's Aura

2nd-level transmutation
Druid, Ranger
Components: V, S
Casting Time: 1 action
Duration: Concentration, up to 1 hour
Range: Self
Area of Effect: Self
Saving Throw: None

You are surrounded by a calming, natural aura that puts animals and sentient plants at ease. During the duration of the spell, you can add 1d6 to your Charisma (Animal Handling) checks.

Nature's Aura

Nature's Repast

3rd-level transmutation
Druid
Components: V, S
Casting Time: 1 action
Duration: 7 days
Range: Self
Area of Effect: Self
Saving Throw: None

For the duration of this spell, the ground itself sustains you, so you don't need to eat or drink. If you lose contact with the ground for more than 1 round, the spell ends.

Nature's Strength

3rd-level transmutation
Druid, Ranger
Components: V, S
Casting Time: 1 action
Duration: Concentration, up to 10 minutes
Range: Self
Area of Effect: Self
Saving Throw: None

For the duration of *nature's strength*, you draw strength from the ground. You have tactical advantage on Strength-based ability checks and skill checks, and your carrying capacity doubles. Your attacks with Strength-based weapons do an additional 1d6 damage. If you lose contact with the earth for more than 1 round, the spell ends.

Nature's Support

6th-level transmutation
Druid
Components: V, S
Casting Time: 1 action
Duration: Concentration, up to 1 minute
Range: Self
Area of Effect: Self
Saving Throw: None

By drawing upon the earth's resilience, you transfer damage that you suffer into the ground. For the duration of the spell, the first 10 points of damage you take from each attack, area effect, environmental effect, or any other source is channeled into the ground you stand on. For example, the slash of a sword might cause a shallow furrow to appear in the ground. The spell ends if you lose contact with the earth for more than 1 round, or when the earth has absorbed 120 points of damage.

Nearsighted

1st-level transmutation
Warlock, Wizard
Components: V, S
Casting Time: 1 action
Duration: Concentration, up to 1 minute
Range: 30 ft.
Area of Effect: 1 creature
Saving Throw: Con / negates effect

Select a creature within range that you can see. That creature must make a Constitution saving throw. If it fails, it becomes nearsighted and has tactical disadvantage on attack rolls against targets further than 20 feet from it. The affected creature can repeat the saving throw at the end of each of its turns; a successful save ends the spell.

Necrotic Feast

1st-level necromancy
Cleric, Wizard
Components: V, S
Casting Time: 1 action
Duration: Instantaneous
Range: Touch
Area of Effect: Self
Saving Throw: None

You touch the corpse of a Small or larger creature that was slain in the past hour. You gain 5 (2d4) temporary hit points, which last until the end of your next rest. The corpse shrivels up and can't be animated.

Enhancement: For each spell slot used higher than 1st level, you can touch an additional corpse and gain 5 (2d4) additional temporary hit points for each corpse you touch.

Necrotic Touch

5th-level necromancy
Cleric, Wizard
Components: V, S, M (flesh from a corpse)
Casting Time: 1 action
Duration: Instantaneous
Range: Touch
Area of Effect: 1 creature
Saving Throw: Con / half damage

One creature you touch must make a Constitution saving throw. If the saving throw fails, the creature takes 6d10 necrotic damage and loses 1d4 points of Strength as its muscles wither. On a successful save, it takes half damage with no other effects.

Enhancement: For each spell slot used higher than 5th level, the spell does an additional 1d10 necrotic damage.

Negative Energy Aura

4th-level evocation
Cleric, Wizard
Components: V, S, M (flesh from a corpse)
Casting Time: 1 action
Duration: 10 minutes
Range: Self
Area of Effect: Self
Saving Throw: None

You surround yourself with an aura of necrotic energy that gives you resistance to necrotic damage. In addition, whenever a creature within 5 feet of you hits you with a melee attack, the attacker takes 2d8 necrotic damage.

Negative Energy Mantle

6th-level necromancy
Warlock, Wizard
Components: V, S
Casting Time: 1 action
Duration: 1 hour
Range: 120 ft.
Area of Effect: Sphere, 20-ft. radius
Saving Throw: Con / negates effect

You select a point you can see within range. A 20-foot-radius sphere of necrotic energy briefly flares around that point, then disappears. Each creature in the affected area must make a Constitution saving throw. If the saving throw fails, the creature can't regain hit points or gain temporary hit points for the duration of the spell.

Net

2nd-level conjuration
Druid, Sorcerer, Wizard
Components: V, S, M (a strand of woven seaweed)
Casting Time: 1 action
Duration: Concentration, up to 1 hour
Range: 120 ft.
Area of Effect: Sphere, 10-ft. radius
Saving Throw: Dex / negates effect

You create a net of seaweed that encloses a 10-foot-radius sphere around a point you can see. The target point must be underwater, but the entire sphere need not be. Each creature in the affected area when the spell is cast is caught inside the net and can't leave the netted area unless it uses an action on its turn to make a Strength saving throw; if the save succeeds, the creature breaks out of the net.

At the start of your next turn, the net collapses inward. All creatures inside it are restrained unless they make a successful Dexterity saving throw.

All trapped or restrained creatures are released at the end of the spell's duration.

Null the Soothing Touch

4th-level necromancy
Cleric
Components: V, S, M (powdered bone)
Casting Time: 1 action
Duration: Permanent
Range: Touch
Area of Effect: 1 creature
Saving Throw: Wis / negates effect

You touch a creature and curse it. The creature must make a Wisdom saving throw against curses. If the saving throw fails, the creature is cursed so that it can't regain hit points from magic. It can still benefit from resting and from nonmagical healing.

The spell can be ended by magic that removes a curse.

Nullifying Cloak

5th-level abjuration
Wizard
Components: V, S, M (a piece of lead)
Casting Time: 1 action
Duration: Concentration, up to 1 minute
Range: 120 ft.
Area of Effect: 1 creature
Saving Throw: Wis / negates effect

You cloak one creature you can see in a faint, silvery shimmer of light that suppresses its attempts to cast spells. The creature can make a Wisdom saving throw. If the saving throw fails, then whenever the creature tries to cast a spell during the duration of *nullifying cloak*, it must make an ability check using its spellcasting ability against your spell save DC. If the check fails, the spell is countered with no effect (the spell slot is expended) and the creature takes 2d6 radiant damage.

Nymph's Aura

6th-level enchantment
Bard
Components: V, S
Casting Time: 1 action
Duration: Concentration, up to 10 minutes
Range: Self
Area of Effect: Self
Saving Throw: None

You take on some of the unearthly beauty and presence of a nymph. For the duration of the spell, you can add 1d8 to your Charisma checks, Charisma-based skill checks, and Charisma saving throws.

Obliterate Soul

7th-level necromancy
Warlock, Wizard
Components: V, S, M (a pinch of bone dust)
Casting Time: 1 action
Duration: Instantaneous
Range: 30 ft.
Area of Effect: 1 living creature
Saving Throw: Con / half damage

Select one living creature you can see. That creature's body is attacked by spirits of the underworld. It must make a Constitution saving throw. If the saving throw fails, the creature takes 8d6 + 20 necrotic damage and its maximum hit points are reduced by the same number; on a successful save, the creature takes half damage and its maximum hit points are not reduced. If the creature is killed by this spell, its soul is ripped from its body and imprisoned on one of the lower planes. If this happens, the creature's soul can be freed only by the use of a *resurrection* or *wish spell*; *raise dead* has no effect on it.

Ogre's Visage

6th-level transmutation
Wizard
Components: V, S, M (a drop of ogre blood)
Casting Time: 1 action
Duration: Concentration, up to 1 hour
Range: Touch
Area of Effect: 1 creature
Saving Throw: Wis / negates effect

One Small or Medium humanoid you touch changes into an ogre-like creature. The targeted creature can choose to make a Wisdom saving throw to avoid the effect. If the saving throw fails or the creature chooses not to make one, it increases in height to 9 feet tall and its ability scores change to Strength 19, Dexterity 8, Constitution 16, Intelligence 5, Wisdom 7, and Charisma 7. Any equipment or armor it possesses grow with it; its weapons do twice their normal number of damage dice.

The creature and its gear return to normal when the spell ends.

One with the Earth

6th-level conjuration
Cleric, Druid
Components: V, S
Casting Time: 1 action
Duration: Concentration, up to 1 minute
Range: Self
Area of Effect: Self
Saving Throw: None

You gain the ability to enter a large block of stone and move magically to another block of stone in the same manner as the *tree stride* spell. Unlike *tree stride*, the nature of the rock you enter and leave determines how far you can move. Use the lower value when moving between different types of material.

Natural Stone: 3,000 feet
Worked Stone: 2,000 feet
Earthen Mound: 1,000 feet
Sand Dune: 500 feet

This spell was first granted to the dwarves by the gods, although it is now known to many other races.

Ooze Bolt

3rd-level evocation
Sorcerer, Wizard
Components: V, S
Casting Time: 1 action
Duration: Concentration, up to 1 minute
Range: 30 ft.
Area of Effect: 1 creature
Saving Throw: None

You shoot a bolt of corrosive ooze at one creature you can see. Make a ranged spell attack against that creature. If it hits, the creature takes 6d4 acid damage immediately and an additional 4d4 acid damage at the end of each of its turns for the duration of the spell.

Enhancement: For each spell slot used higher than 3rd level, *ooze bolt* does an additional 2d4 acid damage on its initial hit.

Open Trail

2nd-level transmutation
Druid, Ranger
Components: V, S
Casting Time: 1 action
Duration: Concentration, up to 1 hour
Range: Touch
Area of Effect: Path, 20 ft. long, 5 ft. wide, 6 ft. high
Saving Throw: None

You gain the ability to open a narrow pathway through thick plant growth. The opening is 5 feet wide, 6 feet high, and 20 feet long. It starts in your space and extends in a direction you choose. The path moves with you as you move, so you always have 15 feet of clear path ahead of you through even the thickest growth. Plants move or bend away from the trail and then close behind you, leaving no sign that anyone passed through. Other creatures have tactical disadvantage on ability checks to track you through areas where you traveled by *open trail*.

Paean of Greater Glory

Otter's Grace

1st-level transmutation
Druid, Ranger
Components: V, M (a fish bone)
Casting Time: 1 action
Duration: 10 minutes
Range: Touch
Area of Effect: 1 creature
Saving Throw: None

One creature you touch gains the grace of an otter. The creature has tactical advantage on Strength (Athletics) checks to swim and can hold its breath twice as long as normal.

Enhancement: For each spell slot used higher than 1st level, you can affect one additional creature.

Outside of Time

8th-level conjuration
Wizard
Components: V, S
Casting Time: 1 action
Duration: 24 hours
Range: 30 ft.
Area of Effect: 1 creature
Saving Throw: None

You shunt one willing creature or object to an extradimensional space where time doesn't exist. Any concentration spells the creature was maintaining end immediately. You decide how long the extradimensional space lasts, up to 24 hours, when you cast *outside of time*.

While it is outside of time, the target creature can't be located with divination magic. Not even a *wish* or *miracle* can bring the target back earlier; it's as if it doesn't exist at all.

When the spell ends, the target returns to the same location it disappeared from. If some other object occupies that space, the target is harmlessly displaced into the nearest open space. For the target, no time has elapsed; it's not even aware it was gone. Any timed or ongoing effects that were active on the target creature (with the exception of spells that were being maintained with concentration) continue from where they left off, since those effects skipped through time with the creature.

Paean of Greater Glory

4th-level enchantment
Bard
Components: V
Casting Time: 1 action
Duration: Concentration, up to 1 minute
Range: 100 ft.
Area of Effect: 1 or more creatures
Saving Throw: None

You fill the air with a powerful song of glory that inspires your allies and bolsters their spirit. Choose any number of willing creatures within range. For the duration of the spell, an affected creature gets tactical advantage on saving throws against being frightened; it adds 1d4 to its attack rolls; and whenever it makes a damage roll and dislikes the result, it can reroll the dice and choose to use either the first or second result.

Paean of the Holy

4th-level enchantment
Paladin
Components: V, S
Casting Time: 1 action
Duration: Concentration, up to 1 minute
Range: 40 ft.
Area of Effect: 1 or more creatures
Saving Throw: None

You fill the air with an angelic chorus. Choose any number of willing creatures within range and one of the options below. For the duration of the spell, each of those creatures benefits from that option.

• *Paean of Glory:* Each creature gains +2 AC and has tactical advantage on Wisdom saving throws.

• *Paean of Judgment:* Each creature does an additional 1d6 radiant damage with weapon attacks and their weapons attacks are magical.

• *Paean of Blessing:* Each creature adds 1d6 to its attack rolls.

• *Paean of Light:* Each creature adds 1d6 to its saving throws.

Pain of Giving

2nd-level necromancy
Warlock, Wizard
Components: V, S, M (eye of a crow)
Casting Time: 1 action
Duration: 1 hour
Range: Touch
Area of Effect: 1 creature
Saving Throw: Wis / negates effect

You touch a creature, and it becomes cursed unless it makes a successful Wisdom saving throw. While cursed, the creature takes 2d6 necrotic damage whenever it uses the Help action, Medicine skill, or restores hit points to another creature with a spell.

The *pain of giving* curse can be lifted by magic that removes a curse.

Paper Tigers

4th-level illusion
Bard
Components: V, S, M (four paper, origami tigers, which are consumed by the spell)
Casting Time: 1 action
Duration: Concentration, up to 1 hour
Range: 30 ft.
Area of Effect: 4 tigers
Saving Throw: None

You release four origami tigers that grow into real-appearing tigers under your control. Only one of the tigers is actually real, however; the others have no more substance than a *mirror image*. The real tiger uses the standard stat block for a tiger. The unreal tigers disappear if they take damage or fail a saving throw. At the beginning of your turn, as a bonus action, you can direct each tiger to move up to its speed, and you can direct the real tiger to attack. Each tiger follows your commands absolutely. The spell ends when the real tiger is killed. All tigers disappear when the spell ends, leaving only scraps of paper.

Pattern Grass

1st-level transmutation
Druid, Ranger
Components: V, S
Casting Time: 1 action
Duration: 1 hour
Range: 120 ft.
Area of Effect: Circle, 20-ft. radius
Saving Throw: None

You temporarily flatten grass, cane, or other soft-stemmed plants in a 20-foot-radius circle around a point you can see within range. Any creatures that are Small or larger in the area are revealed. The soft-stemmed plants recover after the spell is over, but the flattening of the plants makes tracking through the area difficult; Wisdom (Survival) checks for tracking in areas affected by this spell are made with tactical disadvantage. Since the flattened area isn't enormous, a good tracker probably can pick up the trail again at the edge of the affected area unless further steps are taken to prevent that.

Peacebinding

4th-level enchantment
Paladin
Components: V, S
Casting Time: 1 action
Duration: Concentration, up to 10 minutes
Range: Self
Area of Effect: Sphere, 60-ft. radius
Saving Throw: Wis / negates effect

To cast this spell, you must be holding at least one weapon in your hand, and you must sheathe, sling, or drop every weapon you hold as the spell is cast. Each creature within the area of effect must make a Wisdom saving throw. If a creature fails its saving throw, it too must put away its weapons, and it can't attack or cast a spell that adversely affects its target for the duration of the *peacebinding*.

If a creature under the effect of *peacebinding* is attacked, it is automatically released from the effect. If you draw a weapon or attack any creature, the spell ends immediately.

Pepper's Purpose

Enchantment cantrip
Bard, Druid, Wizard
Components: S, M (a pinch of pepper)
Casting Time: 1 action
Duration: Instantaneous
Range: 50 ft.
Area of Effect: 1 creature
Saving Throw: Con / negates effect

One creature you can see sneezes loudly unless it makes a successful Constitution saving throw.

Phantom Accompaniment

2nd-level illusion
Bard
Components: V, S, M (a small candle)
Casting Time: 1 action
Duration: Concentration, up to 10 minutes
Range: Self
Area of Effect: Self
Saving Throw: None

For the duration of this spell, when you play a musical instrument, a phantom ensemble plays along with you. The ensemble can be up to ten performers on any type of instrument, or vocalists. You can add 1d6 to your Charisma ability and skill checks while the phantom ensemble is accompanying you.

Phoenix Cloak

9th-level necromancy
Cleric
Components: V, S, M (a diamond worth at least 500 gp)
Casting Time: 1 minute
Duration: 1 hour
Range: Touch
Area of Effect: 1 to 6 creatures
Saving Throw: None

You touch up to six willing creatures when you cast this spell, binding them all into its shared effect. The next time one of these creatures dies before the spell ends, it returns to life at the beginning of its next turn with 1 hit point as if *raise dead* had been cast upon it, with all the bonuses and penalties conferred by that spell. The *phoenix cloak* spell then ends.

Piercing Vision

4th-level divination
Wizard
Components: V, S
Casting Time: 1 action
Duration: Concentration, up to 1 minute
Range: Self
Area of Effect: Self
Saving Throw: None

You gain the ability to see through up to one inch of metal, wood, or leather while the spell lasts.

Enhancement: When you cast *piercing vision* with a 6th-level or higher spell slot, you can see through up to 1 foot of material.

Pilfer Sleep

1st-level necromancy
Warlock, Wizard
Components: V, S
Casting Time: 1 action
Duration: Instantaneous
Range: Touch
Area of Effect: 1 creature
Saving Throw: Con / negates effect

One creature you touch must make a Constitution saving throw. If it fails the save, you lose one level of exhaustion and it gains one level of exhaustion. It can still gain a level of exhaustion even if you don't have one to transfer, but in that case, the targeted creature makes its saving throw with tactical advantage.

Plant Form

6th-level transmutation
Druid
Components: V, S, M (a jade statue of you, worth at least 150 gold pieces)
Casting Time: 1 action
Duration: Concentration, up to 1 hour
Range: Self
Area of Effect: Self
Saving Throw: None

You take on some of the attributes of plant creatures: your skin becomes like bark and your hair like leaves. Until the spell ends, your base AC becomes 17, you gain resistance to psychic and poison damage, you are immune to stunning, and you have tactical advantage on saving throws against poison.

Player Instrument

3rd-level transmutation
Bard
Components: V, S
Casting Time: 1 action
Duration: Concentration, up to 10 minutes
Range: 100 ft.
Area of Effect: 1 instrument
Saving Throw: None

One musical instrument you can see begins to play as if you were playing it. Make a Charisma (Performance) check to determine the quality of the playing: 1-9 = mediocre; 10-14 = skillful; 15+ = excellent. The instrument plays the music of your choice until the spell ends. For the duration of the spell, the instrument can be the source of any of your abilities that require performance.

Pocket Paradise

7th-level conjuration
Bard
Components: V, S
Casting Time: 1 action
Duration: 24 hours
Range: 100 ft.
Area of Effect: Sphere, 300-ft. radius
Saving Throw: None

You render a performance in song, oration, or music that evokes the image of a lush paradise. As the performance continues, your description grows more vivid in the minds of the viewers, until after one minute all willing creatures within range find themselves physically transported to the location you've described.

The exact design is left to you, but typical paradises resemble balmy tropical islands, silk-strewn seraglios, or crystal towers atop craggy mountains. Whatever the appearance, the total area of the paradise is a 300-foot-radius sphere.

Those within the paradise find themselves the subject of pampered treatment at the hands of a staff of illusory servitors. Delicious food and drink are plentiful. The paradise has a soothing effect on the minds of those within it. Creatures who rest at least one hour in the paradise find themselves cured, healed, or recovered from all exhaustion, fright, poison, and stun.

A creature can opt to leave the paradise at any time before the spell's duration expires. Once someone leaves, they can't return. If you leave, the spell ends and everyone remaining inside is ejected as well, returning to the spot they came from during your performance. Any items you take from the paradise vanish when you leave.

Pollen Cloud

2nd-level conjuration
Druid
Components: V, S, M (pinch of pollen)
Casting Time: 1 action
Duration: Concentration, up to 1 minute
Range: 100 ft.
Area of Effect: Sphere, 20-ft. radius
Saving Throw: Con / negates effect

You create a cloud of pollen and airborne seeds in a 20-foot-radius sphere around a point you can see. The cloud spreads around corners, and its area is lightly obscured. The cloud disappears when the spell ends.

Any creature that is inside the cloud at the start of its turn becomes poisoned unless it makes a successful Constitution saving throw against poison. The condition lasts until the spell's duration ends. Creatures that don't need to breathe are immune to this effect.

A moderate wind disperses the cloud after four rounds. A strong wind disperses it in one round.

Portrait

4th-level divination
Bard, Wizard
Components: V, S, M (paint and brush)
Casting Time: 10 minutes
Duration: Permanent
Range: 30 ft.
Area of Effect: 1 object
Saving Throw: None

You create a picture of the last creature to have touched an object you can see within range. The picture appears to be an oil painting on canvas, representing the creature as it appeared when it touched the object; as a result, the spell can be deceptive if the creature was disguised or had an illusory appearance. The spell will not function if the object was last touched more than a week ago.

Precision of Arms

2nd-level divination
Warlock, Wizard
Components: V, S
Casting Time: 1 action
Duration: Concentration, up to 1 minute
Range: Self
Area of Effect: Self
Saving Throw: None

For the duration of this spell, your attacks become more accurate. You score a critical hit on a roll of 19 or 20, and your critical hits get two bonus damage dice instead of one.

Prey's Scent

5th-level transmutation
Druid
Components: V, S
Casting Time: 1 action
Duration: 24 hours
Range: Touch
Area of Effect: 1 creature
Saving Throw: Con / negates effect

You make a creature smell delicious to carnivores. If the creature fails a Constitution saving throw, all lycanthropes and beasts have tactical advantage on ability checks they make to detect the target for the duration of *prey's scent*. A lycanthrope or beast that is aware of the target must attack it, but it can choose to make a Wisdom saving throw at the start of each of its turns; if the saving throw succeeds, the urge to attack is suppressed until the start of the lycanthrope's or beast's next turn. This saving throw is voluntary.

Profane Link

4th-level necromancy
Cleric, Wizard
Components: V, S
Casting Time: 1 action
Duration: 24 hours
Range: Touch
Area of Effect: 1 undead creature
Saving Throw: None

You create a link between yourself and a willing undead creature you touch. While the spell lasts, you can select the creature as the target of any touch spells you cast, even if you can't physically touch the creature, as long as you are both on the same plane of existence.

Projectile Link

4th-level transmutation
Wizard
Components: V, S
Casting Time: 1 action
Duration: Concentration, up to 1 minute
Range: Self
Area of Effect: 1 projectile
Saving Throw: None

For the duration of the spell, you gain the ability to deliver your touch spells through missile projectiles. When you cast a spell with the range of touch, you can, as part of the same action, make a regular ranged weapon attack. If the ranged weapon attack hits, it does damage as normal and also triggers the effect of the spell.

If the spell normally requires an attack roll to hit, then that roll is considered automatically successful; the ranged weapon attack roll replaces it. Spells that allow saving throws still allow them.

If the ranged weapon attack misses, then the spell is expended with no effect.

Protection from Oozes

1st-level abjuration
Druid
Components: V, S, M (salt)
Casting Time: 1 action
Duration: Concentration, up to 10 minutes
Range: Touch
Area of Effect: 1 creature
Saving Throw: None

You ward one creature against attacks from oozes. For the duration of the spell, oozes have tactical disadvantage on attack rolls against that creature, and the target has resistance to acid damage caused by oozes.

Protection from Paralysis

2nd-level abjuration
Cleric, Wizard
Components: V, S
Casting Time: 1 action
Duration: Concentration, up to 10 minute
Range: Touch
Area of Effect: 1 creature
Saving Throw: None

For the duration of this spell, the target creature is immune to paralysis. If it was already paralyzed, its paralysis ends while the spell is in effect.

Protection from Pressure

3rd-level abjuration
Cleric, Wizard
Components: V, S
Casting Time: 1 action
Duration: 1 hour
Range: Touch
Area of Effect: 1 creature
Saving Throw: None

For the duration of the spell, one creature is immune to all the effects of high pressure caused by being deep underwater, in a pressure chamber, buried under an avalanche or cave-in, and similar situations. The creature also has resistance against bludgeoning damage caused by its surroundings, but not by hostile creatures. The spell doesn't protect against piercing or slashing damage from rocks, trees, or other sharp objects.

Pummel

1st-level transmutation
Druid
Components: V, S
Casting Time: 1 action
Duration: Instantaneous
Range: Touch
Area of Effect: 1 fallen tree branch
Saving Throw: Dex / negates immobilization

You animate a fallen branch as a projectile and launch it at one creature within 30 feet. Make a ranged spell attack against the target creature. If the attack hits, the creature takes 3d6 bludgeoning damage and must make a Dexterity saving throw. If the saving throw fails, the creature's speed becomes 0 until the end of its next turn.

Enhancement: For each spell slot used higher than 1st level, the spell does an additional 1d6 damage.

Purifying Bath

4th-level transmutation
Warlock, Wizard
Components: V, S, M (spirit doll, bath of special oils worth 100 gp)
Casting Time: 1 hour
Duration: Permanent
Range: Touch
Area of Effect: 1 spirit doll
Saving Throw: None

You wash a spirit doll while casting this spell to enhance its power. Any spells that allow a creature to regain hit points can be cast directly on the doll and still affect the creature linked to the doll. Likewise, protection spells can also be transferred to the linked creature through the doll.

Purple Haze

7th-level enchantment
Cleric
Components: V, S
Casting Time: 1 action
Duration: Concentration, up to 1 minute
Range: 60 ft.
Area of Effect: Sphere, 20-ft. radius
Saving Throw: Wis partial

You cause the air in a 20-foot-radius sphere around a point you can see to take on a purplish tinge. Each creature that starts its turn in the area becomes *confused* (per the spell) for as long as it remains in the area unless it makes a successful Wisdom saving throw. If the saving throw succeeds, the creature is not *confused* but it instead becomes poisoned for as long as it remains in the area of the spell.

Push

1st-level evocation
Sorcerer, Wizard
Components: V, S
Casting Time: 1 action
Duration: Instantaneous
Range: 30 ft.
Area of Effect: 1 creature
Saving Throw: Str / negates push

You send a blast of force at one object or creature within range. A free-standing object that no one is holding onto is pushed 10 feet away from you. If the target is a creature or an object that a creature is holding, the creature must make a Strength saving throw. The target is pushed 10 feet if the saving throw fails. Only creatures and objects that are Large or smaller can be affected.

Putrefy Food and Drink

1st-level transmutation
Cleric, Druid
Components: V, S
Casting Time: 1 action
Duration: Instantaneous
Range: 10 ft.
Area of Effect: Sphere, 5-ft. radius
Saving Throw: None (for poisoned food); Con / negates poisoning (for creatures consuming poisoned food)

All nonmagical food and drink within a 5-foot-radius sphere of the spell's target point becomes poisoned. Any creature consuming the food or drink must make a Constitution saving throw or become poisoned for 1 hour.

Quell the Wild

2nd-level illusion
Druid, Ranger
Components: V, S
Casting Time: 1 action

Putrefy Food & Drink

Duration: Concentration, up to 1 minute
Range: Self
Area of Effect: Sphere, 30-ft. radius
Saving Throw: None

For the duration of the spell, you suppress the noise of natural wildlife so that no creature within 30 feet of you can hear it. The sphere moves with you. Note that other noises–the movement or breathing of an assassin or of stealthily creeping orcs, for example–is unaffected.

Quick Change

1st-level transmutation
Bard, Wizard
Components: V, S
Casting Time: 1 action
Duration: Instantaneous
Range: 30 ft.
Area of Effect: 1 or 2 creatures
Saving Throw: Wis / negates effect

You switch your clothing with one other set of clothing that you can see, or you switch any two sets of clothing you can see. If any of that clothing is being worn by a creature that's not willing to be affected by this spell, it can make a Wisdom saving throw. A successful save negates the spell.

Quick change does not exchange magical items or items that are held. Everything else that's nonmagical–armor, cloaks, rings, backpacks, sheathed weapons–is exchanged. Clothing is not resized for the new wearer. If an item can't physically fit on the recipient, it appears on the ground adjacent to the recipient.

Quicken Assassin

9th-level transmutation
Wizard
Components: V, S, M (an item belonging to the target, and raw materials worth 50,000 gold pieces, which are expended in the casting)
Casting Time: 4 hours
Duration: Permanent
Range: Touch
Area of Effect: 1 creature
Saving Throw: None

You create a copy of an individual, and that copy becomes the original person's assassin. The assassin has no soul, but it is a living, breathing creature that is identical in every way to the person it was created to kill. It has all of the skills, feats, powers, and abilities of the original creature, plus enough of its memories and personality to get a +10 modifier on Charisma (Deception) checks to impersonate the intended victim.

The assassin knows that it is a duplicate, and it will do anything to eliminate its target and assume the target's life. You have a telepathic link to it, and it is unquestioningly loyal to you. Once it eliminates the original, the assassin follows your commands. Powerful wizards have been known to replace independent rulers with copies that were completely loyal to their creators.

Unlike normal living creatures, a *quickened assassin* has no soul to give it a strong will to survive. When reduced to 0 hit points, it dies immediately and crumbles to dust.

Quicksand

4th-level transmutation
Druid
Components: V, S, M (a small amount of water and sand)
Casting Time: 1 minute
Duration: 1 hour

Range: 50 ft.
Area of Effect: Cube of ground, 10 ft. square
Saving Throw: Dex / negates effect

You transform a 10-foot-by-10 foot area of ground or normal dirt, sand, or stone floor you can see into a 10-foot-deep pool of quicksand. Creatures on the transformed area when the spell is cast jump to the nearest safe space with a successful Dexterity saving throw. Creatures that fail the saving throw or that enter the quicksand afterward quickly sink into it; their speed is reduced to 5 feet or to their Swim speed, if they have one. Climbing out of the quicksand requires a successful DC 15 Strength (Athletics) check.

The floor returns to its normal condition at the end of the spell. Any creatures or items in the quicksand when the spell ends are squeezed upward and deposited on top of the surface when it returns to normal.

Quill Skin

1st-level transmutation
Druid
Components: V, S
Casting Time: 1 action
Duration: 1 minute
Range: Self
Area of Effect: Self
Saving Throw: None

Your skin grows quills, which provide you with a +1 AC bonus. An adjacent creature that hits you with a melee attack takes 1d4 piercing damage from quills.

Rainbow Spear

4th-level evocation
Sorcerer, Wizard
Components: V, S
Casting Time: 1 action
Duration: Instantaneous
Range: Self
Area of Effect: 3 spears
Saving Throw: varies

You create three spears of varying colors and throw them at one or more creatures within 30 feet. Spears can be thrown at the same target or at different targets. Make a ranged spell attack for each spear. If it hits, roll 1d8 to determine its effect.

D8	Color	Effect
1-2	Red	4d6 fire damage
3	Orange	4d6 acid damage
4	Yellow	2d6 frost damage and speed reduced by 10 feet (Con save negates speed loss)
5	Green	2d6 poison damage and poisoned (Con save negates condition)
6	Blue	4d6 lightning damage
7	Indigo	2d6 thunder damage and stunned (Con save negates stun)
8	Violet	4d6 thunder damage

Effects beyond damage are negated by a successful Constitution saving throw. If the saving throw fails, the creature can repeat the saving throw at the end of each of its turns; a successful save ends the effect.

Enhancement: For each two spell slots used higher than 4th level, you gain one additional spear. If you spend 2 sorcery points when you cast this spell, you can choose the effect of each spear instead of rolling.

Rainbow Staff

5th-level evocation
Sorcerer, Wizard
Components: V, S
Casting Time: 1 action
Duration: 1 minute
Range: Self
Area of Effect: Self
Saving Throw: Special

A staff of shifting, rainbow colors appears in your hand. When you cast *rainbow staff*, and as an action on your following turns, you can make a melee spell attack with the staff against one creature you can reach. If the attack hits, roll 1d8 to determine the effect of the blow.

d8	Color	Effect
1-2	Red	3d6 fire damage
3	Orange	3d6 acid damage
4	Yellow	2d6 frost damage and speed reduced by 10 feet (Con save negates speed reduction)
5	Green	2d6 poison damage and poisoned (Con save negates poisoning)
6	Blue	3d6 lightning damage
7	Indigo	1d6 thunder damage and stunned (Con save negates stun)
8	Violet	3d6 thunder damage

Effects beyond damage are negated by a successful Constitution saving throw. If the saving throw fails, the creature can repeat the saving throw at the end of each of its turns; a successful save ends the effect.

Enhancement: If you spend 1 sorcery point when you hit with this staff, you can choose the effect of the strike instead of rolling.

Raise Island

7th-level conjuration
Wizard
Components: V, S, M (a piece of granite thrown into the sea)
Casting Time: 1 minute
Duration: 7 days
Range: 300 ft.
Area of Effect: 1 rock slab, 1,000 ft. sq., 10 ft. thick
Saving Throw: None

You conjure a slab of bare rock 1,000 feet square and 10 feet thick that floats, immobile, on the surface of a body of water. The water must have enough surface area to accommodate the rock slab; it can't be conjured in a swimming pool, for example.

Raise Shipwreck

8th-level evocation
Wizard
Components: V, S
Casting Time: 1 minute
Duration: Concentration, up to 2 hours
Range: Touch
Area of Effect: 1 ship
Saving Throw: None

You raise one sunken that you touch to the water's surface, where it remains for the duration of the spell. The ship rises at the rate of 10 feet per round. The spell is effective on a vessel of any size. If the ship is broken into pieces, all its different parts are raised, as long as they are all

Raise Shipwreck

in the same general area.

It's important to note that *raise shipwreck* doesn't repair a damaged vessel or reassemble a broken one into a seaworthy craft when the vessel reaches the surface. If it had a hole in the hull, the hole is still there; if it was broken in half, it's still in two pieces. At the end of the spell's duration, a damaged ship is likely to sink again unless other steps are taken to repair it, keep it on the surface, or get it out of the water.

Ravaging Fire

9th-level conjuration
Druid
Components: V, S
Casting Time: 1 action
Duration: Concentration, up to 1 minute
Range: 400 ft.
Area of Effect: Sphere, 100-ft. radius
Saving Throw: Dex / half damage; Con / half damage

You create an eruption of burning rocks and magma in a 100-foot-radius sphere centered on a point you can see. At the beginning of each of your turns, you can use a bonus action to move the sphere 20 feet in the direction of your choice.

Each creature that begins its turn in the affected area or that enters the area must make both a Dexterity saving throw and a Constitution saving throw. If the creature fails the Dexterity save, it takes 6d6 bludgeoning damage from falling rocks. If the creature fails the Constitution save, it takes 6d6 fire damage from the heat. In both cases, a creature takes half damage with a successful save.

Flammable objects burn in the cloud, and stone and metal structures warp and deform. The soil becomes ashen and unable to bear life for the next 1d4 years unless special measures are used to restore it.

Regenerate Plant

2nd-level evocation
Druid
Components: V, S
Casting Time: 1 action
Duration: Concentration, up to 1 minute
Range: 50 ft.
Area of Effect: 1 plant creature
Saving Throw: None

One plant creature you can see gains regeneration. At the beginning of each of its turns, it heals 10 hit points. This ability doesn't work on a turn when the creature took acid or fire damage since its previous turn.

Remember Seas

4th-level transmutation
Wizard
Components: V, S
Casting Time: 1 action
Duration: Permanent
Range: Touch
Area of Effect: 1 ship
Saving Throw: None

You cast this spell on the ship's wheel to make it "memorize" the course you follow for the next 12 hours. The journey thus programmed into the wheel's "memory" remains until it is replaced by a new journey or dispelled. During any future trip through this area, the wheel doesn't need anyone controlling it. Upon command, it can steer itself to any point stored in its "memory." If it passes beyond the boundary of a recorded journey, it begins drifting aimlessly until a pilot or helmsman takes. A ship's wheel can hold only one journey in "memory" at a time.

Reshape Metal

3rd-level transmutation
Wizard
Components: V, S
Casting Time: 1 action
Duration: Permanent
Range: Touch
Area of Effect: 1 metal object up to 50 lbs.
Saving Throw: None

At your touch, a metal object becomes soft and malleable like clay. You can reshape it into any form you want. You must knead and mold the metal to reshape it, but you don't need artistic talent to make it look the way you want. You only need to picture the desired form in your mind, and the magic accomplishes in a single round what your hands can't. Once the object takes its new form, the metal returns to its original hardness in the new shape.

If the item is shaped into a weapon, its damage matches its new form. The spell does not work on an item held by an unwilling creature or on creatures made of metal. It can't increase or decrease the amount of metal in the object.

Resist Channeling

5th-level transmutation
Wizard
Components: V, S
Casting Time: 1 action
Duration: Permanent
Range: Touch
Area of Effect: 1 undead creature
Saving Throw: None

One undead creature you touch gets combat advantage on saving throws against Turn Undead.

Resonant Imbalance

3rd-level evocation
Bard
Components: V, S
Casting Time: 1 action
Duration: Concentration, up to 1 minute
Range: Self
Area of Effect: Cone, 30 ft. long
Saving Throw: Con / negates effect

Your voice creates a reverberating, 30-foot cone of dissonance. Every creature in the cone is incapacitated unless it makes a successful Constitution saving throw. An incapacitated creature can repeat the saving throw at the end of each of its turns; a successful save ends the effect on that creature.

Restore the Undead

3rd-level necromancy
Cleric, Wizard
Components: V, S
Casting Time: 1 action
Duration: Instantaneous
Range: Self
Area of Effect: Sphere, 30-ft. radius
Saving Throw: None

Each zombie and skeleton within 30 feet of you regains all of its lost hit points. This spell does not affect creatures that have been reduced to 0 hit points or those of CR 3 or higher.

Retribution

3rd-level divination
Cleric, Paladin
Components: V, S
Casting Time: 1 reaction
Duration: Concentration, up to 1 minute
Range: Self
Area of Effect: Self
Saving Throw: None

This spell is cast as a reaction after a creature strikes you with a weapon. For the duration of the spell, you add 1d6 to your attack rolls against the creature that struck you. If another creature strikes you during *retribution's* duration, you can re-target the spell and get that bonus against that creature instead.

Revelation Field

7th-level abjuration
Bard, Cleric, Wizard
Components: V, S
Casting Time: 1 action
Duration: Concentration, up to 10 minutes
Range: Self
Area of Effect: Sphere, 30-ft. radius
Saving Throw: None

You create a field of energy in a 30-foot sphere around you that reveals the true forms of everything in it. The field moves with you. All illusions are suppressed for as long as they are in the field, and creatures with altered shapes are perceived in their original form, although the spell doesn't cause them to physically revert to that form. Disguised or invisible creatures are also revealed.

Reverence

5th-level enchantment
Bard, Cleric
Components: V, S
Casting Time: 1 action
Duration: 24 hours
Range: 50 ft.
Area of Effect: 1 creature
Saving Throw: Cha / negates effect

Choose a creature you can see within range. That creature makes a Charisma saving throw. If it fails, it is overcome by such reverence for you that it can take no action that would hurt or adversely affect you, although it is not constrained against attacking your friends. The spell ends if you attack or otherwise attempt to harm that creature.

Righteous Cloak

4th-level abjuration
Cleric, Paladin
Components: V, S
Casting Time: 1 action
Duration: Concentration, up to 1 minute
Range: Self
Area of Effect: Sphere, 30-ft. radius
Saving Throw: None

You create a shining, silver-white cloak of energy that surrounds and protects you. For the duration of the spell, whenever you or an allied creature within 30 feet of you makes an attack roll or a saving throw, add 1d4 to the roll. In addition, any creature that strikes you with a melee attack is blinded until the end of its next turn unless it makes a successful Constitution saving throw.

Rimeshatter

9th-level evocation
Druid, Wizard
Components: V, S, M (a shard of glass)
Casting Time: 1 action
Duration: Instantaneous
Range: 250 ft.
Area of Effect: Sphere, 30-ft. radius
Saving Throw: Con / half damage

You fill a 60-foot sphere centered on a point you can see with bitter, freezing cold. Each creature in the affected area must make a Constitution saving throw. If the saving throw fails, the creature takes 8d6 + 20 damage and is restrained until it escapes or the spell ends, as it is encased in ice. On a successful save, the creature takes half damage and is restrained until the end of its next turn.

A restrained creature can escape by using an action and making a successful Strength check against your spell saving throw DC.

A creature reduced to 0 hit points by this spell dies instantly when its body shatters into frozen chunks.

Rock Bolt

1st-level conjuration
Wizard
Components: V, S
Casting Time: 1 action
Duration: Instantaneous
Range: 30 ft.
Area of Effect: 1 creature
Saving Throw: Str / negates being knocked prone

You create a rock and throw it at a creature you can see within range. Make a ranged spell attack roll against the target. If it hits, the spell does 4d6 bludgeoning damage and the creature must make a Strength saving throw or be knocked prone.

Enhancement: For each spell slot used higher than 1st level, the spell does an additional 1d6 damage.

Rooted in Place

2nd-level transmutation
Druid
Components: V, S
Casting Time: 1 action
Duration: Concentration, up to 1 minute
Range: Touch
Area of Effect: 1 creature
Saving Throw: Con / negates effect

One creature you touch must make a Constitution saving throw. If the saving throw fails, its legs (or their equivalents) sprout roots that force their way into the earth, anchoring it in place. The creature can't move or be moved for the duration of the effect.

As an attack, the creature can try to cut the roots; they have AC 8 and 3d6 hit points, and are immune to all but slashing and fire damage. When damage is done to the roots, the rooted creature takes identical damage. The creature is free to move and the spell ends if the roots are fully severed.

Sacred Aegis

7th-level transmutation
Cleric
Components: V, S
Casting Time: 1 action

Duration: Concentration, up to 1 minute
Range: 30 ft.
Area of Effect: Self plus 1, 2, or 3 creatures
Saving Throw: None

You summon from the heavens a great spear of white light that touches you and up to three creatures of your choice that you can see. For the duration, each creature touched by the light emits dim light in a 10-foot radius and has tactical advantage on Strength, Dexterity, and Constitution saving throws. In addition, affected creatures add 1d6 to their attack rolls.

Sacred Champion

5th-level transmutation
Cleric, Paladin
Components: V, S
Casting Time: 1 action
Duration: Concentration, up to 10 minutes
Range: Touch
Area of Effect: 1 creature
Saving Throw: None

For the duration of the spell, one creature you touch has tactical advantage when it makes an attack roll against a fiend, and fiends suffer tactical disadvantage when they make attack rolls against the *sacred champion*.

Safeguarded Slumber

2nd-level necromancy
Wizard
Components: V, S
Casting Time: 1 action
Duration: 7 days
Range: Touch
Area of Effect: 1 creature with 0 hps
Saving Throw: None

You touch a creature that has 0 hit points. For the duration of the spell, the creature is locked in a protective coma; it doesn't need to make death saving throws (even when it takes damage), and it doesn't need food or water to survive. The affected creature still shows signs of life, though an observer might need to look closely to detect them. The spell ends when the creature regains hit points.

Sanctified Reverie of Arms

2nd-level transmutation
Paladin
Components: V, S
Casting Time: 1 action
Duration: Concentration, up to 1 minute
Range: Self
Area of Effect: Self
Saving Throw: None

You combine religious meditations with weapon training to greatly enhance your fighting ability. For the duration of this spell, whenever you use an attack action, you can make one additional attack. You must chant throughout the duration of this spell; the effect ends if you are unable to do so, and you can't cast other spells while chanting.

Sand Blast

3rd-level conjuration
Sorcerer, Wizard
Components: V, S, M (a pinch of sand)
Casting Time: 1 action
Duration: Instantaneous
Range: Self
Area of Effect: Cone, 30 ft. long

Saving Throw: Dex / half damage

Hot sand blasts in a 30-foot cone from your outstretched hand. Every creature in the cone must make a Dexterity saving throw. If the saving throw fails, the creature takes 6d6 fire damage and is blinded until the start of your next turn. If the saving throw succeeds, the creature takes half damage and is not blinded. The blast extinguishes open flames such as candles, torches, and even small fires in the cone.

Sandbody

2nd-level transmutation
Druid
Components: V, S, M (a pinch of sand)
Casting Time: 1 action
Duration: Concentration, up to 1 minute
Range: Self
Area of Effect: Self
Saving Throw: None

You transform your body into sand. For the duration of the spell, you gain resistance to slashing and piercing damage and you have tactical advantage on Dexterity (Stealth) checks made in sandy environments.

Sanguine Creatures

7th-level necromancy
Cleric
Components: V, S
Casting Time: 1 action
Duration: Concentration, up to 1 hour
Range: 50 ft.
Area of Effect: 3 beasts
Saving Throw: None

You use your blood as a catalyst to create mystical creatures based on living animals. You can conjure up to three beasts of challenge rating 3 or lower. Sacrifice up to 10 hit points when you cast the spell. Each creature gains triple the amount you sacrificed as temporary hit points. The creatures also have +2 AC.

The creatures are friendly to you and your companions. They act as a group on their own initiative, and obey verbal commands you give them (as bonus actions on your turn).

The creatures vanish when the spell ends or when they are reduced to 0 hit points.

Scalding Sea

4th-level evocation
Sorcerer, Wizard
Components: V, S
Casting Time: 1 action
Duration: Concentration, up to 1 minute
Range: 150 ft.
Area of Effect: Cylinder, 30 ft. radius, 50 ft. high
Saving Throw: Con / half damage

You cause a large body of water to emit scalding steam. The steam cloud rises upward in a 50-foot-radius, 30-foot-high cylinder from a point you can see within range. Each creature in the steam cloud at the start of its turn takes 4d6 fire damage, or half damage with a successful Constitution saving throw.

Scent Mask

2nd-level abjuration
Druid, Ranger, Wizard
Components: V, S
Casting Time: 1 action
Duration: Concentration, up to 1 hour

Sanguine Creatures

Range: 30 ft.
Area of Effect: 1 creature
Saving Throw: Con / negates effect

You suppress all odor emanating from a creature you can see, unless it makes a successful Constitution saving throw. A willing creature can choose to fail the saving throw.

For the duration of the spell, the affected creature can't be tracked or detected by scent. If the spell is cast on a creature that has an odor-based special ability, such as a troglodyte, that ability doesn't function, but the creature can repeat the saving throw at the end of each of its turns; a successful save ends the spell.

Enhancement: For each spell slot used higher than 2nd level, you can affect one additional creature.

Scintillating Doom

9th-level evocation
Sorcerer, Wizard
Components: V, S
Casting Time: 1 action
Duration: Concentration, up to 1 minute
Range: 50 ft.
Area of Effect: Cube, 20 ft. square
Saving Throw: Dex partial

You create a field of multicolored rays bouncing around inside a cubic area 20 feet on a side, formed around a point you can see. Each creature that starts its turn in the affected area or enters it must roll 1d8 to determine which color of ray strikes it, and apply the appropriate result from the following table. Every result on the table also calls for a Dexterity saving throw.

d8	Effect
1–Red	The target takes 8d8 fire damage, or half damage with a successful Dexterity saving throw.
2–Orange	The target takes 8d8 acid damage, or half damage with a successful Dexterity saving throw.
3–Yellow	The target takes 8d8 lightning damage, or half damage with a successful Dexterity saving throw.
4–Green	The target takes 8d8 poison damage, or half damage with a successful Dexterity saving throw.
5–Blue	The target takes 8d8 cold damage, or half damage with a successful Dexterity saving throw.
6–Indigo	The target is restrained if the Dexterity saving throw fails. A restrained creature makes a Constitution saving throw at the end of each of its turns. The restraint ends when it accumulates three successes, or it becomes petrified when it accumulates three failures, whichever happens first. Successes and failures don't need to be consecutive.
7–Violet	The target is blinded if the Dexterity saving throw fails. At the start of your next turn, it must make a Wisdom saving throw; a successful save ends the effect, but a failed saving throw transports the blind creature to a plane of the GM's choosing.
8–Two rays	The target is struck by two rays; roll twice more, re-rolling results of 8.

Scorching Air

7th-level evocation
Sorcerer, Wizard
Components: V, S
Casting Time: 1 action
Duration: Instantaneous
Range: 150 ft.
Area of Effect: Sphere, 40-ft. radius
Saving Throw: Con / half damage

You cause the air in a 40-foot-radius sphere centered on a point you can see to heat to intense temperature for an instant. Each creature in the area when the spell is cast must make a Constitution saving throw. If the saving throw fails, it takes 5d8 + 20 fire damage and gains two levels of exhaustion. On a successful save, it takes half damage and gains one level of exhaustion.

Searing Flash

7th-level evocation
Sorcerer, Wizard
Components: V, S
Casting Time: 1 action
Duration: Instantaneous
Range: 50 ft.
Area of Effect: 1 creature
Saving Throw: Con / half damage

One creature you can see within range must make a Constitution saving throw as a bright bolt of light streaks from your hand to its eyes. If the saving throw fails, the creature takes 8d6 + 20 radiant damage and is permanently blinded; on a successful save, it takes half damage and is not blinded.

Searing Projectiles

4th-level transmutation
Wizard
Components: V, S
Casting Time: 1 bonus action
Duration: Concentration, up to 1 minute
Range: Self
Area of Effect: 1 missile weapon
Saving Throw: None

Your ranged weapon glows with fire. For the duration of this spell, each missile you fire does an additional 2d6 fire damage on a successful hit.

See the Ephemeral

3rd-level divination
Warlock, Wizard
Components: V, S
Casting Time: 1 action
Duration: Concentration, up to 10 minutes
Range: 60 ft.
Area of Effect: Self
Saving Throw: None

You gain the ability to see the dreams of sleeping creatures within range. You can also see creatures that exist in the Dreamlands, such as night hags. The amount of information you learn from what you see depends on the time spent studying the subject.

One round: You determine the presence or absence of dreams.

Two rounds: You determine how many sleepers are dreaming and the emotional intensity of the dreams. You also learn the number and relative power of dream creatures within range.

Three rounds: You determine the exact nature of the dreams of one

creature within range, and determine the exact location and types of dream creatures within range.

At the GM's option, you can learn one significant fact about a dreamer for each minute you spend observing that creature's dreams.

In settings without a Dreamland, this spell applies to the Ethereal Plane.

Serpent Hands

6th-level transmutation
Druid, Wizard
Components: V, S
Casting Time: 1 bonus action
Duration: Concentration, up to 1 minute
Range: Self
Area of Effect: Self
Saving Throw: Con / negates poisoned condition

Your hands transform into serpent heads. As an action on your turn, you can make a melee spell attack with your hands. If you hit, the target takes 5d8 poison damage and becomes poisoned. At the beginning of each of its turns, a poisoned creature makes a Constitution saving throw; on a successful save, it is no longer poisoned.

For the duration of the spell, you can't hold items or cast spells that have somatic components.

Serpent's Gaze

1st-level enchantment
Bard, Warlock, Wizard
Components: V, S
Casting Time: 1 action
Duration: Concentration, up to 1 minute
Range: 30 ft.
Area of Effect: 1 creature
Saving Throw: Cha / negates immobilization for 1 turn

You select a creature you can see and fix it with your gaze. For the duration of the spell, the targeted creature must make a successful Charisma saving throw at the start of each of its turns or its speed becomes 0 until the start of its next turn.

Shade Swarm

6th-level necromancy
Wizard
Components: V, S
Casting Time: 1 action
Duration: Instantaneous
Range: Self
Area of Effect: Cone, 30 ft. long
Saving Throw: Con / half damage

You summon a horde of wrathful, screaming spirits that fly away from you, engulfing all creatures in a 30-foot cone. Each creature in the affected area must make a Constitution saving throw. If the saving throw fails, the creature takes 6d6 necrotic damage and its maximum hit points are reduced by the same number. On a successful save, the creature takes half damage and suffers no additional effect.

Shadow Bolt

3rd-level necromancy
Sorcerer, Wizard
Components: V, S
Casting Time: 1 action
Duration: Instantaneous
Range: 100 ft.
Area of Effect: 1 creature
Saving Throw: None

You direct a bolt of shadow at one creature you can see. Make a ranged spell attack roll. The creature takes 5d10 necrotic damage if the attack hits.

Enhancement: For each spell slot used higher than 3rd level, *shadow bolt* does an additional 1d10 necrotic damage.

Shadow Embrace

2nd-level abjuration
Bard
Components: V, S
Casting Time: 1 action
Duration: Concentration, up to 1 minute
Range: Self
Area of Effect: Self
Saving Throw: None

You cloak yourself in swirling shadows that enclose you like a cloak and move with you. You are lightly obscured, and you can add 1d4 to your saving throws while the spell is in effect. The shadows disappear when the spell ends.

Shadow Form

4th-level transmutation
Warlock, Wizard
Components: S
Casting Time: 1 action
Duration: Concentration, up to 1 minute
Range: Self
Area of Effect: Self
Saving Throw: None

You transform yourself into shadow-stuff. For the duration of the spell, you can fit through openings of 1 square inch or larger, you have a +10 bonus on Dexterity (Stealth) checks, and you have resistance to bludgeoning, piercing, and slashing damage from nonmagical weapons.

However, while in shadow form, you can't speak or interact with anything in a physical manner.

If you occupy a space that's too tight for you when the spell ends, you are displaced to the nearest space where you'll fit; you take 1d6 bludgeoning damage for each 5 feet you were displaced to reach that spot.

Shadow Sight

2nd-level divination
Wizard
Components: V, S
Casting Time: 1 action
Duration: Concentration, up to 1 hour
Range: Self
Area of Effect: Special
Saving Throw: None

By peering into a nearby shadow, you can see out of any other shadow within 30 feet of you as if you were standing in that shadow. You are aware of all shadows you could use for this effect, even if your line of sight to them is blocked.

Shadowbind

4th-level evocation
Wizard
Components: V, S
Casting Time: 1 action
Duration: 10 minutes
Range: 100 ft.
Area of Effect: 1 to 6 creatures
Saving Throw: Wis / negates effect

You target up to six creatures that you can see. Each creature must be adjacent to (within 5 feet of) at least one other creature targeted by this spell. Each targeted creature must make a Wisdom saving throw. If the saving throw fails, its shadow becomes quasi-real and merges into the shadows of all the other creatures that failed their saving throws.

For the duration of the spell, creatures with merged shadows must remain within 5 feet of at least one other creature with a merged shadow. For the sake of simplicity, all of the creatures can move together on the turn of whichever creature comes last in the initiative order, at the speed of the slowest creature in the group. There are likely to be gaps of more than 5 feet between creatures, caused by creatures making successful saves. Affected creatures must move to become adjacent to other affected creatures at their first opportunity.

Each affected creature can repeat the saving throw at the end of its turn; a successful save ends the effect for that creature. The spell ends entirely when only one creature is affected by the spell.

Shadowstaff

8th-level necromancy
Wizard
Components: V, S
Casting Time: 1 bonus action
Duration: Concentration, up to 1 minute
Range: Self
Area of Effect: 1 staff
Saving Throw: None

You imbue a staff you hold with necrotic energy. When you successfully hit with it, the staff does an additional 6d6 necrotic damage and you gain temporary hit points equal to half of the damage taken by the target.

Shattering Cry

5th-level evocation
Bard, Sorcerer, Wizard
Components: V, M (a small piece of crystal)
Casting Time: 1 action
Duration: Instantaneous
Range: Self
Area of Effect: Cone, 50 ft. long
Saving Throw: Con / half damage

You let out a powerful, magically-enhanced shout that affects a 50-foot cone emanating from your space. Each creature in the cone takes 8d8 sonic damage, or half damage with a successful Constitution saving throw. A creature made of glass or crystal has tactical disadvantage on its saving throw.

The shout shatters mundane, unattended objects made of crystal or glass. Attended items of that sort only shatter if their possessor fails his or her saving throw.

Shield of Crackling Fire

7th-level abjuration
Wizard
Components: V, S
Casting Time: 1 action
Duration: 10 minutes
Range: Self
Area of Effect: Self
Saving Throw: None

Shadowstaff

You surround yourself with an aura of electrical sparks and flames. For the duration of the spell, you gain resistance against lightning and fire damage. If you are struck by a melee weapon attack by a creature within 5 feet of you, the attacker takes 2d8 fire damage plus 2d8 lightning damage.

The flames shed bright light in a radius of 10 feet around you, and dim light to a further 10 feet.

Shield Open Flame

Abjuration cantrip
Bard, Druid, Wizard
Components: V, S
Casting Time: 1 action
Duration: 1 hour
Range: 30 ft.
Area of Effect: 1 flame
Saving Throw: None

You create a protective shield of force around one flame. That flame can't be extinguished by nonmagical breezes or gusts of air.

Shifter's Bane

2nd-level transmutation
Ranger
Components: V, S
Casting Time: 1 action
Duration: Until dawn after a full moon
Range: Self
Area of Effect: Self
Saving Throw: None

This spell can be cast only on the night of a full moon. For the duration of the spell, any weapon you wield is considered to be made of silver, and you have tactical advantage on Charisma (Bluff), Wisdom (Perception), Wisdom (Insight), and Wisdom (Survival) checks that deal with or are focused on lycanthropes.

Shroud the Shadow

1st-level transmutation
Warlock, Wizard
Components: V, S
Casting Time: 1 action
Duration: Concentration, up to 10 minutes
Range: 30 ft.
Area of Effect: 1 creature
Saving Throw: None

One creature you can see within range casts no shadow. If the target of the spell is a shadow creature, it is incapacitated unless it makes a successful Constitution saving throw. It can repeat the saving throw at the end of each of its turns; a successful save ends the spell.

Signal Flare

1st-level evocation
Druid, Ranger, Wizard
Components: V, S
Casting Time: 1 action
Duration: 5 minutes
Range: 100 ft.
Area of Effect: Sphere, 20-ft. radius
Saving Throw: None

You shoot a bright light resembling a flare to a point you can see within range. The flare gives off bright light in a 20-foot radius and dim light for an additional 20 feet. The light drifts 10 feet toward the ground at the start of each of your turns. The source of the light is immaterial; it can't be picked up, thrown, carried, or moved in any way after it's initial "launch" or once it reaches the ground. It can be extinguished by the caster before the end of the spell's duration as a bonus action.

Silver Bones

3rd-level transmutation
Wizard
Components: V, S
Casting Time: 1 action
Duration: 24 hours
Range: Touch
Area of Effect: 1 skeleton
Saving Throw: None

One skeleton you touch gains resistance against bludgeoning, piercing, and slashing damage from weapons unless they're either magical or silver, for the duration of the spell.

Enhancement: For each spell slot used higher than 3rd level, you can affect one additional skeleton.

Silver Shield

4th-level abjuration
Paladin
Components: V, S
Casting Time: 1 action
Duration: 1 hour
Range: 20 ft.
Area of Effect: Self and allied creatures within range
Saving Throw: None

You and each creature you choose within range is surrounded by a protective silver aura. Each creature affected by the aura gains a +5 bonus to AC for the duration of the spell. The effect ends for a creature when it attacks or casts a harmful spell.

Silver Spear

2nd-level conjuration
Druid, Sorcerer, Wizard
Components: V, S, M (a silver needle)
Casting Time: 1 action
Duration: Instantaneous
Range: 30 ft.
Area of Effect: 1 creature
Saving Throw: None

You conjure a shimmering spear and throw it at one creature you can see. Make a ranged spell attack against the target creature. If it hits, the spear does 3d10 piercing damage and is treated as a silver weapon.

Enhancement: For each spell slot used higher than 2nd level, the spear does an additional 1d10 damage.

Skull Bomb

5th-level necromancy
Cleric, Wizard
Components: V, S
Casting Time: 1 action
Duration: 1 minute
Range: Touch
Area of Effect: 1 skull
Saving Throw: Con / half damage

You imbue one humanoid skull with explosive force. When the skull is thrown against a solid object, it explodes in a 20-foot-radius blast. Each creature in the blast area must make a Constitution saving throw. If the saving throw fails, the creature takes 6d8 necrotic damage and can't regain hit points until it completes a short or long rest. With a successful save, the creature takes half damage and suffers no additional effect.

The skull explodes when the spell's duration expires, if it has not exploded before then.

Sleep of Power

7th-level transmutation
Wizard
Components: V, S, M (two silver coins)
Casting Time: 1 bonus action
Duration: See text
Range: Self
Area of Effect: Self
Saving Throw: None

Sleep of power must be cast on the same turn that you cast any other spell of level 6 or lower that has a duration longer than instantaneous. You fall into a deep, trancelike sleep in which you do not age, breathe, or need food or water. For the duration of the sleep, your other spell doesn't expire, even if it requires concentration.

When you cast *sleep of power*, you must indicate conditions that will cause you to awaken. You always awaken if you take damage or if the original spell ends (by being discharged or dispelled, for example).

This spell is typically used by wizards to provide an ongoing benefit to another adventurer; for instance, an *Immunity to Energy* spell could be maintained throughout an extended trip to the plane of fire. NPC wizards typically charge large sums of money and magic items to cast this spell.

Slime Bucket

5th-level conjuration
Cleric
Components: V, S
Casting Time: 1 action
Duration: Instantaneous
Range: 150 ft.
Area of Effect: Cylinder, 10-ft. radius, 40 ft. high
Saving Throw: Dex / half damage

You conjure a glob of heat-absorbing slime at a point you can see in the air. It then spreads and extends hairlike filaments downward throughout a 10-foot radius, 40-foot high cylinder. Each creature in the area takes 8d6 cold damage, or half damage with a successful Dexterity saving throw.

The slime can't freeze water; it just sinks slowly if it falls into water.

Enhancement: For each spell slot used higher than 5th level, the initial damage increases by 1d6.

Slimeball

4th-level evocation
Sorcerer, Wizard
Components: V, S, M (a vial of acid)
Casting Time: 1 action
Duration: Instantaneous
Range: 150 ft.
Area of Effect: Sphere, 20-ft. radius
Saving Throw: Dex / half damage

You shoot a ball of slime from your hand to a point you can see. The ball then explodes into a 20-foot-radius sphere. Each creature in the affected area must make a Dexterity saving throw. If the saving throw fails, the creature takes 6d6 acid damage immediately and 2d6 acid damage at the end of its next turn. On a successful save, a creature takes half damage immediately and 1d6 acid damage at the end of its next turn.

Enhancement: For each spell slot used higher than 4th level, *slimeball* does an additional 1d6 damage immediately. For each

107

sorcery point you expend when casting the spell, the additional damage persists for an extra round. The maximum number of sorcery points that can be expended equals one-half the level of the spell slot used, rounded down.

Slow Draw

1st-level transmutation
Bard, Wizard
Components: V, S, M (a vial of glue)
Casting Time: 1 action
Duration: Concentration, up to 1 minute
Range: 30 ft.
Area of Effect: 1 weapon
Saving Throw: Wis / negates effect; Str / negates effect

One weapon you can see sticks in its sheath. Drawing the weapon requires a successful Wisdom saving throw. Only the spell's caster can draw the weapon without making a save. The spell has no effect on a weapon that isn't in a sheath or a scabbard when the spell is cast.

Slur

2nd-level transmutation
Cleric, Warlock, Wizard
Components: V, S
Casting Time: 1 action
Duration: Concentration, up to 1 minute
Range: 50 ft.
Area of Effect: 1 creature
Saving Throw: Con / negates effect

You impede the speech of a creature you can see. The creature must make a Constitution saving throw. If the saving throw fails, its speech becomes slurred and imprecise; other creatures must make an Intelligence saving throw against your spell save DC to understand what the affected creature is saying. In addition, the affected creature can cast a spell with a verbal component only if it makes a successful ability check matching its spell-casting ability against your spell save DC; the spell slot is not expended if the ability check fails.

An affected creature can repeat the Constitution saving throw at the end of each of its turns. A successful save ends the effect.

Smart Arrow

3rd-level divination
Ranger
Components: V, S
Casting Time: 1 bonus action
Duration: Concentration, up to 1 round
Range: 150 ft.
Area of Effect: 1 creature
Saving Throw: Wis / negates effect

Select a creature you can see within range. For the duration of the spell, you can make missile weapon attacks against that creature even if it is not in your line of sight, as long as it is within range of the weapon. Your missiles can swerve around corners, go up and down stairs, and even seek out alternative paths to the target if a door is closed. They ignore cover and concealment. Only a creature that has blocked all possible routes from you to it is safe from your missiles.

Smothering Cloud

2nd-level evocation
Sorcerer, Wizard
Components: V, S, M (a small piece of worn cloth)
Casting Time: 1 action
Duration: Concentration, up to 1 minute
Range: 50 ft.
Area of Effect: Sphere, 10-ft. radius
Saving Throw: Con / partial

You create a thick, roiling mass of gray clouds in a 10-foot-radius sphere around a point you can see. Creatures inside the cloud can't breathe, and fires inside the cloud are extinguished. The cloud also prevents other air-based phenomena, such as *stinking cloud* spells or a troglodyte's stench, from affecting those inside it.

You can choose to anchor this spell on a creature when you cast it. The creature must make a Constitution saving throw. If it fails, the cloud moves with it. If it succeeds, the spell is centered on a spot just behind the target.

The cloud's area is heavily obscured. It lasts for the duration of the spell or until a wind of moderate or greater force disperses it.

Snakes into Staves

4th-level transmutation
Cleric, Druid
Components: V, S
Casting Time: 1 action
Duration: Concentration, up to 1 minute
Range: 50 ft.
Area of Effect: 1 to 6 snakes
Saving Throw: Con / negates effect

You transform up to six snakes you can see into staves. Each snake must make a Constitution saving throw when the spell is cast; a successful save negates the effect on that snake. Small snakes become clubs and large snakes become quarterstaffs, which can be used as weapons.

This spell only works on snakes classified as beasts. The staves revert to snakes when the spell ends.

Solar Flare

8th-level evocation
Cleric
Components: V, S
Casting Time: 1 action
Duration: Instantaneous
Range: 150 ft.
Area of Effect: Cylinder, 15-ft. radius, 60-ft. tall
Saving Throw: Dex / half damage; Con / not blinded

You summon a vertical column of divine fire from the heavens. Each creature in a 15-foot-radius, 60-foot-tall cylinder centered on a point within range takes 6d6 fire damage plus 6d6 radiant damage, or half damage with a successful Dexterity saving throw. Each creature in the cylinder or within 15 feet of it that can see the fire is permanently blinded unless it makes a successful Constitution saving throw.

The light from the *solar flare* affects creatures as if it were true sunlight.

Solar Fury

6th-level evocation
Druid
Components: V, S
Casting Time: 1 action
Duration: Concentration, up to 1 minute
Range: Self
Area of Effect: Self
Saving Throw: None

Your body glows intensely, giving off bright light in a 60-foot radius and dim light for a further 60 feet. For the duration of the spell, you gain resistance to fire damage. You also radiate heat in a 20-foot radius; each creature that begins its turn within 20 feet of you takes 4d6 fire damage, or half damage with a successful Dexterity saving throw.

Solar Spear

4th-level evocation
Sorcerer, Wizard
Components: V, S
Casting Time: 1 action
Duration: Instantaneous
Range: 120 ft.
Area of Effect: 1 creature
Saving Throw: Con / partial

A bolt of light streaks from your hand to a creature you can see. Make a ranged spell attack against that creature. If you hit, the creature takes 5d8 radiant damage and must make a Constitution saving throw. If the saving throw fails, the creature is blinded. A blinded creature can repeat the saving throw at the end of each of its turns; a successful save ends the blindness.

Enhancement: For each spell slot used higher than 4th level, the spell does an additional 1d8 damage.

Song Barrier

6th-level evocation
Bard
Components: V, S
Casting Time: 1 action
Duration: Concentration, up to 1 minute
Range: 150 ft.
Area of Effect: Wall, 80 ft. long, 20 ft. tall, 5 ft. wide
Saving Throw: See text

You cause the air to vibrate with music concentrated in a wall up to 80 feet long, 20 feet high, and 5 feet wide. The wall forms in an area you choose within range. It must be straight along its entire length. Creatures in the area occupied by the wall when it's created make Dexterity saving throws. A successful saving throw indicates the creature can immediately move to an adjacent unoccupied space; if the saving throw fails or the creature has nowhere to go, the wall forms around it. The wall doesn't obscure vision or block movement physically.

When you cast the spell, you choose whether the song is melodious or cacophonous.

The melodious song causes one side of the wall that you choose to emit a pleasing melody that entrances those that can hear it; the other side is silent. Every creature within 30 feet of the melodious side of the wall that can hear the song must make a Wisdom saving throw at the beginning of each of its turns. If the saving throw fails, the creature must move toward the wall by the shortest, safest route until it is within the wall.

A creature that enters the melodious wall or ends its turn inside it must make a Wisdom saving throw. If this saving throw fails, the creature falls unconscious for as long as it's inside the wall. If it takes damage, it can repeat the saving throw; it awakens on a successful save. A creature never needs to make more than one saving throw against the wall's effect per turn.

The cacophonous song causes one side of the wall to emit thunderous, damaging vibrations while the other side remains silent. Each creature that ends its turn within 30 feet of the wall takes 3d8 thunder damage and is deafened until the start of its next turn, or half damage with no deafening if it makes a successful Constitution saving throw. Being unable to hear the wall doesn't protect a creature against the damage, which is caused by vibrations affecting the creature's whole body.

The interior of the cacophonous wall is even more dangerous; any creature that enters the wall or ends its turn there must make a Constitution saving throw (no more than one saving throw per turn). If the saving throw fails, the creature takes 8d6 thunder damage, is permanently deafened, and is stunned until the beginning of its next turn. A successful save halves the damage and the creature is not deafened or stunned. Creatures that are already deaf are immune to the stunning but still take the damage.

Song of Vengeance

5th-level abjuration
Bard
Components: V, M (a ruby worth at least 1,000 gp, which is consumed in the casting)
Casting Time: 1 action
Duration: 1 minute
Range: Self
Area of Effect: Sphere, 30-ft. radius
Saving Throw: Con / negates effect

You create a magical song that resonates with your physical state in a way that hurts your enemies when they hurt you. Whenever you take damage, each creature within 30 feet of you takes 2d8 thunder damage, or no damage with a successful Constitution saving throw, as the song picks up your pain and throws it back in concentrated, musical form at those around you.

When you cast *song of vengeance*, you can nominate up to six creatures to be unaffected by its magic; those creatures are not damaged by the spell.

Sonic Boom

1st-level transmutation
Bard
Components: V, S
Casting Time: 1 bonus action
Duration: Concentration, up to 1 minute
Range: Self
Area of Effect: 1 weapon
Saving Throw: None

You gain the ability to turn your weapon strokes into concussive blasts transmitted through the air. For the duration of the spell, you can make melee weapon attacks against creatures up to 20 feet away from you as if they were adjacent, and the attacks do thunder damage instead of their usual damage type.

Soul Shatter

5th-level necromancy
Wizard
Components: V, S, M (gems worth at least 500 gp, which are consumed in the casting)
Casting Time: 1 action
Duration: Instantaneous
Range: Touch
Area of Effect: 1 creature
Saving Throw: Con / negates effect

You send waves of negative energy coursing through the body of one creature you touch as you cast this spell. The target must make a Constitution saving throw. If the saving throw fails, it loses 1d6 points of Charisma and is incapacitated for 1 round for every point of Charisma it lost; it recovers at the beginning of your turn after the appropriate number of rounds. (For example, if the creature lost 1 point of Charisma, it is stunned until the beginning of your next turn.)

Soul Shield

2nd-level abjuration
Wizard
Components: V, S
Casting Time: 1 action
Duration: 1 hour
Range: Self
Area of Effect: Self
Saving Throw: None

You siphon some of your life force into a shimmering shield of light around yourself. Sacrifice any number of your hit points (up to your current total -1) when you cast the spell, and you immediately gain twice as many temporary hit points. You must leave yourself at least 1 "real" hit point. While any of those temporary hit points remain, you get tactical advantage on Dexterity and Constitution saving throws. Remaining temporary hit points disappear when the spell ends. The spell ends immediately if all the temporary hit points are lost.

Soul Strike

8th-level necromancy
Cleric, Wizard
Components: V, S, M (the heart of a humanoid killed in the last week, which is consumed in the casting)
Casting Time: 1 action
Duration: Instantaneous
Range: 100 ft.
Area of Effect: Sphere, 40-ft. radius
Saving Throw: Wis / half damage, not stunned

You cause negative energy to fill a 40-foot-radius sphere around a point within range, which claws at the souls of all creatures exposed to it. Each living creature in the affected area must make a Wisdom saving throw. If the saving throw fails, the creature takes 8d10 necrotic damage and is stunned for 1d4 rounds; on a successful save, the creature takes half damage and is not stunned.

A stunned creature makes a Constitution saving throw at the end of each of its turns; a successful save ends the stun.

A creature killed by *soul strike* can't be raised by any magic less powerful than an 8th-level spell.

Sound Worm

3rd-level enchantment
Bard
Components: V, S
Casting Time: 1 action
Duration: 1 minute
Range: 60 ft.
Area of Effect: 1 creature
Saving Throw: Wis / negates effect

Your shouted words, aimed at a creature within range, reverberate and disrupt the target. The creature becomes unable to maintain concentration on spells for the duration of *sound worm* unless it makes a successful Wisdom saving throw. Any spell cast by the creature with a duration of concentration ends instantly, and it can't cast spells requiring concentration. The creature can repeat the Wisdom saving throw at the end of each of its turns; a successful save ends the effect.

Speak with Objects

3rd-level divination
Cleric, Wizard
Components: V, S
Casting Time: 1 action
Duration: 10 minutes
Range: Self
Area of Effect: Self
Saving Throw: None

You can communicate telepathically with objects, whether they are inanimate or animated objects and constructs. You can ask questions and receive answers from objects. An inanimate object's sense of its surroundings is quite limited, so it can't give detailed descriptions of creatures, recognize specific individuals, or answer questions about events outside its immediate vicinity. They are most attuned to sound (vibration) and touch, but have very limited or nonexistent vision. They can sense powerful smells, but nothing subtle. Inanimate objects seldom volunteer information; they only respond to direct questions.

The spell doesn't make animated objects or constructs more friendly or cooperative than normal. Furthermore, they don't lead interesting inner lives and they're prone to making comments that seem inane to sentient creatures (but might make sense within the confines of some unfamiliar logic). If an animated object or construct is friendly toward the caster, it probably is willing to do a favor or service for the caster, within its limited ability (as determined by the GM).

Spectral Archers

4th-level conjuration
Wizard
Components: V, S
Casting Time: 1 action
Duration: Concentration, up to 1 minute
Range: Touch
Area of Effect: 1 creature
Saving Throw: None

When you touch a creature, five shadowy duplicates appear around it. The duplicates are quasi-real; they take up no space, can be moved through by allies and enemies, and can't be damaged, though they can be dispelled.

The next time the targeted creature makes a ranged weapon attack, the duplicates make identical attacks against targets of the creature's choice. The creature makes attack rolls against each target and does damage to them as if it were making the attacks. The spell then ends and the duplicates disappear.

Speed Undead

2nd-level necromancy
Cleric
Components: V, S, M (a drop of quicksilver)
Casting Time: 1 action
Duration: Concentration, up to 10 minutes
Range: Touch
Area of Effect: 1 undead creature
Saving Throw: None

You imbue a willing undead creature with unnatural speed and grace. For the duration of the spell, the undead target gains a +2 AC bonus, has tactical advantage on Dexterity saving throws, and its speed increases by 10 feet.

Enhancement: For each spell slot used higher than 2nd level, you can affect one additional undead creature.

Spell Inhibitor

6th-level abjuration
Wizard
Components: V, S, M (a pinch of powdered adamantine worth 10 gp)
Casting Time: 1 action
Duration: 1 minute
Range: Self
Area of Effect: Sphere, 100-ft. radius
Saving Throw: None

You disrupt magical energy around yourself. The effect moves with you.

Any spellcaster that casts a spell within 100 feet of you must make an ability check using their spell-casting ability against your spell saving throw DC. If the check fails, the spell takes effect as if it were cast using the minimum slot level that could be used to cast it rather than the slot that was actually used. In addition, if the spell has a variable effect, it has a -1 penalty on each die, to a minimum of one.

Spectral Archers

Spell Kill

3rd-level transmutation
Warlock, Wizard
Components: V, S
Casting Time: 1 action
Duration: Instantaneous
Range: 120 ft.
Area of Effect: 1 creature
Saving Throw: Spellcasting ability / negates effect

A silvery ray of energy shoots from your hand to one creature you can see. That creature loses one 4th-level spell slot as if the spell was cast unless it makes a successful saving throw using its spell-casting ability. If it has no 4th-level spells, it loses a 3rd-level slot instead; if it has no 3rd-level slot, it loses a 2nd-level spell; and so on. *Spell kill* has no effect on creatures that don't have spell slots.

Enhancement: *Spell kill* can be cast using a spell slot of 3rd level or higher. It wipes out a spell slot one level higher than the slot used to cast *spell kill*.

Spell Legs

5th-level transmutation
Wizard
Components: V, S
Casting Time: 1 action
Duration: Concentration, up to 1 minute
Range: 120 ft.
Area of Effect: 1 spell
Saving Throw: None

You gain control of one non-instantaneous, area effect spell within range whose area is not centered on an object or a creature, such as *stinking cloud* or *flaming sphere*. When you cast *spell legs*, and at the beginning of each of your turns, you can move the targeted area of effect up to 20 feet in any direction.

If the original spell has a duration of "concentration," you must make an opposed ability check at the beginning of each of your turns, pitting your spellcasting ability against the original caster's. You can move the spell if you win the contest; otherwise, the spell behaves normally.

Spellcaster's Refusal

5th-level abjuration (ritual)
Cleric, Wizard
Components: V, S
Casting Time: 1 action
Duration: 24 hours
Range: 120 ft.
Area of Effect: 1 portal
Saving Throw: None

You create an invisible barrier that wards one point of entry (a hallway, doorway, window or the like). The entryway can be no more than 20 feet across. You must be able to see the area affected and it must be in range. For the duration of the spell, no creature with spellcasting ability can pass through the portal, but non-spellcasting creatures are not affected. You and up to three creatures you nominate when you cast the spell can pass through the portal as if *spellcaster's refusal* was not in effect.

Enhancement: For each spell slot used higher than 5th level, you can create one additional barrier.

Spilling of Blood

6th-level necromancy
Wizard
Components: V, S, M (a few drops of blood)
Casting Time: 1 action
Duration: Concentration, up to 1 minute
Range: 50 ft.
Area of Effect: 1 creature
Saving Throw: Con / negates effect

You cause a gaping wound to open in the body of a living creature. At the beginning of each of the target's turns, it must make a Constitution saving throw. If the saving throw fails, the creature takes 5d6 necrotic damage and loses 1 point of Constitution.

The spell ends if the creature regains hit points or if it makes two successful Constitution saving throws against this effect. The saves don't need to be consecutive.

The spell has no effect on creatures without blood.

Spirit Blast

2nd-level necromancy
Sorcerer, Wizard
Components: V, S
Casting Time: 1 action
Duration: Instantaneous
Range: 120 ft.
Area of Effect: 1 creature
Saving Throw: None

You sacrifice part of your life force to create a bolt of energy that you immediately hurl at a creature you can see. Sacrifice any number of hit points (up to your current total -1) and make a ranged spell attack against the target. If it hits, the bolt does radiant damage equal to the hit points you sacrificed plus 5d6.

Enhancement: For each spell slot used higher than 2nd level, the bolt does an additional 1d6 damage.

Spirit Cartographer

2nd-level conjuration
Wizard
Components: V, S
Casting Time: 1 action
Duration: 8 hours
Range: 30 ft.
Area of Effect: 1 spirit
Saving Throw: None

You summon a Tiny, corporeal creature from the Plane of Law that accurately maps any area you traverse. Its attributes are identical to a sprite's, except it has Perception +8 and passive Perception 18. In combat, it always takes the Dodge action and never attacks.

The spirit cartographer hovers above the person who summoned it and can see anything you see (plus a bit more, sometimes). Whenever you pass within 5 feet of a secret door, a concealed panel (including trapdoors on the floor and ceiling), or another feature that can be detected with sharp senses, the GM makes a Wisdom (Perception) check to determine whether the spirit cartographer notices the feature and records it on the map. Because it remains completely silent at all times, characters won't know about these "extras" until they take the time to examine the spirit's map.

The spirit vanishes and the spell ends if the spirit is reduced to 0 hit points. The map the spirit has drawn remains.

Spirit Disk

8th-level evocation
Wizard
Components: V, S
Casting Time: 1 action
Duration: Concentration, up to 1 minute
Range: 120 ft.
Area of Effect: 1 creature
Saving Throw: None

You evoke a spinning disk of force that streaks toward one creature you can see. Make a ranged spell attack. If it hits, the creature takes 10d10 force damage. If you roll a natural 20 to hit, roll the d20 again. If the result of the second roll is another 20, the creature loses a limb, the same as if it had been struck by a *sword of sharpness*.

Once launched, the *spirit disk* remains hovering near its target. As an action, you can attack again with it on each of your turns. The target, however, can't be changed.

Spirit Doll

5th-level transmutation
Warlock, Wizard
Components: V, S, M (a doll, a piece of hair from the mark, and a ruby worth at least 1,000 gp, which is consumed in the casting)
Casting Time: 10 minutes
Duration: 7 days
Range: Touch
Area of Effect: 1 doll
Saving Throw: None

You turn an ordinary doll into a *spirit doll*, which is attuned to another creature whose lock of hair was woven into the doll during the casting. This creature is referred to as the "mark" or as the linked creature.

For the duration of the spell, the mark must subtract 1d4 from its saving throws against spells cast by you while you possess the doll. The mark is also subject to other spells that make use of the *spirit doll*.

When the spell ends, the doll disintegrates.

The link between the doll and the mark is inactive if both are on different planes of existence, but that that doesn't sever the link; it becomes active again when both are on the same plane of existence.

Spiritbreaker

6th-level abjuration
Warlock, Wizard
Components: V, S, M (a specially prepared document)
Casting Time: 3 rounds (see text)
Duration: See text
Range: 50 ft.
Area of Effect: 1 fiend
Saving Throw: Cha / partial

This spell allows you to inflict wracking pains on a fiend, usually in order to exact a service from it. If the creature refuses and you continue the spell, it is eventually banisehd to its plane of origin.

To cast this spell, you must have a specially prepared document that contains the fiend's true name; without that, the spell fails automatically. You can start and pause the reading at any time, so long as no more than 10 rounds have elapsed since the spell was started. You can end the casting at any time by simply not finishing the reading of the document.

When you begin reading the document, the subject feels great discomfort and must make a Charisma saving throw. If the saving throw fails, the creature is unable to attack or to move from its location by any means. A successful save allows the creature to move normally (including retreating to its home plane) if it isn't prevented from doing so, but the *spiritbreaker* spell still renders it powerless to attack.

During the second round of reading, the subject feels great pain coursing through its body and it loses one-fourth of its current hit points.

At the start of the third round of reading, the subject loses one-half of its current hit points as the pain intensifies. At the end of the third round, the creature is condemned to its home plane. It remains confined there, unable to be summoned to your plane, unable to leave its own plane, and in wracking pain, for ten years. From this point forward, the creature is your sworn enemy. Unfortunately, its confinement to its home plane doesn't prevent the creature from sending its minions and servitors to deal with you.

Material Component: The specially prepared document mentioned above must contain the true name of the fiend the spell is being used against. The document itself costs 1,000 gp for the paper or parchment, special pens, and other materials. The ink used to scribe the document must be made from powdered rubies (totaling at least 5,000 gp) and the blood of a fiend.

Note that a fiend's true name is not easy to come by. Many (particularly in the case of demons) go by more than one name on the various planes of existence, and some don't even know their own true names. No fiend ever voluntarily reveals its true name to anyone, especially a spellcaster from the Material Plane.

Spiteful Images

3rd-level illusion
Bard, Wizard
Components: V, S
Casting Time: 1 action
Duration: Concentration, up to 1 minute
Range: 120 ft.
Area of Effect: 1 creature
Saving Throw: None

Choose one creature you can see that has *mirror image* or similar image-duplicating magic in effect. Those images immediately turn and attack the creature. Make an attack for each image, using your melee spell attack bonus. Each hit does 2d6 force damage to the target creature.

Images always know which is the original creature and never attack other images. In addition, enemies of the target no longer have any difficulty distinguishing the target from his or her images; all attacks can be directed against the actual creature without risk of hitting an image (unless the attacker wants to hit an image, of course).

Spyworm

3rd-level conjuration
Druid
Components: V, S
Casting Time: 1 action
Duration: 8 hours
Range: Touch
Area of Effect: 1 creature
Saving Throw: Con / negates effect

A small worm grows beneath the skin of a creature you touch if it fails a Constitution saving throw against disease. While the worm is under the target's skin, you can hear any sounds the target hears as though the worm was one of your ears, as long as you and the target are on the same plane of existence.

A *spyworm* can be removed by any effect that cures disease. It shrivels into nothingness when the spell ends.

Squeaking Floor Alarm

3rd-level illusion
Cleric
Components: V, S, M (a rusty hinge)
Casting Time: 1 action
Duration: 8 hours
Range: 30 ft.
Area of Effect: Square area, 10 ft. by 10 ft.
Saving Throw: None

You cause a 10-by-10-foot section of ground to squeak loudly when it's stepped on. Creatures that are trying to move silently can avoid triggering the noise with a successful Dexterity (Stealth) check against your spell save DC. The noise can be heard clearly within 100 feet, regardless of barriers.

Steam Bolt

3rd-level evocation
Druid, Sorcerer, Wizard
Components: V, S
Casting Time: 1 action
Duration: Instantaneous

Range: 150 ft.
Area of Effect: 1 creature
Saving Throw: None

You create a superheated bolt of steam and propel it at one creature you can see. Make a ranged spell attack roll against that creature. If it hits, the bolt does 8d6 fire damage and the creature must make a successful Dexterity saving throw or drop whatever it is holding.

Steam Cloud

4th-level evocation
Sorcerer, Wizard
Components: V, S
Casting Time: 1 action
Duration: Concentration, up to 1 minute
Range: 150 ft.
Area of Effect: Sphere, 20-ft. radius
Saving Throw: Con / half damage

You call up a billowing cloud of superheated water in a 20-foot-radius sphere within range. The area of the cloud is lightly obscured. Each creature that starts its turn in the cloud or enters the cloud takes 4d6 fire damage, or half damage with a successful Constitution saving throw. The area of the cloud is also quite slippery; any creature moving through it on the ground must make a successful Dexterity saving throw when it begins its move or fall prone.

At the beginning of each of your turns, the cloud moves 10 feet directly away from you. The cloud lasts for the duration of the spell or until a strong wind disperses it.

Steel Butterflies

4th-level conjuration
Wizard
Components: V, S
Casting Time: 1 action
Duration: 1 hour
Range: Self
Area of Effect: Cone, 30 ft. long
Saving Throw: Dex / half damage

You conjure numerous steel butterflies, which you release in a 30-foot cone. Each creature in the cone takes 10d4 slashing damage, or half damage with a successful Dexterity saving throw. Fey creatures have tactical disadvantage on the saving throw, and they are also stunned until the end of your next turn if the saving throw fails.

Enhancement: For each spell slot used higher than 4th level, the damage increases by 5 points.

Stench of Death

2nd-level transmutation
Druid
Components: V, S
Casting Time: 1 action
Duration: 1 hour
Range: Self
Area of Effect: Sphere, 20-ft. radius
Saving Throw: None

A pungent odor surrounds you. Beasts with an Intelligence of 3 or lower will not approach within 20 feet of you for the duration of the spell, unless they are eaters of carrion.

Sticky Tongue

2nd-level transmutation
Druid
Components: V, S, M (a frog)
Casting Time: 1 action
Duration: Concentration, up to 1 minute
Range: Touch
Area of Effect: 1 creature
Saving Throw: None

You transform the tongue of a willing creature so it becomes long and sticky, like the tongue of a frog.

For the duration, the creature can use a bonus action to make a melee weapon attack against one target within 10 feet. If the attack hits, the target is grappled. The tongue can grapple only one creature at a time, and a creature using its tongue to maintain a grapple can't speak or attack anything else with its tongue.

The grappled target can use an action to make a Strength (Athletics) or Dexterity (Acrobatics) check against your spell save DC to escape.

Enhancement: When you cast *sticky tongue* with a 3rd-level or higher spell slot, you can affect one additional creature for each slot level above 2nd.

Stonefast

4th-level abjuration
Cleric, Druid, Wizard
Components: V, S, M
Casting Time: 1 action
Duration: 1 day
Range: Touch
Area of Effect: 10,000 cubic ft. of stone
Saving Throw: See text

You touch stone and ward up to 10,000 cubic feet of it, making it immune to transmutation spells and impassable to creatures that meld or pass through stone. A creature already within the stone is trapped there unless it makes a successful Constitution saving throw, in which case it is expelled to the nearest empty space.

A simple way to envision the volume of this spell is 10 cubes, each 10 feet on a side (10 x 10 x 10). Bricks, mortared stone, and other constructions that are made of stone but are not solid stone are resistant to the effect; only half the normal volume is affected.

Storm of Vitriol

9th-level evocation
Sorcerer, Wizard
Components: V, S
Casting Time: 1 action
Duration: Instantaneous
Range: 1 mile
Area of Effect: Sphere, 100-ft. radius
Saving Throw: Dex / half damage; Con / negates effect

You create a compressed globule of vitriol at a point you can see within range, which then bursts into a 200-foot-sphere of caustic acid, corroding and dissolving anything in the area. Each creature in the affected area takes 6d10 + 20 acid damage, or half damage with a successful Dexterity saving throw. Each creature must also make a Constitution saving throw; if it fails, they are incapacitated for 1d4 rounds by the burning fumes. Creatures who don't breathe or that are immune to acid damage are unaffected by the second effect.

Strength of the Wyrm

8th-level transmutation
Cleric, Wizard
Components: V, S, M (scale from a dragon)
Casting Time: 1 action
Duration: Concentration, up to 1 minute
Range: Touch
Area of Effect: 1 creature
Saving Throw: None

Storm of Vitriol

One willing creature you touch increases its Strength to 25 and its Constitution to 19 for the duration. A creature that has a higher score in either ability keeps its innate score; its ability score isn't lowered because of this spell.

Stupefy

4th-level necromancy
Bard, Wizard
Components: V, S
Casting Time: 1 action
Duration: Instantaneous
Range: 30 ft.
Area of Effect: 1 creature
Saving Throw: Int / half damage

You psychically attack one creature you can see. The creature must make an Intelligence saving throw. If the saving throw fails, it takes 6d6 psychic damage and loses 2 points from Intelligence, Wisdom, and Charisma. If the save succeeds, it takes half damage and suffers no ability score loss. Lost ability points are restored after the creature's next short or long rest.

Summon Undead

3rd-level conjuration
Cleric, Wizard
Components: V, S
Casting Time: 1 action
Duration: Concentration, up to 1 hour
Range: 60 ft.
Area of Effect: See text

Saving Throw: None

You summon undead creatures from Orcus's realm that appear in unoccupied spaces you can see within range. The undead creatures disappear when their hit points drop to 0 or when the spell ends.

Roll initiative for the creatures when they arrive. They are considered your allies and companions. The undead follow your verbal commands, which you can issue as bonus actions. If the undead are not commanded, they don't take actions except to defend themselves from hostile creatures.

If your concentration on the spell is broken, the undead immediately turn against you and your companions; they do not disappear until an hour has passed since you summoned them.

You can choose what appears from among the following.
- One undead of CR 2 or lower
- Two undead of CR 1 or lower
- Four undead of CR 1/2 or lower
- Eight undead of CR 1/4 or lower

Enhancement: For each spell slot used higher than 3rd level, the challenge ratings of the undead you can summon increase by one step for each slot level above 3rd (1/4 to 1/2 to 1 to 2 to 3, etc.).

Swirling Leaves

2nd-level abjuration
Ranger
Components: V, S
Casting Time: 1 action
Duration: Concentration, up to 1 minute
Range: Self
Area of Effect: Self
Saving Throw: None

You surround yourself with swirling leaves that lightly obscure you for the spell's duration.

Tattoo Object

5th-level transmutation
Wizard
Components: V, S
Casting Time: 1 action
Duration: 24 hours
Range: Touch
Area of Effect: 1 object weighing up to 50 lbs.
Saving Throw: None

With a touch, you convert one nonmagical object into a tattoo that appears on the body of a willing creature within 10 feet. The object must weigh no more than 50 lbs. The tattoo shows the object at one-twelfth of its normal dimensions; the spell fails if such a tattoo can't physically be placed on the creature.

Either you or the recipient can end the spell by using a bonus action. The object then reappears, either in the hand of the spell's recipient or adjacent to them, if desired.

Enhancement: When you cast *tattoo object* with an 8th-level or higher spell slot, you can affect magical objects. Their magical abilities are suppressed while in tattoo form.

Taunt

2nd-level enchantment
Bard
Components: V, S
Casting Time: 1 action
Duration: Concentration, up to 1 minute
Range: 30 ft.
Area of Effect: All humanoid enemies
Saving Throw: Wis / negates effect

You call out insults and challenges that irritate and enrage nearby creatures, forcing them to direct all their attacks against you. Each enemy humanoid within 30 feet must make a Wisdom saving throw. If the saving throw fails, it can't move away from you and any attack it makes or offensive spell it casts must include you as one of the targets. At the end of each of its turns, an affected humanoid can repeat the saving throw; a successful save ends the effect on that creature.

Tenacious Blade

3rd-level conjuration
Warlock, Wizard
Components: V, S
Casting Time: 1 bonus action
Duration: Concentration, up to 1 minute
Range: Self
Area of Effect: 1 dagger
Saving Throw: None initially; Con negates effect

You create a metal dagger in your hand that is treated as a magical *dagger +1*. Upon striking a creature, the blade breaks off and remains stuck in the creature. The affected creature must make a Constitution saving throw at the start of each of its turns. If the saving throw fails, the creature takes 2d6 piercing damage and is incapacitated until the end of its turn. If the saving throw succeeds, the blade drops out of the wound and disappears, ending the spell.

Tendrils of Night

9th-level conjuration
Sorcerer, Wizard
Components: V, S, M (black pearl worth at least 500 gp, which is consumed in the casting)
Casting Time: 1 action
Duration: Concentration, up to 1 minute
Range: 150 ft.

116

Area of Effect: Circle, 5-ft. radius
Saving Throw: Dex / negates effect

You create a portal to an eldritch realm inside a 10-foot circle that opens in the floor centered on a point you can see. Creatures standing on the portal when it opens can make a Dexterity saving throw to jump to the nearest safe space and avoid being drawn through the portal inadvertently.

Immediately after the portal appears, four 30-foot-long tendrils emerge from it. When you cast the spell and at the beginning of each of your turns, each tendril tries to grapple one creature; you select the targets. Make a melee spell attack for each tendril. If it hits, the target is grappled and dragged 10 feet toward the portal. Instead of attacking, a tendril that already has a creature grappled drags it another 10 feet closer to the portal. Grappled creatures can escape by making appropriate ability checks against your spell saving throw DC.

Creatures that fall or are pulled into the portal no longer exist on the plane where *tendrils of night* was cast; they are inside the eldritch realm where the tendrils originate. They must make Constitution saving throws at the start of each of their turns. If the saving throw fails, the creature takes 4d6 necrotic damage and its maximum hit points are reduced by the same number. As an action, the creature can try to escape by making a Strength check against your spell saving throw DC; if it succeeds, it appears in the unoccupied space closest to the portal.

When the spell ends, creatures pulled through the portal reappear in the portal's space, alive or dead.

Thorn Snare

2nd-level transmutation
Druid
Components: V, S
Casting Time: 1 action
Duration: 1 minute
Range: 50 ft.
Area of Effect: Four 5-ft. by 5-ft. by 3-ft. high thickets
Saving Throw: Dex / negates damage for 1 turn

You cause a dense thicket to grow instantly. The thicket is 3 feet tall, covers 100 square feet of ground, and must be at least 5 feet wide at every point. (A simple way to think of this is four squares, each 5-by-5 feet horizontally and 3 feet high.) The thicket must be continuous; no portion of it can be separate from the rest. The thicket is difficult terrain to move through. The first time a creature moves in the thicket each turn, it must make a successful Dexterity saving throw or take 1d6 piercing damage from thorns.

Torrent

6th-level conjuration
Cleric, Druid
Components: V, S
Casting Time: 1 action
Duration: Instantaneous
Range: Self
Area of Effect: Cone, 60 ft. long
Saving Throw: Dex / half damage

You conjure a 60-foot cone of water from your hands. Each creature in the area must make a Dexterity saving throw. If the saving throw fails, the creature takes 7d6 + 15 bludgeoning damage and is pushed 30 feet away from you. On a successful save, the creature takes half damage and is not pushed.

Touch of Madness

8th-level enchantment
Wizard
Components: V, S, M (a handful of coal dust)
Casting Time: 1 action
Duration: Instantaneous
Range: 150 ft.
Area of Effect: 1 creature

Saving Throw: Wis / negates effect

The judgment of a creature you can see is overwhelmed with contradictory images and impulses. The creature takes 4d6 psychic damage and must make a Wisdom saving throw. If the saving throw fails, the creature's Wisdom score becomes 1, it can't cast divine spells, and it becomes incredibly trusting, always following the last order given to it by anyone unless doing so would cause self-harm.

At the end of every 30 days, the creature can repeat the saving throw to end the effect. The spell can also be ended by a *greater restoration*, *heal*, or *wish* spell.

Track Magic

4th-level divination
Ranger
Components: V, S
Casting Time: 1 action
Duration: Concentration, up to 8 hours
Range: Self
Area of Effect: Self
Saving Throw: None

You gain the ability to track magical auras. You can follow the trail of any creature that is affected by ongoing spells or is carrying magical items. You must still make Wisdom (Survival) checks to follow the trail, but terrain and weather conditions have no effect on your tracking ability.

Tracker's Gaze

5th-level divination
Cleric
Components: V, S
Casting Time: 1 action
Duration: 8 hours
Range: 200 ft.
Area of Effect: 1 creature
Saving Throw: None

Select one creature you can see within 200 feet. For the duration of the spell, you can see the creature clearly, regardless of distance, cover, lighting, or even magic, as long as the creature is within the range of your normal vision. Obstacles still block your vision, but unless the creature has total cover, you can still perceive it clearly. *Tracker's gaze* doesn't allow you to see the true form of polymorphed creatures, but it does allow you to see the exact location of creatures affected by *mirror image* and similar displacement effects.

Tranquil Grove

8th-level conjuration
Druid
Components: V, S, M (an acorn)
Casting Time: 1 action
Duration: 12 hours
Range: 50 ft.
Area of Effect: a single glade or copse up to 30 ft. in diameter
Saving Throw: None

You create a small green glade or copse of trees that exudes peace and tranquility. Any creatures that take a long rest in the grove regain all hit points and hit dice as normal, and they are cured of all diseases, they recover fully from exhaustion, and all poison in their systems is neutralized.

The grove also contains enough food to feed ten Small or Medium creatures. Finally, the grove and everything inside it are invisible to all creatures outside the grove except for those you allow to perceive it.

Up to ten creatures can rest in the grove at one time. The spell can only be cast outdoors.

Transfer of Vigor

5th-level transmutation
Cleric, Druid, Warlock, Wizard
Components: V, S
Casting Time: 1 action
Duration: Concentration, up to 1 hour
Range: Touch
Area of Effect: 1 creature
Saving Throw: Con / negates effect

You touch a creature and attempt to gain its physical prowess. The creature can make a Constitution saving throw if it chooses to. If the saving throw fails or if the creature didn't make a saving throw, you exchange Strength and Constitution scores with the target for the duration of the spell. *Transfer of Vigor* ends if either you or the target drops to 0 hit points.

Transform Boulder to Pebble

4th-level transmutation
Druid, Wizard
Components: V, S
Casting Time: 1 action
Duration: Permanent
Range: 50 ft.
Area of Effect: 1 boulder
Saving Throw: None

You transform one natural boulder you can see into a pebble no more than 1 inch in diameter. The boulder can be no more than 1,000 cubic feet (a cube 10 feet on a side, or a sphere 12 feet in diameter). The boulder remains in pebble form until the magic is dispelled. The spell has no effect on creatures of living stone or on man-made objects; the target must be a boulder in its natural state.

Enhancement: For each spell slot used higher than 4th level, you can affect an additional boulder.

Transform Pebble to Boulder

4th-level transmutation
Druid, Wizard
Components: V, S
Casting Time: 1 action
Duration: Permanent
Range: Touch
Area of Effect: 1 pebble
Saving Throw: None

You transform one pebble you touch into a boulder up to 1,000 cubic feet in volume (a cube 10 feet on a side, or a sphere 12 feet in diameter). If you throw the pebble as part of the spell, it transforms in flight, and you can make a ranged spell attack against one creature within 30 feet. On a hit, the boulder does 6d10 bludgeoning damage.

Transform Zombie

5th-level necromancy
Wizard
Components: V, S, M (a bone from a ghoul)
Casting Time: 1 action
Duration: Permanent
Range: Touch
Area of Effect: 1 zombie
Saving Throw: None

One zombie that you touch becomes a ghoul. If you previously had control of the zombie, you retain control of the ghoul.

Transmute Gold to Steel

6th-level transmutation
Wizard
Components: V, S
Casting Time: 1 action
Duration: Permanent
Range: Touch
Area of Effect: 20 lbs. of gold
Saving Throw: None

You transmute up to 20 lbs. of gold into a strong substance that appears to be gold but has the strength of steel.

Soft, easily worked gold can be shaped into complex forms or razor-thin blades and then given the strength of the highest-grade steel with this spell. The metal created by the spell is free from any flaws or imperfections and is ready for immediate enhancement. It also holds enhancements better and longer than less-pure forms of steel. The exact effects of this are left to the GM.

Transparent Steel

6th-level transmutation
Wizard
Components: V, S
Casting Time: 1 action
Duration: Permanent
Range: Touch
Area of Effect: 100 lbs. of steel
Saving Throw: None

You transmute up to 100 lbs. of steel so that it becomes transparent. Visually, it is indistinguishable from high-grade glass, but it retains all of its other properties. Weapons made of transparent steel get a +1 bonus to hit creatures that rely on sight, as they have trouble seeing and countering the weapon.

Tree Ladder

1st-level transmutation
Druid, Ranger
Components: V, S
Casting Time: 1 action
Duration: 1 minute
Range: Touch
Area of Effect: 1 tree
Saving Throw: None

One living tree that you touch instantly grows ladderlike holds, allowing it to be climbed easily by humanoid creatures. The DC to climb the tree drops to 5. The handholds are sturdy enough to hold 500 lbs. of weight. The spell has no effect if cast on a tree creature.

Tremorsense

2nd-level divination
Druid, Ranger
Components: V, S
Casting Time: 1 action
Duration: 1 minutes
Range: Self
Area of Effect: Self
Saving Throw: None

You gain tremorsense, enabling you to detect moving creatures that are in contact with the ground (or other solid or liquid surroundings) within 30 feet of your location. You must be on the ground (or in contact with the same liquid or solid) for the ability to work. Creatures detected this way can be "seen" as clearly as if you were using your eyes.

Twig Torture

4th-level transmutation
Cleric, Warlock, Wizard
Components: V, S, M (a personal object belonging to the caster, twine left outside during a full moon)
Casting Time: 1 action
Duration: 8 hours
Range: 1 mile
Area of Effect: 1 creature
Saving Throw: Wis / negates effect

You form a crude representation of a humanoid creature from dead twigs. Something belonging to the target must be incorporated into the twig doll. The creature must make a Wisdom saving throw. If the saving throw fails, the twig doll is mystically linked to the targeted creature.

As an action, you can break or burn parts of the twig doll to injure the linked creature. A maximum of 10d6 force or fire damage can be inflicted on the linked creature. The damage can be done all at once, or in smaller amounts at a time. For example, you could spend an action to inflict 1d6 fire damage on your turn. On your next turn, you could do 5d6 force damage. This leaves 4d6 damage that could be inflicted at a later time.

The doll is destroyed and the spell ends when 10d6 damage has been done.

Twisted Magic

3rd-level enchantment
Bard, Wizard
Components: V, S
Casting Time: 1 action
Duration: Concentration, up to 1 hour
Range: 50 ft.
Area of Effect: 1 creature
Saving Throw: Wis / negates effect

Choose a creature you can see. The creature must make a successful Wisdom saving throw or become temporarily cursed. The next time the creature casts a spell, the player chooses the level of spell they wish to cast, but the actual spell cast is selected randomly from all their prepared or available spells of that level. If they have only one spell to choose from at that level, then it has an unusual, reduced, or unexpected effect; the Wild Magic table can be used for inspiration, but the changes should never be beneficial to the caster.

If *twisted magic* is cast on a player character, it's recommended the GM make the character's Wisdom saving throw so the player can't be sure whether the character is under the spell's effect. Although the spell that gets cast could be chosen randomly, GMs with a flair for the dramatic can instead choose a specific spell for its absurd or disastrous result in the current situation.

Twitch

1st-level enchantment
Bard, Wizard
Components: V, S
Casting Time: 1 action
Duration: Concentration, up to 1 minute
Range: 30 ft.
Area of Effect: 1 creature
Saving Throw: Wis / negates effect

One creature you can see within range begins twitching its fingers uncontrollably. While the spell is in effect, an affected creature must make a successful Wisdom saving throw to cast a spell with a somatic component; if the saving throw fails, the intended spell fails and the spell slot is expended. An affected creature also must make a Wisdom saving throw before making a Dexterity check that requires fine control of the hands, such as using thieves' tools; if the saving throw fails, the Dexterity check fails automatically. A successful Wisdom saving throw ends the spell effect.

Umbral Images

3rd-level illusion
Wizard
Components: V, S
Casting Time: 1 action
Duration: 1 minute
Range: Self
Area of Effect: 3 images
Saving Throw: None

This spell works the same as *mirror image*, but the images are infused with shadow energy so they don't disappear immediately when struck. Instead, an image is destroyed only by an attack that does 10 or more damage.

Umbral Storm

8th-level necromancy
Wizard
Components: V, S
Casting Time: 1 action
Duration: Instantaneous
Range: 400 ft.
Area of Effect: Sphere, 20-ft. radius
Saving Throw: Con / half damage and exhaustion

You create a spherical storm of necrotic energy surrounding a point you can see, with a 20-foot radius. Each creature in the area must make a Constitution saving throw. If the saving throw fails, it first loses all temporary hit points and then takes 5d6 + 30 necrotic damage; on a successful save, the creature does not lose temporary hit points and takes half damage.

Umbral Strike

3rd-level necromancy
Wizard
Components: V, S
Casting Time: 1 action
Duration: 1 minute
Range: Touch
Area of Effect: 1 creature
Saving Throw: Wis / negates effect

Tendrils of shadow-stuff under your control infiltrate into the aura of a creature you touch. The creature makes a Wisdom saving throw. If the saving throw fails, or if the creature is willing to be affected, you can cast touch spells on the creature as long as you can see it, regardless of whether you can actually touch it.

Umbral Touch

4th-level necromancy
Cleric, Wizard
Components: V, S
Casting Time: 1 action
Duration: 1 minute
Range: Self
Area of Effect: Self
Saving Throw: None

You gain a Strength-draining attack. As an action, you can make a melee spell attack against one creature within your reach. If you hit, the creature loses 1d4 points of Strength. If the creature is reduced to 0 Strength, it dies; 1d4 rounds later, it reanimates as a shadow under your control, with the stats of a standard shadow.

Umbral Transformation

6th-level transmutation
Wizard
Components: V, S
Casting Time: 1 action
Duration: Concentration, up to 1 hour
Range: 30 ft.
Area of Effect: 1 object weighing up to 50 lbs.
Saving Throw: Wis / negates effect (see text)

You transmute one nonmagical object of up to 50 lbs. that you can see into shadow-stuff. If the item is attended, its possessor can make a Wisdom saving throw; on a successful save, the item is unaffected. Otherwise, the item is transformed.

A shadow item has an indistinct, shadowy hue when in dim light, but it can be used normally in such light. In bright light and darkness, the item becomes barely visible, insubstantial, and useless; it functions only in dim light. A shadow-stuff item is destroyed instantly if it is exposed to true sunlight.

If you maintain concentration on this spell for the full hour, the transformation becomes permanent.

Umbral Weapon

5th-level necromancy
Wizard
Components: V, S
Casting Time: 1 bonus action
Duration: Concentration, up to 1 minute
Range: Self
Area of Effect: Self
Saving Throw: None

You reach into nearby shadows and use them to create a blade made of shadow-stuff. The blade can resemble any weapon you are proficient with. For the duration of the spell, you can wield the *umbral weapon* like a normal melee weapon, but you use your spellcasting ability and spell attack bonus when attacking. The weapon does 3d8 necrotic damage, and the target loses 1 point of Strength unless it makes a successful Constitution saving throw. The *umbral weapon* gains a +3 bonus to damage for every point of Strength it drains. A creature reduced to 0 Strength by this blade dies instantly, and rises in 2d4 rounds as a shadow.

The blade disappears if you let go of it, but during the spell's duration, you can create it again in your hand with a bonus action.

Unchained Melody

1st-level transmutation
Bard
Components: V
Casting Time: 1 bonus action
Duration: 1 round
Range: Self
Area of Effect: Sphere, 30-ft. radius
Saving Throw: None

Until the end of your next turn, each creature within 30 feet of you can add 1d4 to its ability checks made to escape from a grapple or other restraint.

Undead Alteration

2nd-level illusion
Wizard
Components: V, S, M (sinew from a mammal and a drop of quicksilver)
Casting Time: 1 action
Duration: 10 minutes
Range: Touch
Area of Effect: 1 undead creature
Saving Throw: None

You give one undead creature you touch the appearance of a skeleton or a zombie. A creature that uses its action to investigate the monster can determine its true nature with an Intelligence (Investigation) check against your spell save DC.

Undertow

2nd-level evocation
Wizard
Components: V, S
Casting Time: 1 action
Duration: Concentration, up to 1 minute
Range: 50 ft.
Area of Effect: Cube, 20 ft. square
Saving Throw: Str / negates effect

You create a powerful undertow in a 20-foot cube centered on a point you can see. Any creature swimming in the area must make a successful Strength saving throw or be pulled underwater and restrained. A creature can use its action to make a Strength (Athletics) or Dexterity (Acrobatics) check against your spell save DC; it breaks free from the restraint if the check succeeds, but it becomes restrained again if it's still in the undertow at the end of its turn.

Undetectable Charm

2nd-level abjuration
Bard, Wizard
Components: V, S
Casting Time: 1 action
Duration: 24 hours
Range: 50 ft.
Area of Effect: 1 creature
Saving Throw: None

One magical charm effect on one creature you can see becomes undetectable by magical means, such as *detect magic*.

Undulating Earth

3rd-level transmutation
Druid, Wizard
Components: V, S
Casting Time: 1 action
Duration: Concentration, up to 1 minute
Range: Self
Area of Effect: Cone, 60 ft. long
Saving Throw: Dex / negates effect

You touch the ground at your feet and cause it to ripple in a 60-foot cone away from you in the direction of your choice. For the duration of the spell, the ground continues rippling and shaking. The area is treated as difficult terrain and every creature in the area must make a successful Dexterity saving throw at the end of its turn or fall prone. Objects fall over, but structures and rooted plants are unaffected.

Unfasten

3rd-level transmutation
Bard, Wizard
Components: V
Casting Time: 1 action
Duration: Instantaneous
Range: 120 ft.
Area of Effect: Cylinder, 10-ft. radius, 10 ft. high
Saving Throw: Dex / negates effect

You cause all buckles to become unbuckled and all clasps to become unclasped in a cylindrical area 10 feet high and with a 10-foot radius, around a point you can see. An affected creature can negate the effect on

121

itself with a successful Dexterity saving throw. Armor that's unfastened by this spell remains on the creature wearing it, but the creature's AC is reduced by 2 until it spends an action refastening it. The spell only affects clothing, armor, and other accoutrements such as pouches and backpacks. It does not affect locks or latches.

Unfettered Steed

1st-level transmutation
Paladin
Components: V, S
Casting Time: 1 action
Duration: 10 minutes
Range: Touch
Area of Effect: 1 mount
Saving Throw: None

For the duration of the spell, one mount takes no speed penalty from wearing armor.

Unholy Glare

5th-level necromancy
Cleric
Components: V, S
Casting Time: 1 action
Duration: Concentration, up to 1 minute
Range: Self
Area of Effect: Sphere, 30-ft. radius
Saving Throw: Con / negates effect

Your eyes glitter with unholy fury. For the duration of the spell, each non-evil creature within 30 feet of you that can see you must make a successful Constitution saving throw or be paralyzed until the start of its next turn. Unless surprised, a creature can avert its gaze to avoid the saving throw, but it suffers the usual penalties for attacking an unseen target if it attacks you before the start of its next turn.

Unstoppable Tracker

3rd-level transmutation
Ranger
Components: V, S
Casting Time: 1 action
Duration: Concentration, up to 8 hours
Range: Self
Area of Effect: Self
Saving Throw: None

For the duration of this spell, you have tactical advantage on Wisdom (Survival) and Wisdom (Perception) checks, and you don't suffer penalties from exhaustion. When this spell ends, you gain one level of exhaustion.

Unyielding Durability

5th-level transmutation
Wizard
Components: V, S
Casting Time: 1 action
Duration: 10 minutes
Range: Touch
Area of Effect: 1 object up to 20 lbs.
Saving Throw: None

One item you touch, which can weigh no more than 20 lbs., becomes unbreakable and can't be damaged for the duration of this spell. If the item is subjected to a *disintegrate* effect, it is unaffected but this spell immediately ends.

Vengeful Environs

5th-level transmutation
Druid, Ranger
Components: V, S
Casting Time: 1 action
Duration: Concentration, up to 1 minute
Range: 150 ft.
Area of Effect: Cylinder, 40-ft. radius, 20 ft. high
Saving Throw: None

From a point you can see, you raise a cylinder of magical energy with a 40-foot radius and 20 feet in height. All plants and animals inside the affected area become infuriated, so that they bite and sting and lash out against all nearby creatures.

Every creature that begins its turn inside the affected area takes 3d6 + 10 piercing damage from bites, stings, and lacerations. Creatures in the affected area also make concentration checks with tactical disadvantage.

Animals and swarms of insects are drawn to the area affected by *vengeful environs*, so killing a few of them doesn't lessen the spell's effect. An area-effect attack that hits AC 5 and does at least 20 points of damage, however, clears a 5-by-5-by-5-foot cube of infuriated creatures inside the spell's area; once cleared this way, that zone doesn't refill.

Vermin Swarm

4th-level conjuration
Wizard
Components: V, S
Casting Time: 1 action
Duration: Concentration, up to 10 minutes
Range: 60 ft.
Area of Effect: 1 or more swarms
Saving Throw: None

You summon one or more swarms of creatures that appear at the points you select within range. They can appear in spaces occupied by other creatures, but those creatures can make Dexterity saving throws; on a successful save, they jump to the nearest safe square.

Choose one of the following options when you cast the spell.
- One swarm of CR 2 or lower
- Two swarms of CR 1 or lower
- Four swarms of CR ½ or lower
- Eight swarms of CR ¼ or lower

Only swarms categorized as beasts can be summoned. A swarm vanishes when its hit points drop to 0 or when the spell ends.

Swarms obey your mental commands and move on their own turns; roll initiative for them when you cast the spell. If you don't issue any orders to a swarm, it stays where it is but attacks creatures in its space.

Enhancement: When you cast *vermin swarm* with a 7th-level or higher spell slot, you summon double the normal number of swarms. If you use a 9th-level spell-slot, you get triple the normal number.

Vigil of Enlightenment

2nd-level divination
Paladin
Components: V
Casting Time: 8 hours
Duration: Instantaneous
Range: Self
Area of Effect: Self
Saving Throw: None

After kneeling in unceasing prayer for eight hours, you are granted a vision of what your deity would have you do.

The vision granted may be symbolic or simply obscure; you must demonstrate your wisdom by interpreting the vision correctly. For example, a vision of a beggar huddled before a crumbling, forgotten tower on a windswept heath may be symbolic of a disgraced noble bloodline that you should aid, or it might be a vision of a physical tower to which you must journey.

A *vigil of enlightenment* is often expected as atonement from paladins who have shown cowardice, weakness in devotion, laxity in duty, or who have disappointed their deity or their order in any other way. But it is also useful to those who face difficult trials, who don't know how to proceed on a challenging quest, or who simply want a new "mission" to further the interest of the sometimes inscrutable entity they serve.

Although you can cast *vigil of enlightenment* again before completing an errand shown to you previously, doing so is considered ungrateful and a sign of weak faith.

Vile Vintage

5th-level transmutation
Cleric, Druid, Wizard
Components: V, S, M (powdered gemstones)
Casting Time: 1 action
Duration: Permanent
Range: Touch
Area of Effect: 1 container of wine, up to 1 cubic ft.
Saving Throw: None

You transform up to 1 cubic foot (7.5 gallons) of wine into poison. The wine must be in a container, and all of the wine in the container must be affected for the spell to work; the spell fails if it is cast on just 7.5 gallons of wine in a full, 50-gallon barrel. The wine can be poisoned with any of the game's standard, ingested poisons. The material component cost is the same as one dose of the poison.

Vines of Binding

4th-level conjuration
Druid
Components: V, S
Casting Time: 1 action
Duration: 1 minute
Range: 30 ft.
Area of Effect: 4 vines
Saving Throw: Dex / negates effect

You create up to four vines that spring from your fingers and attempt to wrap themselves around creatures you can see within range. You select each creature that will be affected. A creature be targeted by more than one vine.

Each target must make a Dexterity saving throw for each vine that attacks it. If the saving throw fails, the creature is restrained and falls prone; it is wrapped up securely by the vine.

A creature restrained by a vine can escape by using an action to make a Strength (Athletics) or Dexterity (Acrobatics) check against your spell save DC. Each restraining vine must be escaped individually. Vines can also be cut; each one has AC 15 and 10 hit points, and they are immune to all but slashing, acid, and fire damage.

Vines that miss their targets or that the target escapes from quickly wither and turn to dust, as do all remaining vines when the spell ends.

Violent Scream

5th-level evocation
Bard, Sorcerer, Wizard
Components: V
Casting Time: 1 action
Duration: Instantaneous
Range: Self
Area of Effect: Cone, 30 ft. long
Saving Throw: Con / half damage

You scream and emit a 30-foot cone of damaging sound. Each creature in the cone takes 8d8 thunder damage and is deafened for one minute, or takes half damage and is not deafened with a successful Constitution saving throw.

Enhancement: For each spell slot used higher than 5th level, *violent scream* does an additional 1d8 damage.

Voice of Confession

4th-level enchantment
Bard
Components: V, S, M (a shiny gold coin)
Casting Time: 1 action
Duration: 10 minutes
Range: 30 ft.
Area of Effect: 1 creature
Saving Throw: Cha / negates effect for 1 question

One creature you can see becomes enchanted by your voice so that it has a very hard time lying to you. You can ask up to seven questions of the creature. The creature must answer each question truthfully unless it makes a successful Charisma saving throw; the saving throw is repeated for each question. Creatures that can't be charmed are immune to the effect of this spell.

If you ask the creature the same question twice, it doesn't make a new saving throw but uses the same result as the previous time you asked. This quirk of the spell can be overcome by framing the question differently and winning a contest between your Charisma (Deception) check and the creature's Wisdom (Insight) check. For example, asking "How many ogres are in the giant king's army" twice won't accomplish much; if the creature was able to lie the first time, it can lie again the second time. If the creature answered "fifteen" and you then ask, "Does the giant king's army include fifteen ogres," it triggers a contest. If the creature wins the contest, it uses the earlier saving throw result (if that save succeeded) or makes a new one (if the previous saving throw failed). If the creature loses the contest, those results are reversed.

Voice of Memories

5th-level enchantment
Bard
Components: V, S
Casting Time: 1 action
Duration: 3 minutes
Range: Touch
Area of Effect: 1 creature
Saving Throw: Wis / negates effect

You weave magic into you voice or music as you attempt to hypnotize one living creature you can see. The creature must make a Wisdom saving throw. If the saving throw fails, its unconscious mind comes under your control. You have a period of three minutes in which you can instill false memories or cause the target to forget painful experiences. New memories are somewhat fragmented, but the target's mind fills them in, actually making the spell more effective over time.

A new memory that goes against the target's real experiences allows the creature to make another Wisdom saving throw to reject the "memory" as nothing but a dream. For example, a paladin who "remembers" committing an infamous local murder is likely to question that memory's veracity.

This spell can be used to set up a "patsy" to take the blame for a crime, or it can be used to help erase and ease painful memories so that an individual can move back into normal life after a horrible trauma. The spell reveals no information about memories in the target's mind; the spellcaster is well-advised to become familiar with the creature's background before trying to erase or add memories.

Volley of Thorns

3rd-level evocation
Druid
Components: V, S
Casting Time: 1 action
Duration: Instantaneous
Range: Self
Area of Effect: Cone, 60 ft. long
Saving Throw: Dex / half damage

You project a blast of sharp thorns in a 60-foot cone from your outstretched hand. Each creature in the cone takes 6d6 piercing damage, or half damage with a successful Dexterity saving throw. A target whose AC (including cover bonuses) is equal to or greater than the spellcaster's save DC takes half damage from the spell normally, or no damage with a successful Dexterity saving throw.

Enhancement: For each spell slot used higher than 3rd level, the damage increases by 1d6.

Volley Spell

7th-level abjuration
Wizard
Components: V, S, M (a bent willow wrapped with strands of gut)
Casting Time: 1 action
Duration: 8 hours
Range: Touch
Area of Effect: 1 creature
Saving Throw: None

You weave a ward of protection about one willing creature. That creature gains the ability to use its reaction to turn one spell that allows a saving throw back at the spell's caster.

The target of the reflected spell makes a saving throw against it. If the save is successful, the spell rebounds again, back to the original target. That creature then makes its own saving throw, and if successful, the spell rebounds again. The spell continues to rebound between the original caster and the original target until one or the other fails its saving throw; at that point, the spell takes full effect and stops rebounding. If this hasn't happened by the time six saving throws have been made (three from each target), the spell dissipates harmlessly.

In the case of an area effect spell, only that portion of the spell that would affect the warded creature is volleyed; the rest of it goes off and affects other creatures in the original target area as normal. If several creatures in the area of effect are warded by this spell, the original caster could take the effect of the spell several times over!

Wail of Fate

5th-level necromancy
Bard, Cleric, Sorcerer, Wizard
Components: V, S
Casting Time: 1 action
Duration: Instantaneous
Range: Self
Area of Effect: Cone, 30 ft. long
Saving Throw: Con / negates effect

You project a scream of doom at all creatures in a 30-foot cone. Each creature in the cone must make a Constitution saving throw. If the saving throw fails, the affected creature must roll on the table below to determine the effect of the spell.

d4	Effect
1, 2	The creature is permanently deafened.
3	The creature is incapacitated and can't move. It can repeat the saving throw at the end of each of its turns; a successful save ends the effect.
4	The creature suffers both effects above.

In addition, a creature that fails its saving throw has tactical disadvantage on attack rolls. It can make a Wisdom saving throw at the of each of its turns; a successful save ends the tactical disadvantage.

Wailing Dirge

3rd-level enchantment
Bard
Components: V, S
Casting Time: 1 action
Duration: Concentration, up to 10 minutes
Range: 30 ft.
Area of Effect: Sphere, 30-ft. radius
Saving Throw: Wis / negates effect

You perform a piece of haunting music that sends those who hear it into states of deep depression. Each humanoid creature within range and capable of hearing the music must make a Wisdom saving throw. If the saving throw fails, the creature suffers crushing sadness; it is incapacitated, unable to move, and it has a 50% chance of dropping everything it is holding. While the effect lasts, the creature can do nothing but lament its misfortune.

The spell ends if an affected creature is attacked. If any action is taken that would normally cause a creature to react violently, it make another Wisdom save to break free of the spell.

Walk in the Moonlight

3rd-level transmutation
Cleric, Druid
Components: V, S
Casting Time: 1 action
Duration: 1 hour
Range: Self
Area of Effect: Self
Saving Throw: None

For the duration of the spell, you gain the ability to walk on surfaces illuminated by unfiltered moonlight as if they were horizontal, solid floors. For instance, you could walk across water where an unbroken strip of moonlight shined on its surface, or you could walk up a moonlit wall as if it were a level floor.

Wall of Blood

4th-level conjuration
Wizard
Components: V, S
Casting Time: 1 action
Duration: 1 minute
Range: 100 ft.
Area of Effect: Wall, 40 ft. long, 20 ft. high, 1 ft. thick
Saving Throw: Dex / negates dropping; Con / negates
    incapacitation

Blood pours from your hands and forms into a heaving, queasy, crimson wall of blood. The flat, vertical, 12-inch-thick barrier appears where you designate; its entire lower edge must be supported by a solid, reasonably flat surface. The entire wall must be within the spell's

Wall of Blood

range, and it must be 1 foot thick and 20 feet high along its whole length. Within those restrictions, it can bend however the caster chooses.

Objects and creatures can pass through the liquid wall. It lightly obscures everything behind it. Anything that passes through it becomes coated with thick, slippery fluid. Any creature that passes through the wall must make both a Dexterity saving throw and a Constitution saving throw. If the Dexterity saving throw fails, the creature drops any items it is holding. If the Constitution saving throw fails, the creature is nauseated by the experience; it becomes incapacitated until the end of its next turn. Creatures that enjoy the taste of blood or that have no sense of taste and smell are immune to the nauseating effect.

Wall of Water

3rd-level conjuration
Druid, Wizard
Components: V, S, M (a vial of water)
Casting Time: 1 action
Duration: 10 minutes
Range: 100 ft.
Area of Effect: Wall, 30 ft. long, 20 ft. tall, 5 ft. thick
Saving Throw: None

An immobile curtain of water springs into existence in the area you designate. The wall must be contiguous, it must be at least 5 feet thick along its entire length, you must be able to see the whole thing, and all of it must be within 100 feet of you. The wall need not be anchored on its sides, but the bottom of it must touch the ground everywhere (it can't bridge gaps in the ground). The wall can be composed of saltwater, freshwater, or brackish water, depending on the water used for the material component.

A wall of water is up to 30 feet long, 20 feet high, and 5 feet thick. A simple way to envision this is as six 5-by-5-foot squares of water, each 20 feet high. Alternatively, the "wall" can be conjured as a hemisphere of water 30 feet in diameter and 15 feet tall at the center.

The wall can't be conjured so that another object or a Small or larger creature is inside it.

No spell effect or missile (magical or mundane) can pass through the wall. Creatures on one side of the wall are heavily obscured from the other side. Creatures can enter and move inside the wall as difficult terrain. Flame creatures take 3d6 cold damage if they start their turn inside the wall or enter it during their turn.

When the spell ends, the water disappears entirely.

Warrior's Touch

4th-level transmutation
Warlock, Wizard
Components: V, S
Casting Time: 1 action
Duration: Concentration, up to 1 minute
Range: Touch
Area of Effect: 1 creature
Saving Throw: None

One willing creature that you touch gains a +1 bonus on weapon attack rolls and gets tactical advantage on Constitution checks and Constitution saving throws. The creature also gains 20 temporary hit points.

Water Double

3rd-level transmutation
Wizard
Components: V, S
Casting Time: 1 action
Duration: See text
Range: Touch
Area of Effect: 1 body of liquid
Saving Throw: None

By touching a body of liquid ranging in size from a goblet to an ocean, you cause the liquid to form an exact duplicate of the first living creature to cast a reflection on its surface. The liquid holds the spell until it's triggered, and does not evaporate while so enchanted.

When a creature casts a reflection on the liquid, an exact double rises from the liquid in the same round. The double is as large as the amount of water allows, up to the same size as the original creature. For example, if the enchanted liquid is contained in a goblet, then the double can be only about 6 inches tall.

Once it appears, the double remains for 10 rounds. The water double's speed is twice that of the original creature. It can't use any of the creature's equipment, spells, attacks, or special abilities. Being amorphous, it can flow through cracks and openings as small as one-half-inch square. It can't be damaged or physically destroyed, but it can be dispelled.

The water double tries to touch the creature it resembles, moving toward it by the shortest available route. It must make a successful melee spell attack to touch its original, using your melee spell attack bonus. If it misses, the double collapses into a puddle and the spell ends. If it hits, the double spreads across the target's body, engulfing it in a film of crushing water; the target takes 2d6 bludgeoning damage at the start of each of its turns. After taking the damage, the target can make a Constitution saving throw; a successful save ends the spell.

Watery Blood

5th-level necromancy
Cleric, Druid
Components: V, S
Casting Time: 1 action
Duration: See text
Range: Touch
Area of Effect: 1 creature
Saving Throw: Con / negates effect

One creature you touch must make a successful Constitution saving throw or be cursed; its blood becomes watery and doesn't clot normally. Whenever the creature takes piercing or slashing damage, it begins bleeding profusely. It suffers one-fourth of the original damage (rounded down) at the end of each of its turns until it regains hit points, or until it or an adjacent ally binds the wound by spending an action and making a successful Wisdom (Medicine) check against your spell save DC.

Weaken Fiendish Will

5th-level enchantment
Sorcerer, Wizard
Components: V, S
Casting Time: 1 action
Duration: Concentration, up to 3 rounds
Range: 50 ft.
Area of Effect: 1 fiend
Saving Throw: None

You attempt to force compliance from a fiend you can see. In most cases, it's wise to confine the creature in a *magic circle* or restrain it with a *planar binding spell* so it can't attack you while you cast *weaken fiendish will*. The targeted fiend gets no saving throw against this spell.

• From the moment this spell is cast until the start of your next turn, the target creature feels uneasy and suffers a –2 penalty to Wisdom and Charisma saving throws.

• In the second round, the creature becomes nervous; it suffers a –4 penalty to Wisdom and Charisma saving throws.

• In the third round, the creature feels a dull pain envelop its body; it suffers a –6 penalty to Wisdom and Charisma saving throws.

• For the next thirty minutes after the spell ends, the creature suffers a –6 penalty to Wisdom and Charisma saving throws against spells you cast.

If your concentration is broken while maintaining this spell, you are automatically dominated (per *dominate person*) by the fiend.

Weapon of Retribution

3rd-level evocation
Paladin
Components: V, S

Casting Time: 1 action
Duration: 10 minutes
Range: Touch
Area of Effect: 1 weapon
Saving Throw: None

You call upon your deity to imbue one weapon with the power to seek justice against a specific, evil-aligned opponent. You choose the target at the time of casting; they don't need to be present. You don't need to know the target's name, but it must be a creature you can identify, such as "the gnoll king's champion" or "the fomorian who slew Sir Pelgram."

The next time the *weapon of retribution* attacks the chosen target, its wielder gets tactical advantage on the attack roll and a hit does an additional 6d8 radiant damage.

Weather Calming

3rd-level conjuration
Druid
Components: V, S
Casting Time: 1 minute
Duration: 1 hour
Range: Self
Area of Effect: Sphere, 30-ft. radius
Saving Throw: None

You create an area of calm, pleasant weather in a 30-foot radius around yourself, regardless of what the weather beyond is like. Within this bubble the temperature is mild and the air pleasantly warm or cool (your choice), even if a blizzard or a hailstorm is raging outside. This can't produce sun on a cloudy day, but it does provide shade on a sunny day, as if the bubble were tinted.

If *weather calming* is cast inside an area affected by *control weather* or other, higher-level weather-controlling magic, the caster must make a spellcasting ability check. The DC equals 10 + the level of the weather-controlling magic being countered. *Weather calming* fails and the spell slot is expended if the spellcasting check is unsuccessful.

Web Orb

1st-level evocation
Wizard
Components: V, S
Casting Time: 1 action
Duration: Concentration, up to 1 minute
Range: 50 ft.
Area of Effect: 1 creature
Saving Throw: Dex / negates efffect

You project a small, gray glob of fluid from your hand at a creature you can see. The creature is struck by the glob unless it makes a successful Dexterity saving throw.

When it hits its target, the glob expands into a small net of sticky webbing as strong as fine steel wire. A Large or smaller creature struck by the net is restrained. A restrained creature can use its action to make a Strength check against your spell save DC; if the Strength check succeeds, the webs burst and the spell ends.

A thin line of webbing trails from the net to your hand. As an action, you can make an opposed Strength contest against the restrained creature. If you win the contest, you pull the creature 10 feet closer to you; otherwise, it remains where it is. In either case, the creature remains restrained.

Weeping Wounds

3rd-level necromancy
Cleric
Components: V, S, M (iron filings)
Casting Time: 1 action
Duration: Concentration, up to 1 minute
Range: 120 ft.
Area of Effect: 1 creature
Saving Throw: Con / negates effect

You open the wounds on one creature you can see within range. For

127

the duration of the spell, the targeted creature must make a Constitution saving throw at the start of each of its turns if it is not at full hit points. If the saving throw fails, it takes 3d6 necrotic damage as its wounds tear open and bleed profusely. The affected creature or an adjacent ally can use an action to make a Wisdom (Medicine) check against your spell save DC; a successful check ends the spell.

Whirlwind of Gore

3rd-level necromancy
Cleric
Components: V, S, M (small vial of blood)
Casting Time: 1 action
Duration: Concentration, up to 1 minute
Range: 120 ft.
Area of Effect: Cylinder, 15-ft. radius, 40 ft. high
Saving Throw: Wis / negates fright

You create a great storm of blood and gore in a 15-foot radius, 40-foot high cylinder at a point you can see. Every creature in the storm must make a Wisdom saving throw; if it fails, the creature becomes frightened of the storm for the spell's duration.

The area of the storm is heavily obscured.

Every creature that starts its turn inside the storm or that enters the storm must make a Constitution saving throw. If the saving throw fails, the creature takes 2d8 acid damage and is blinded until the start of its next turn. If the save succeeds, the creature takes half damage and is not blinded.

Whisper Wind

3rd-level divination
Cleric, Wizard
Components: V, S
Casting Time: 1 action
Duration: 8 hours
Range: 120 ft.
Area of Effect: 1 creature
Saving Throw: None

You create a magical link between yourself and one willing creature you can see. For the duration of the spell, you can hear anything that creature says, no matter how far it moves away from you or how softly it speaks, as long as you are still able to see them. The spell is not broken by brief periods when you can't see the target (though you can't hear the target when it's out of sight), but if you lose sight of it for more than 10 minutes, the spell ends.

Willful Transformation

2nd-level transmutation
Cleric, Paladin
Components: V, S
Casting Time: 1 action
Duration: Concentration, up to 1 minute
Range: Self
Area of Effect: Self
Saving Throw: None

For the duration of the spell, you can use your Wisdom score and modifier in place of your Strength, Dexterity, or Constitution score and modifier. Choose which ability score will be replaced when you cast the spell.

Wind Speak

1st-level divination (ritual)
Druid, Ranger
Components: V, S
Casting Time: 1 action
Duration: Instantaneous

Range: Unlimited on the same plane
Area of Effect: 1 creature you know
Saving Throw: None

You whisper a short message of no more than 15 words into the air, and the wind blows it to the ears of one creature you know. You must be in a place where the wind can blow freely (outdoors or in a building with large, open windows) when you cast the spell, and the target must be in a similar location when the message arrives; otherwise, the spell fails. The message travels 1 mile per round (10 miles per minute, or 600 miles per hour).

Wine Fount

3rd-level conjuration
Cleric
Components: V, S, M (a handful of grapes, which are consumed during casting)
Casting Time: 1 action
Duration: Permanent for created wine; Concentration, up to 3 rounds for geyser
Range: 30 ft.
Area of Effect: 10 gallons of wine or a cylinder, 5-ft. diam, 10 ft. high
Saving Throw: None or Dex / avoids effect

You can choose one of two modes for this spell when you cast it.

Create Wine: You create up to 10 gallons of wine of a type and quality of your choosing. You can choose the characteristics of the wine to suit your specifications (acidity, bouquet, color, etc.), but you can't raise or lower the alcohol content beyond the normal range for that type. The spell doesn't create containers for the wine, but it appears inside whatever nearby empty bottles, jugs, skins, or tub you designate. Once it's created, this wine is completely normal in all regards.

Dionysian Geyser: You slam your staff or another object onto the ground and cause a 10-foot tall, 5-foot diameter cylinder of wine to gush from a point on the ground within range. If the space is occupied by a creature, it must make a successful Dexterity saving throw to avoid taking 4d6 bludgeoning damage and being knocked prone and pushed 10 feet away from the geyser in a direction you choose. The same saving throw must be made by any creature that starts its turn in the geyser or that enters it.

The geyser can be maintained with concentration for up to 3 rounds.

Wings of Heaven

3rd-level transmutation
Paladin
Components: V, S, M (a feather)
Casting Time: 1 action
Duration: 2 hours
Range: Touch
Area of Effect: 1 horse
Saving Throw: None

Your horse grows wings and can fly like a pegasus (fly speed 90 feet). The spell ends if another creature tries to use your horse as a mount without you also riding it.

Wisdom of the Divine

2nd-level divination
Cleric, Paladin
Components: V, S
Casting Time: 1 action
Duration: Concentration, up to 8 hours
Range: Touch
Area of Effect: 1 creature

Saving Throw: None

For the duration of the spell, one willing creature you touch can add 1d4 to its Wisdom checks and Wisdom saving throws. In addition, the creature has one additional 1st-level spell slot, which it can use to cast divine spells.

Wise Defense

3rd-level divination
Cleric, Paladin
Components: V, S
Casting Time: 1 action
Duration: 10 minutes
Range: Touch
Area of Effect: 1 creature
Saving Throw: None

A creature you touch gains insight into the actions of its foes. For the duration of the spell, the creature can use its Wisdom modifier in place of its Dexterity modifier for calculating Armor Class, and it can substitute Wisdom saving throws for Dexterity saving throws.

With the Wind

1st-level evocation
Sorcerer, Wizard
Components: V, S
Casting Time: 1 action
Duration: Concentration, up to 1 hour
Range: Touch
Area of Effect: 1 ranged weapon
Saving Throw: None

One ranged weapon you touch doubles its range for the duration of this spell, as the air moves around its missiles to propel them farther.

Wither Limb

9th-level necromancy
Cleric
Components: V, S
Casting Time: 3 rounds
Duration: Instantaneous
Range: 30 ft.
Area of Effect: 1 creature
Saving Throw: Con / negates effect

Choose a limb (either arm or leg) of one creature you can see. The creature must make a Constitution saving throw. If the saving throw fails, the limb withers, drops from the creature's body, and crumbles to dust. A creature with only one leg drops prone and its speed is reduced to 5 feet per round.

The limb can be regrown by use of the *regenerate* spell or comparable magic.

Wolf's Hearing

2nd-level transmutation
Druid, Ranger
Components: V, S
Casting Time: 1 action
Duration: 10 minutes
Range: Self
Area of Effect: Self
Saving Throw: None

For the duration of the spell, your hearing sharpens so that you have tactical advantage on Wisdom (Perception) checks that rely on hearing.

Wolf's Howl

2nd-level enchantment
Druid, Ranger
Components: V, S
Casting Time: 1 action
Duration: 1 round
Range: 50 ft.
Area of Effect: All beasts within range
Saving Throw: None

You howl like a wolf, frightening beasts within 50 feet of you. Roll 8d8; the result is how many hit points of beasts can be affected by the spell. Beasts with 1 hit die must be affected first, then beasts with 2 hit dice, then 3 hit dice, and so on. Within that restriction, you choose the order that beasts are affected.

Each beast affected by the spell becomes frightened until the start of your next turn, and must spend its turn moving as far away from you as it can.

Woodland Shriek

1st-level abjuration
Druid
Components: V, S
Casting Time: 1 action
Duration: 8 hours
Range: 30 ft.
Area of Effect: Circle, 20-ft. radius
Saving Throw: Dex / alarm is not triggered

You imbue nonintelligent plants and bushes in a 20-foot radius with the ability to shriek loudly if a Small or larger creature enters the warded area. The creature can go unnoticed if it makes a successful Dexterity saving throw, but it must be a conscious effort at sneaking; a creature can't "accidentally" go unnoticed by the plants. The shrieking plants are audible up to a mile away. Once the alarm is triggered, the plants shriek for 30 seconds, then the spell ends.

Other than the size minimum, the spell is entirely nonspecific. Any creature that meets the size criterion, such as deer, foxes, and children, will set it off.

Words of Thunder

6th-level evocation
Bard, Sorcerer, Wizard
Components: V, S
Casting Time: 1 action
Duration: Instantaneous
Range: Self
Area of Effect: Sphere, 60-ft. radius
Saving Throw: None

When uttered, the *words of thunder* rises to a tremendous pitch and wash outward as a tangible boom of sound in a 60-foot radius centered on you. All other creatures in the sphere with 30 or fewer hit points are permanently deafened and are incapacitated until the end of your next turn, with no saving throw. Creatures with 31 to 60 hit points are deafened for 1 minute, but not incapacitated. Creatures with more than 60 hit points are unaffected.

You can cast *words of thunder* even if you are in a zone of magical silence. In this case, the spell destroys the *silence* effect but has no effect on creatures.

Wound Reading

2nd-level divination (ritual)
Cleric, Druid, Ranger
Components: V, S

Casting Time: 1 action
Duration: Instantaneous
Range: Touch
Area of Effect: 1 wound
Saving Throw: None

By touching a willing, wounded creature, you gain a mental image of what inflicted the injury (a specific person, monster, trap, and so on). If the victim didn't see what wounded him or her, you must make a successful DC 10 Wisdom (Medicine) check to gain specific information; if the check fails, you learn only the general type of the attacker (beast, fiend, monstrosity, etc.).

Wrack the Mind

9th-level necromancy
Wizard
Components: V, S
Casting Time: 1 action
Duration: Instantaneous
Range: Touch
Area of Effect: 1 creature
Saving Throw: Int / negates effect

Your hand glows with crackling black and red energy as you touch one creature within reach. The creature must make an Intelligence saving throw. If the saving throw fails, the creature loses 2d6 points of Intelligence (to a minimum of 3) and must roll on the following table to see how it is cursed. On a successful save, the creature loses half that amount of Intelligence and suffers no additional effect.

d6	Curse Effect
1	The target is frightened of you.
2	The target develops a severe phobia to a common object. Anytime the target is within 15 feet of the object and is able to perceive it, he or she becomes frightened until the object is again more than 15 feet away. You choose the subject of the phobia. The object should be common, but not ubiquitous. For example, "wooden spoons" would be an appropriate subject, but "shoes" would not.
3	The target automatically fails Intelligence checks.
4	The target is confused (per the *confusion* spell).
5	The target suffers amnesia and is unable to recall details of its past or cast spells.
6	The target's mind regresses to a childlike state.

The curse effect can be ended by *remove curse* or comparable magic, and *greater restoration* or comparable magic can repair the ability loss. Otherwise, the effects of this spell are permanent.

Wyvern Guard

2nd-level abjuration
Cleric
Components: V, S
Casting Time: 1 action
Duration: 8 hours
Range: 50 ft.
Area of Effect: 1 mist wyvern
Saving Throw: None

You create a bank of swirling, nearly insubstantial haze that quickly takes the shape of a wyvern in an unoccupied space you can see. The wyvern is Large and has a reach of 10 feet, but it can't leave the space where it was created.

When a creature moves into or starts its turn in the reach of the wyvern, the wyvern guard attacks it. Make a melee spell attack against the target. If it hits, the target takes 1d8 piercing damage and is paralyzed. A paralyzed creature makes a Constitution saving throw at the end of each of its turns; the paralysis ends on a successful save.

The wyvern guard disappears and the spell ends when the wyvern makes a successful attack.

In areas of bright light, the wyvern is clearly visible. In dim light, a DC 15 Perception check is needed to notice the wyvern at distances of 30 feet or more. In darkness, the wyvern is effectively invisible.

Xenophobic Rage

8th-level enchantment
Bard, Cleric, Wizard
Components: V, S
Casting Time: 1 action
Duration: Concentration, up to 8 hours
Range: Self
Area of Effect: Sphere, 50-ft. radius
Saving Throw: Wis / confused 1 round

You sow chaos by drawing upon the secret fears of any number of creatures you can see to make them instantly aggressive toward anyone not of their own race. Each creature must make a Wisdom saving throw. If the saving throw fails, the creature feels the full effect of this spell; on a successful save, the creature is confused (per the *confusion* spell) until the start of your next turn.

Targets that failed their saving throws become homicidal against creatures of different races. They have no allies except creatures of their own race, even if those creatures were their enemies before *xenophobic rage* was cast. Affected creatures must use all of their powers to the best of their ability to destroy the nearest enemies they can see.

Each time an affected creature reduces another creature to 0 hit points or kills it, it can repeat the Wisdom saving throw; a successful save ends the spell's effect on that creature.

Yellow Smoke

3rd-level conjuration
Wizard
Components: V, S
Casting Time: 1 action
Duration: Concentration, up to 1 minute
Range: 90 ft.
Area of Effect: Sphere, 20-ft. radius
Saving Throw: Con / negates effect

You create a 20-foot-radius sphere of yellow gas centered on a point you can see. The cloud spreads around corners and its area is heavily obscured. The gas dissipates when the spell ends.

Each creature that starts its turn in the cloud must make a Constitution saving throw against poison. If the saving throw succeeds, the creature is unaffected by the gas until the start of its next turn. If the saving throw fails, the creature is poisoned for as long as it's in the cloud and for another 1d4 rounds after it leaves the gas. Creatures that don't need to breathe or that are immune to poison are immune to this effect.

A moderate wind disperses the cloud after four rounds; a strong wind disperses it after one round.

Zephyr of Death

8th-level necromancy
Wizard
Components: V
Casting Time: 1 action
Duration: Concentration, up to 1 minute
Range: Self
Area of Effect: Cone, 100 ft. long

Zephyr of Death

Saving Throw: Wis / 4d8 necrotic dmg and not frightened

You send a zephyr that whispers hate and despair in a 100-foot cone. Each creature in the cone takes 4d8 necrotic damage and must make a Wisdom saving throw. If the saving throw fails, the whispers gather around the creature and it is frightened of you for the duration. The whispers gnaw at the creature's mind, attempting to drive it to death.

While a creature is frightened by the *zephyr of death*, it must make a Wisdom saving throw at the start of each of its turns. If the saving throw fails, the creature takes 4d8 necrotic damage and is incapacitated until the start of its next turn. On a successful save, it remains frightened, takes half damage, and is not incapacitated. A creature that makes three successful saves, which don't need to be consecutive, overcomes the spell and the effect ends for them.

Zombify Self

4th-level necromancy
Wizard
Components: V, S, M (a piece of zombie flesh)
Casting Time: 1 action
Duration: 10 minutes
Range: Self
Area of Effect: Self
Saving Throw: None

Your flesh becomes corrupt and dead as your body transforms into that of a zombie. You become immune to poison, paralysis, stun, disease, and unconsciousness for the duration of the spell. You also lose 4 points of Dexterity and have tactical disadvantage on Charisma checks used to interact with others.

You can end the spell as a bonus action. When the spell ends, you take 5d8 necrotic damage, or no damage if you make a successful Constitution saving throw.

Zone of Ablation

5th-level abjuration
Paladin
Components: V, S
Casting Time: 1 action
Duration: Concentration, up to 1 minute
Range: Self
Area of Effect: Self
Saving Throw: None

For the duration of the spell, whenever you are struck by a weapon attack, you take the minimum damage possible from the attack (as if all dice rolled the lowest possible number). This doesn't affect spell damage rolls or effects that don't do hit point damage.

Zone of Metamagic Minimization

8th-level abjuration
Cleric, Wizard
Components: V, S
Casting Time: 1 action
Duration: Concentration, up to 1 minute
Range: 50 ft.
Area of Effect: Sphere, 20-ft. radius
Saving Throw: None

You create a zone of purple-hued air in a 20-foot-radius sphere around a point you can see. Within this zone, all damage caused directly by spells is minimized; each damage die is treated as having rolled a 1. The spell doesn't reduce damage from effects that inflict damage indirectly, such as damage from conjured weapons and creatures, or damage from bonuses; for example, a spell that causes 4d6 + 20 damage is reduced to 4 + 20 damage by a *zone of metamagic minimization*.

Appendix - Wizard Spells by School

Cantrips (Level 0)

Abjuration
Shield Open Flame

Divination
Detect Charm
Itemize

Enchantment
Befuddle
Pepper's Purpose

Transmutation
Alter Normal Fires
Assassin's Mark
Burden
Decorate Object
Encrypt
Ferment

Level 1

Conjuration
Assassin's Coin
Bubble Net
Dragon's Gauntlet
Gossamer Webbing
Mucilage
Rock Bolt

Divination
Know the Mark

Enchantment
Malicious Intent
Serpent's Gaze
Twitch

Evocation
Acid Wind
Caustic Spittle
Earthen Blast
Fiery Grasp
Flaming Bolts
Flash of Light
Frostfire
Ice Bolts
Impressive Blow
Push
Signal Flare
Web Orb
With the Wind

Illusion
Bewitch
Enhance Oration
Morph Shadow
Muddy Appearance

Necromancy
Commune with Shade
Debilitate
Grave-Touched Weapon
Hives
Necrotic Feast
Pilfer Sleep

Transmutation
Copy
Dead Man's Hands
Decrypt
Erase
Farsighted
Fiery Cloth
Fire Burst
Flame Water
Lasting Breath
Nearsighted
Quick Change
Shroud the Shadow
Slow Draw

Level 2

Abjuration
Bolster Mental Fortitude
Delude
Faerie Ward
Frame
Protection from Paralysis
Scent Mask
Soul Shield
Undetectable Charm

Conjuration
Boarding Plank
Gaze Mirroring
Ironshot
Net
Silver Spear
Spirit Cartographer

Divination
Combat Mind
Detect Curse
Detect Illusion
Precision of Arms
Shadow Sight

Enchantment
Character Flaw
Damage Morale
Dream Speaker
Hesitate
Insomnia
Inverted Compass

Evocation
Bead of Blazing
Bead of Frost
Charged Missile
Death March
Ethereal Blade
Ethereal Strike
Fiery Shield
Flame of Chaos
Flameswell
Force Wave
Frost Snap
Ghostly Throttle
Ignite
Molten Strike
Smothering Cloud
Undertow

Illusion
Menace
Undead Alteration

Necromancy
Blood Bath
Death Rattle
Ghostly Howl
Glowing Bones
Pain of Giving
Safeguarded Slumber
Spirit Blast

Transmutation
Air Forge
Augment Flames
Augment Skeleton
Biting Blade
Blindfold
Blood Geyser
Blunt the Edge
Brittle
Burn the Sight
Buttress
Dragon Scales
False Gold
Glide
Melt
Slur

Level 3

Abjuration
Blackout
Protection from Pressure

Conjuration
Aerial Pilot
Binding Chains
Blinding Ash
Explosive Cloud
Glass House
Sand Blast
Summon Undead
Tenacious Blade
Wall of Water
Yellow Smoke

Divination
Detect Land
Link Perception
See the Ephemeral
Speak with Objects
Whisper Wind

Enchantment
Babel's Curse
Bad Luck
Lustful Gaze
Twisted Magic

Evocation
Anchor
Arcane Spear
Barbaric Yawp
Blade Song
Blinding Flare
Breath of the Dragon
Cacophony
Chaos Bolt
Electromagnetic Storm
Far Strike
Frost Shards
Hard Water Blast
Ooze Bolt
Steam Bolt

Illusion
Battle Double
Spiteful Images
Umbral Images

Necromancy

Bone Trap
Cause the Bends
Delay Death
Finger Missile
Hemophilia
Infuse Weapon
Life Leech Weapon
Restore the Undead
Shadow Bolt
Umbral Strike

Transmutation

Air Breathing
Air Bridge
Charged Touch
Heat Flesh
Reshape Metal
Silver Bones
Spell Kill
Undulating Earth
Unfasten
Water Double

Level 4

Abjuration

Aetheric Shield
Bastion
Bead of Luck
Charge
Deflect Ram
Lock Form
Mark of Ownership
Stonefast

Conjuration

Abiding Webs
Air Sphere
Aura of Tsathogga
Bubble Goop
Creeping Eye
Endless Abyss
Gallows Tree
Instant Exit
Spectral Archers
Steel Butterflies
Vermin Swarm
Wall of Blood

Divination

Circle of Scrying
Multiple Shot
Piercing Vision
Portrait

Enchantment

Association
Bait
Fumble
Megalomania

Evocation

Bead of Blasting
Enduring Missiles
Fiery Blast
Flames of Purification
Negative Energy Aura
Rainbow Spear
Scalding Sea
Shadowbind
Slimeball
Solar Spear
Steam Cloud

Illusion

Distance Distortion
Fire Fascination
Maligned Performance

Necromancy

Bloodburn
Infirmity
Infuse Shadow
Iron Bones
Mind Carve
Profane Link
Stupefy
Umbral Touch
Zombify Self

Transmutation

Bladelust
Corpulent Bloat
Desail
Dig
Earthburst
Flames of Darkness
Fluid Form
Force Corporeality
Hard Water Weapon
Iceform
Iron Rope
Projectile Link
Purifying Bath
Remember Seas
Searing Projectiles
Shadow Form
Transform Boulder to Pebble
Transform Pebble to Boulder
Twig Torture
Warrior's Touch

Level 5

Abjuration

Arcane Shield
Cone of Silence
Mystic Negation
Nullifying Cloak
Spellcaster's Refusal

Conjuration

Dark Empowerment
Devouring Darkness
Earthen Snare
Foggy Flying Carpet

Enchantment

Euphoric Ecstasy
Fugue
Mantle of Dread
Weaken Fiendish Will

Evocation

Arcane Retribution
Dance of Seduction
Dark Curtain
Jolt
Rainbow Staff
Shattering Cry
Violent Scream

Necromancy

Blades of Bone
Blood Purge
Bloody Tentacles
Clot
Donor
Ethereal Blast
Ethereal Shield
Grim Resilience
Heat Bone
Necrotic Touch
Skull Bomb
Soul Shatter
Transform Zombie
Umbral Weapon
Wail of Fate

Transmutation

Absorb Object
Blood Blade
Corrupt Water
Divine Burden
Forced March
Lower Spell Resistance
Mark of Fire
Mark of Ice
Mark of Ooze
Memento
Resist Channeling
Spell Legs
Spirit Doll
Tattoo Object
Transfer of Vigor
Unyielding Durability
Vile Vintage

Level 6

Abjuration

Bead of Iron
Spell Inhibitor
Spiritbreaker

Conjuration

Cold Fog
Hound of Hell
Ice Sled

Divination

Instant Fluency

Enchantment

Death's Imposition
Lost Wanderer

Evocation

Acid Blast
Fangstorm
Lightning Storm
Lightning Wheel
Words of Thunder

Illusion

Confounding Battlefield
Illusory Illusion
Judicious Concealment

Necromancy

Adamantine Bones
Black Exhalation
Crew with the Dead
Curse of Infirmity
Death Gaze
Ebon Water
Extract Life
Life Shot
Negative Energy Mantle
Shade Swarm
Spilling of Blood

Transmutation

Blade Bond
Breach Defenses
Change Dust to Water
Change Water to Dust
Chilling Gaze
Claws of Digging
Dust of Death
Farvision
Fiery Constrictor
Giant's Potency
Glass Window
Inflict Lycanthropy
Merge into Art
Ogre's Visage
Serpent Hands
Transmute Gold to Steel
Transparent Steel
Umbral Transformation

Level 7

Abjuration

Containment Orbs
Divine Disconnection
Immunity to Energy
Revelation Field
Shield of Crackling Fire
Volley Spell

Conjuration

Crawling Chaos
Dancing Daggers
Magma Eruption
Raise Island

Enchantment

Interdiction

Evocation

Acid Storm
Chain Enervation
Ebon Lightning
Electrical Storm
Forceful Crush
Liquid Fire
Mangling Foot
Scorching Air
Searing Flash

Necromancy

Cone of Decay
Create Crypt Thing
Obliterate Soul

Transmutation

Acid Swamp
Burning Rain
Chronal Displacement
Create Iceberg
Deep Freeze
Establish Foundation
Hovership
Icebreaker
Sleep of Power

Level 8

Abjuration

Zone of Metamagic Minimization

Conjuration

Outside of Time

Enchantment

Imbue Passion
Touch of Madness
Xenophobic Rage

Evocation

Ebonflame
Halt Aging
Ice Geyser
Raise Shipwreck
Spirit Disk

Necromancy

Dark Geyser
Death Bringer
Deny Succor
Destined Doom
Greater Curse
Life Leech
Shadowstaff
Soul Strike
Umbral Storm
Zephyr of Death

Transmutation

Elemental Infusion
Fuse Joints
Glass into Iron
Impart Strength
Strength of the Wyrm

Level 9

Abjuration

Arcane Censure
Hide the Soul

Conjuration

Crag Warrior
Curtain of Fire
Tendrils of Night

Evocation

Conflagration
Rimeshatter
Scintillating Doom
Storm of Vitriol

Necromancy

Wrack the Mind

Transmutation

Eternal Sleep
Quicken Assassin

This printing of *The Book of Lost Spells* is done under version 1.0a of the of the Open Game License, below, and by license from Mythmere Games and Necromancer Games.

Notice of Open Game Content: This product contains Open Game Content, as defined in version 1.0a of the Open Game License, below (the "Open Game License"). Open Game Content may only be Used under and in terms of the Open Game License.

Designation of Open Game Content: Other than as set forth in the declaration of Product Identity, below, all text contained within this product (including monster names, stats, and descriptions) is hereby designated as Open Game Content, with the following exceptions:

1. Any text on the inside or outside of the front or back cover or on the Credits or Preface pages is not Open Game Content;

2. Any advertising material — including the text of any advertising material — is not Open Game Content;

3. Any material contained in the "Credit" section of each monster is not Open Game Content. See the "Note on the 'Credit' Section," below;

Use of Content from *Tome of Horrors* Series: This product contains or references content from the *Tome of Horrors Revised*, *Tome of Horrors II* and *Tome of Horrors III* by Necromancer Games, Inc. Such content is used by permission. Further, some content reprinted here from the original *Tome of Horrors* and/or *Tome of Horrors Revised* contains content owned by Wizards of the Coast and is used under the Open Game License.

Designation of Product Identity: The following items are hereby designated as Product Identity as provided in section 1(e) of the Open Game License:

Any and all material or content that could be claimed as Product Identity pursuant to section 1(e), below, is hereby claimed as product identity, including but not limited to:

1. The name "Necromancer Games" and "Frog God Games" as well as all logos and identifying marks of Necromancer Games, Inc. and Frog God Games, including but not limited to the Orcus logo and the phrase "Fifth Edition Rules, First Edition Feel" as well as the trade dress of Necromancer Games products and similar logos, identifying phrases and trade dress of Frog God Games;

2. The product name *Quests of Doom Volume 1*, *Fifth Edition Foes*, *Tome of Horrors, Tome of Horrors Revised, Tome of Horrors II, Tome of Horrors III* and *Tome of Horrors Complete* by Necromancer Games, Inc. as well as any and all Necromancer Games Inc. and/or Frog God Games product names referenced in the work;

3. All artwork, illustration, graphic design, maps, and cartography, including any text contained within such artwork, illustration, maps or cartography;

4. The proper names, personality, descriptions and/or motivations of all artifacts, characters, races, countries, geographic locations, plane or planes of existence, gods, deities, events, magic items, organizations and/or groups unique to this book, but not their stat blocks or other game mechanic descriptions (if any), and also excluding any such names when they are included in monster, spell or feat names, and also excluding any of the foregoing if the material is already Open Game Content;

5. Any other content previously designated as Product Identity is hereby designated as Product Identity and is used with permission and/or pursuant to license.

6. All logos and identifying marks of Mythmere Games and Matthew J. Finch, any trade dress, identifying words or phrases of Mythmere Games or Matthew J. Finch products and similar logos;

OPEN GAME LICENSE Version 1.0a

The following text is the property of Wizards of the Coast, Inc. and is Copyright 2000 Wizards of the Coast, Inc. ("Wizards"). All Rights Reserved.

1. Definitions: (a) "Contributors" means the copyright and/or trademark owners who have contributed Open Game Content; (b) "Derivative Material" means copyrighted material including derivative works and translations (including into other computer languages), potation, modification, correction, addition, extension, upgrade, improvement, compilation, abridgment or other form in which an existing work may be recast, transformed or adapted; (c) "Distribute" means to reproduce, license, rent, lease, sell, broadcast, publicly display, transmit or otherwise distribute; (d) "Open Game Content" means the game mechanic and includes the methods, procedures, processes and routines to the extent such content does not embody the Product Identity and is an enhancement over the prior art and any additional content clearly identified as Open Game Content by the Contributor, and means any work covered by this License, including translations and derivative works under copyright law, but specifically excludes Product Identity; (e) "Product Identity" means product and product line names, logos and identifying marks including trade dress; artifacts; creatures; characters; stories, storylines, plots, thematic elements, dialogue, incidents, language, artwork, symbols, designs, depictions, likenesses, formats, poses, concepts, themes and graphic, photographic and other visual or audio representations; names and descriptions of characters, spells, enchantments, personalities, teams, personas, likenesses and special abilities; places, locations, environments, creatures, equipment, magical or supernatural abilities or effects, logos, symbols, or graphic designs; and any other trademark or registered trademark clearly identified as Product identity by the owner of the Product Identity, and which specifically excludes the Open Game Content; (f) "Trademark" means the logos, names, mark, sign, motto, designs that are used by a Contributor to identify itself or its products or the associated products contributed to the Open Game License by the Contributor; (g) "Use", "Used" or "Using" means to use, Distribute, copy, edit, format, modify, translate and otherwise create Derivative Material of Open Game Content; (h) "You" or "Your" means the licensee in terms of this agreement.

2. The License: This License applies to any Open Game Content that contains a notice indicating that the Open Game Content may only be Used under and in terms of this License. You must affix such a notice to any Open Game Content that you Use. No terms may be added to or subtracted from this License except as described by the License itself. No other terms or conditions may be applied to any Open Game Content distributed using this License.

3. Offer and Acceptance: By Using the Open Game Content You indicate Your acceptance of the terms of this License.

4. Grant and Consideration: In consideration for agreeing to use this License, the Contributors grant You a perpetual, worldwide, royalty-free, non-exclusive license with the exact terms of this License to Use, the Open Game Content.

5. Representation of Authority to Contribute: If You are contributing original material as Open Game Content, You represent that Your Contributions are Your original creation and/or You have sufficient rights to grant the rights conveyed by this License.

6. Notice of License Copyright: You must update the COPYRIGHT NOTICE portion of this License to include the exact text of the COPYRIGHT NOTICE of any Open Game Content You are copying, modifying or distributing, and You must add the title, the copyright date, and the copyright holder's name to the COPYRIGHT NOTICE of any original Open Game Content you Distribute.

7. Use of Product Identity: You agree not to Use any Product Identity, including as an indication as to compatibility, except as expressly licensed in another, independent Agreement with the owner of each element of that Product Identity. You agree not to indicate compatibility or co-adaptability with any Trademark or Registered Trademark in conjunction with a work containing Open Game Content except as expressly licensed in another, independent Agreement with the owner of such Trademark or Registered Trademark. The use of any Product Identity in Open Game Content does not constitute a challenge to the ownership of that Product Identity. The owner of any Product Identity used in Open Game Content shall retain all rights, title and interest in and to that Product Identity.

8. Identification: If you distribute Open Game Content You must clearly indicate which portions of the work that you are distributing are Open Game Content.

9. Updating the License: Wizards or its designated Agents may publish updated versions of this License. You may use any authorized version of this License to copy, modify and distribute any Open Game Content originally distributed under any version of this License.

10. Copy of this License: You MUST include a copy of this License

www.ingramcontent.com/pod-product-compliance
Lightning Source LLC
Chambersburg PA
CBHW081328090726
47907CB00010B/2410

* 9 7 8 1 6 2 2 8 3 5 1 5 7 *